NIGHT OF THE HORNS

Lawyer Robert Race has always been a straight-arrow guy, taking on underdog cases against all odds. He believes in his client's innocence. But one night his confidence is shattered when racketeer Kresnik forces him to collect a suitcase at the docks, and Race stumbles into a world he didn't know existed. He runs into his old flame, Ginny, who for some reason now despises him. He is confronted by his neighbor Paul Taylor's wife, Laura, who confesses that her husband has been having an affair with Race's wife, Eve, right under his nose. His protégé, Tony Fontaine, has been acting strange, and even his father-in-law, Sam Alford, taunts Race that he has been living with his head in the sand. Tonight Race learns a lot about his life. But his trip to the docks is only the beginning. Soon his life is completely turned upside down— because tonight he finds himself on the lam for murder!

CRY WOLFRAM

John Molson is an expatriate American living in France where he is currently bodyguard to an old millionaire named Craddock. Life is good. He's got a new girl named Julie. What does it matter that she keeps warning him about her brother, while spending the evening hovering over that suave bastard, Roger Lascelles? If it isn't love, it's the next best thing. But Molson's reverie is shattered when Craddock announces they are driving down to Spain where there's a deal to be finalized involving some lucrative mining rights. No sooner do they arrive but Craddock is murdered, Molson is framed, and every unsavory character in town is after him—Colonel Parker, dangerous double-crosser; Chivas, Craddock's rival; Vidal, sadistic chief of police, Luiz Hernandez, disgraced bullfighter—and most dangerous of all, sweet Louise, who holds the key to the whole deal!

D0925768

DOUGLAS SANDERSON BIBLIOGRAPHY

Dark Passions Subdue (US, 1952)

Final Run (UK, 1956) aka
Flee from Terror (US, 1957) and
Un bouquet de chardons (Fr, 1957)
both as by Martin Brett

Night of the Horns (UK, 1958) aka
Murder Comes Calling (US, 1958)
as by Malcolm Douglas

Cry Wolfram (UK, 1959) aka *Mark it
for Murder* (US, 1959) and *La semaine
de bonté* (Fr, 1958) as by Martin Brett

Catch a Fallen Starlet (US, 1960)
aka *The Stubborn Unlaid* and
Cinémaléfices (Fr, 1960)
as by Martin Brett

Lam to Slaughter (UK, 1964) aka
As-tu vu Carcassone? (Fr, 1963)
as by Martin Brett

Black Reprieve (UK, 1965) aka
White Man Dead and *Couper cabèche*
(Fr, 1964) as by Martin Brett

No Charge for Framing (UK, 1969)

A Dead Bullfighter (UK, 1975)

As Martin Brett

Exit in Green (US, 1953) re-written as
Murder Came Tumbling (UK, 1959)

Hot Freeze (US, 1953) aka
Mon cadaver au Canada (Fr, 1955)
and *Heisser Schnee* (Germany, 1975)
as by Malcolm Douglas

Darker Traffic (US, 1954) aka *Blondes
are My Trouble* (US, 1955) and
Salmigonzesses (Fr, 1956)

Flee from Terror (US, 1957) aka
Final Run (UK, 1956) and *Un bouquet
de chardons* (Fr, 1957).

The Shreds published as
Sables-d'or-les-pains! (Fr, 1958)

The Dead Connection published as
La came á papa (Fr, 1961)

A Dum-Dum for the President
(UK, 1961) aka *Estocade au Canada*
(Fr, 1961)

Shout for a Killer published as
Chabanais chez les pachas (Fr, 1963)

Score for Two Dead published as *Le
moîne connait la musique* (Fr, 1964)

As Malcolm Douglas

Prey by Night (US, 1955) aka *A boulets
Rouges* (Fr, 1956) as by Martin Brett

Rain of Terror (US, 1955) aka *And All
Flesh Died* and *Le Fête a la grenouille*
(Fr, 1956) as by Martin Brett; and
Alptraum auf Italienisch (Germany,
1975) as by Malcolm Douglas

The Deadly Dames (US, 1956) aka
Du Rebecca chez les femmes (Fr, 1956)
as by Martin Brett

Pure Sweet Hell (US, 1957) aka
Zum Sterben hat jeder mal Zeit
(Germany, 1975)

Murder Comes Calling (US, 1958) aka
Night of the Horns (UK, 1958) as by
Douglas Sanderson; and *Ruh in
Frieden, lieber Schatz* (Germany,
1974) as by Malcolm Douglas

Night of the Horns

∙ ∙ ∙ ∙ ∙ ∙ ∙

Cry Wolfram

by Douglas Sanderson

STARK
HOUSE

Stark House Press • Eureka California

NIGHT OF THE HORNS / CRY WOLFRAM

Published by Stark House Press
1315 H Street
Eureka, CA 95501, USA
griffinskye3@sbcglobal.net
www.starkhousepress.com

ISBN: 1-933586-72-9
13-ISBN: 978-1-933586-72-4

Book design by Mark Shepard, shepgraphics.com
Cover art by Gregory Shepard
Proofreading by Rick Ollerman

First Stark House Press Edition: June 2015
FIRST EDITION

Douglas Sanderson: Pure Sweet Hell

By Gregory Shepard

Douglas Sanderson loved to travel. You could almost chart his travels in the books he wrote. Growing up in England, he first moved to Canada, where his first five novels were set. Then off to Europe—Yugoslavia and Spain, in particular—where he set his next four novels. Then back to Canada for one more mystery. Next, he took a trip around the States, which gave him the background for two more books. Then back to Europe again, where most of his final books were set—with the exception of one in Cuba and another in Africa—and including four novels that were published only in France. But really, it all started in Canada.

Sanderson had just published his first book, *Dark Passions Subdue*, with Dodd, Mead and Company. It got a few good notices. Sanderson himself called it "an analysis of Puritanism in Montreal's high society," and that is certainly one way of looking at it. It is also a frank look at a group of gay men who jockey for the attention of an effete artist. Banned in England, the book did not sell well. But interestingly enough, the fellow whom Sanderson used as a model for his main character made him a bet that he couldn't write a hardboiled thriller. As Sanderson paraphrased it in a 1990 interview with Lucas Soler for *El Temps*: "Mickey Spillane has sold 32 million copies of his books. I'll bet you ten dollars you cannot write a thriller as he does."

The bet was on. Sanderson claimed that he had never read a tough guy thriller before, though in fact he had already published one mystery, *Exit in Green*, featuring a somewhat hapless main character, not at all in the Spillane mold. As the story goes, Sanderson went out to a local drugstore and did a bit of quick research in the paperback stand. He met some members of the Canadian Mounted Police. They shared stories about local drug dealers. Douglas had his hook. The result was *Hot Freeze*, a story of drug smuggling in Quebec. His publisher didn't want him to use his real name because they were still trying to build a reputation around "Sanderson." For *Exit in Green* he had used a name that had a family history, albeit a tricky one—Martin Brett—which he again employed for *Hot Freeze*.

For the "Martin Brett" anecdote, we must leave Canada and go back to Eng-

land, where Ronald Douglas Sanderson was born on August 20th, 1920, in
Beltinge, Kent, and grew up in a large family with three brothers (one a half-
brother) and two sisters. While he was still a child, his father abandoned them,
leaving his mother bring up the family. She and Douglas did not get along, two
temperaments at opposite extremes. She was the hard-headed pragmatist, he
the temperamental artist. And she had a family to feed. After Père Sanderson
left, a Mr. Brett began visiting the household, and after each one of his visits,
there would always be more to eat in the house. So, when it came time to pick
out a pseudonym for his first thriller, Sanderson chose "Martin Brett" as a way
of letting his mother know that he full well knew what was going on back in
Kent.

World War II began in 1939. Sanderson was only 20 when he joined the Merchant Navy and the RAF. But due to a perforated eardrum—caused, Sanderson claimed, by regular beatings from his father—he did not pass the medical
test to become a pilot. Instead, he started writing and performing, directing theatrical comedies for the troops. He even acted in a stage presentation of "Rope,"
which Alfred Hitchcock later turned into a distinctive film.

Sanderson also wrote articles for the RAF magazine, then edited by René
Brabazon Raymond, better known as thriller writer James Hadley Chase. It was
Chase who first suggested that Sanderson start writing novels instead of plays.

In spite of this fortuitous suggestion, Sanderson joined a theatre company in
London after the war. However, his mother still didn't approve of his artistic
pursuits. And like many a brow-beaten son, Douglas moved as far away as possible, immigrating all the way to Canada and Montreal in 1947, where he
eventually became a naturalized citizen. Here he did what he could to keep the
wolf from the door—worked in a jeweler's shop, at a radio station, and in a Kel-
logg's factory. Somewhere along the line Douglas hooked up with the Canadian
Broadcasting Corporation, and began to write radio comedies.

As Sanderson said in his interview with Lucas Soler, "For fourteen months
I was writing an half an hour comedy every week." It was then he made his first
attempt at writing a novel. Feeling that his writing was too derivative, too
strongly influenced by the authors he admired, he soon gave it up. But he tried
again, and this time produced *Dark Passions Subdue*. The biography on the dust
jacket flap could have almost been written by Sanderson himself:

"His interests, now and always, have always been as wide as the
world, and his travels have taken him over many areas.

"But what he has seen is unlikely to result in any pleasant trave-
logues. A keen and pitiless eye for dishonesty, a fierce distaste for self-
deception—be it his own or anyone else's—and the very considerable
dramatic-satiric gift that is revealed in this first novel, can be expected
to provide us with provocative and disturbing books for years to come.

"Mr. Sanderson is a terrifying critic of the social scene. His Montreal frauds can be found in big cities everywhere. His hero's crisis is the crisis not of an individual, but of an era.

"This book is neither temperate nor kindly. It can not be flippantly read, or easily forgotten. The author's vast rage against the synthetic and cruel, emotional life, and the 'splendid isolation of the mind' that he finds everywhere, are conveyed with a sharp irony that will be felt long after the book is put away. His picture of utter vindictiveness, gathering force behind the façade of friendship, is shocking, terrifying, and disconcertedly recognizable."

The book definitely feels very personal to the author, as first novels so often do. It is at once verbosely overwritten, and a hothouse of restrained passions. There is no question but that he is railing against his restrained English upbringing. The flap copy goes on to explain the plot:

"Engaged by the sanctimonious hostility of his home life, Stephen lives in emotional and intellectual isolation until he meets Fabien—a wealthy, cultured and hedonistic young foreigner. Through Fabien he envisages a dazzling new way of life in which 'warm human contact would penetrate the intellect while embracing the heart,' and he sets out to intrench himself with his new friend by disposing of two great obstacles—his own inadequacy and a rival named Duncan. Stephen's campaign, increasingly feverish and tortured, abject and malevolent, provides a brilliant and haunting study of homosexuality in process of development."

The feverish quality to the writing lends passion to Sanderson's story of a young man awakening to his own talents and desires. Sanderson definitely evidenced a strong sympathy for some (though not all) of his gay characters. His son, John Douglas Sanderson, said that later in life he had many gay friends in Spain, "some of whom worshipped him as a father figure." Perhaps, in a more general sense, his true sympathies lay with the outsider in society, with a definite distaste for class consciousness and the thwarting of the artistic urge which can be traced back to his mother's rejection.

In fact, the thing that really hits the reader when encountering Sanderson's writing for the first time, is the anger and urgency which he uses to propel each story along. The Sanderson mysteries aren't always solved by cool intellectual minds interested in cracking a puzzle, but sometimes by sheer force of will, by frantic, haunted men with much to lose, and nothing less than their lives and freedom to gain. Sanderson's plots involve lots of running and chasing and falling and smashing and shooting. And after all that misery, it isn't even the solving of the mystery that really counts—though the payoff is always there—it's the getting out alive, which for most of Sanderson's main characters is the real challenge.

As Kevin Burton Smith observes in a recent introduction to David Montrose's *The Body on Mount Royal* (Ricochet Press, 2012), Sanderson's main characters are "desperate lone wolves [who] seemed to be always on the verge of losing it—politically, emotionally, even psychologically." This is a perfect description. As Smith says, Sanderson's books are "darker and messier," than the competition, propelled at a breakneck urgency.

Dark Passions Subdue was published in 1952, first by Dodd, Mead, then by Avon Books in a 1953 paperback edition. *Exit in Green*, Sanderson's first actual mystery was published in hardback only by Dodd, Mead in 1953 (and then expanded as *Murder Came Tumbling* when it was published as a hardback in England in 1959 by Hammond, Hammond & Company). The story concerns a fretful Boston playwright recovering from nervous exhaustion in a resort in the Laurentian Mountains who encounters murder when a British stage actress who is vacationing nearby is found dead. The tone of *Exit* is rather playful, almost teasing, and the action fairly restrained as Sanderson felt his way into this new medium.

Right after *Exit in Green* came *Hot Freeze* (also published by Dodd, Mead in hardback in 1954) the book which presumably won him his $10 bet, and introduced us to Montreal PI, Mike Garfin. In the words of Kevin Burton Smith from his introduction to the Stark House edition of *The Deadly Dames*, Garfin is a "former Royal Canadian Mounted Police officer of French-Canadian and Irish-Canadian ancestry who becomes a private investigator with an office in Montréal's centre-ville and an apartment in the Notre-Dame-des-Grâce district." Or, in the words of paperback publisher Popular Library from their back cover blurb: "Big Mike Garfin, hired to tail a degenerate playboy, follows his quarry into a notorious sin-spot only to fall into a hornet's nest of kill-crazy underworld hoodlums. Here is a passionate suspense thriller written at machine-gun tempo!"

Quite a change for an author whose first book was a "brilliant and haunting study." But by now, Sanderson had found his footing and was off and running, and getting good reviews to boot. The *New York Times* critic called *Hot Freeze* "entertaining…the tempo is fast" and *The Saturday Review Syndicate* said "it's a rough winter in Montreal when Op. Mike Garfin takes on a case for a quality gal." Not ecstatic reviews, but much more positive than the drubbing Sanderson took on his first novel. He had found his niche.

Hot Freeze dealt with the drug trade and was quickly followed that same year by another Garfin thriller, *The Darker Traffic*, which was reprinted in paperback in 1955 by Popular Library as *Blondes Are My Trouble*, this time focusing on prostitution. For anyone who thought Montreal was a quiet, genteel city to the north of New York, *Hot Freeze* and *The Darker Traffic* set them straight. In *Traffic* "the story combines fancy floozies, sizzling smooching and gore…Fast paced action with a surprise climax," according to the critic from

Tulsa World.

The following paragraph from the back cover of *Blondes are My Trouble* should give the reader a good example of Sanderson's brisk, declarative approach to thriller writing:

> "I slid the girl to the floor. She fell like dead meat, her dress up above her knees. At the same moment, Yellow-Head went after the pair of hoods. The blackjack whistled. One thug went down. The other guy swung around. The blackjack hit him right in the mouth. He was out cold. Yellow-Head grinned at me. 'We're in, pal.' I nodded. We were in, all right."

Mickey Spillane would be proud. Sanderson's career really began to take off. By this point, he had left Canada and was travelling around Europe, settling in Spain, where he met his wife, Fina, and where his son, John, was eventually born. And this is where he bid adieu to Mike Garfin for awhile. As Sanderson pointed out in the Soler interview for *El Temps* in 1990, "I am a writer with no imagination who can only write about places and people I know. Mike Garfin, for instance, is based on a corporal of the Canadian Mounted Police I knew really well. When I started travelling...Mike Garfin made no sense anymore."

Sanderson's next book, *Prey by Night*, was set in Spain. It was also his first book written for the lucrative Gold Medal market. Gold Medal Books was the premier paperback publisher of the 1950s both in terms of sales and quality for the men's thriller market. Published in 1955, *Prey by Night* was also the first book to utilize yet another name change for Sanderson. Skipping over his contractual relationship with his original agent for a lucrative side deal, he was now Malcolm Douglas, named after his favorite brother, Malcolm Frank Sanderson. But Sanderson proved to be an uneasy traveler, often developing a love-hate relationship with each new locale he'd settle in. These telling passages from *Prey* say it all:

> "The road was like almost any other road in Spain—twisting like boiled macaroni, the only one in the district, and very bad. Spanish road-builders have a conviction that any distance tween two points should be made as long as possible...
> "There's nothing like that scenery anywhere else in the world. Range after towering range of peaks, sun-smitten Spanish rock, every shade from bright yellow to a purple almost black. Once in a while, thousands of feet below in the foothills, you catch a glimpse of man-made terracing, where people are trying to suck a living from the dry soil by growing olive trees. Tough people."

Prey by Night tells the story of a young smuggler named Bill Williams who is being forced out of business by a larger group called the Association. Over the course of a couple days, he has to find out who is out to get him, while keeping one step ahead of his partner Paco, who is murderously upset that Bill has fallen in love with his sister Maria. Like most of the Sanderson thrillers, this one never stops moving. Williams has his boat shot at, another boat exploded under him, and his car driven off the road; he's been roughly interrogated by the police, chased by a Spanish bull, and survived a knife fight. It's almost beside the point when he finally discovers who the bad guy is. By the end of the book, we're just relieved that he and Maria can finally sail off into the sunset, because they've just been through two days of hell. If *Prey by Night* is one of Sanderson's best thrillers, it is also a poignant love story, perhaps reflecting his own burgeoning love affair with Fina, the woman who in June of 1957 would become his wife, and with Spain itself.

The notices continued to come in. A writer for *The Naperville Sun* called *Prey by Night* "one of the most exciting...adventure yarns we've ever read," and that fellow from *The New York Times* was back with the opinion that this was one "tough action tale." Sanderson kept the folks at Gold Medal happy.

Rain of Terror came next, another Malcolm Douglas thriller published by Gold Medal in 1955, this one set in a small Italian mountain village south of Naples. The area is being deluged by rain and newspaper reporter Jake Abbott is sent up the flooded mountain with a photographer to write about the disaster. Jake is having an affair with his boss's wife and eventually they all end up in this small village where the water is knocking hell out of everything and everybody. Jake's boss is killed, an old World War II treasure is discovered, Jake is implicated and no one is who they seem.

This is one of Sanderson's most frantic novels yet. Weather always plays a major role in his books—a heatwave here, freezing snow there—but this book unleashes the full fury of Nature's hell as the characters dodge or are engulfed in rivers of water, mudslides, falling buildings and even a flooded automobile tunnel. In the following passage, Sanderson combines action with weather in a scene that leaves the reader winded:

"The figure continued to advance, and Jake Abbott knew he was going to die. He wanted to dig himself in the earth. His scrabbling hand touched a large piece of stone. He snatched at it and straightened up and flung it with all this strength. Angelo gave a tiny scream of surprise. The gun clattered to the ground.

"Jake ran. He cleared the arch and the heavens seemed to split. There was a brief roar, like the concert of a thousand caged animals. The rain was hammering down with renewed intensity. The gun barked again, strangely muffled. Jake couldn't get his breath... In the thundering of rain he couldn't tell whether he was still pursued or not."

Before the end of the day, Jake is being pursued not only by Angelo but the local police, while all hell continues to break loose from the skies. In 144 short pages, Sanderson takes the reader on a trip to the Seventh Level and back again.

It was during this time, while living with Fina and his young son, John, in Alicante, Spain, that Sanderson decided to move his family back to Canada, where they would live until 1963. While there, according to son John, Sanderson "wrote some articles that he read aloud in a local radio station about life in Spain, what the wedding in Alicante had been like, etc." Wherever he lived, he loved to talk about somewhere else.

This brings us to the next Malcolm Douglas novel, *The Deadly Dames* (1956), and the return of his Montreal private eye. As he said, Sanderson liked to write about what he knew and decided to write another Mike Garfin mystery set in his old stomping ground. Unfortunately, Garfin belonged to Dodd, Mead, or least another agent, and for contractual reasons, Sanderson had to change his character's name to Bill Yates for Gold Medal. Same over-sized detective, same milieu, but different name. And this time he gives his character a heatwave to deal with. And not just any heatwave—the mother of all heatwaves. Yates catches his image in a shop window: "six feet, brown hair, brown eyes slightly poached, and a hundred-ninety pounds, every one of them sweating."

Yates is first hired by a lush to tail his wife, whose mother-in-law then attempts to hire him away before she is hit by a bus. After that, things get messy. Yates is hired by the wife, whose sister gets in on the act, and pretty soon the bodies start to pile up. Eventually everyone is out to kill Yates. There is always a high body count in Sanderson's books, and the hero always seems to be the logical scapegoat. But in this case, Yates also has to do battle with rampaging mosquitoes. Stripped to his shorts in order to find out the identity of a body lying in a canoe on a nighttime lake, Yates encounters true torture:

> "I kicked, not using my hands, gliding forward. My feet touched oozy bottom... In the stillness I heard the low whining of the insects. I almost swallowed my gorge.
>
> "The boat started up with a roar. A bullet plucked the water beside me. I dived into the forest.
>
> "...I put my forearms in front of me and pushed at the high undergrowth and the bracken whipped me. My bare feet twisted on the uneven ground. The boat roared closer. A bullet slapped into the woods. The mosquitoes came.
>
> "They came in a cloud of millions. The needles pierced my skin and I went wild and the panic was worse than the pain because I couldn't get away from them... The whine of the insects rose to a scream."

Once again, Mother Nature wreaks havoc on our hero, and it's a toss-up whether he gets a worse deal from the mosquitoes or the guys who are chasing him.

Sanderson lived with his wife and son in Montreal for two years but the travel urge was as strong as ever. In 1958, he took a solo trip through the United States. This gave him the background for *Night of the Horns* and *Catch a Fallen Starlet*, both set in Southern California. In between his Gold Medal books and before the California novels, however, he produced one more book from his European travels. This was *Final Run*, published in hardback by Secker & Warburg in London in 1956 under his real name, and reprinted in the U.S. in paperback by Popular Library as *Flee from Terror* by Martin Brett.

This time Sanderson gave us an Eastern European spy novel, utilizing his experiences travelling around Yugoslavia (around the same time he was in Spain gathering ideas for *Prey by Night* and *Rain of Terror*). In *Final Run*, an expatriate American named John Gregory is offered ten grand for a mission behind the Iron Curtain by an old spy named Blishen. The spy's wife offered her body to double-cross him. His best friend betrayed him. The secret police want to beat the hell out of him. Written in an extremely abrupt, declarative style, this is Sanderson at his darkest and most cynical. This is also one of his most political novels as he lashes out at both the country and its leader, Tito:

> "I once knew a man who liked Yugoslavia. He always talked of it with
> a defensive passion. ...He used to say that if religion was right and he
> was due for Hell, he expected to open his eyes after death in a replica of
> Ljubljana. There'd be no devils, no flames, no heat, no cold, nothing.
> Just a great grey drabness and over it all an electric sign spelling out the
> name of SATAN. In Ljubljana the sign says TITO."

He further makes his point by describing this street scene: "The workers were going home. I didn't hear a cheerful voice or a single sound of laughter. It was chilling. The only time an inhabitant shows animation is where he's drunk, which is often, and early." And just in case the reader doesn't get the point the author is trying to make about the drabness of the town, there is this: "I took my drink to a far table. I rolled back the cloth and watched the flies ascend. I sat down. The flies came back." By this point, Sanderson is beginning to sound more like Camus than Spillane. Or as the critic for *The Spectator* put it: "As pretty a talent for torture scenes as Ian Fleming. There is an echo of Hemingway *staccato* in the prose."

Like *Rain of Terror* and *Prey at Night*, *The Final Run* most of the action takes place over a 24-hour period, mainly at night, with a plot that involves a mad dash from situation to situation, each one seemingly worse than the one before—and each one involving lots of pain and discomfort for the main character before the final twist of betrayal is revealed at the end.

His fourth book for Gold Medal produced the climax of his European chase thrillers, the aptly named *Pure Sweet Hell* in 1957. This one is set in Alicante, Spain, where Sanderson would eventually return to and live the rest of his life. The settings are all places he knew well. The set-up involves an FBI agent named Bishop who is trying to break a drug ring by finding out who is smuggling cocaine into the country. He is under cover as part of a merchant ship's crew. When they land, the rest of the night becomes one long chase (another 24-hour dash through hell) down alleys, into bars, over fences and into various hell-holes as he tries to track down his lead. Bishop has stuffed a wad of bills into his shoes to purchase the drug, so his feet are in constant pain from the pressure, and it's hot and miserable. He eventually finds his man, right under his nose the entire time, but nearly kills himself doing so. It's the perfect setting for a Sanderson book, and one of the high points of his writing career.

Sanderson's own favorites, according to his son John, were *Prey by Night* and *Night of the Horns*. The latter title is another split-by-line book, published in England under its original title and under the author's real name. In the U.S. it was published as *Murder Comes Calling* and was the last of the "Malcolm Douglas" thrillers from Gold Medal. In it, Sanderson tries something a little different by creating a protagonist who is both naïve, clueless and just a little exasperating in his holier-than-thou attitude. Lawyer Robert Race has a good practice helping people he knows to be innocent; and he is married to a beautiful woman that makes other men envious. But Race has taken on a shady client by the name of Kresnik who wants him to pick up a suitcase for him and hold it in his apartment until he sends someone to get it. Race would like to refuse but Kresnik threatens to reveal their relationship. That night, while Race is retrieving the suitcase, someone jumps him, and in one evening his entire life is turned upside down. He is slapped and rejected by an old flame, told off by those he thought respected him, threatened by Kresnik's henchmen, accused of murder and worse of all, finds that his beautiful wife has been less than faithful.

In its own frantic way, *Night of the Horns* has much in common with *Pure Sweet Hell* as Race races from one situation to another, uncovering facts along the way in one revelatory night of hell on earth (it is never named, but the city here feels like San Diego). He finds out that his protégée, the man he got off on a murder charge, was guilty all along. He finds out that his morally indignant father-in-law has some nasty secrets. He finds that love can come from the least likely of places. But mostly he finds out that he has been living a lie, that everything he believes is wrong. The pell-mell pacing doesn't detract from the sting in its tale, making this one of Sanderson's best, and quite possibly the apex of his writing career.

After *Horns* comes a real mystery of a book. His next novel, *The Shreds*, was only published as *Sables-d'or-les-pains* in France as part of the Serie Noire from

Gallimard in 1958 under the Martin Brett pseudonym. The French title is a play on words, referencing the coastal town of Sables-d'Or-les-Pins on the coast of Brittany. Sanderson had four of his books published in French only, and as far as I know, none of them ever existed in English editions, nor have the original manuscripts ever been found. In fact, we only know the original English titles from the copyright page of the French editions. And it's particularly frustrating for his English-only fans because Sanderson was now writing at the top of his form.

But as son John pointed out, Sanderson "sold mostly in France." Invited to a convention there some years later, Sanderson was surprised that so many people showed up with stacks of his books to be signed.

Following *The Shreds* came *Cry Wolfram*, published in England in 1959 under the Sanderson name by Secker & Warburg, and in the U.S. as *Mark it for Murder* by Avon Books. This is a much lighter book than its predecessors, as evidenced by this almost-playful opening:

> "The night outside was filled with sea-sounds and the smell of flowers. The Regatta Club was full of cigarette smoke and expensive perfumes with an underwaft of perspiration. There was a band playing French jazz, loud but good, and a big-chested girl at the microphone singing loud but no good. The dancing couples were crammed hard together and an aerial view of the floor would have looked like a snood of boiling porridge.
>
> It was two o'clock in the morning. I should not have been there."

Like *Pure Sweet Hell*, the action is set in a Spanish coastal town (referred to only as "the capital city of the province") where Johnny Molson, hired as nursemaid and bodyguard to an old, hardened millionaire named Craddock, finds himself in the middle of a financial swindle involving the supply of wolfrum, or tungsten. There are also two women involved, as is so often the case, one to tempt and the other to taunt. As usual, Molson soon finds himself unjustly accused of murder, and before long is subjected to ill treatment at the hands of the local police:

> "My jacket was pulled up, my legs were clamped. I lay there like a stretched pelt. The rubber hose whistled through the air and hit me across the kidneys. The agony was incredible."

Though the pace is no less frenetic than his previous few novels. *Cry Wolfram* is leavened by occasional touches of humor that was completely missing from the last few books—for example, a drunken gypsy wedding that comes out of nowhere and provides Molson a brief opportunity to recover from his beating. You can't help but think that *Cry Wolfram* could have been hatched as a Hollywood film plot, with its tireless hero and bittersweet ending. It makes sense when you consider that the next Sanderson novel, *Catch a Fallen Starlet*—published in paperback by Avon Books in 1960—was set right in the middle of Hollywood.

As his son John pointed out in his introduction to the Stark House edition of *Pure Sweet Hell*, Sanderson loved the movies. James Cagney was a particular favorite. In *Fallen Starlet*, the main character, Al Dufferin, is a former script writer who had left Hollywood after a scandalous death in which he had been involved. Now he has returned to work on a new writing deal which naturally leads to murder. As John points out, Sanderson himself had had a bad film experience when veteran director Marion Gering came over to Spain to talk about turning *Prey by Night* into a movie. After many meetings and letters, Gering turned down the proposal. Dufferin reflects much of Sanderson's cynicism about the Hollywood machine, as well as the author's disdain for television, which he considered a threat to the cinema.

Once the Sanderson family moved back to Spain, while Franco was still in control (he died in 1975), Sanderson wouldn't allow a TV set in the house. As John mentioned in one of many emails, his dad was a very popular author in Europe, but none of the Sanderson novels were published in Spain. The reference to cocaine trafficking alone in *Pure Sweet Hell* would have landed him in jail because Franco denied the existence of any such illegal drug activity. Sanderson certainly didn't want Franco's propaganda invading his house, so instead of television, the Sanderson father and son would spend a lot of time at the local movie theatre.

Sanderson's last great mystery thriller was *A Dum-Dum for the President*, which also happens to be Mike Garfin's final appearance. Though still set in the Montreal area, *Dum-Dum* feels very international in scope—no surprise after all of Sanderson's travels—since it involves Garfin's discovery of a deposed South American president hiding out on Mount Royal from his political enemies. Very much a hardboiled thriller, Sanderson also interjects a strong dose of cynical politics into the story as he did in *Final Run*. Until Stark House reprinted it in paperback in 2006, *A Dum-Dum for the President* had been a fairly rare Sanderson novel, only available in a British hardback edition published by Hammond, Hammond & Co. in 1961.

Two years later, in 1963, Sanderson left Canada for good and moved his family permanently back to Alicante, Spain. Gone were the U.S. paperback deals. The next three books, in fact, were only published in France by Gallimard. The *The Dead Connection* came out first as *La came á papa* (1961; loosely translated as "Drugs for Daddy"), followed by *Shout for a Killer* as *Chabanais chez les pachas* (1963; "Chabanais at the Pashas") and finally *Score for Two Dead* as *Le moîne connait la musique* (1964; "The Monk Knows the Score"). Like *The Shreds*, these three novels had no non-French editions and we only know their original English titles from the copyright pages of the Gallimard books.

After this, there were only four more Sanderson thrillers which came out in England in small hardback printings intended for the library trade from Robert Hale Ltd. *Lam to Slaughter* (1964) is the story of a young man being chased across Europe by some shadowy figures when he ditches the safety of his uncle's care for that of a dubious friend. *Black Reprieve* (1965) is a political thriller about a group of escaped prisoners in Africa, one of whom is a traitor. *No Charge for Framing* (1969) takes the action to Cuba for an unabashed spy novel featuring escaped cons, warring government agents, two American girls and a Cuban assassin.

By now, Sanderson was no longer writing in top form. There were moments, but the edge was off. The last novel, *A Dead Bullfighter* (1975) feels more cantankerous than thrilling, returning Sanderson back to Spain for a tale of political corruption set against the world of bullfighting. The ability to tell a good tale is still there, but the immediacy of the prose is gone. Son John admits that his dad had been drinking pretty heavily in his later years, only quitting in 1995, twenty years after his wife Fina had left him and moved back to Montreal. In Sanderson's own words, from his interview with Soler, "I have some Irish blood so I have always drunk a lot."

Nor had Sanderson made a lot of money from his books. He was never really able to keep his family comfortable with his book income. Sanderson's younger brother, Frank, was a successful businessman, according to John, and transferred money to his brother which allowed him to live off the interest in his later years. He did start one more book, a story about drug trafficking from Colombia, but never got around to finishing it. As in many a case, alcohol eventually replaced the creative urge. And though he was never in any physical pain, his later years were spent with very little to do.

Fortunately we have so many great hardboiled thrillers that he did write during his lifetime: the Mike Garfin books and the Gold Medal novels, in particular. Sanderson seemed to write at a fever pitch. He put his characters through trial by torture. These are dark, sometimes dream-like stories about men who search in the night for a small bit of information that they think will set them free. Most of them find a bit of redemption at the end, and some even walk off into the sunset with the girl. But Sanderson always made them work for it, as hard on his characters as he was on the people around him. In fact, he could be quite the curmudgeon when he wanted to. As he confessed to Soler in his final interview, "I hate the English; I guess that is why I became Canadian."

Sanderson wrote from the gut. As Kevin Burton Smith says of his writing, "his twisted and often nightmarish tales of obsession stand up amazingly well, even half a century later, and still boast a passionate no-holds-barred immediacy that's hard to deny." Like fellow thriller writers Cornell Woolrich and David Goodis, Sanderson could bring nightmares to life with a crazy kind of logic. As a man, Sanderson loved the outdoors; he loved canoeing, sailing and skiing. As an artist, he loved classical music, art and decorating, and the Mediterranean. As a writer, however, he travelled down some very dark paths, reveling in the twisted by-ways, the ill-lit corners of the night—and of the soul. Sanderson died in Alicante, Spain, in 2002 at the age of eighty-two—irascible, irritating, argumentative, colorful and opinionated—and one hell of a great thriller writer.

—February 2013
Eureka, CA

Sources:

Douglas Sanderson interview with Lucas Soler in *El Temps*, Spain, 1990.

John Sanderson introduction to *Pure Sweet Hell/Catch a Fallen Starlet* (Stark House Press, 2004); plus various email exchanges.

Kevin Burton Smith introductions to *Pure Sweet Hell/Catch a Fallen Starlet* (Stark House Press, 2004) and *The Deadly Dames/A Dum-Dum for the President* (Stark House Press, 2006).

Night of the Horns

by Douglas Sanderson

For Marjorie
with affection

PART ONE

1

I sustained the bright mood all the way back from the jail. When I reached my office and flopped into the chair my false confidence waned. I faced up to the fact that my client was going to lose his case. He had the wrong witnesses against him.

Few people disbelieve the evidence of children. Place a child in court, especially a little girl, and everyone is so anxious to protect her that usually she finishes by giving no real evidence whatever. There's nothing concrete to combat and the case gets lost on unstated implications. And if you cross-question her the jury hates you and takes it out on your client.

This case had little girls to the number of three.

I gazed out of the window at a spring evening, a small horned moon rising like a sliver of Edam cheese over the buildings down by the port. I got depressed. My depression depressed me further. To enter court without confidence means that your client has lost before you start.

It was not a question of money. Garcia wasn't paying me; he was one of what Eve called my charity cases, the sort I took only when I was convinced of the client's innocence. I was convinced about Garcia. Losing the case wasn't going to hurt so much as the idea of an innocent man finishing in jail. Garcia had a cruel sentence coming up. I could feel it.

I swivelled in the chair, turned on the desk light, examined the urgent mail left stacked by Miss Cleaver. I had enough work to last me six months: I should have been satisfied. I couldn't get Garcia out of my head. I thumbed the pile of letters, took the two unopened ones from the bottom. The first was marked Strictly Personal.

It was from Mrs. Danvers; old, rich, bitch and eldritch. Her daughter-in-law was poisoning her with daily doses of strychnine and if I took the case to court I could name my own price. I dropped her letter in the wastebasket and picked up the other marked Personal. I knew just by looking what it contained.

Five others had arrived in the recent past with the same barbed-wire handwriting, the same cheap envelope. I ripped it open.

"I going to get you any day now for what you done to my bruther. You going to be sorry when I kill you."

A long list of dirty names. Unsigned.

It might be anyone, a legion of people dating back to when I was assistant

D.A. It could be a crank having no connection with me, a man who wrote this sort of thing as a pastime. It was my duty to inform the police. But the poor devil was obviously uneducated, probably mentally ill, and I'd find it hard to forgive myself if the police actually caught him.

The phone rang.

I said, "Robert Race speaking."

"Eve Race speaking. It is now past seven o'clock. At eight-thirty we are due at my Papa's place for dinner. Get your skates on, sweet, so I can fix you up neat in your bib and tucker and we can be on time for once."

"Incidentally, I love you," I said.

"You should. Now come home."

"Listen, Eve. You mustn't get mad. I'm up to my eyes. I'll be working till midnight. My apologies to your father, and see if he cares a hoot so long as you're there."

She wailed. I loved her to idiocy even on the phone. "Get here or I'll divorce you. I'll give the case to another lawyer. I've bought a voluptuous new dress specifically designed to rouse a mad lust in you. I want you panting after me."

"Around midnight I'll pant like a steam shovel. Honey, I can't get away."

"Charity case?"

"Partly."

"Damn you and damn your Robin Hood complex. Poor Maid Marian has to live like a grass widow." She laughed. I was forgiven. She said, "I guess a maiden couldn't be a widow. Okay, lovey, I'll await the chopper at midnight."

"Yeeeow!" I said. "Any messages?"

"Someone phoned that Mr. Al Kresnik wants to speak to you. Shady business, no doubt. I said you were still at the office."

"I was probably down at the jail. Anything else?"

"Nothing."

I said, "Oh hell, this is Wednesday, Tony Fontaine's night to come to supper. Get hold of the kid and put him off."

"What? Oh, he already phoned. I told him we were going out. He can come Monday."

"He upset?"

"What do you care?"

"Okay, then there's nothing on my mind except all this work and being in love with you. 'Bye, dear."

"Adios, my wooden Adam."

Fifteen minutes later I had the end of a pencil in my mouth, my feet on the desk, I was leaning back and thinking about Eve. The kick is supposed to be gone after the first six months of marriage. It's a logical, biological conclusion. In the days when I believed it I didn't know I was going to marry Eve. I didn't know this world had any Eves.

I forget which orphans the Charity Ball was in aid of. Being an orphan myself I bought a ticket. We met there. We fell in love like a cannon going off. I'd recently quit the D.A.'s office, I was broke, I wasn't even a struggling young lawyer, I was merely writhing. She was the only child of Sam Alford, already retired and reputedly very rich.

His wife had recently died. He objected to the marriage. But I wanted Eve and she wanted me and in the end she won because he idolised her. We were married at eleven in the morning.

Sam Alford and I declared a sort of truce. The fact that he didn't really like me had one good result. He never tried to help me, rich as he was. He threw no business my way. He let me accomplish everything on my own and I was grateful. I knew he continued for a while being generous to Eve, giving her lump sums to spend on herself. But even that had stopped six months ago. The only thing that didn't change was his jealousy of me.

Perhaps he had cause for it: I was so very happy. After two years of marriage the kick not only remained, it increased. Each time I made love to her was more potent than the last. Merely to watch her undress was like being belted by a mule. And when she lay in my arms and put her fingertips to my spine I knew why I'd always be faithful to her. No other woman could compare even in my imagination.

I chewed harder on the pencil, slumped deeper in the chair and thought the pleasant thoughts of a lustful husband. I eyed the work with distaste for five minutes, fighting a losing battle. I wanted my Eve.

I dumped the papers back into the incoming tray, tidied the desk, put away the pencils, stood up and got my hat. I couldn't find the keys. I made a resolution to do something about my absent-mindedness. I discovered the hole in the lining of my trouser pocket, retrieved the keys from under the desk, dusted myself, checked the safe, took a last look around and got to the door.

The phone rang.

I debated whether to answer it, and hoped it would stop ringing. They never do unless you're running from the bath. I remembered the things Eve said about my being a work slave and her being a grass widow and I felt like a weakling. I answered the phone anyway.

Jordan said, "Race?"

He had a thin, sharp, snorting voice as if he spoke through only one nostril. I didn't know his exact capacity, but he seemed to be one of Kresnik's larger satellites.

"Good evening," I said. "I was just leaving."

"You're not now. You're gonna wait. Mr. Kresnik's coming up to see you."

I never liked Jordan. Now his tone riled me. I said, "I've got urgent business. That's why I'm leaving. Tell Mr. Kresnik I'll get in touch with him in the morning."

"Mr. Kresnik'll get in touch with you tonight. You'll do like he says, shyster."

"Mr. Jordan," I said stiffly, "Mr. Kresnik is an important and appreciated client. However, there are other people who have an even stronger call on me. I'm going to see one of them now. I assume from the fact that Mr. Kresnik can wait an hour that he doesn't want a *habeas corpus ad subjiciendum*. Anything else can be taken care of tomorrow. Goodnight."

I hung up.

The worry about Garcia came back.

I put on my hat, locked the office, went down in the elevator. Mrs. Mendoza was washing the main lobby and she gave me a big white Mexican smile. We said goodnight. I went round to the lot, got the car and drove toward home.

2

Waiting for the red light to change I saw Paul Taylor over on the other corner flagging madly at every passing cab. He looked irritable, out of temper, slightly stewed as usual, and I considered leaving him to it. He saw me and came on a jay-walking run. The decision was out of my hands.

He slid in beside me, smelling like a vat of bourbon. He said, "Tried getting a taxi in this town this time of the evening?"

"What happened to the car?"

"Laura took it to the hairdresser."

"Buy another."

"Another Laura? Oh my God, you mean there are others?"

"Another car."

"Some of us lawyers are still poor," he snapped. The light changed. He grunted and sank back in the seat. "I don't feel so bad. If the impeccable Robert Race can be late, so can I."

"What's this?"

"We're both dining tonight with my client—your father-in-law. That's why Laura had the hair done."

A bunch of Mexican kids I knew were playing on the far sidewalk. I waved to them. They didn't see me. Taylor said, "How come Alford didn't give his business to you and keep it in the family? I wish he had."

"He wanted me to stand on my own feet," I said. "I've always appreciated it."

"Pretty speech. Chum, if I relied on Alford I'd be on relief. I figured I'd got a rich tycoon. His business consists of an occasional lease and a peanut transfer in shares. Take him any time you want. And if you're wondering why I go to dinner with him, that's Laura's idea. She likes the social altitude."

"Maybe you're still poor because you talk about a client's private business."

Taylor turned his head and looked at me with contempt. "Rip off the Fauntleroy collar, Race, you don't fool anyone. You're in a straight racket. You pick cases like this Garcia guy, defend them free and let the resultant publicity pull you in great hunks of business. You make sure of the publicity by picking the most sensational cases. You work for nothing, pose as a do-gooder, every-one thinks you're honest and that means more business because people are afraid of all lawyers except the supposedly honest ones. You're a real smart cookie, Race."

"Smart? It might be I defend these cases because I believe the people involved to be innocent."

He looked out of the window. He gave a short laugh. "You holy bastard, you never drop the pose for a minute, do you? Innocent like that Tony Fontaine kid?"

"Why pick him especially?"

"Attempted robbery with violence while he was jugged up with tea."

"Look," I said. "I took the case because there was a marijuana drive on at the time. Tony Fontaine was going to be rail-roaded to jail as an example. He never smoked a reefer in his life."

"And you got him off the robbery with violence because the principal witness suddenly decided he might have made a mistake in identification. What did you do—pay the old guy?"

My conscience twitched.

I said, "Would you like a good belt in the nose?"

"Okay," he waved a hand, "okay, we're neighbours, let's not fight. Eve and Laura made up their quarrel, let's not start another." He rubbed his jaw. Sud-denly he scrubbed at it ferociously. "I'm jealous of you."

The scar on my conscience still tingled. I said, "About Tony Fontaine. I had confidence in the kid and he's proved right. He's at college now, getting good marks. One day he's going to amount to something. I shall be proud to have helped him out of the gutter."

"Out of the gutter," Paul Taylor sneered. "I wonder if you know how god-damned Epworth League and goddamned revolting you sound when you use that tone of voice. And who's paying Fontaine's college fees?"

I kept silent.

"That's my answer. Ask what I think, the punk's got it good. He's found a sucker. Always at your apartment, wears your cast-off clothing, comes to sup-per twice a week—"

"I didn't ask what you think. Lay off! The kid's maybe a little wild, but how were you at twenty."

"Me, I never was twenty. I was thirty-five when I was born; thirty-five and disillusioned and poor. It'll get worse. I'll stay disillusioned and poor, but I'll get to be sixty."

He tossed his cigarette from the side window. "Nuts! Don't listen to me! I'm having one of my misanthropic spells. I hate the whole rotten world and every-thing in it. Most of all I hate you. You're successful. You're hard as nails, fit as a fiddle, belong to the Rackets Club and play lunchtime squash three times a week. This a new second car?"

"Yes," I said. "Stop beefing. You do well enough. You live in the apartment below mine, we both enjoy the same living conditions, I've got a gorgeous wife, you've got a gorgeous wife—"

"You can have her. I'll swap for yours. Like in one of those sensational tabloid cases you'll be defending one of these days."

I said, "You really do want that belt in the nose."

"Oh Christ, forget it! Thanks for the ride home."

We drew up in front of the apartment block, went together through the entrance to the elevator. The cage ascended and I was thinking how things had changed, how Taylor and I used to be close friends. The relationship between our wives had cooled off six months ago for no reason I could fathom and Paul had joined the movement by getting nasty with me. The breach between Eve and Laura was now apparently healed, but he clearly wanted to stay nasty.

The elevator stopped with a little pop at the fifth floor. He glanced at his watch. "Three quarters of an hour to get there. Our wives'll play hell."

"Yours maybe, not mine. It's a pleasant surprise. She doesn't know I'm coming."

He stared at me a second and flittered his eyelids. "Well, call down for us when you go. We'll all arrive together."

"Sure." I went up to the next floor and along the corridor to the apartment. No key. I went twice through all my pockets. Car keys, office keys, safe-deposit key, but no latch key. I'd probably left it at the office. Eve was going to rib me.

I stabbed the buzzer and waited. She didn't answer.

I wondered if she were having one of the customary heart-to-heart phone chats with her father. I buzzed again. I felt foolish because maybe she'd already left for her father's house and I would have to go down and get the janitor. Then I figured she hadn't heard me because she was taking a bath or back in the bedroom changing. I put my finger on the button and held it there.

She called something from the back of the apartment. I heard her coming. The safety chain rattled as she unhooked it, the door opened, and there she was in her kimono, blue eyes wide, golden hair mussed, no shoes on her feet. All my chromosomes set up individual little howls.

"You!" she said, and stood on tip-toe. She flung her arms around my neck and kissed me, the door still open. We held it. She laughed. She murmured something about the neighbours and drew me inside. She said, "You lecherous wolf, you couldn't resist the thought of that dress." She was going to kiss me again. Her eyes widened with horror. "No! Don't tell me it's midnight already."

"We've three-quarters of an hour. Mix us both a martini."

She sank beside me on the settee. Under the kimono she was naked and beautiful. "No time. I have to dress. I stretched on the bed for my ten minutes therapeutic beauty relaxation and fell asleep. Been ringing long?"

"I want that martini."

"Dad'll float you in gin when we get there." She nuzzled my neck. We held tight and kissed deep and I tried to ease her onto the floor. She started giggling. She wriggled away.

"You told me midnight, I'm geared to midnight. Behave or I'll slap you."

Down in the street a man began shouting something. It sounded to me like a love song. Anything right then would have sounded like a love song.

"Eve," I said, "I love you so much it's an ache."

"I know. And it's nice. Ever figure how lucky we are?" She leaned over me and put a hand to the side of my face and looked deep into my eyes. "I love you too, Mr. Race. I've been thinking. Pretty soon we'll have to start making that baby."

I felt very happy. "You mean it this time?"

She nodded.

"Then let's get changed and on our way. Never let it be said any child of ours was made on the quick." I stood up. "Can we afford one?"

"About. Paul Taylor's been telling me this evening how rich we are. He doesn't know our overheads."

"Nor how much we have in the bank," she said. "The last time I looked it was a hundred-and-thirty-three dollars. No cents. Plus two hundred dollars emergency fund in your shirt drawer. Babies cost more."

"We'll manage."

She struck a languishing pose. "Because we have each other. And this thing is bigger than both of us."

"It will be if you don't stop looking at me like that." I moved to pat her backside.

I heard what the man in the street was shouting. I remembered the threatening letters and the fear rose in my throat like bile. I shoved her hard toward the bedroom door. I shouted, "Get out of here!"

3

Her face went deathly white. She said, "What is it?" I was at the sideboard, fumbling for the gun in the drawer. She saw what I was doing. Her voice rose to a scream. "Bob, what is it?"

The voice in the street was still shouting. I heard the noise out on the fire escape. "Into the bedroom," I snapped. I shoved her again. I jumped for the window.

Anti-climax.

Tony Fontaine's grinning face appeared at the other side of the glass. He waved, twiddled his fingers and tapped on the pane. I jerked the window open.

"You goddamned fool," I snarled, "what the hell you think you're doing?" I watched his eyes go wide in surprise. He stood there on the fire escape pained and apprehensive like a kid about to be whipped. I got the reaction.

I started to laugh. I said, "Who's the guy hollering down there? A cop?"

He nodded. His confidence slowly returned. He began grinning again. "Yeah, he's been threatening to put a bullet up my rear end. He's on the point of pulling the trigger. Come out and tell him I'm not a burglar."

I squeezed onto the escape and leaned over the rail. Down in the quiet street a cop was standing quite alone with a gun in his hand, his head tilted back. I recognised him.

I shouted, "Skelly, it's okay. The kid's a screwball. Thanks for being on the job."

"Whatever you say, Mr. Race." He muttered something else I couldn't hear, shrugged his shoulders and started walking away. A light stabbed out on the floor below. Paul Taylor's voice called, "What's going on up there?"

"Nothing," I said, and got back into the apartment and shut the window.

Eve had her back to the frame of the bedroom door, hands clutching her kimono together. The three of us stood in a little pocket of silence and stared at one another. Suddenly she sucked in a deep breath, her eyes crinkled, she began to giggle.

She had the most infectious giggle in the world. Tony joined in first, and I did, and we laughed like fools till the tears ran down our faces and we were weak. She said, "Tony, you dolt, what were you doing out there? Don't you know I'm afraid of prowlers. I even had the chain on the door when Bob came home."

He fought down a residual gurgle of mirth. He was wearing one of my old suits and I thought it looked better on him than it ever had on me. He said, "Mrs. Race, I'm sorry. I'm a nut. I'm studying too hard. I thought it was a good gag to come to supper via the fire escape."

I was putting away the gun. I said, "Didn't Eve tell you on the phone we were going out?"

He was a very good-looking boy, very boyish looking. He ran a hand through his dark curly hair and looked helpless. "That what you said, Mrs. Race? My fault, I didn't understand. I've got the bad habit of trying to read and telephone at the same time."

"God preserve me from absent-minded people," Eve said, and came across and put an arm around my shoulders. "My handsome hunk of a husband will go out one day without his pants."

She kissed me lightly on the mouth. I saw Tony's face. He was feeling out of it. I said, "Don't fret, kid, you'll get this too after you're married."

"I do all right." He jutted his chin with adolescent pride. "Me and some of the boys are going down to Santapola for the week-end. We got some Mexican girls down there."

Eve released me. She said lightly, "Tony, confine that sort of conversation to the times when I'm not here. I'm a little bit of a stuffed shirt. I don't like it."

He grinned. He looked as if he had the world on a string, and that was right at his age. "Sorry again, Mrs. Race, sorry about making the mistake over supper, I'll push along now and can I come as usual on Monday?"

"Sure," I said, and banged his shoulder. "Think I've got another suit you can pick up. Don't study too hard in the interim."

Eve arched her eyebrows. "At Santapola?"

I said, "Tony, how's your mother?"

"She's okay. Still a little sick, but maybe I can change all that when I get out of college." He reached as if to touch my arm, then dropped his hand. "I'll change a lot of things when I get out of college."

I knew what he meant. He was a good kid and I liked him. I said, "Nuts! Now beat it!" I took him to the door. At the elevator he looked back and waved.

Eve had gone to the bedroom. I went in and started undressing and threw my clothes on the rumpled bed where she'd been sleeping. I said, "Honey, you're too hard with Tony. Why did you drop on him like that when he mentioned the girls? It's natural at his age. At any man's age, if he's a bachelor."

She was standing on her kimono, examining her naked body in the full-length mirror. She was Venus. She said, "I'm jealous. You pay too much attention to him. I think he takes advantage of you." She turned her head. "For the love of Peter, get cracking. We'll be late."

I stripped right off. I said, "We're going to pick up Paul and Laura. I drove him home tonight, slightly tight as usual. He tells me you and Laura are pals again. What was the original quarrel about?"

She lunged at me and fetched a tremendous whack across my bare backside. "Stop talking! Into the shower! I'm about to emerge in my new dress."

I grabbed her. "Don't want to wrestle?"

"I hate you!" She groaned. "Oh, Robert Race, how I hate you."

I was towelling myself in the bathroom when she appeared at the doorway. I said softly, "Wow!" The dress was low cut and the colour turned her eyes to amethysts. I caught my breath and just stared. I said, "The desired voluptuous effect."

"Animal," she said. "Here comes the chopper to chop off his head." It was a private joke between us. We smiled and I felt very married and I was happy. She said, "Okay, Race, my feminine ego is sated. I'll empty the pockets of your other suit or you'll forget everything."

I heard the keys and loose change chinking on the bed. I called, "Hole in the right-hand pants pocket." I finished drying myself, stood at the door and contemplated the wonderful back view of her. She felt my eyes. She turned slowly, lips parted. She looked frightened.

In her hand was the letter.

She said quietly, "Who is going to kill you for what you did to the brother?" She tried to smile. "Spelt with a 'u'."

I'd forgotten it was stuffed in my pocket. I went across and took it from her. "Nothing. All lawyers get things like that."

"You've never told me."

"No need."

She stared at me large-eyed, seeing me over a long distance. "If anything happens to you," she said, and suddenly flung her arms convulsively around me and pulled my head down to her breast. A sob escaped her. "Bob! My honey!"

I was thinking of the fire escape, the way Tony Fontaine has been able to enter, the ease of it. The letter writer might get at me through Eve. The thought dissolved my guts.

I disengaged myself. "You'll crumple your voluptuous new dress." I kissed her.

After a while, looking very smart, we went down and picked up Paul and Laura. I left word with the janitor where I'd be if anyone wanted to contact me. We arrived late.

4

Jeff Pastor was at the dinner; lieutenant of police. There were fifteen of us altogether, young to youngish, mostly professional, all known to one another. What my father-in-law, Sam Alford, would call a "damn near ideal dinner party but too goddamn small."

Sam liked to entertain lavishly. I'd thought at first it was loneliness. I learned later that he was just as prodigal when Eve was still at home. After dinner I watched him move smiling among his guests, putting arms around shoulders, happy as a fly on sugar, the perfect match for the somewhat over-spectacular surroundings of his house. Until he opened his mouth.

He was elegant as a Bellini Doge and talked like someone out of Francois Rabelais. At times it seemed every second word was hell or goddamn. He was over sixty. I think he was trying to compensate failing vigour with extra vigour of speech.

I was grieved, though not too much, that he didn't like me better, and slightly annoyed that he thought it my fault we hadn't yet produced a child. During dinner he didn't once speak to me.

When the meal was over he shepherded us all into the big library. There were too many maps and globes, but a good half mile of shelves contained some good books. Sam would have preferred little talking groups so that he could drift from one to the other sucking up the honey, but someone started an apathetic four of bridge and three others, including Eve, played Scrabble.

Paul Taylor's voice rose above everyone else's. He'd been guzzling steadily through dinner and was pretty far gone. I could remember a time when he never got drunk. Now he was seldom anything else.

I was twenty yards around the second shelf, a drink in my hand, looking at some nicely bound translations of Cicero, Euripides, Aristotle, et cetera—and

Rabelais. I was reaching for Tacitus. Sam Alford came up behind me.

"Nothing like 'em," he said. "Hell of a lot more sex than in the goddamn tabloids. Makes your hair stand on end." He laughed in his belly. "Ovid's my boy, except for that story about Myrrha and Cinyras. Makes me think of me and Eve. Can you imagine her creeping into bed to seduce her poor old father?"

It was the sort of thing he liked to say. Once it shocked me. Now I thought, not for the first time, that he was a dirty old man.

"The advantage of education," he said, "is you can talk about sex without being called smutty. You, Robert. When you gonna give me that grandchild? God damn it, you're betraying Eve. You'll have trouble on your hands if you don't hurry."

I said, "Eve's happy enough. She knows I love her."

He stared at me. "You bloody prune! Someone ought to soak you for a week to bring you up to size. How's business? Making money?"

"Some."

On the other side of the room Paul Taylor was getting drunker. He said, "Paul and Laura, like the names of two characters in a stinking sudsy soap-opera. With modifications, of course. The unsuccessful not-so-young lawyer and the aging, long-suffering spouse worrying about Paul's other wife."

He syruped his voice like a radio announcer. "At the same time tomorrow we bring you another heart-warming instalment of tears and laughter and life." The syrup went. He said bitterly, "The time to really listen in is when we get back to the apartment tonight. Or any other night."

Laura turned her head from the bridge table. She was faintly tragic-looking— the Lady of Shalott with a Challion haircut and a Macy's mezzanine gown, her face pale under the red hair. She said, "Paul, stop strip-teasing. No one's interested in seeing your slips. Play your game."

"Tell 'em what my game is."

Eve reached across the table, lightly touched his arm. "Paul, there's no such word as 'convrey.' Take that turn again."

"The guy's a lush," Sam Alford said. "When'd he start that racket?"

I didn't want to talk about him. He was none of my business. I was saved by Jeff Pastor.

I said, "Hi. How are things at Headquarters?"

"The same." He lit a cigarette and looked at the end of it. "I understand we clash in court tomorrow. I'm giving evidence. It's a dirty case. Why'd you take it?"

"Because the guy's innocent. Let's save the discussion till the case is cleared."

Sam Alford's ears pricked up. "You talking about the Mex—Garcia? Sure, the guy's as guilty as hell. You know me, I never condemn anyone for his sex life— a man can couch a swan and give it eggs if he likes. So long as it's an adult swan. A man who fools with little girls ought to be doctored."

I said, "This is interesting. Jeff's worked up a load of circumstantial evidence

from a dozen witnesses and feels sure Garcia is guilty. I've met Garcia, his family, the few friends he has, I've talked to them all and I'm convinced he's innocent. How do you take your stand without knowing anything?"

"Good question," my father-in-law said. "Here's a good answer. I read the
papers. The guy's forty-two. His wife's twenty-one. Proves he likes fresh meat.
He's got two kids. They're both little boys. Means he's got neither sensibility
nor responsibility toward little girls. Means he's guilty."

It was making me cringe. I said, "You left out two more important points. He's
poor. He's a Mexican."

"And for a pretty smart boy," Sam Alford said, "you're a pretty damn stupid bastard." He turned to Jeff Pastor. "My son-in-law's got a couple of dog-
mas. All the rich are sons-of-bitches except for the odd one like me, and all the
poor are nature's noblemen by instinct and natural eugenics. He was once poor
himself. He's hanging on to it. Another dogma is that any member of a minority
group is automatically victimised."

I said, "Jeff, would you have worked so hard if Garcia had been native-born
like his wife?"

He sucked his cigarette. He didn't look at all as a cop is supposed to look. He
said, "I got a good American name. Put the accent on the second syllable I got
a good Mexican name."

I looked into his tanned face. He had sharply defined eyebrows and deep
brown eyes. I felt foolish. I said, "The question was insulting. Sorry. One cor-
rection: I'm still poor."

Over at the table Paul Taylor had developed hiccups, his voice coming in sta-
catto rushes. "Trouble with me, I haven't been successful. Should have been like
that wonderful young lawyer Robert Race. Tell you something. I been like
Robert Race. I been just like him."

His wife led a card. "Shut up, Paul! Play Scrabble!"

He didn't look at her. He said, "Evie, you've put 'adult.' I can add to that and
make adultery. Like to commit adultery with me?"

Eve smiled. She said coolly, "Paul, you're a sweetie." She said it well. I not only
loved her as my wife, I liked her as a woman.

Sam Alford muttered, "Last time that bastard comes here. I'm going to get
him away from my daughter." He strode over to where they were playing Scrabble. "Anyone here spell 'metamorphoses'?"

I turned back to Jeff Pastor. He was drinking his gin slowly. "Wanted to see
you, Jeff," I said. "Would you rather I left it till business hours?"

"Shoot!"

"I'm getting these." I pulled the anonymous letter from my pocket. "This is
the sixth. It occurred to me that the writer might get at Eve."

He read it without changing expression. He said, "Yeah, these are nasty. Old
crimes and old sins cast long shadows. Any ideas?"

"It maybe dates back to when I was assistant D.A. I've been prosecution evidence a few times since then and I can let you have a list. One thing. The writer's pretty obviously sick in the head. Can you operate on an unofficial basis—sort of just warn the guy when you find him?"

Pastor took another sip of gin. His brown eyes hardened. He said, "Race, you're a slop. You're Doctor Pangloss himself. All alone in a little Leibnizean lily-garden where everybody's really a good guy at bottom and nobody must get hurt. Know something? When you were with the D.A. we used to make bets on how long it'd be before your eyes opened. We all lost. When the job began to get sordid and nasty you quit. You're a success now because the sort of professional life you lead would make good reading in the cheap magazines. Everybody loves a guy who loves everybody else because life's easier that way. I'll tell you something else. Somebody once figured that in defending all these bad characters you're really defending yourself, that you've got something on your conscience. I just hope it's nothing to do with your client Mr. Kresnik. I'd watch that guy if I were you. Headquarters watches him, and watches him pretty closely."

I said, "That was a long speech. What about the letter?"

"I proceed officially or not at all."

I took it and thrust it back in my pocket. "Let's talk about something else."

The bridge four had quit playing. Paul Taylor was making too much noise. Sam Alford put a disc of Viennese waltzes on the phonograph and a couple tried to dance. Laura drifted toward us.

She was not a beautiful woman but she was good looking enough and took pains with herself. I was happy she and Eve were friends again. She smiled brightly at Jeff and me, but her eyes had a hollow look. She said, "Hello men. Isn't there a drug called anabuse that wives slip secretly to their husbands to stop them drinking?"

I said, "Maybe he's got business worries."

She looked at me strangely. "You, of course, never worry at all."

I thought of Garcia. I shrugged. "You're looking lovely tonight Laura."

"First time I've been told that in months. Six, to be precise."

Someone touched my arm. Sam Alford's servant said, "Telephone, Mr. Race. They say it's urgent. Will you take it in the hall?"

I excused myself and followed him out. I picked up the phone. It was Jordan again.

His voice sounded a little different. Maybe he was talking through the other nostril. I said, "What is it?"

"Mr. Smart-Aleck? Get down and see Mr. Kresnik. Right now!"

"Mr. Jordan, I'm busy. I'll contact Mr. Kresnik in the morning."

"You'll—ing well do it now, Buster. You're in trouble. You get here right away or...."

He stopped. The phone was still connected. I waited. The hard, smooth voice came on, cold and impersonal as an unmarked tombstone. "Mr. Race, my invitation was more polite but it amounts to the same thing. This is very, very urgent."

He'd never spoken to me over the phone before. I said, "Good evening, Mr. Kresnik."

"I'm in the office back of the *Caracol*. Enter by the alley."

"If it's that urgent."

"It's that urgent. I'm waiting."

I returned to the library. The Scrabble game had crumbled. There was no conversation, no music, Paul Taylor was holding the floor, swaying from side to side and being drunk. I beckoned to Eve. Sam Alford took advantage of the diversion and said something loud. General conversation started again.

Paul remained in the centre of the floor. He looked very much alone. All at once I was sorry for him.

"What a lousy party," Eve whispered. "We going?"

"Honey, I'm sorry, it's a case. I don't know how long I'll be so go home when you're ready, be careful and don't wait up for me. I'll be making money for us."

"Oh." She made a wry face. "I really am sorry for this Garcia man, but right now I hate his guts. Never mind. Run along. I'll say goodbye to Dad and the others for you." She reached up and gave me a tiny kiss.

"I'll leave the car," I said. "I love you."

"Know you do. Get out!"

I went into the hall. The servant called me a cab and it arrived in three minutes.

5

I did some thinking on the drive across town. Maybe Jeff Pastor was right. I could be criticised for having Kresnik as a client. People talked about Kresnik.

He ran the local race-track and a couple of night-clubs, had an interest in various businesses including a large car-servicing depot. Rumour said he was a racketeer, that he was mixed up in the numbers racket, had run narcotics, had even run girls across the Mexican border. Nobody offered proof. He had no criminal record.

He was not a type I liked. He was too cold, too businesslike, completely impersonal, lacking in what seemed the normal human weaknesses. But he was polite in his way, paid promptly and well, never offered any business that wasn't strictly legal. And I had to be grateful to him for one fact: he had come to me unsolicited and unrecommended when I broke with the D.A.'s office and badly needed clients. He said he was looking for an honest lawyer. He'd heard I was just that. He brought a lot of business.

I paid off the cab and walked the last block. On the other sidewalk the neon sign of the *Caracol* blinked against the night. The big snail was in red and green.

The horns kept shooting out of the head then slowly drooping like disconsolate lily-stalks. The sign was amusing and called attention. I crossed over and entered the back alley.

I appreciated Kresnik's point. I was well-enough known in the city to be recognised if I went through the front. No man wants it known he's calling a lawyer late at night.

At the back door an old man was expecting me. He led me down a passage, past the dressing rooms of the floor-show people, into the corridor with the thick carpet. Music came from the front, the faint sound of applause. The old man knocked, pushed open the door of the office, I walked in, there were four of them present.

The door closed behind me.

Kresnik was at his desk. He had light grey eyes like bleached flints, a small moustache, powerful shoulders and a thick-set body that made him appear short until he stood up. He waved me to a chair without a greeting. He looked at me as if I'd already been there two hours.

Against the wall, elbow on a sideboard, stood Jordan—his hair bright as flax, his body like a rail. He had a small, experienced rictal sneer that he must have practiced since childhood. The hand in his pocket held a gun. I wondered if he had a licence. The man standing at the other end of the sideboard, like the second lion rampant in a coat of arms, was a pale-faced nondescript with dirty hair whom I'd often seen with Kresnik but whose name I didn't know. The third man sat in a chair.

He was small and neat. He had light straight reddy-blonde hair that meant his face also should have been pale. It wasn't. He was sunburned almost black. His hands were work roughened and unduly large. He wore a neat flannel suit of a strict cut and glaring black-and-white shoes, but he was unmistakably a sailor. He reminded me of photographs I'd seen of Truman Capote, the author. Which made it droll because he was trying to look like a toughie. His eyes were narrowed, jaw thrust forward. He wasn't in any way convincing.

I said, "Good evening," and sat down.

We had a full minute of silence. Kresnik clipped the end of a cigar, lit it and blew out blue smoke. There was no air in the room and the cloud hovered motionless. Jordan was watching me with malice.

Kresnik said, "Okay, Race, I want a man to do a job. I've picked you. I'm going to give you a chance to earn five hundred dollars. Wanna help?"

"That's what lawyers are for."

Jordan sniggered and bobbed his head, the light skating over his flax. The man with dirty hair stared at me fixedly. Truman Capote screwed up his face like a lap-dog in a bad temper.

Kresnik said, "You're to run an errand for me. Nothing much and five hundred bucks at the end. I'll pay that to a man I can trust."

"Thanks for the compliment. What sort of errand?"

"Very simple." He blew a second cloud of smoke. It hovered beside the first and they drooped like a pair of incorporeal breasts. "Very little to it. Tomorrow night at —" He looked inquiringly at Truman Capote.

"Eleven-thirty to eleven forty-five." There was something wrong with the little guy's voice.

"Yeah," Kresnik said. "We'll let you know the exact time tomorrow. Take your car and go out to Pier Thirty-Seven. That means you don't have to go through the harbour gate. Wait over near the oil-refinery shed where it's dark and this guy'll bring you a suitcase. Drive it straight home. Got a back entrance to your apartment?"

"An alley and some service stairs."

"Use 'em. Don't let anyone see you. Keep the suitcase in your apartment till I tell you. It may be an hour, it may be a week. Got all that?"

"It was easy. Now tell me what's in the suitcase."

Jordan said, "None of your —ing business."

A silence fell. Kresnik blew more smoke.

I remembered the stories I'd heard about him. I took it very slowly. I said, "This is interesting. For five hundred dollars I risk losing my licence by helping you smuggle something into the country. Are you nuts?"

"A thóusand."

I could hear the music from out in the club. I said, "Goodnight," and started to rise from the chair.

Jordan whipped out of the corner like a striking snake. He hit my face and I sat down again. Multi-coloured ice-cream sundaes sloshed behind my eyes.

Truman Capote said, "Hit the bastard again." He forgot himself in the excitement and I realised about his voice. He was an Englishman trying to talk American. He really said, "'It the bauhstud agahin."

Jordan did it, but harder.

I put my hands to my face and slumped to the side. The world has misfired somewhere. It was all, as they say, like a bad dream.

I waited for the fudge to clear. The band out front was reviving rock-n-roll. Capote parted his lips and showed small pearly teeth. Kresnik watched the pluming smoke of his cigar. The dirty-haired man with the pale face hadn't moved an inch.

"You'll do it," Kresnik said comfortably.

"I won't."

Jordan took a leisurely step forward to slug me again. I swung upright and slammed a fist in his guts and the breath rushed out of him and he fell over Truman Capote's legs. The Englishman gave a little whinny. Jordan sat down jarringly on the floor. A gun jabbed into my back because the dirty-haired man had moved at last.

He said, "Siddown again."

I sat down again. I was frightened. This wasn't my league or my game.

Jordan picked himself from the floor holding his belly, venom in his eyes. Capote looked like a child seeing all its dreams come true. The other man was motionless again, behind me, holding the gun to my neck. Kresnik put down his cigar.

"Now let's talk it over sensible."

"Talk yourself black," I said. "No smuggling."

"Suppose I say it's not smuggling. That the case contains no drugs, no contraband...."

"Suppose you say it's not illegal."

"Okay, I'm saying it."

"I'm believing it. That's why you've got these elaborate arrangements fixed for late at night. I can talk to you straight, Kresnik, because we just severed our connection and you're no longer a client. I'm not helping. I don't care how much you offer or how tough your hoods get. I assist in nothing illegal. I don't jeopardize my licence. Now I'll go home."

The gun pushed coldly at the back of my neck. I stayed where I was. We had another silence. Kresnik picked up his cigar again and the smell of it was beginning to make me feel sick. He spoke and I nearly retched.

"Let's talk about Tony Fontaine."

My mouth turned to papyrus and the scar on my conscience opened like a new wound.

"Marijuana and attempted robbery with violence," Kresnik said. "You took the case because the kid was getting a raw deal. That's what the publicity said. No evidence on the dope charge and only one uncertain witness for the robbery, an old man named Lopez. An old pauper named Lopez. He decided not to give evidence."

"He wasn't certain."

"He got a hundred dollars."

There was no spit in my mouth. I tried to swallow. I couldn't. I croaked, "Not the way you make it sound, Kresnik. He needed the money to help him with a debt."

"A hundred bucks. So you lose your licence anyway. You buy Lopez for a C, I buy him for a G. Or two G's, or three. I don't know the Fontaine kid, but I've met poor old Lopez and he's a nice old guy. He'll say you bribed him, corruption of justice, suborning of witnesses. I guess there'll be a board of inquiry."

He smiled gently. "Why we talking like this, Race? I never asked you to do anything illegal, did I? I'm not now. All you do is collect the suitcase and take it home. Nothing to it. You'll do it."

"No."

"Sure you will. For a pal."

There was a torn place in my cheek where Jordan had hit me. I sucked at it. I thought of the world without my practice. I thought of Eve. I looked at Kresnik and he had me and he knew it. He repeated, "You'll do it."

"I don't know," I said, and got up.

"Don't want to rush you, Race, just think it over and I'll call you in the morning. If we reach a nice agreement I'll pay you...."

"Nothing," I said. "Keep your money to buy the guy over there a shampoo." I got to the door.

Jordan said to my back, "One day I'll fix you, Buster."

I turned around. "Watch I don't decide to fix you. All of you."

Kresnik said impersonally, "And leave by the back way."

I shut the door.

I went down the carpeted corridor and I was angry and frightened and I could barely see. I went toward the sound of the music. I was going to leave by the front way or any other way I wanted. When the dressing room door opened I was already too shaken to register any more shock.

The girl stepped out and turned her head and froze into position and stared at me.

I came to a standstill. I thought of what Jeff Pastor had said about old sins and long shadows. It was my night for them.

The girl was Virginia Ferrer.

6

She opened and shut her mouth twice and narrowed her eyes and unfroze herself. She gave a hard laugh. "Well, see who's here! Don't say you were coming to pay a visit."

I shook my head. I was still coming out of a daze. I didn't even think to say hello. I said, "You working here?"

"I ain't saving souls."

She had on a glittering sequined show dress. Her hair was dyed raven black. She was still very pretty. She continued gazing at me and suddenly shifted her weight from one foot to the other as if she were nervous. She said, "Well, what's new? How is it after all this time? I hear you're a respectable married man with a family."

"No family," I said. "How are things with you?"

She had been drinking and she was a little high. "You mean you care?"

I flushed. "I was just leaving."

"Don't have to run away from me any more, I got no hold on you." She gave me a hard glittering smile. "I'm not on for ten minutes yet. How about a drink for old time's sake."

I nodded. "Sure." I followed her out to the club.

There weren't many people and we got an empty table over near the lobby. The floor was clearing. The waiter brought us drinks and we sat and half-looked at one another. There wasn't anything to say.

She made a try. Her laugh was metallic. "After the way it was an' we can sit here like strangers."

"A long time ago," I said.

"Yes."

The lights dimmed. The band struck up. Ten girls pranced out with G-strings, nipple beads, and rhinestoned snail-shells on their backs. The number was energetic and obscene. It was old. It had been used with the same costumes more than a year before when the *Caracol* first opened. Kresnik was losing his originality.

Ginny Ferrer held up her empty glass. "You're still a slow drinker. Did you change at all?"

"I don't know."

"I didn't." She put the glass down. Then she said, "I still loathe your guts." Her face in the dim light was cast from stone. She said, "I can still startle myself awake at night and go hot with hatred at you. I won't ever forget it."

"I'll go now," I said.

"Not this time. This is one time you don't get away. I been drinking. You make a move and I'll holler the goddam joint down."

"As you like, Ginny."

She shook her head wearily. "Ah, what's the use. Whatever I say you'll sit there like a mummified virgin. Nothing could ever touch you." She laughed again. It wasn't pleasant. "Tell me one thing, just for my collector's album. Did I take your virginity? You sure took mine, in no uncertain manner."

"It's not doing any good to talk about it now."

"Of course not," she grated cynically. "Let's all forget about it. That dirty nasty unpleasant operation. You could never bear even to think about it, could you?"

"I offered to marry you," I said in a low voice.

"Yeah, and the tone in which you offered." In her face only her lips were moving. "Still no family, huh? Your wife having operations too?"

I said, "If you're short of money...."

"You can just shut your filthy mouth," she said slowly. "You're so consciously noble it makes me sick. That built-in sense of decency only works when you punch the switch."

I said, "I'll leave."

A man took a few paces in from the lobby, stood by our table, waited for the lights to go up. On the floor the chorines unhooked the snail-horns from their heads, used them for a final obscenity and cantered off. The band blared to a halt. There was a ripple of unenthusiastic applause. The lights flared and the man standing by the table looked down at me and opened his mouth and blinked his eyes.

He said, "Hello, Bob."

It was Tony Fontaine.

I looked glassily at him. I felt myself turning red. I moved my lips a few times and said, "Hello, Tony. Where do you get the dough to come to joints like this?"

He went right on blinking. He glanced over his shoulder. I followed his gaze and Eve came out of the ladies' cloakroom and bore down on us.

I was afraid to look at Ginny Ferrer's face. I stood up feeling frozen. I said, "Hello, Eve. What are you doing here?"

She smiled. It was a thin smile. She said in a strained voice, "Why, hello. And what are you doing here?" Then she sort of froze into position. She stood and looked down at Ginny and the band began to play more rock-n-roll.

I said, "Honey, this is Miss Virginia Ferrer. My wife. The lad is Tony Fontaine. Let's all sit down."

We did. We sat in a nerve-tearing silence and I tried desperately to catch the eye of a waiter. They were all looking the other way. Eve made a sort of bracing motion. She cleared her throat. She said, "What a relief to get away from that party. Paul broke it up by being sick against a bookcase."

"Sounds gay," Ginny Ferrer sneered.

Eve switched on a friendly smile. It was fantastic to watch her work. She said in an intimate way, "Paul's all right, it's just that his wife doesn't give him any peace. He's compensating. You know how it is."

"I guess so," Ginnie said less certainly.

Eve turned directly to me for the first time. "I didn't want to go home to an empty apartment, love, so I drove around to take a little air. Who do I see in the street but Tony! What does he tell me except that he saw you come in here! I came too—to look. Tony, by the way, is a little crocked."

"It's a slander." Tony broke into his big boyish grin. "Stop depleting my stock in front of this beautiful doll."

Ginny smiled back. She could handle this sort of thing. "You won't like me so well in a minute. I'm going to sing."

"A singer?" Eve's voice rose enthusiastically. "How exciting and wonderful! That was my ambition once, but there was a drawback. I had no voice. But how like my husband! He'll talk for hours about his dreary old clients. Glamorous and beautiful people like you he keeps to himself."

She giggled. "That's done it! Now I'm the prying wife."

Suddenly they were all smiling.

"Nothing of the sort," Ginny said. "He had no reason to mention me. We haven't seen each other for years till tonight. We were pals when he was working in his first law office. I was a waitress at the joint he used to come and eat. I worried because he didn't eat enough."

"He still doesn't," Eve said. Her intimate tone was like an arm round Ginny's shoulders. "How does he compare now to the way he was?"

The hard smile came back. "He's the same."

"The perennial boy wonder," Eve said. "When I'm hewn with wrinkles he'll still look twenty-one. Horrible thought. Wait till the babies start coming, that'll age him."

Ginnie Ferrer turned her head slowly and stared at me.

"Drinks?" I said.

Eve leaned nearer. "I know nothing about his early life. He never talks. How about dinner at the apartment some time next week?"

The couples were clearing from the floor. Ginnie said, "Gee, that'd be nice. Could I phone you?"

"Any time. Arrive early and divulge all the deep dark secrets before he gets in from the office. He's always late."

"I'm not waiting till then," Tony Fontaine said. "I'm sticking around till the show finishes then I'm taking Miss Ferrer for a long refreshing walk in the park."

"There's another show after this, sonny-boy. And I'm too old for you." But she liked it. She looked toward the bandstand. She said, "My cue's coming up. I have to go back afterwards and talk to Mr. Kresnik."

She got to her feet, held out her hand. "Goodbye, Mrs. Race. It's certainly been a pleasure. Goodbye, fellas." She took a step away, then turned back and looked at Eve. "You're miles too good for him," she said, then she went slowly across the centre of the empty dance floor. The drummer guyed her, faintly stroking his brushes in time to the movement of her hips.

I said, "Let's go."

"What for?" Eve's eyebrows shot up. She grinned. "Oh. Home to bed. Where can we drop you, Tony?"

"I'm staying." Eve had spoken the truth. He was a little crocked. He gazed dreamily into her eyes. "I'm going to wait for the babe. She is a dish of the purest porcelain."

Eve said a little sharply, "Don't you have to study tomorrow?"

He continued gazing and didn't answer.

I said, "This is an expensive joint, Tony. What you using for money?"

He shrugged. His teeth glittered. "I been making some dough. Little jobs I do. I got a very able body."

"Well, I'm sure it's none of my concern." Eve got to her feet and started toward the ladies' room. I slipped Tony ten dollars. I followed. The lights went dim. A spot stabbed. Ginny Ferrer began to sing.

It was a little minor-key half-blues all about deserted love. I waited at the cloakroom door and I was thinking Ginny's voice was better than in the days when we took long walks in the dark and she used to sing to me. It was all a long time ago. There was no point in harking back. The world changes, a man has to change with it.

I took Eve's arm and we went out to the car.

I drove slowly. It was a fine night and not too late and there was still traffic and people around. The demolition guys were night-working at the corner of

Main and Bronson. A long line of watchers, mostly men, stretched along the sidewalk. I had a bursting headache. I said, "Like a drive along the sea-shore?"

"I thought you were raring for bed. Why the tearing hurry to leave the *Caracol?*" She turned to be. "I don't care what you think, I am a prying wife."

"It was true," I said. "I haven't seen her since long before I married you."

"Odd. I thought from the way she looked she was in love with you. I was furious with jealousy. Oh well. Change the subject. Tony Fontaine is a bore. He was getting on my nerves."

At that moment he was on my nerves. But I couldn't blame him that he was indirectly responsible for the mess I was in. I said, "Why get so acid with him? He's all right."

"I suppose so." She snuggled up and put her head on my shoulder. "Something worrying you, Bob?"

"Nothing."

"So long as it's not that girl. Mr. Race, how could you? A waitress! She's not even pretty. Is she older than I am?"

At four-thirty in the morning I still wasn't sleeping. I had violent nervous pains in my duodenum. I went to the kitchen, drank off a glass of bicarbonate and water, and when I returned Eve was sitting up in bed with the light on.

"All right," she said. "You nearly kicked me to death, tossing and turning. Is it this Garcia case tomorrow?"

"In part." I sat on the bed.

"What's the other part?"

"Unimportant."

She reached up and pulled the hair on my chest. I winced. She said, "Robert Race, you're looking like death and I'm worried sick about you. After all your talk you didn't even kiss me goodnight. I want to help."

"No."

"Please!"

"All right."

I told her.

She lay back on the pillow. She looked faintly frightened and very thoughtful. She said, "It's bad. You fool. I never knew you'd done that for Tony. You lovable fool."

I lit a cigarette. The smoke intensified the constricting pain in my stomach.

"Kresnik's capable of anything, even murder," she said, "if you can believe what you hear. You'll just have to go through with it. Maybe it's not so bad. He's told you it's not illegal and it's only for once. How long do you keep the suitcase here?"

"I don't know. An hour. A month."

She took the cigarette from my mouth and puffed at it. She stubbed it out in the ashtray by the bed. She looked at me a moment then reached up and drew me down. Her breasts were soft and firm. She smelled good. In her arms were peace and forgetfulness. I reached overhead and turned off the light.

I dozed off afterwards, thinking of the baby we'd have.

She let me sleep soundly till nine-thirty. She brought me breakfast in bed and she looked replete and fresh and beautiful. She went off to draw me a hot bath.

I lay in a cocoon of drowsiness. It was pleasant. I thought of what lay ahead and the pain leapt back into my duodenum as if someone had thrown an assegai.

It was going to be a bad day.

7

Garcia got six years.

The court was cleared for the evidence of the little girls. I questioned them as best I could, then I saw I was working for the prosecution. The public filed back in, outraged by the thought of a filthiness too black for it to hear. The mood communicated to the jury. That was it.

Garcia was a bad witness in his own defence. His frightened incoherence helped him little, his accent less, and me not at all. I tried. I couldn't concentrate. I had Kresnik at the back of my head. I was endeavouring to figure a way out of his job. There wasn't one. The verdict came in at seven in the evening.

I sat afterwards in an office at the back, waiting for the reporters to disappear, thinking of Garcia's lined anguished face as they took him off, wondering what I could do for his young wife. He was innocent. It was an instinctive knowledge like my certainty of Eve's love, like the existence of God and like the way I'd been right to help Tony Fontaine no matter what the outcome. There was no longer any way I could help Garcia.

A cop came and said someone was trying to get me on the phone. My mouth dried, but I told him to switch the call through. It was Sam Alford.

He said, "Okay, bring Eve here for the evening and forget everything. I just heard the result. I'm sorry for you."

"Thanks. I can't join you. I have to return to the office and clear up some work. You'll be doing me a favour if you'll entertain our girl by herself for the evening. Can I tell her to come out?"

"Sure you can't come yourself?"

"Too busy."

I smoked a cigarette, then called Eve.

She said brightly, "How's the tummy?"

"Thanks. I lost the case."

"Darling, I'm sorry. Anything I can say?"

"Nothing. I love you. Look, I won't be home to dinner so drive out to your father's. I lost an evening's work last night. I have to catch up. I'll eat out somewhere."

"Bob, are you worrying about this other thing?"

"Yes."

"You going to do it?"

"Yes."

"They phoned half an hour ago. I said I didn't know where you were. You're to call the *Caracol* as soon as possible."

She paused. She said, "I'm not going to Father's. Let me stay with you on this thing. Let me drive down to the port with you."

"You'll stay out of it," I said. "Go play some of the old man's Viennese waltzes. He's got a complete new recording of the *Fledermaus*."

"I hate the *Fledermaus*. What time will you get back?"

"I don't know. You come home about one o'clock. Keep your fingers crossed."

"Yes," she said. "I'll be praying. Here comes the chopper. I love you."

I lit another cigarette. The pain in my stomach had gone and I felt limp. I called the *Caracol*. Jordan's voice was a sneering whine.

"I like this. This is nice. I call 'dung' and you have to lump on the shovel. All right, Buster, here's the details. The time's fixed for eleven-thirty. On the point. Call us the moment you get back to your apartment. We want a double check. Got that? How you liking it?"

I hung up without answering. Only five minutes afterwards did I realise that he hadn't even bothered to check if I was going through with the job. Kresnik must have been pretty sure of me. It was like seeing myself in a new light.

The courthouse was nearly empty. My feet echoed along the marble corridors. I nodded to a couple of people and went outside and down the steps into the gathering dusk. I intended getting a sandwich in the bar across the street.

Someone shouted my name.

I jumped a mile. My nerves were foul. I turned, and Jeff Pastor was coming down to me, and the panic didn't abate. I was suddenly afraid of policemen.

"I'll buy you a drink," he said. A faint grin spread over his dark face. "You looked in court as if you needed one." He led me across the road by the arm, the way a cop leads a prisoner.

In the bar I had a Western sandwich and a small beer. Jeff drank a double Scotch and I envied him his stomach. He lifted the glass to me, arching his eyebrows. He said, "Hard feelings?"

"None."

"Even you can't acquit a guilty man."

"Nuts. Thousands of guilty men are acquitted every year. Garcia is innocent. The middle-aged blonde you put in was just another neurotic willing to perjure herself for the sake of the publicity. The kids didn't know what they were talking about. At that age one grown-up looks like another."

"But the jury convicted." Jeff Pastor sucked his upper lip. "Christ! Six years. Four and a half with time off for good behaviour, maybe a parole. I doubt it. Not for a man who interferes with kids."

I said, "I know you cops have a special hatred for guys like that. This time you allowed it to blind you. What about Garcia's own kids? You've interfered with them, with their whole lives. What about his wife?"

He drained off his drink and called for another. I refused. He said, "I thought when the wife broke down and talked about how she loved him it would sway the jury. It did. The wrong way. She's an American-American, not a Mex. They figured she was another victim. I shouldn't be surprised if some of the guys on the jury thought Garcia was a hot stuff Latin lover and felt inferior by comparison. They went out for their revenge."

"They didn't stay out long," I said. "I shall appeal."

"On what grounds?"

I sagged. I said, "There must be some good in the guy or he wouldn't inspire so much love from a girl like his wife."

"Nuts! You're back in your little flowery paradise. Come out before the petals wither; shrink your great bleeding heart a little. The uttermost bastards can inspire love. There's a million possible reasons. Maybe the guys on the jury were right and Garcia really is hot stuff in bed. Maybe that's why she loves him." Pastor grinned sardonically. "I'll hate to see you the day you have to wake up. And it'll come as sure as Tuesday. Have another beer."

"I have to go."

"Any more anonymous letters?"

I shook my head.

I was wrong. I drove to the office and when I got upstairs another letter was waiting.

I stared at the barbed handwriting. In the dirtiest language yet it told me my time was coming soon. I tore up letter and envelope, threw them into the basket, and the poor devil of a writer never seemed less important. The important thing was what I was about to do for Kresnik. I couldn't think straight. The worry grew to an engulfing ache.

The sliver of moon over the downtown buildings was larger, duller than last night, the horns on it sharper. The time was out of joint. Last night seemed a year ago. I sat and thought and began to feel sorry for myself and saw the danger of it. I swung back to the desk to bury myself in work for two or three hours.

I turned on the lights, put my wristwatch beside me. I took up some papers relating to a client's transfer of some Fidelity Fund shares. A swelling sense of guilt remained.

After a while I became half conscious of the second worry, buried deep in the first and gnawing like a maggot in an apple. I tried to attribute it to Garcia, to the fact that I'd been too preoccupied to give him a first-class defence. The gnawing continued. I dug deeper. I found the cause.

Ginny Ferrer. The hard bitter face she wore. The hatred with which she looked at me.

8

The clock on the dashboard said eleven twenty-two. I turned from Marimon into Descanso and drove slowly past the harbour gate. The air smelled of ships, cargoes and ocean. Through the harbour fence I saw the stevedores still working a cargo at Pier Seven. The winches stuttered, the old harbour train moved tiredly along the tracks toward the farther warehouses, spitting a fountain of sparks from its stack. I drove on.

My heart was in my throat, I was frightened of what I had to do, I wanted to back out, I was more frightened of what Kresnik could do to my life. I told myself he couldn't be as powerful as that. The new Chief of Police had closed down the numbers racket, the race track now had official supervision, the local nightclubs had been failing for the past year.

I got consolation from nothing. He was powerful enough to lose me my licence.

Somewhere at sea a ship's siren started weeping. The smell of oil on the air got stronger. A gathering mist was murking the small moon. The oil company buildings were dim shapes, and the open railroad track I must cross gleamed dully like the spoors of twin snails. The dashboard clock said eleven twenty-six. I wound down the side window.

There was no warning. A man leapt out of the darkness ahead. He had a flashlight. The beam glinted on the buttons of his uniform. He was a cop. I drew to a halt.

He advanced heavy-footed. He said, "Where you going, Mac, what you heading off the road for?" The ship's siren wailed again. The train chuffed slowly back from the far end of the harbour. I sat without answering. The light flashed in my face.

He said brightly, "Evening, Mr. Race."

I peered beyond the beam. I could remember the face but not the name. I twisted my mouth into a smile. "Hi! Nice night."

"Yeah. But it'll rain. Sailor on one of the boats said so, and those guys know. It's all the same to me, I'm going home. The relief can get wet."

I said, "I didn't know you boys did a regular patrol round here."

"Yeah, we didn't once. It's part of the new guy's campaign. He thinks there's smuggling from Mexico. I think he's nuts. Why'd they smuggle through a port when they got hundreds of miles of badly policed frontier?"

"You're right," I said.

"Yeah. The guy's run out of other things to clean up." The cop peered in the car. "Midnight yet?"

"It wants half an hour."

He made himself comfortable with his elbow on the window. "Taking a drive?"

"I had a hankering to see some ships. Wanted to fancy myself on a cruise. I been working too hard today."

"Yeah, the Garcia case, wasn't it? They tell me the dirty bastard got six—a couple years for each of the poor little kids. It's not enough. Why'd you be taking on a case like that, Mr. Race?"

"Somebody had to."

"Yeah, I guess. I hear you didn't give him such a good defence."

"Would you have done?"

He reached in, punched my shoulder and laughed. "Yeah, I get the point. Yeah." He straightened, peered at the clock again. It was eleven thirty-four. He said, "Relief was late last night. He should be early tonight, by rights. I'm going."

"I should," I said. "Goodnight."

I lit a cigarette and listened to his receding footsteps. My hands were shaking. I stubbed out the cigarette in the ashtray and drove on.

The oil company buildings loomed darkly. I wondered if Truman Capote was still waiting. The car bumped slowly over the rail tracks, and the train was halfway around the harbour, coming toward me. I coasted another hundred yards, drew into the shadow of the warehouse. I braked. I turned off the lights.

It seemed an eternity. It was barely two minutes. He made no footfalls. The small shadow glided past the side window and he whispered, "I'm putting it in the back." He closed the boot again without slamming it. He came noiselessly back to the window and hissed in his funny accent, "Okay, get going." Then he stiffened.

He croaked, "Wait!" He opened the door and scrambled in beside me and the door didn't shut properly. I heard the soft chuff of approaching footsteps. He said quietly, "Bleeding hell!" Then without warning he put his arms around me and held me tight and laid his cheek alongside mine.

He was wearing his English cut suit. It was tight under the armpits. His body was hard and lumpy like a sack of smooth rocks. He pinioned me and I didn't move and the other footsteps whispered nearer and then stopped.

The other guy was coming on tiptoe. One of his boots squeaked. He came right to the window, looked in and said, "Hey, you two!"

The little guy broke from my arms. He said, "Oh dear!" and his English voice sounded effeminate. My insides squirmed and I could hardly breathe. The man looking in was a watchman.

He gave the door a tremendous kick. I heard the catch snap shut. He said hoarsely, "You couple of dirty perverts, get out of here before I run you in for trespassing." He kicked again. I thought of the coachwork. He roared, "Go on get out, you dirty corrupt bastards."

I snapped the car into fast reverse. I reared a full half circle and the tires squealed and I headed for the tracks. The train was almost on us. I should have waited. I panicked. The guy behind us was still shouting and I was afraid he'd change his mind and raise an alarm. I stamped the accelerator. I hit the tracks and bounced. We skimmed the cow-catcher and the train hissed and screeched and the engineer joined the shouting party. I got on the road and swung past the harbour gate. The little Limey lounged back on the seat and crossed his knees, flashing his black and white shoes.

He was being the ice-cold type. He said from the corner of his mouth, "Just kidding back there. Even if I wasn't you're not the type I'd go for." He laughed with self-delight. He rolled his shoulders. "You blokes over here ain't the only ones can think fast."

I said, "We're not saying 'blokes' this year except on the east coast."

"You're a smart bleeder, ain't you," he sneered, very tough.

"You're a phoney bleeder. Where's it from, the movies?"

We were heading back toward the main town. I turned into an empty cross street and pulled over to the curb. "Far as you go. Out!"

"Oh no." He lengthened both "o" sounds. "I come this far, I'm sticking with you. We'll go up to your apartment and wait for that phone call. Got any rye?"

Eve would be out of her mind with worry. I wasn't going to mix her in any further. I leaned across him and opened the door. "Shove off."

"What you so anxious about? Got something up your sleeve?"

"An arm," I said, and climbed out. The street was deserted. I walked around the car and looked at the scratches and the small dent where the watchman had kicked. Then I pulled the door open wide and reached inside. I was tired and fed up and frightened. I took Truman Capote by the shoulders and yanked. His scalp scraped the door frame.

He scuffed his feet on the sidewalk and tried to find a purchase. He gave me a mouth full of knuckles. He was tough as a wild pony and as small. I clutched him hard and lifted him by the lapels and the groin and flung him through the air. He hit the wall, bounced to the sidewalk and sprawled full length.

He started to get up. He thought better of it, or he couldn't. I said, "Terribly sorry and all that sort of thing," and got in the car and left him there. At the end of the short street I looked back.

He was tough all right. He was on his feet again and running after me like a harrier. I reefed round the corner. He was lost from sight.

The murk in the sky was thickening. The moon was lost. I drove slowly down the main street and tried to adjust myself back into the ordinary world. I didn't do so well. On the sidewalk the slim Mexicans in bright suits and the fat Mexicans in dark suits floated through the thinning crowd like contrapuntal ghosts. Two drunk sailors brawled on a corner. A blonde hustler stood in a shadowy doorway and tried to look like the incarnation of waiting sin.

I had no contact with any of them. The case in the boot was a talisman expelling me from the normal. I had a sudden howling ache for company. I needed a drink. I pulled up at the next bar.

I walked round the car and locked the boot with the ignition key and went in. There were three other customers. It was as gay as a Haitian morgue on a wet Monday midnight. I sat on a high stool, shook a bit and drank two slow scotches. Nobody wanted to talk. The barman looked as though he might be a great wit, but he wasn't going to bother with the joint nearly empty. I caught a glimpse of myself in the mirror. I looked as if I'd just come round from having nasty operations performed on me.

I needed Eve. I went back to the car and started for home. The job was over. I drove five minutes and then, for no reason, the Bomb went off in my head and I sat in the resultant mushroom cloud. I went more empty with each succeeding hundred yards. I saw what I'd got myself into. I was the world's prize chump.

Lopez, the witness against Tony Fontaine, the old guy to whom I'd given the hundred bucks—he still existed. Kresnik could buy him any time he wanted. Lopez was on tap, and so was I. I could be threatened with loss of licence whenever Kresnik felt like it.

Worse, I was in deeper than before. I'd established a precedent. Because of what I'd just done the hold was tighter. Kresnik could put the screws on when he thought fit—so could Jordan, so could the dirty-haired one, so could Truman Capote. Tonight might be the first of a long series of nights. I'd be performing like a circus horse any time one of them liked to crack my licence.

I let it sink in. I surveyed the prospect. There was only one way out. Go to the cops. Now.

I took it slowly and I felt dirty, but I was only human. I had a wife. I had to protect her. This way.

Return to the apartment, open the suitcase, see what was inside. Whatever it contained, call the cops, call Jeff Pastor, tell him. Explain that I'd never had any intention of going right through with the job, that I'd gone this far as a public-spirited citizen, as a lawyer who wanted incontrovertible evidence and could get it only by laying hands on the suitcase.

I went over it several times. Tell the truth about everything except my original intention because a lie is its own trap. I began to feel less lonely. I turned into my own quiet street, still tensed up, but with the kind of entirety that was my normal condition. For the first time in tweny-four hours I had contact again with my known world. I drove past the front entrance and round to the side street where we sometimes parked one of the cars on nights we were too lazy to go to the garage.

I locked the doors from inside, got out, locked the last door with the key. It was after midnight. There was no one on the street and not many lights in the surrounding buildings. The noises from downtown seemed hushed. My rubber soles whispered round to the rear of the car. I unlocked the boot.

I hadn't seen what Truman Capote put in. I think I was half expecting anything from a dead body to a brick of contraband gold. It was a suitcase, ordi-

NIGHT OF THE HORNS

nary imitation leather of a type mass-produced and sold in thousands. I lifted it out by the handle.

It wasn't too heavy—just enough to be packed with clothes for a couple of weeks vacation with maybe a few extra pairs of shoes. I hefted it in my right hand and entered the alley. I was no longer frightened or anything else out of the way.

The alley was the length of the short block and fairly wide. It was reasonably well lighted by the street lamps shining in from either end. It was empty. I walked swiftly with my shoes making little gritty noises. I got a third of the way along. I stopped outside the door to the service stairs.

It was normal precautions. I lifted my right foot and pushed the door open sharply. Nobody. The light high in the ceiling above the stone stairs was dim, but enough to see by. I put out my left hand to keep the door open, I walked in softly. No premonitions. Nothing. I lifted my foot to the first stair and a thunderbolt hit the back of my head.

My eyes fell out.

I couldn't see. I did a slow pirouette in a nightmare adagio and the case fell from my fingers and whatever it was hit me again on the side of the jaw. I left the earth. I flew blind through whining black storm clouds and the cold stone floor slammed my cheek. Hands like big land crabs scuttered all over me and ran through my pockets. I took off again on a longer darker flight.

I was a small ball. An engine was running because in my rubberized interior was the illusion of vibration. There wasn't sight, sound, smell or touch, only a great empty darkness. I fancied someone was whispering, but the words were pockets in nothing like the quacking on air of voiceless ducks. I tried to move.

I had no arms or legs. I opened my mouth and screamed for help, but I was without lips and no sound came. An infinitesimal spot of white light inside me continued screaming. It went out. I was flying again, downward this time. At the very bottom Garcia was waiting, stretched out on a slab and flayed and tortured.

It all ran together. There were no vibrations, only the washing of a tired sea. The land crabs entered and wandered and I changed my weight and flew out and my face struck. It wasn't the stone floor. It was grass and gravel.

I could have moved then, if I could have tried. Effort was away on Proxima Centauri. I'd have done better had I been able to see, but my eyes were gone forever. I had no defence.

The hands lifted and I swung like a cod fillet and my head hit hard bone. The sea sang. I changed weight again and the crabs nipped and pinched and the bone was rigid against my palms. The vibration started.

It purred and roared. It purred again. It settled. I knew now it was an engine, but that didn't bother me. I was alone. I was content. The little white light came on.

It grew to a great size and then it exploded. The bone under my hands was a steering wheel and the sea roared and was real and I tried lazily to lift my eyelids. The car jolted and I knew what was happening to me.

I screamed. I forced at my eyelids. The vibrations stopped, the car bucketed at the edge of the cliff and plunged down toward the sea and I screamed louder and I was blind. I flung myself at where the door must be. I felt the handle under my hand. That was all.

The darkness returned.

9

Something clacked rhythmically near my ear and a choir of off-key voices began the Anvil Chorus from *Trovatore*. I lay and listened a while. The rain pelted down and I was soaked and I was thinking that the sailor had been right, whoever the sailor was. I couldn't think.

I gathered a few resources and wrenched up my eyelids.

A dirty wet night in Autumn. I knew the time of year because someone nearby was burning a mountain of wet leaves. I couldn't smell them, but the smoke drifted thickly across my eyes. The clacking went on. The singing stopped.

I operated an antiquated pulley system in my neck and turned my head. A crooked hand lay about an inch from my eyes. The anvil noise was coming from the watch on the wrist. I lay and tried to tell the time by extra-sensory perception. Useless. I gave a couple of quiet chuckles because I had fooled them by getting my sight back, then I opened my mouth and screamed like a nut case.

I quit by biting my tongue. I was all right then. There were no more leaves, the smoke cleared, nothing remained but the sound of the sea below and the sheeting rain splatting mud all around me. I tried to remember what had happened to me. It was like trying to conjure a small sardine out of a large ocean. I said, "Eve," smiled to myself, twitched my shoulder, twitched my knees and was on all fours. My head fell off and rolled away. I started to crawl up the slope.

I knitted one, purled two, the mud sloshed, I slithered, it was like climbing a great chute. After several trials I got the hang of it. Dig toe-caps in mud, crouch like rabbit to be sure purchase is firm, put arms above head, face in mud, stretch till your hands encounter something they can hold, drag feet once more to crouch, start the whole silly process again.

Simple. Get knock-happy with a couple of whacks on the head and everything is child's play. So long as you don't try something really difficult, like wiping your nose or rubbing mud out of your eyes.

I got lost a couple of times in the next half hour. I needed a good Sherpa. It wasn't as unpleasant as all that because the voices came back and sang the Pilgrims' Chorus from *Tannhauser* accompanied by music played on a piano with a feather duster. When I got to the top they changed to a short lullaby and I went off to sleep again for a few minutes, or maybe an hour. I woke to grass and gravel on my face again. I was back where I started. Almost.

I walked. I was tottery, but ambulant. My head was somebody's old racksack stuffed with pistols that kept going off, but that didn't matter because I was going home to Eve. I reached the road, and when I had staggered so far that the rain was drowning the sound of the sea I recognised where I was. Fourteen miles out on the far side of town. No houses, just familiar trees and hillocks. Not a long trip. All I needed was a car. My own was somewhere in the sea.

That sobered me.

I was having my third shaking fit when I got to the lone house. It had a picket fence and was a frame house standing back from the highway with a lot of dark green trees dripping on it. I couldn't find any sort of gate so I went over the fence. A sign on the front porch said *J. P. Plackett.*

Mr. Plackett must have been a Quaker, or something equally trusting. The ten year old car was in a barn-type outhouse. The barn was unlocked. The car keys were in the ignition.

I opened the doors wide, backed, turned on the lawn, still not knowing where the gate was, and drove through the picket fence. It sounded like the break-up of a log jam. Quaker or not, Plackett had a clear conscience. He didn't even wake up, so far as I could see. I zoomed toward town.

Halfway there I squinted at my watch. Five thirty-five—presumably in the morning because there was no traffic. Eve would be out of her head with worry.

I abandoned the car two blocks away from the apartment. When I was nearly home I realised I was entering again by the back alley—the finger of Fate beckoning me to discover something. I pushed open the door at the bottom of the service stairs and discovered nothing beyond small circular evidence that a couple had dropped in off the street. I climbed one flight of stairs, went through to the elevator and up to the sixth floor. In the corridor I automatically reached for the key.

I patted myself over. A nice casual accidental murder. Everything in my pockets was intact except for the car keys. I even found the latch key. I let myself in quietly in case she was sleeping. I stood and breathed the goodness of being home, then I went into the bathroom from the kitchen side and took stock.

There was a lump the size of a pigeon's egg on the back of my skull. I was plastered from top to bottom in mud. I felt myself over and nothing seemed broken except my neck. I stripped and examined the bruises and I had Africa on my hip and the Andes across my knees.

I got under the shower, boiled myself five minutes, froze myself. I stepped out, dried off, rubbed myself from head to foot with a giant Christmas-gift bottle of after-shave lotion I'd been trying to get rid of for two years, got clean pyjamas from the linen cupboard, vested myself and practised a few steps up and down. Apart from creaks and aches I didn't feel bad.

I stepped into the dark bedroom.

I could smell the nice night perfume she used. I fumbled toward the bed.

Kresnik, cops, cars, everything, could wait a while. I stumbled over a pair of her slippers and thought she might wake up. I took the last two steps and was at the bed and it was empty.

I turned on the light. The bed hadn't been slept in. I sat on it. My head began gnawing. Eve had taken my advice to stay out of it and spent the night at her father's house. I went out to the phone and called Alford's number.

The servant sounded sleepy. I said, "Mrs. Race staying with her father?"

"I can check, sir. Can I call back?"

"Okay."

I thumbed the book, found the number of Mr. J. P. Plackett. He had a low pleasant voice that sounded as though he'd already done a day's work.

"Mr. Plackett," I said, "I took your car a while back. It's parked down on Bayard West with the key in the right hand glove compartment. On the way out I smashed your picket fence. I'll be sending you a hundred dollars by mail for repairs. That all right?"

"More than all right," he said. "I'll be repairing the fence myself. Just send fifty. Was the car of some use? Got your difficulties solved?"

"Thanks," I said. "Goodbye."

"Thanks to you."

I put down the receiver. Five seconds later the phone rang again. I snatched it.

The voice said, "Bob, I have to talk to you. I heard you come in. Can you get down here?"

"Laura?" I asked.

"Who else?"

"What's the matter?"

She gave a hysterical giggle. "I'm nearly out of my head. Can you come at once?"

"I'm waiting a phone call," I said. "Eve's not here."

"I'll come up."

"That's a good idea. I'm starved. You can cook me some breakfast."

She said, "I'll get some clothes on."

I opened the front door and went into the bedroom. I was still dressing when I heard her enter and go into the kitchen. I smelled the cooking. I was back sitting by the phone when she called me. The table in the dining recess was set with a red checkered cloth and she'd made bacon and eggs and toast and there was coffee on the stove.

I said, "What's the matter?"

She sat opposite me. She had on a green dress that went well with her red hair, but there were dark purple smudges under her eyes. She said, "There's something in what my grandmother used to say. In moments of crisis, eat first and talk afterwards. Shut up and eat!"

I ate. I listened for the phone. She cleaned nearly everything from her plate before she spoke again. She got up and poured coffee. She was going to take her own time in telling me what was bothering her, and I didn't mind. My own worries had clamped back like a suit of lead. She was acting as a counter-irritant.

She said, "Everything would be nice and neat if you and I were in love. Unfortunately we're not."

In the other room the phone rang.

I went out. Sam Alford said, "What's this about Eve?"

"You shouldn't have got out of bed, Sam," I said. "The servant could have called me. I just wanted to check Eve was there."

He said, "She's not."

"What?"

"She's not here."

I couldn't speak. His voice rose. "What's it about?"

"When did you see her last?"

"When she left last night around eleven o'clock. She was here for a couple of hours. I asked what the hell this is all about."

I said, "She's not here either. She hasn't been here all night."

He paused. He spoke in a low voice. "If you've let anything happen to that girl of mine I'm gonna —ing well murder you."

I hung up.

My throat had constricted. I didn't realise I was back in the kitchen until I stood there looking down at Laura Taylor. She stared back to me. She said in a grating voice, "Something new?"

I said, "I don't know where Eve is."

She put down her coffee cup. She picked up a napkin and dabbed at herself and the muscles of her face were twitching. Her mouth fell open. She couldn't contain herself.

She flung back her head and shoulders and screamed with laughter. She sounded as if she would never stop. I gaped at her. I dragged her upright and shook her but the laughter went on. I said, "What is it?"

The words choked from her throat. She was laughing and crying together like a madwoman. "You don't know where Eve is?" she asked crazily. "You don't know? You fool, you poor blind silly goddamn fool, I know where she is. She's run off with my husband. She's run off with Paul."

I slapped her across the face with both hands. She stopped laughing. She sat down again and picked up her coffee cup and started to drink.

10

In the silence she gazed at me as if I were a marionette whose head she had accidentally torn off. She said, "Sit down, Bob." She glanced into her cup, rose, fetched the pot from the stove and set it on the table. We sat facing one another.

"You didn't know," she said, "I'm sorry. I wouldn't have broken it to you that way." She tried to laugh again. It was different to her previous laughter and even more unpleasant. She said, "I was certain you'd known for the past nine months."

I whispered, "You lying bitch."

She sipped at her coffee, drew back from the cup as if the liquid were scalding. She said, "I phoned all his usual hangouts. When it got to three o'clock in the morning I came up here and buzzed the doorbell for half an hour. She wasn't in either. Then I knew. Crafty little tart."

I said, "Laura, finish the coffee and leave."

"Oh, for God's sake," she snapped, "stop bleating! We're stuck in this together." She sipped again. "I think you did know. If you'd once acted like a man this wouldn't have happened. Okay, so it's Paul's fault too, but he's weak. He didn't have a chance once she sunk her hooks in him."

I started to shake. "Don't talk about that drunken no-good bastard in my house."

"He's all that now," she said. "He never used to be. It started six months ago when she told him he couldn't come up here to bed any more. He's been no good ever since."

She looked into her coffee cup again. With a sudden motion she flung it across the room. It hit the stove and fell to the floor in a shattering of china and spilled coffee. She said, "He's still in love with her. I've tried every means I know how. I knew I hadn't won him back, but I thought she was tired of him. She was only waiting."

I said, "Leave, Laura. Get out before I throw you out."

She took no notice. She said, "I guess this six months was an illusion I built up. I never thought about phoning his office to check what time he was leaving. I suppose he was going up in the elevator and stopping at the sixth floor instead of the fifth, then coming down at leisure. I thought he wasn't making love to me any more because he didn't like me. He was worn out, of course. They must have worked to a time-table. He wouldn't want to be nearly caught again. You wouldn't know about that, I guess, about the time you arrived home unexpectedly and he had to come down the fire escape. That's how I first found out for sure."

She put her arms on the table and lowered her head. She began to weep. She said, "Oh hell, I'm still in love with him."

In the other room the phone rang.

I walked like an automaton. Sam Alford said, "Let's get this straight. What about Eve?"

I hung up.

In the kitchen Laura was still weeping. I sat staring at the phone because I knew it would ring again. In a while it did.

I said, "Hello?"

"We been ringing all night," the nasal voice said. "So you're finally there. Now git here!"

"Jordan," I said, "I'm busy."

"Ain't you always." He sniggered incredulously. "I got to hand it over to you, Race, I never thought you had it in you. But the fun's over. Get to the house."

"I'm busy," I said dully.

He said, "Your wife won't like more waiting. She's tired already."

It sank in slowly. I said, "What did you say?"

"We took precautions, Buster. She's been here all night. She plays a mean hand of poker, but she's gotten fed up with it. She wants hubby to come and take her home. He can do that if he brings the suitcase."

I said, "Yes. I'll be there."

I was trying to light a cigarette, waving goodbye to my nose with a lighted match. The footsteps came along the corridor. The front door banged open against the wall. I was stupefied enough to feel certain it was Eve.

Paul Taylor staggered in.

He felt his way along the wall. His eyes were out of focus. He waved at me. He was crocked to the point of paralysis and his tongue sputtered and hung out. He said, "No one home. Came up for you to give me a drink."

He crossed the room in a staggering run and crashed into the kitchen. I went after him. He said, "Laura, Laura, Floradora, what you doing here? Pour me a beer." Then he fell into a chair and dragged at the table cloth. All the crockery crashed to the floor.

She didn't move. She gazed at me across the room. She looked as if she were staring through a mile of water. Under the red hair her flesh had turned green.

"I know where Eve is," I said.

"Evie-stevie in the garden of Eden." Paul crashed his fist on the table. He leaned forward confidentially. "Been celebrating, Laura, wait till you hear. I landed one of the biggest clients in the State. He likes me. He loves me. He took me to the biggest goddamn party you ever saw. We're gonna be rich, Laura. You'll be rich, I'll be rich, just like the great Robert Race. I'll be a rich-bitch lawyer."

She didn't look at him. She remained staring at me with eyes like phlegm. She said, "I didn't know what I was saying. I got hysterical."

Paul Taylor said, "Huh?"

Her voice shot upwards. "It was all a big lie. I was gibbering. I was off my head."

I went across and lifted Paul Taylor to his feet by the front of his jacket. I said, "Taylor, I want to know about the time I came home early and you went down the fire escape."

He blinked. He tried to get his eyes into focus. He shook his head drunkenly. "Who told you?"

I crunched his nose. He jerked. He said, "All right, I've been waiting for a chance like this." I hit him again. Laura came screaming at me with her claws out. I managed to shove her off. I flung him across the room.

He doubled over and his head hit the sink. He fell to the floor and the blood spurted all over from his scalp and his nose. She ran to him and tried to pick him up by the shoulders. He turned his head. He vomited into her lap. I left them.

I closed the front door behind me. The phone rang. I went along the corridor and down in the elevator.

11

The guy in the garage had been on all night. He had pouches under his eyes. It was his own garage and when I got into the Buick he was meticulously checking me out on a thumby looking sheet of paper.

I said, "What time did Mrs. Race bring this in last night?"

It didn't come as casually as I wanted. He didn't notice because he liked being asked questions like that. He ran off to his office, got another thumbier sheet, came back smiling. He said, "Eleven twenty-three."

I nodded. I drove out into the morning.

The rain was finished, the sun struggling up. The sky was aquamarine and the air pure. No one was about to enjoy it except milkmen, early risers, a drunk sitting on a doorstep. I wasn't enjoying it.

I drove north out of town, up the hills to the Elwood residential district. The houses got fewer and larger and they had big gardens. There were bright coloured flowers growing along the roadside, palm trees set in graceful avenues. The residents deserved it. Their taxes were tremendous.

I got high enough to see the city lying small below me, the harbour like a saucer. I turned off into a badly paved track, the palm trees got scrubbier, the avenue was principally of cactus. The air was even clearer here, birds sang somewhere, I could see the big blue sierras farther north. The track petered out and I pulled up at the gates.

They were wide open. There was no one in the gatekeeper's lodge. I went through and up the long driveway and there were no other cars in sight. I climbed out. Back down the drive a small figure appeared and was shutting the gates. It didn't affect me one way or the other. I took a last look at the clear sky and rang the bell.

The door opened at once. The elderly Mexican houseboy gave a withered white smile and stood back for me to pass. I stepped over the threshold. Jordan put a gun in my back.

He patted me, frisking me for a weapon. He said, "Where's the case, Buster?" I didn't answer.

He said to the houseboy, "Look in the car." He prodded me across the white arcaded hall to a corner arch and we entered the carpeted room. Eve said, "Bob, darling."

She started to get up. She looked at the others and sat down again.

There was a stale feeling that the room had been up all night. The air was thick with cigar smoke and in the corner was a table with cards and poker chips. Truman Capote and the man with dirty hair were over by the window. They'd been watching for me. Kresnik was sprawling shirt-sleeved in an armchair with his belly pushing at the top of his pants. Leaning over the back of him, fooling with his hair, was Ginny Ferrer.

She gave no sign of recognition. I looked last at Eve. The houseboy's footsteps came across the hall and his singsong voice said, "Nothing in the car." He went away again. Kresnik heaved himself upright. There was a stirring, but nobody spoke. Eve looked about her and said in a small bright voice, "I've won an awful lot at poker. I made them pay up. We'll celebrate tonight."

The gun bored into my back. "Where's the case?" Jordan asked.

Kresnik said easily, "Not that we anticipated any trouble, but we're always on guard. We snatched your wife outside the garage last night after she put the car away. A sort of hostage. Now you're both here just tell me what you done with the stuff and you can both go away."

Ginny Ferrer studied her fingernails. Truman Capote made a terrier-like gesture of impatience. Eve said nothing. "I want to speak to my wife," I said. "Alone." None of it meant much. I was watching them all through a dream. Kresnik billowed smoke, screwed up his eyes, put down his cigar and nodded. He said, "Take 'em downstairs." He stayed behind with Ginny Ferrer. The others came across the hall in convoy. We went down a flight of nine broad stone steps and halted while they unfastened a narrow door on a landing. I stepped inside. Eve came behind me. It was a large room. It had a narrow bed, a chair, three baseball pictures on the wall and no window. The door was without a lock and fitted flush with the wall. A bolt slid on the outside. We were alone.

She whispered, "Bob, what's happening?" She put her arms around me.

I wrenched at her wrists and pushed her hard and she thumped down on the bed. She looked up at me from great wide eyes and put a hand to one side of her face. She said, "Bob, you don't look well. You all right?"

I was staring out at her from a diving-bell, somewhere in the deepest ocean. I said, "I've found out about Paul Taylor."

Her expression remained unchanged. The hand didn't move. She said, "What's he done?"

I couldn't take it. I reached down and seized her throat and I squeezed. I shook her. The blonde hair fell over her face. "You tell me," I said. "About the time he went down the fire escape. About six months ago when you told him he couldn't sleep with you any more. About how it was going on just the same because he was leaving his office early and sneaking up to you. About how you were able to say you loved me all the time. You dirty rotten whore."

A puppet-master sat in my head and pulled the controlling tendons of my hands. My fingers tightened. She didn't resist, she didn't try to speak. Her face congested and she drooped to one side like a sawdust doll. Her hair brushed my wrists.

I couldn't do it.

She fell full length on the bed and lay gasping. I wanted to run to her and comfort her and kiss her. I couldn't do that either. I stood like an image, loving her and hating her with every part of me. She lifted herself up.

She said, "Laura. That stupid woman!" The two large tears welled from my wife's eyes and ran down her cheeks. Thus on the sandy banks of Nile, weeps the deceitful crocodile. I didn't know where the couplet came from. It sneered in my head. I said, "Laura cried, too."

"Well she might." Eve wiped a hand across her face and put her feet to the floor. She pushed back her hair. She said, "All right. Do I tell you or aren't you going to believe me? You appear to have made up your mind."

"I'm listening," I said.

She nodded. "I can guess how you feel. I was a little surprised when I first learned about it. I should have told you long ago."

"What?"

"Laura has accused Paul of affairs ever since they married. Possibly she's right, but that's his business. When she ran out of candidates for the Jealousy Stakes she elected me, possibly because I was near. I didn't know about it till Paul warned me to be on my guard. I wasn't flattered. He's not exactly my saucer of tea."

Her eyes were candid and unwavering. "I didn't tell you: you have enough worries. As for the fire escape incident, it's true. Paul was up one evening, the only evening, telling me Laura's latest manoeuvre. He heard your key in the door and panicked. He was on edge through Laura, he thought you might kick up a row, she'd come in on your side and things would blow up generally. He didn't want that. He's in love with her, bitch though she is. Hence the fire escape."

She massaged her throat. "Not a very good story. It's the only one I've got. She saw him come through the window, took it as outright proof of what she's been saying, I went down to see her, we had a row and I didn't speak to her for months. I made it up again because I thought she'd found someone else to be suspicious about. Apparently I was wrong."

"You should have told me before."

"Why?"

I said, "I thought you'd run away with him."

"Is that why you took all night getting here?" She managed to smile and I loved her. "Were you scouring the country for me? Bob, after two years of marriage this is pretty flattering and exciting."

"Paul admitted it."

"Admitted what? How could he?"

I thought of his words. He had asked who told me about the fire escape, nothing more. I said, "Does your neck hurt?"

She got to her feet and held out her arms. She raised her mouth to be kissed. Because of the habit of marriage, or despite it, there was no resisting her.

She murmured in my cheek, "Yes, indeed, it hurts. I love it. It's the biggest compliment you ever paid me."

We broke apart. She smiled at me. "Settle the business with Kresnik. We'll go home to bed."

"It's not that easy."

"Why not?"

"I got knackered last night. The case was stolen."

"What?" She put the tips of her fingers in her mouth and stared at me in bewilderment. "Who?"

"I don't know. Maybe the guy who was writing me anonymous letters. He tried to kill me."

I went over and banged on the door with my open hand.

The guy with dirty hair was unaccompanied except for a Luger. The houseboy smiled from the front door as we were shepherded back across the hall and into the room. They were in the same positions as before, except that Ginny Ferrer was in Kresnik's lap. Once again she didn't look at me. He pushed her off as we entered.

"Good." He stood up. "You've settled your private business. Now where's the suitcase?"

I said, "I don't have it. It was stolen from me."

Nobody moved. Kresnik slowly lifted a hand and rubbed his jaw. He needed a shave. "Well," he said, "that's that. Any idea who it was?"

"None."

He nodded slowly. He shrugged philosophically. "It's not important. Nothing of value." He smiled at Eve and shrugged again. He looked helpless. "Sorry to have kept you here all night."

"That's all right." Ginny sank into Kresnik's chair, looking at her nails again. Eve smiled at him. She went to the table and picked up her handbag. "It was new and different," she said. "And I did win eighty-three dollars."

"You can go home now."

She put a hand on my arm.

"Not your husband."

The hand tightened. Kresnik said, "I want to talk to him a bit longer. Another business."

"I'll wait."

I said, "No. You need some sleep. I'll be along later."

She still held me. I walked with her into the hall. Ginny stayed sunk in the chair. The rest trailed behind without guns, but too close for comfort. I wasn't fooled. They hadn't held Eve hostage all night for a case full of nothing.

I removed her hand. "The car's outside. I'll come down in a cab."

"We'll drop you," Kresnik said politely. "A small point, Mrs. Race. I know you won't be silly and contact the police. There's still this touchy question of your husband's licence."

The houseboy opened the door.

I said, "Call your father. He's worried."

"Of course." She was doing a good job, but her fright wasn't hidden. She reached up and kissed me lightly on the cheek. Jordan guffawed.

I said, "Till later."

"Yes."

The door closed behind her. The Mexican smiled. I was getting tired of his smile. We all stood perfectly still and listened to the car go down the drive.

Kresnik said, "Okay, where's the suitcase."

"Stolen."

They were grouped around me in a circle; Kresnik, Jordan, the man with dirty hair, Truman Capote. The little Englishman said, "I told you last night the sod was up to something. He was too bloody anxious to get rid of me."

Kresnik said, "Yeah. This what you meant when you said you'd fix all of us, Race? Where is it?"

"Stolen."

His big fist hit me in the mouth and I staggered backwards. Capote caught me by the shoulders. He spun me round. He took his turn. They all took turns.

They pounded me.

The blood ran from my lips and down my chin. I hadn't enough strength to lift my arms. Ginny Ferrer came out of the room and leaned against an arch and watched. She said coldly in a faraway voice, "Ruin the bastard!"

I scissored at the knees and went out.

12

I explained to Garcia that he must have patience. He was weeping. I put my hand on his shoulder and said I'd get him out, then I opened my eyes and the light-bulb swooped down from the ceiling and scorched my eyeballs.

The next time I tried it was better. Not much. I wanted to wipe away the sweat on my forehead. My hands wouldn't move. I turned my head on the pillow and Jordan smiled down at me and said something like, "Gyah gyah gyah." My ears popped.

He drifted across and shifted the middle baseball picture on the wall. He spoke into the microphone concealed behind it. I heard him this time, though still indistinctly. He said, "He's with us, boss."

He let the picture drop. He smiled again. Truman Capote hove out of the mist and stood beside him. I closed my eyes.

The phony accent said, "Look at him! Played out! I don't wonder his wife was getting in the pit with some other bloke." He lightened his voice to a falsetto. "Paul! Oh Paul! Give it to me, Paul! I can't get enough of it, Paul! Okay, sugar, here it comes."

I jerked. I tried to fling myself off the bed. The ropes held. They both laughed. Jordan said, "She's a dollie. Wouldn't mind laying her myself."

"You might get the chance. Once they start taking on the old belly-drummers they never stop."

Kresnik said, "Quit that."

I opened my eyes.

He entered the door sideways. Ginny Ferrer was behind him. She stopped over the threshold and leaned against the wall and she didn't mind looking at me now. In her eyes was absolutely nothing.

Kresnik said, "Your fault, Race. We didn't know we'd be listening in on your marital difficulties."

"She didn't look difficult to me," Jordan said.

"I told you to quit." Kresnik sat on the edge of the bed and leaned over me. His face was so close I could see the volcanic pores of his skin. He said, "Okay, Race, where you stashed the case?"

The mist was clearing. I tried to get the cobwebs out of my head. I said, "Listen carefully. I carried out all your instructions. I got back to my apartment and someone slugged me. They tried to kill me. They took me out to Maribor and drove me over the cliff. You can check by looking for my car. It's in the sea."

"A nice story. I don't believe it. The part about the car might be true. What's the price of a car compared with what you'd be gaining? But you've overlooked one small point, Race. The stuff in the case is no good to anyone who can't distribute it. I can stop distribution any time I want. Think it over."

I said, "What's in the case?"

His nostrils flared wide. His flinty eyes blazed. Behind the temper he looked suddenly scared. "Don't overplay it. You're in no position. Tell us where the stuff is and we'll forget the unpleasantness. I'll give you a bonus."

I said, "I was robbed."

His hands came up. My insides cringed. He flexed his fingers, rubbed the side of his nose and let the hands fall again. "You weren't," he said. "I'll tell you why. One other small point. No one except us in this room knew anything about the job. Unless you blabbed."

"I didn't." I was lying. I told Eve. But she hadn't done anything. She couldn't. She'd been a prisoner right here in the house.

For a sick moment I thought he'd read my thoughts. He turned to Jordan. "Did you call the wife?"

The flaxen head nodded. "She was out."

"Try again later. He has to talk to her, tell her he's all right." Kresnik looked down at me again. "Who's in with you on this?"

"No one."

"I draw the obvious conclusion."

"Sure. Someone in this room robbed me. Or the guy with dirty hair. Where's he?"

The fist landed. I thought my jawbone had snapped. Small red worms wriggled swiftly through my head and spiralled behind my eyes. I moaned. Ginny Ferrer sucked air through her clenched teeth. Kresnik said, "Untie him."

Jordan and Capote held one arm apiece and hauled me up on my india-rubber legs. The room nearly disappeared.

"Anything to add?" Kresnik asked.

I peered through ripples at Ginny Ferrer. Expression had finally come to her eyes. She was frightened. I said, "There are people here don't like me."

Capote twisted my arm. "You can say that again."

"It would bore me. We'll take you for a start. There was plenty of time after I threw you out of the car last night to get to my house and wait. Or take Jordan. Take Ginny...."

"Take this!" Kresnik snarled.

His fist planted so far in my belly it touched my spine. I opened my mouth and rolled up my eyeballs with a click. I wanted to lie down and die. The guys holding my shoulders wouldn't let me. I did a small buck-and-wing, went up on my toes and hung.

Kresnik chucked me under the chin, lifted my head. "Want to tell me anything?"

"Take it easy. You'll rupture my ulcer."

"Hard guy." He slapped me twice with his flat hands. He simultaneously opened his temper and closed his fists. He played tick-tack-toe on my face and I went "Uh uh uh!" My upper vertebrae opened and closed like the pleats of a concertina.

I saw Ginny Ferrer leave the wall. She grabbed Kresnik's arm. She shouted, "Al, not so much! Al, you're killing him!"

I took a nap.

I made some trips into the hither and yon. I lay a long while wondering what time of day it was. Someone came into the darkness with me and I thought it was Garcia. He lifted me by the nape of the neck and gave me a long dribbly drink of water.

There may have been a time lapse. I don't know. I opened my eyes and the pale-faced guy was leaning over me with a hypodermic needle the size of an Indian lance.

He hadn't yet washed his hair. He was flaked thick with dandruff and I thought some of it would fall on me. The prospect wasn't pleasant. I closed my eyes and went on more voyages. They weren't so good, either. They all ended with me hiding in an empty suitcase and peering out through the keyhole and watching Eve and Paul Taylor.

Kresnik said, "Beat it, Ginny, you're due at the Club. Gimme a kiss."

I mustered all my strength and raised my eyelids by force. Kresnik being kissed was something I had to see. The door shut and the light swung from side to side like a fake harvest moon in a corny musical number. The bed creaked as Kresnik sat down beside me. He said, "He ready, Charlie?"

Dirty-hair floated by like a motorless rocket ship. So his name was Charlie. He said, "I guess so. His eyes are open."

Kresnik's face came close. I felt the air jetting from his nostrils. From this distance his skin looked like the lava-field of a volcano. He looked deep in my eyes. He lowered his voice. He said, sepulchrally, "You're gonna tell me the truth, Race. You can't help yourself. You understand?"

It was like something out of Inner Sanctum. I had an insane urge to giggle. I couldn't even bat my lids.

He said, "You're gonna talk. You stole the suitcase. Where you hidden it? Tell me!"

I had neither a voice nor the strength to use one. I lay and watched him lap his lips and swirl around a bit. He turned his head. He said, "Goddam stuff don't work. You sure you give it to him right, Charlie?"

"Like the doc told me."

"Why didn't you bring the guy with you?"

"He wouldn't come. He was scared."

"Jordan call the wife?"

"Yeah. She still ain't there. "

"We'll have to get this guy out of here."

Kresnik pointed his nose at me. He re-started the intoning.

I could see clear up his nostrils to his scalp. He said, "Race, you're gonna live your experience again. You just pushed Scrine from the car. You're driving away swiftly. Where you going?"

The English sailor's name was Scrine. It wasn't a name I liked. It didn't suit him so well as the other. I said clearly and distinctly, articulating every syllable, "I prefer Truman Capote."

My lips didn't move and no words came out.

Kresnik snarled, "Charlie, you fouled this up. The guy's out cold."

"His eyes are open," Charlie said. "Is he dead?"

Kresnik leaned so close I thought he was going to give me a cigar-reeking kiss.

He said softly, "Just lie there, baby. Your wife wants you out of the way. She's in bed with this other guy, this Paul. She ain't answering the phone because she's all tangled up."

If I jerked my head I could break his nose. I tautened all my fibres. I strained. The fibres snapped like old string. I didn't move a millimetre.

He said, "How you like it? The guy'll be about taking off his pants. Now he's taking off his shirt. He's standing there. He's got more than you got. Your wife likes it even if you don't. Oh boy, she loves it!"

I started a noiseless scream. I kicked and struggled. I was a prisoner in my own rigid skin. Vultures tore at my liver, my bones pulverised, a fire was lit under me. I couldn't move. Kresnik put a big hand across my throat.

He said, "Quit stalling," The fright was back and he looked desperate. He said, "You can hear me, you bastard, I can see it in your eyes. Where you hid the suitcase? Where? Where?"

He picked me up by the gorge and shook me like a mat. He rat-tatted the back of his hand across my face and my head boomed like the gong in the Teahouse of the August Moon. He snarled, "I'm gonna work on you, you bastard. You'll sing your guts out."

He started a second tattoo. I hated to cheat him, but there was no remedy. I faded back into the ink.

I went with Garcia and we did a couple of shifts in a couple of mines. First it was Siberia and all salt. I couldn't see anything for the whiteness. Then we went over to Pennsylvania and Garcia was howling and I was trying to hew him out of the solid coal face. I couldn't see anything for the blackness.

I drove a pick through my own head. Garcia moved and shouted from a long way off and I booted down a dark alley toward the shaft. I ran so hard I couldn't breathe. I stood looking up at nothing with my head breaking and my lungs bursting to suffocation. The cage came down.

It had a little hook on the bottom. I clung to it with three fingers. I swooped to the top in two seconds and left my stomach behind. I still couldn't breathe. I opened my eyes and the darkness was complete. The reason for not breathing was a hand over my mouth and blocking my nostrils. I tried to struggle.

The voice hissed in my ear, "No noise. No noise. No noise."

In a while I nodded. The hand went away. I lay quiet and sucked down air by the cubic mile.

The figure rose from its knees at the bedside. There was movement around my hands and feet. The ropes fell away, the pressure went, but I continued to lie still. My arms and legs were dead. I didn't think I could ever stand up again. Back came the lips from the darkness. They made more whispering. "Take it easy. The bed creaks. The microphone. Jordan's up in the other room. You okay?"

I nodded. I concentrated very hard and tried to pump blood into my extremities by will power. I gritted my teeth and eased one foot to the floor. I shifted the inside leg inch by inch, got the second foot to the floor alongside the other, and shifted my weight.

The bed plucked and twanged like an orchestra of harps. I fell over.

There was a hiss of breath. The hands came down and tried to yank me upright. I got to my knees, pitched forward, rolled and managed to rise to my feet. The door opened.

She was silhouetted against the dim light, beckoning frantically with a gun. She wore a street dress and an old pair of canvas running shoes. I slid after her. The footsteps echoed across the hall above us.

She stopped and slipped the bolt on the door. I remember thinking how smart that was. She dragged me round the corner and down six steps of the second flight of stairs. She pressed the gun into my hand, flattened me against the wall. Jordan was almost on top of us.

His footsteps went from one to eight. He stopped in front of the door and did nothing and the silence rang like a bell. I went back up my six steps. I put my nose around the corner. He had his ear to the door and his back to me. I took two steps more and tapped his shoulder.

He turned so hard I didn't have to use force. The gun butt in my hand slammed his jaw and crunched and he went unconscious with his eyes open. I caught him on the way down. I slid the bolt and dragged him into the room. I dropped him on the bed.

The second lot of footsteps pattered across the hall. The Mexican houseboy called, "Ebryt'ing okeh?"

I couldn't have sounded like Jordan if I practised a year. I kept mum.

He came down the stairs very slowly. Jordan moaned on the bed behind me. I had visions of him leaping on my back. I gripped the gun butt.

The Mexican's head came round the door. I whacked him.

I ought to be ashamed. He was too small for such treatment. He gave a singing little whine and I whacked him again. He put his chin on my arm and went to sleep and I tossed him on the bed on top of Jordan. I went out and bolted the door.

She was still waiting around the bend of the stairs. I whispered, "Two. Any more?"

She shook her head.

We went farther down, through a basement and up again, her running shoes going slap-slap-slap. The air opened to us with a sky full of stars. It was night. That was a surprise. We ran across a back lot until we had to stop at the wall. She said, "We got to get over. There's still a guy down at the gate."

It was a high wall. I couldn't make it. I looked around for something to stand on. I said, "How strong are you?"

"Try."

I took off my shoes, tied them and held the laces between my teeth. She made a half stoop. I felt mean as hell but I climbed on her shoulders. She wavered. I got my hands on the top of the wall and dragged up. I saw the car waiting the other side and nearly died of fright. There was no one in it.

I bent right back over the wall and got her wrists. She scraped herself a bit, but I pulled her up beside me and then it was nothing. I jumped down first and lifted my arms and when I held her I remembered for a moment how it had been a long time ago.

We got in the car. She eased the brakes and we coasted noiselessly down the slope.

I said, "Thanks, Ginny."

13

She said, "I managed the wall by standing on the roof of the car. It was easy."

She had changed from her running shoes and was driving again. She could drive like Juan Fangio. We slid through traffic like a sea-snake through oil. We were sticking to the back streets and I was keeping my head down.

I said, "Why did you do it?"

"Because it was easy and I needed the exercise."

"I don't get it. You're a pal of Kresnik's."

"I'm his mistress," she said.

She gave the wheel a little twist. The tires hummed. She said, "It sort of goes with the job of singing at the *Caracol*. He's not all that bad. He's generous, he's given me my own apartment...."

I said, "Yes, you're in a tough profession. There must be times when...."

"Shut your trap!" Her teeth showed. "I don't need you making excuses for me. I know what I'm doing. You're the only guy I ever walked into with my eyes shut."

We drove a while in silence. We were getting near the outskirts of the main town.

I said, "You still didn't say why you came over the wall."

She sneered. She said, "Okay, here's the way you want to hear it. All these years I've still been in love with you. When I saw you the other night I got that old feeling. When they beat you up I couldn't bear to see my precious boy getting hurt. Wait while I turn on the radio. There's maybe a band playing *Hearts and Flowers*."

I gazed steadily to the front. She shot me a look from the corner of her eye. She said, "Okay. Charlie got the idea of feeding you this truth drug. Charlie don't talk much, but when he does everything he says is screwed up. He was going to pump a gallon of the stuff in you. Al Kresnik would have let him. He wants that suitcase bad. They might have killed you between them, then Al would have been in trouble. I don't want that. I like Al. He's a good meal ticket. And just for the record I enjoyed seeing you beat up, I revelled in it. You've had it coming for years."

"I know how you feel."

"Don't start understanding me again."

I said, "What's in the suitcase?"

She drew to the side of the road and pulled up. She put an arm on the back of the seat and looked at me steadily. "You don't know?"

"No."

"You didn't swipe it?"

"Did you?"

Cars flicked by like volleys in a pin-ball machine.

I said, "Did you haul me out of that room to pump me? You're wasting your time. I don't have a thing to tell."

She slapped my face. Her nose screwed up and then her eyes and then she flung her arms around me and sobbed on my chest. I held her tight. For no reason I tilted back her head and kissed her.

She said, "I don't know what's in the case, but you'd better find it pretty soon or Al Kresnik'll kill you." I moved. She thought I was going to kiss her again. She shoved me off.

She said harshly, "Quit that any time you like. You got an ever-loving wife. You kicked up enough hell when you thought she was two-timing you."

She started the engine. A slow fire burned under my skin. I'd forgotten how they'd eavesdropped through the microphone. The ache came back.

"That was a backfire for everyone," she said. "Al Kresnik put you in that room because he thought you might talk to her about the suitcase. He figured maybe she was mixed up in it."

"She wasn't."

"Sure not. Anyone could see that. She's a sweet person. She's also a smart cookie. When they brought her in last night she never cracked a wink that we'd met before. She hardly spoke to anyone all through the poker game. She just sat there winning."

"What time did they bring her in? Who did the bringing?"

"Charlie and Jordan, about half past eleven. I was leaving to be in time for the midnight show."

"Who stayed with her afterwards?"

"I don't know. Like I told you, I left for the show."

"One of the boys had the chance of robbing me." I touched her arm. "You really don't know what's in the case?"

"I was at the Club," she said angrily. "I'm supposed to be there now for the second show. It's going on midnight. Al Kresnik or anybody else finds I'm missing they'll put two and two together and my life won't be worth a snapped girdle. No, I don't know what's in the case."

We went around by the Fruit Market, down Belleville. I said, "Take the third on the right. You can drop me. I live two blocks from there."

"I know where you live," she said testily. "I read about you in the papers."

She turned into the shadowy side street and drew up. "Don't stay home too long. When Kresnik finds you're gone he'll be on your tail. Warn your wife. You want this gun?"

"I won't need it." I opened the door. "Does your second show always go on at midnight?"

"Round about. The orchestra stalls along if I'm late. Why?"

She reached out and touched my wrist. "Anything else I can do to help, call Bel-Air 6-54326. Or the Club. You got any plans?"

"Yes. I'm going to call the cops."

"Remember me to your wife," she said, and slammed the door and let in the clutch. She drove away swiftly. I walked a block and turned left. I didn't feel so bad as I'd expected.

Our car was parked on the street. It meant Eve was home. I found the latch key, went to the first floor via the service stairs, took the elevator from there. The building was very quiet. I opened the door of the apartment and the gnawing came back. There was no light.

I said, "Eve!"

I had an impression someone was there with me. I snapped on the switches. No one. I called again: "Eve!"

I knew she wasn't home, but I went through all the rooms. The bedroom was tidy. In the kitchen was a used glass, gin, vermouth, some drying olives where she'd made herself a martini many hours ago. I poured a slug of the gin, changed my mind, threw it down the sink. I went out to the phone.

The servant answered. I said, "Mrs. Race with her father?"

"Mr. Alford's alone, sir. Would you like to speak to him?"

"It doesn't matter."

I broke the connection, dialled again and waited. When the receiver lifted there was music at the other end and two men laughing in the background. Laura Taylor said, "Yes?"

"Eve with you?"

"Why, no. No, Bob, she isn't." Laura hesitated. "I want to talk to you, Bob, I have to apologise. Can I see you tomorrow? We're busy now."

I hung up.

I went into the bathroom and studied myself. I took a wash. There was nothing much wrong with my face except a swelling of the nose and a blue contusion on my upper left eyelid that didn't show if I kept the eye wide open. I slapped the knees of my trousers where they'd got dusty going over the wall, straightened my tie and went downstairs. Laura Taylor opened the door.

She saw who it was and closed the door again so that her face was showing. She said pleadingly, "Bob. Tomorrow. For God's sake don't make trouble now. It's the first time he's been normal for months. It means so much."

I pushed the door and strode in past her.

They were sitting opposite one another in easy chairs, Paul Taylor and a pros-perous looking old man with white hair and the seamed face of a tout. They were drinking big drinks and the radio was playing. Paul Taylor looked over his shoulder, saw me, half rose, and the colour seeped up his face to the cut on his forehead. He said nervously, "Hello, Bob."

The old man tilted the skin of his forehead questioningly. He had no eye-brows.

Behind me Laura said breathlessly, "Mr. Crossland, this is our neighbour Mr. Race. Mr. Race is also a lawyer. Mr. Crossland is Paul's very most important client. I suppose I should be angry with him for keeping Paul out all last night, but I think's he's much too sweet." She gave a pathetic quack. "Drink, Bob?"

"No."

The old man billed his lips and went "Kyeh kyeh kyeh!" He was laughing. He said, "You're in the wrong company, young fella. Should a been with us last night. Dusk till dawn. Solid. Always say you can't trust a man who don't know how to take his liquor. Kyeh kyeh kyeh! Learn to drink a bottle of bour-bon and I might throw a little of my business your way, too. I got plenty to throw."

Paul Taylor moved his lips a few times. "Mr. Crossland's a very, very im-portant man and a great business personality. Kedgeree Mine Development, Dallas-Duluth Housing, Toledo Minerals...."

He tailed off. He looked at me with the entreaty of a spaniel. The old man stared at the dusty knees of my trousers.

"Sure about the drink, Bob?" Laura asked.

I turned on her. "I want to know if you've seen Eve today. Either of you?"

"Why no. No we haven't. We haven't moved from the apartment. I've been looking after Paul. He had a headache."

"Fell down and cracked his head when he was boozed. Kyeh kyeh kyeh!" I was glad the old man wasn't my client.

Laura said, "I think I heard her moving around about nine o'clock this morning. But we haven't seen her."

"Sorry to have butted in. Goodbye."

The old man said, "Stay if you want a drink. A guy who can't drink is a boob."

Paul Taylor had recovered his composure. "Yeah, a boob," he said.

I left.

At the moment the police were out of the question. Back in the apartment I picked up the phone and dropped it again. Sam Alford would have called back if he wanted to talk to me. I went into the bathroom, took another wash and had a shave. I went out to the kitchen, gave myself a sandwich and a pint of milk and sat looking at the dusty knees of my trousers. They offended me.

The newspapers were always remarking on the way I dressed. I liked to be halfway neat. I decided to change. I finished eating, wiped my mouth, turned off the light and went into the bedroom.

I opened my cupboard.

All my suits were in ribbons.

They had been slashed with a razor, without method, great criss-cross cuts on every article of clothing. I stood and stared at them. I tried to wet my dried mouth. I crossed the room and opened Eve's wardrobe.

I knew then.

She had left behind the clothes she didn't like. Her wedding dress hung at the back wrapped in plastic. I went through the drawers. Stockings, underclothes, nightdresses, all gone. I opened my own drawer, put my fingers among the shirts. The two hundred dollars emergency fund was gone. I knew the gun wouldn't be there even before I went to the sideboard. I was right.

I changed my shirt. Back in the kitchen I poured half a tumbler of neat gin and drank it down. I shuddered. I hadn't understood her all our married life. I didn't know the first thing about her.

I went down in the elevator and out by the front way, advertising myself. I didn't give a damn about Kresnik now, only insofar as he was indirectly involved. I went out into the street and searched for nine blocks. Skelly, the patrol cop, was sauntering down the sidewalk.

I brushed his shoulder. I stopped. I said, "Why, hello Skelly. How are things?"

"Okay with me." He grinned. "Not so good with you, I hear. Your client got the book thrown at him yesterday. How'd you come to take on a case like that?"

"Somebody had to."

"You're too good-hearted, Mr. Race, you let 'em deceive you. The dirty bastard, they should a shot him."

I said, "Lay off the gun law. You nearly shot my dinner guest the other night. How come you saw him. You must have good vision."

"Average, Mr. Race. It wasn't so hard. He came out of your window and stood on the fire escape landing like he was peering in. Then he starts coming down the escape like he's trying not to make any noise about it. I shouted at him. I was gonna grab him when he got to the bottom. The little bastard ran up again. A kid, was he?"

"Playing a joke," I said. "A friend of ours. How's the wife, Skelly?"

"I'm not married. I live with my sister."

"That's right, I forgot. Give her my regards. Be seeing you."

He said, "Don't take any more dud clients."

I headed back toward the apartment. On the fifth street I saw an open drugstore and went inside to the phone booth. The music and laughter was still going on in the background at the other end. I said, "Laura?"

"Hello, Bob." She was jumpy as a pulse.

I said, "The husband's always the last to know. When Eve gave Paul the brush six months ago...."

She interrupted in a desperate whisper. "Can't you forget it? I was gibbering, I was out of my head, I didn't know what I was saying."

"Well make a note of what I'm saying. If you don't tell the truth I'll come straight to the apartment and start the biggest goddamned brawl you ever saw in your life. Got that?"

"Yes," she said.

"Why did Paul get the shove-off?"

She didn't answer. The music came louder. Maybe Paul Taylor had turned up the radio. I couldn't hear anyone laughing any more.

I said, "Because she'd found another guy?"

"I don't know."

"All right, you got a brawl on your hands."

"Wait!" she said. "If you know about it why are you asking me? Don't you know who he is?"

"Paul does," I said. "Paul called him a punk. Paul hates him. Goodbye, I won't bother you again."

I stood there and chewed my own mouth and choked up. All that giggling when he came in off the fire escape: laughing at me, the two of them, sharing their dirty little secret. The way he always called her Mrs. Race. And the blind accident of the *Caracol*, when Eve claimed he had seen me going in. He hadn't seen me. I'd entered by the back way. Eve asking me almost immediately if I wanted to go home to bed.

How much more?

Six months. Six whole filthy lying deceitful months! Him opening his pants. Her pulling up her clothes.

I opened the phone book, found the name and made a note of the address. I went round the block, got the car and headed across the town.

14

The narrow street was in the Mexican quarter of town. The time was after midnight, the crowd still thronged thick, some of them drunk, most of them laughing. It was Friday night. Pay night. Nobody answered my ring at the door.

I rang again. A guitar was playing high in a tenement on the opposite side of the street. A guy was singing a Latin deserted-lover song, his artificially hardened voice pitched somewhere just under his scalp. A smell of cooking, deep-fried in olive oil wafted down the block. I pushed open the door and walked in.

There was a dim light in the ceiling. Badly concealed in a curve of the stairs a couple was in an advanced stage of making love. The girl was about eighteen and the boy about fifteen. The boy lowered his head and made uncomfortable grabs at himself. The girl wasn't embarrassed.

"Mrs. Fontaine?" I said.

"First floor, left hand."

I scraped past them up the narrow staircase. They whispered together and the boy said loudly, "No!" I went along a stinking landing and there was only one door on the left so I rapped it with my knuckles. I tried to guess how many people lived in the building.

I'd met Mrs. Fontaine twice before, once at the court, once at my office when she heard that I'd pay Tony's college fees. She had struck me as elderly, dignified, ill and pathetic. I guess I wanted her to be like that.

She opened the door.

She had on a negligee and a slip. The negligee showed most of the slip and the slip showed most of her breasts. Her feet were bare, her hair hadn't been combed in a while, her eyes were bleary and the rye on her breath would have knocked down a dray horse. I don't know where I'd got the idea she was elderly. She was around forty or forty-five. She had the same face as her son.

A radio in the apartment was playing at the top of its speaker. I raised my voice to a shout but she couldn't understand me, either through noise or rye. She hung on the door and blinked. She gave up. She made a majestic flourish and swept me in.

She hollered, "Looie, turn down the goddam radio!"

The guy on the sofa wore pants, socks, a long sleeved undershirt and a tumbler of whisky. He turned his head and blinked suspiciously at me from bright brown eyes. That was his only movement. He shouted, "Who's this?"

"How should I know?" She fixed the radio so that it only shrieked. It was playing a mambo. The guys in the orchestra cried, "Oooogh!" She smiled at Looie, twitched her shoulders and buttocks in time to the music and pivoted to me. The recognition dawned in her eyes.

She screamed, "Why it's Mr. Race. What you doing here this time of night, Mr. Race? Looie, for Christ's sake sit up like a gentleman. This is Mr. Race."

Looie said without moving, "And who the hell is Mr. Race?"

"Mr. Race," she said. "The lawyer. Tony's friend."

"You telling me that no good son-of-a-bitch got any friends? Stop surprising me!"

Mrs. Fontaine drew the negligee tighter around her. She said with withering dignity, "You can stop talking like that about my Tony or you can get the hell out of here. I'm his mother. Those things reflect on me."

"That's right," Looie said calmly, and belted off his drink. "And you can tell me to get out of this joint when I stop paying the rent. We all straight now?"

I looked directly into his bright brown eyes. I said, "Looie, I'm new in from the desert. How about a drink?"

"A fellow prospector." He heaved off the sofa, went to the table, poured one for himself and one for me. The glass had thumb prints. He lay the dead bottle tenderly on the floor, hooked a fresh one from somewhere under the table, broke the seal, handed me my glass and said, "America expects every man to do his duty."

The drink nearly choked me. He poured me another. He slapped my arm and went back to the sofa. Mrs. Fontaine said, "What about me?"

"You," he said, "can go — yourself."

"I prefer a drink."

She swayed across, helped herself and swayed back. The radio said "Oooogh!" She gave a great elaborate wink and I winked back. She wriggled her shoulders. She threw back her head and crowed with laughter.

"Shows how wrong you can be about a person, don't it?" she said. "Tony always said you was a stuffed shirt without any stuffing. You're okay."

"Tony's opinions are all shot," I said. "I, for instance, think Looie's a good joe. Tony says Looie's a no-good lazy jerk."

"Yep! That's what I am." Looie swung his feet to the floor and sat up straight. "A no-good lazy jerk who works fifty hours a week to give me and Lil some of the pleasures of life. And what does that little bastard do? Sneak thieves from the stores, lays all the gratis broads in the neighbourhood and pretends he's too good for everybody else because he goes to college twice a week."

"Shut up, Looie," Mrs. Fontaine said. "Mr. Race is paying the college fees."

"What's it to me who's paying the college fees?" The brown eyes leered a little. "Why are you paying the college fees? 'Cause he's pretty?"

"Looie," I said, "lay off that line. We're not gonna quarrel about Tony. You and me's got the same opinion."

"That right?" His face glowed with pleasure. He shot a triumphant look at Mrs. Fontaine. "He in trouble?"

"Bad trouble."

"There y'are, Lil," he said. "Did I tell you when he came round here this morning in that goddam new car, or didn't I?"

Mrs. Fontaine didn't have a wriggle left. Her mouth hung slackly. "It was an old car."

"It was a second-hand car hopped up and it cost at least six hundred bucks."

"A Plymouth," I said.

"A Mercury. Repainted bright green. Green as peas. Ain't that just like him! Okay, tell me! He stole it!"

"Yes," I said.

"The lying bastard said it belonged to a friend of his and they was going away for the week-end."

"To Santapola."

"How the hell do I know where they gone."

"Mrs. Fontaine, does he know anyone in Santapola?"

She didn't wink any more. She was looking at me with half fear and half hatred.

I said, "He mentioned the place a couple of nights ago. If I can catch him and bring back the car by tomorrow night there won't be any trouble. Otherwise…."

She said, "I got a cousin there. She's married to a guinea name of José Ruso. They run a bar called the Flamenco."

"Thanks."

"Will there be trouble?"

"I don't know."

"Do all you can to make it," Looie said heartily. "Come again any time. I like the sort of news you bring."

She spat a dirty word and lifted the bottle from the table and flung it at him. He caught it with a slap in the palm of his hand and pulled up his legs and stretched out again on the sofa. I closed the door behind me. Down at the curve of the stairs the ranging girl was back with a man old enough to be her grandfather.

I went out to the street and round the corner to where I'd parked the car.

I wouldn't have gone there, but I needed money. The servant showed me into the library.

Sam Alford was reading Tacitus on Imperial Rome. I could almost guess by the expression on his face which passage he was at. He looked up, pointed to a chair, grunted and went back to the book. I didn't sit down.

He said, "Stop standing there like Banquo's ghost. What you want?"

"Lend me five hundred bucks."

He laid the book on his knees, fished a wallet from his pocket and extracted some notes. "Hundred and fifty. No more in the house." The suspicion of a grin flicked across his face. "Going on a wing-ding?"

"Sort of. To look for Eve."

"She off somewhere?"

I said levelly, "You know she is. I phoned an hour ago to see if she was here. It meant I was worried. It meant you should have worried. You weren't. You didn't call me back. Where is she?"

The grin spread. He made no attempt to hide it. "I don't know. Good luck to her wherever she is. I hope she enjoys herself. She deserves it."

I said, "The guy's twenty years old. Eve's twenty-seven." I wanted to shock him, surprise him into something. He merely went on grinning. "And you're thirty-four," he said. "You might as well be seventy-four, the sort of husband you've been. You know how long you lasted? Three months! If you'd slept with her before you got married she'd have found out sooner and not married you. You were useless. And on top of everything else you didn't want a baby. That really washed you out."

I had no stomach. I said, "She seems to have told you everything."

"Everything!" he said triumphantly. "She always has. I brought her up that way. I got a relationship with my daughter that no one else can ever take from me, you least of all. You couldn't even fulfil the position of husband." He snorted contemptuously. "Husband! A red-blooded girl like Eve had to go else-where."

"Crimson-blooded," I said. "Where is she?"

He ignored me. He said, "It's time somebody told you where to get off, little Willie Milquetoast. You married Eve for what you thought was my money. You didn't get any. You had my girl living like a goddamned slavey. I threw good business your way and you still kept her short, in bed and out of bed. I helped her all I could, any way I could. You continued to sit on your skinny ass and do nothing. You didn't buy her clothes, you took her out once a month, you neg-lected her. You asked for all you got, Willie. You walked right into it. Serves you goddam right!"

"She's told a good story." I had a big lump in my throat that I couldn't swal-low. I said, "I'm still in love with her."

"Oh Christ! Quack quack! Get the hell out of here."

"Where is she?"

"I wouldn't tell you if I knew. She came here this morning and said she was going away. She'll let me know where she is when it suits her."

His grin became a leer. He said, "The kid she spent last night with must be pretty hot stuff to persuade her to skip off like that at a moment's notice. I'm glad of that. I didn't think so much of Paul Taylor and some of the others she's had."

I said, "She really does tell you everything."

"Beat it!" He picked up the book and started to read.

I said, "But she didn't spend last night with any guy. She was a prisoner out at Al Kresnik's house—Al Kresnik, the race-track boy, the racketeer."

He lowered the book to his knees. He said slowly, "What was she doing there?"

"Being held as safeguard for my good conduct. I was carrying out a job for Kresnik down at the port, collecting a smuggled suitcase from an English sailor."

He stared at me incredulously. "You?"

"Me. Kresnik's a client of mine. He applied a little blackmail. Everything mis-fired, for him and for me. Somebody robbed me of the case and sent me for a short ride over a high cliff."

My father-in-law started to get up. His face had gone white as a fall of snow. "Who?"

"Make your guess. I'd told Eve about the job. She could have told Tony Fontaine. She was at Kresnik's house at the time of the robbery, but Fontaine was still in circulation. A guy who hates me enough to slash up all my suits just because I've given him some hand-me-downs, hates me enough to send me over a cliff. Eve didn't tell you she was skipping with him until this morning because she didn't know until this morning if the robbery was a success. She'd just been released by Kresnik. She found the plan had worked out and hit the road with

Fontaine. I'm still trying to figure two things. Why Kresnik let her go and what was in the case."

Sam Alford's voice shook. He said, "You lying, fabricating twisted son-of-a-bitch. You're trying to get her in trouble with Kresnik."

"I'm the one in trouble," I said. "He's looking for me. He thinks I stole the suitcase."

"You did." Sam Alford swung a fist. I ducked. It was the first fist I'd ducked in a long while. He raised his arm and stood panting, all his teeth bared. He looked newly off his head. He said, "I'll fix you!" and strode out across the hall. I heard him at the phone. I went after him.

He said, "I want to talk to Al Kresnik. Now! Sam Alford calling."

I went straight out through the front door and got in the car. I left at forty and when I was outside the city limits I raised to seventy-five.

I figured I should be in Santapola around nine in the morning.

15

It wasn't a good journey. There were few trees on the way down, but a bird sat singing in every one. Cuckoo! The word of fear, unpleasing to a married ear.

When I shot the birds the sign from the *Caracol* switched on behind my eyes and flickered there for two hundred miles. The horns of the snail kept shooting up and wilting, shooting up and wilting. I was poor boring old King Mark, mumbling and droning, on and on. And his wife out in the woods getting laid by another guy to the sound of a million violins.

There was ruined vanity mixed up in it, the implied sneer, the indictment of my sexual prowess. There was humour. A husband with horns is a comic character. I didn't laugh. I was trying impossibly to compute the other men I didn't know about, thinking that everything she'd said to me, everything she'd done with me, she had said and done with them. Her hair and eyes, the curves of her body, the lazy laugh when she was finally satisfied. They knew it all as well as I did. My Eve. An illusion. A deception so profound. I wanted to spit on her. I wanted to kill her.

Santapola not so long ago was a cow town. Lean rangy cowboys descended from their horses and spurs clinked in the streets. Lithe handsome Mexicans said witty things in funny English, plunked guitars and sang liquid songs. Everyone was a crack shot. Everyone drank rotgut whisky.

There are no horses now and all the cowboys are on film in the local movie house. The songs come from juke-boxes in a long line of sleazy, neon-lit bars on the main street. There are still crackshots, but living in a border town they aim at something else, foregathering in upstairs rooms to heat small organs with marijuana. The one thing unchanged is the scorching wind that blows from the desert across the border. And the noise. Santapola is a hell of a noisy town.

I got there at ten-thirty. I was a mess. I was caked with dust and my skin felt like sandpaper and I needed a bath. My eyes were bunged. I was nearly dead from lack of sleep. I couldn't get rid of the idea that I was on a wild goose chase.

I drove around a warren of scabrous side streets filled with playing children, found a dingy little hotel called the Albero. It was the sort of place you visited for a passionate hour. You couldn't get a bath unless you hired a room and paid in advance. I hired one and paid.

The water wasn't hot, but I felt physically better afterwards. I returned to the room, sat on the bed in my underwear. I listened to the traffic and the yelling kids outside and wondered how anyone in the town ever got any sleep. Then I stretched on the bed and went to sleep. I dreamed about Garcia. It was five-thirty when I awoke.

Dusk was coming. In the street the same kids squalled the same howls. I dressed carefully, wished I had a clean shirt, went down and left the key. I walked around till I found a place where I got a shoe-shine and a shave. In a drugstore I had soup, spaghetti, sandwiches, coffee, checked the Flamenco Bar in the phone book, stood by while the clerk explained with paper, pencil and a writhing tongue exactly where the street was.

I drove slowly, looking for a second-hand Mercury with a bright green respray job. There wasn't one. I could still be on a wild goose chase.

The town degenerated into a squatty slum of crumbling adobe. Up ahead was the office of the border guards, Mexico beyond. I parked the car, got out and walked. Amid all the stinks you could feel the harsh clean smell of the desert. It was getting pretty near night.

The Flamenco was long narrow dirty and dark—a standup joint with a few tables squeezed against the wall so that when you stood at the bar for a drink the sitting customers were served with your rear-end. There was a door at the far end, and a big clock, not going, put up on the wall in the days of the Emperor Maximilian. There was no juke box and no customers.

The guy behind the bar gave me a big smile as I entered. I said, "Hola! José."

"Hola! yourself." The smile was lit with gold all along the left side. He had dried white spit caked at both corners of his mouth and his face was a mass of deep cracks like a forgotten old brown boot recently recovered and re-polished. He was old enough to go grey on either side of his thick hair, but instead he'd gone blue. It may have been the grease. He wasn't big, but he was wiry. He was tough. He had a quick eye.

"Beer?"

"Yeah." I was almost sitting on the back of a chair. "Tony around?"

It was Mexican beer. He drew it carefully and piled a big head of suds. He placed it in front of me and put his hands down behind the bar.

"What Tony?"

"Your wife's cousin, or something. I'm supposed to meet him here."

"What for?"

"We going into the desert to shoot butterflies."

"Ha ha!"

I sucked off the beer suds. We weren't getting anywhere. I tried again.

"His mother sent me. Mrs. Fontaine. She was taken pretty sick last night with some sort of internal trouble. The doctors are going to operate. It's a fifty-fifty chance. She wants Tony back there, naturally."

He said, "Don't you like the beer?"

I drank it.

He drew me another careful one and set it on the bar. He put his hands back to their original position. He wasn't smiling any more. He called, "June!"

The door opened at the other end.

She looked more like November. She was a lean black-clad birch tree of a woman with no leaves. She said, "Whadya want?"

"Guy says your cousin Lil's sick."

"What's that to me?"

"Wansa know I seen Tony."

"Did you?"

"No."

"He ain't been here since last year. What else?"

"Nuttn."

She shut the door.

The Mexican said, "Satisfied?"

"No."

I put down the beer glass, rested my hands on the bar. "You're not curious enough."

"I ain't a curious guy."

He had the pauper look about him, as if he'd lived poor all his life from dollar to dollar. There was a last method. I said, "Tell me where he is and you get five hundred bucks. Paid now."

He scratched some of the dried spit from the corner of his mouth and examined his fingernail. He said, "Listen, *chamaco*. You tell me two stories. You supposed to meet him here. You got sent by his mother. Or you flash a badge or you ain't got no authority for these questions."

"I got five hundred long green juicy bucks."

"I tell you where to put them."

I looked at him. I said, "What you holding down there, a lollipop?" His hand came up fast. I was ready.

I grabbed his wrist and pushed the hand higher. I brought it over in an arc and smashed it down on the bar. The gun fell to the floor by my side. I kicked it down the far end of the room.

His other hand came over. He was at a bad angle. I nearly pulled his arm from the socket. I bent both his wrists over the edge of the bar and bore down and watched the brown leather of his face go two tones lighter. He struggled. He was strong enough but he wasn't desperate. I was. I said, "Start again. Where's Tony Fontaine?"

He didn't say a word.

The door at the other end opened on noiseless hinges. The woman took a pace forward, bent effortlessly and scooped the gun from the floor. She said, "Okay, Wisie, let him go!" It was a big gun.

I jammed hard on the wrists. The Mexican howled with pain and fell back against the shelf of bottles. I grabbed behind me and snatched the chair and ran down the bar with it at chest level. She was still making up her mind about pulling the trigger.

The chair legs hit her like spikes. She staggered back into the room, banged a table and started to fall to the floor. I let go the chair, grabbed her wrist. She coiled like a ferret and tried to bite me. I slammed her jaw, her teeth went click, she let go the gun and I wheeled around and José changed his mind about jumping on my back. He came to a screeching halt. He jabbed his fingertips at the ceiling.

I said, "Come in and shut the door."

The woman picked herself up from the floor. I lined them both against the wall and there wasn't much space because the ten feet by ten room contained a cooking stove, two cupboards with shelves, a plain wooden table in the centre and four chairs. There was another room beyond with an unmade bed in it. That was the extent of the house. Everything had an aura of garlic and a layer of dust.

The woman said, "What's this getting you?"

"It could get you five hundred dollars."

She laughed contemptuously.

Out in the bar somebody called, "Ain't there no service here?"

I waved them into the bedroom with the gun. It was even smaller than the other room. They stood huddled in a corner at the far side of the bed and the Mexican still had his hands in the air. He was a lot more frightened than his wife. She wasn't frightened at all.

She said, "Now what?"

Her husband lowered his eyes. He saw me watching and looked at the ceiling.

I tossed the draped blankets to the other side of the unmade bed, reached my foot underneath and hooked my toe into a handle. I dragged the suitcase out. Ordinary, imitation leather, mass produced and sold in thousands. There was as much dust on it as might gather in a day.

I made a quick stoop and lifted it to the bed. I snapped the catches and raised the lid. The inside was clean. It was empty.

"Now what?" the woman repeated.

"Who does it belong to?"

"My aunt Sophie in Biloxi."

Her husband started to lower his arms. The door opened. The guy from the bar walked in.

He said, "What goes on? Someone declare prohibition?" He was a cocky little rooster of a man. He saw the gun and turned grey.

He breathed, "Trouble?"

The woman laughed. She sounded genuine. "Nothing to it, Ernie. Mac was demonstrating how someone held up a bank back in Kokomo. Ain't that so, Mac?"

She looked at me. She had my number. She walked past me. There was nothing I could do. Her husband lowered his arms.

He laughed. The rooster laughed. Everybody laughed except me. I put the gun in my pocket and followed them out to the bar. She said, "Set 'em up for everyone, Joselito. I need one."

"The night is young," the rooster said.

"And Mac's so beautiful," she said.

The little man put his beak in his glass. He crowed, "Where's the guy was here last night? The guy spending all the dough?"

"You mean Philip?" the woman asked. "He left after you passed out."

"Didn't leave his blonde, did he? Some dish. I could use some of it. How they hit a joint like this?"

I said, "The guy with the bright green Mercury?"

"Mercury, was it?"

The woman reached under the bar and I reached in my pocket. She drew out a phone with a long trailing cord. She said, "Think I'll call the cops."

The little guy choked on his drink. "Cops? Here?"

She lifted the phone from its cradle and stuck her finger in the dial. "Sorry you can't stay, Mac."

I took the rooster by his small shoulder. I said, "Was he driving a green Mercury?"

"Who? Him? How the hell do I know, it was night time." His eyes went round as marbles. He rolled them in his head so he wouldn't have to look at me.

"Was it green?"

"I told you I don't know. It was night." He tried to struggle free. He said, "June! Call them cops!"

I let him go. She started to dial. I turned around and walked out.

It could have been any suitcase. The blonde and the free-spender could have been any couple passing through, newlyweds on a honeymoon. I didn't dwell on that aspect. I concentrated on what to do next. I had to do something or go nuts.

I got back to the drugstore and the clerk asked me if I'd found the place. I said I had. He told me long-distance was pretty free at this time of the evening. I went into the booth and placed the call and came back for a glass of milk to quieten the ache in my stomach. A man and a woman made local calls while I was waiting. I had visions of the operator being unable to contact me. I got desperate. When the phone rang finally I had fire in my solar plexus.

"Ginny," I said, "this is Bob Race."

She made a little hissing sound. "They told me it was from Santapola."

"I'm here looking for that suitcase. Did you find out what was in it?"

"I'm afraid to ask. Al's losing his marbles. He's raging around like a crazy wolf. He knows you got away." She took a breath. "Jordan's in hospital with a broken jaw. They're out for your guts, Bob. There's a whole bunch of guys looking for you. You gotta be careful."

"I am," I said. "Ginny, find out what was in the suitcase. Help me. I got nowhere else to turn. I'll call you back in a while."

She didn't answer.

I said, "Has Kresnik said anything about my wife?"

Her voice came like flung acid. "You chiselling weak-kneed bastard. After what you did to me, a cheap little waitress who wasn't good enough to marry you. Now you're out on a limb and you come crawling back like a...."

I hung up. I didn't want to hear any more.

I opened the booth door, shut it again, lifted the phone and jiggled the cradle a few times. The operator came on. I said, "That long-distance line still open?"

"Yeah."

"Put me through to the exchange supervisor at the other end."

I listened to the voices, tried to think of the name of the supervisor I'd met in the D.A.'s office when the bookie phone scandals were on. At the far end a woman said, "Hello?"

"Miss Kolanski?"

"She doesn't work here any more, sir. She got married. This is Miss Birell. Can I help?"

I said, "This is Mr. Race—Mr. Robert Race, the lawyer. I'm down here in Santapola with my father-in-law, Mr. Sam Alford. We've come to meet my wife. Mr. Alford got a long-distance call from her today. She gave him a number and we're supposed to call her again from here. The number has been lost. Could you check the records and find out where she called from? Mr. Alford's own local number is Glenview 8-80080."

She said, "One moment."

The girls were hello-ing at the other end. I wondered what percentage were double-crossing their men. Miss Birell said, "Yes, here we are. Long distance, person-to-person, from Campello, Mexico. The number...."

She broke off short. Her voice hardened. "One minute, Mister. That call was made only half an hour ago. Mr. Alford wasn't there to answer and the call's still on. What's the game? You're not Mr. Race."

I replaced the receiver.

I went out, got in the car, drove toward the border post. Campello was two hours over the border, the other side of the desert. I put the Mexican's gun far under the driver's seat.

The guys at the border talked for a couple of minutes, told me not to lose too much money in Campello's gambling joints and waved me on.

I hit the desert.

PART TWO

16

I had given up. I stumbled on the step, lurched against the door, the light went dancing and glinting all along the rows of bottles and the other three customers turned in my direction. The bartender said wearily, "Back again?"

I nodded stupidly. I curled my fingers over the edge of the bar to keep my balance. "Another double," I said. "Where are some more places to go?"

He examined me doubtfully. He made up his mind and grudgingly poured the drink. He said, "I already told you all the joints there are. All ninety-five. Now go book yourself a room and get a nice night's sleep and stop bothering me. Beats me you're still walking."

"Have to walk," I said. "Have to keep looking." And I had to keep drinking because it made things a little less bad, a little more supportable. I said, "I'm looking for a second-hand Mercury…."

"Painted green. Yeah. There's a blonde dame in it with her brunette brother. You told me that eleven times in three hours. We're all getting bored."

The farthest customer laughed. "Her brother?"

"That's what the man says. Leave him alone, he's suffering. He'll suffer worse in the morning when he wakes up and finds his head." The bartender shrugged, turned back to me. "You're drinking your last drink, Mister. Pay up and get out. Why don't you try the *Tortuga?* Make you sleep better. Anyone'll tell you where it is."

This time all the guys laughed. I realised dimly that the *Tortuga* might be a private joke. I wanted to explain that I wasn't so dumb as they thought. I said no words because my tongue wouldn't move fast enough. I slapped some money on the bar and staggered outside.

The dark night was made gaudy by the gambling signs, stretched in a neon spectrum down both sides of the main street. They flickered and jigged like the sign of the *Caracol.* In the open-fronted slot-machine joints the conflicting juke-boxes blared loud. The fiercest was a mambo. I hesitated a moment. I put my forehead against a squat pot-bellied palm tree and was sick. A passing woman turned her head sharply away in disgust.

I was a little more sober after that. Not much. I wondered whether to return to where I'd left the car. I'd been searching the town on foot all evening. They were nowhere. If they were here at all they must be in bed. I'd had that thought for a while now. No amount of drink could blot it out.

I needed more. I went slowly past a line of tall new hotels and back into the west side gambling district.

I was learning something. I knew how Paul Taylor must have felt, sleepless in the bedroom below, thinking of Eve in my arms. I knew now why he'd got drunk so often. Poor Paul Taylor. Poor Robert Race.

Then I hated myself for going back to what Jeff Pastor called my Leibnizean lily-garden. Poor Paul Taylor was a dirty no-good double-crossing bastard. Robert Race was a cuckolded husband without a spine.

The hatred surged so fiercely I was nearly sick again. I put out my hand and stopped the passing man by the shoulder. I said, "Where's the *Tortuga?*"

He was small and neat and had rimless spectacles. He recoiled, maybe from the smell of my breath. He muttered something I couldn't understand and jerked himself free and walked on briskly. I couldn't be bothered to hate him as well. I was saving all that for the lovebirds. I walked on.

Nothing was real. The slot machines rattled and clinked and the night was awful with jarring music. Under the flashing signs of the flashy gambling joints the uniformed doormen waited on short flights of steps. This, I told myself, was Mexico. Then the night and the noise and the people all turned into illusions.

I stopped on the corner. I thrust out my arm and blocked the way of a big man nearly a head taller than I. I said, "Where's the *Tortuga?*"

He looked me over slowly. His lips twisted without mirth. He said, "Witty boy, eh?" then he chopped down on my arm and slammed me against the corner and I stood there sobbing because I thought my ribs were broken. He walked slowly away, dusting his hands, very erect, very proud of himself.

The other figure materialised beside me.

"You wann woman?"

I didn't answer. He was a warty little guy. He had long hair. I didn't like him. I straightened up and felt my ribs and I walked down the side-street away from the main stem. The Mexican trotted alongside.

"I find you tortuga very good and clean. The husband of my sister he works far away. She is lonely. Twenty dollars."

Without lights the side-street was almost dark. It was like walking immediately into the country. The dwarf palm trees looked like giant pineapples and the desert smell was strong. The only gambling house stood back from the road, exclusive and discreetly lit, fronted by a gravel strip crowded with cars.

The Mexican said, "Fifteen dollars."

The bright pea-green Mercury was the fifth car from the right.

I was drunker and then more sober. I went along the gravel strip thinking the car was too bright green, too obviously a respray job, that they hadn't been very smart about it. The doorman made a tentative movement. He didn't like my prowling. I ascended the steps to meet him and I said, "Get rid of this guy. He's bothering me." The Mexican scuttled away into the night.

I said, "I'm going inside. Keep your eye on that green car. If anyone tries to take it let me know immediately." I extended five dollars.

The man shook his head. He was a Mexican with a lot of Indian in him and he was very handsome and very big. He gave me the same doubtful look I'd got from the bartender. Then he grinned. He said in impeccable English, "Use it to play, sir. I'll take five per cent of the winnings. Good luck."

He came in behind me. He gave the high sign to two bulgy men in evening dress and retreated again. The men made no move.

I didn't know much about gambling joints, but this seemed a high-class one. At one end was a long bar with four barmen behind and high stools in front. There was roulette down the centre, craps in the corner and leading to an upstairs room at the far end a gilt staircase with music wafting down it. There were about fifty people present. I studied them. I didn't know one of them. I walked the length of the hall to the stairs.

Halfway up I remembered I'd left the gun from Santapola under the driving seat of the car. It didn't matter. I could do what I had to do with bare hands. I wasn't in any way excited.

The upstairs room was bigger. There was another bar, more roulette and some card games. The music came from five guys in red polka-dot shirts with frilly sleeves. The guy on his feet was carrying the main melody on a marimba. There were more people here but all strangers, so I went in and searched the men's room then I waited outside the ladies' room for ten minutes. Nobody appeared.

I went back downstairs and out to the main entrance. The car was still there. The doorman said, "Going so soon?"

"No. Don't forget to keep your eye on that car."

I returned inside. If I stayed by the first roulette table I could see everyone that came and went. I waited. I wasn't feeling anything. I didn't even know any more what I'd do when I saw them.

The drink rose in my throat and I shuddered. The two bulky men in evening dress moved in on either side of me.

They drew me a little apart. They could have been twins, though their faces weren't alike. The one wearing a flower on his lapel said in a crocodile-skin voice, "Can't stay unless you play, bud."

I nodded. It was all the same to me. I went back to the table and drew all the money from my pocket. There was eighty-one dollars and I had no further use for it. I put it all on a single square.

I didn't see the number. I only noticed the croupier squint at me. I smiled at the bulky men and looked again at the entrance.

People came in and out, but not Eve and not Fontaine.

Something touched my shoulder. It was the croupier's rake. I remember thinking it was impolite of him. The other people round the table stared at me and the croupier said, "You won, sir." He pushed back my money and some chips.

"Good," I said. Then I put everything on a black square. It may have been the same one as before. I didn't know and I wasn't much interested. The ball went clicking around the wheel. I looked at the door.

He said, "You won again, sir."

"Leave them," I said. "Keep leaving them." I walked out through the entrance, past the doorman and down the steps to the green Mercury.

Both doors were locked. No luggage inside, no article of Eve's I could recognise, nothing at all. The footsteps came behind me and the doorman said, "Your car, sir?"

"No. Friends of mine. They mustn't get away without my seeing them."

His face was wooden. I sort of liked him. He said, "Friends? You don't look so friendly."

"That anything to you?"

"Just we don't want trouble."

"Don't try to make any."

I brushed past him, back up the steps and in the door.

There was a big mob milling around the first table. Some of them must have run down from upstairs. They were making a lot of noise and a haggard old woman was shouting above the rest, "Spin it! The guy told you to leave it on. About time somebody won something in this crooked joint. Spin it!"

Over their heads I saw the croupier look questioningly at a small neatly dressed man with a neater moustache. The small man nodded. The croupier spun the wheel again.

It seemed it didn't turn very long. It whirred a little and clacked and then it stopped. There was a long pause—as if no one breathed. A man said in a reverent whisper, "Jesus! He won again."

The croupier looked across and saw me.

He nudged. He nodded his head. The small man came scurrying. He said, "Sir," and though he must have been saying it a long time it came hard to him. "Sir, you realise we cannot accept play if the player is not present to watch the wheel. You've caused a disturbance, sir."

"So I'll watch the wheel."

He quivered. He said flatly, "We have a house limit. Perhaps you'd like to withdraw some of what you've won."

No one was playing any more. Everyone was watching. The two bulky men eased discreetly in my direction. The doorman's calm voice said behind me, "You want the guy put out?"

"Certainly not!" The small man shook his head frantically. "No, no! Why should I want him put out?"

"He's drunk. He was looking for a fight with some people who left a car outside. It's all right now. They've left."

I swung around and slung a punch at him. The big man with a flower popped up beside me and caught my wrist. The small man said desperately, "All right, leave the gentleman alone. He wants to play again."

"I don't," I said. "Who was in the car?"

"What's it to you?" the doorman asked.

I went back to the table and looked at the croupier. Somewhere back of his dead eyes was humour. He was approving of me. He scraped his rake and pushed the pile of chips toward me and I tossed five of them back to him. The crowd gasped. I walked across to the tellers cage and the two bulky men and the small guy closed in with me.

The small guy was talking a stuttering blue streak. I didn't listen to him. The man behind the grill said, "Twenty-eight thousand nine hundred dollars." He gave me a lot of crisp new notes.

I crammed them all in my pocket except five-hundred's worth. I walked back to where the doorman was still standing.

I said, "Who was in the car?" I held out the money.

His face lost its woodenness. He blinked slowly and wet his upper lip. "A chunky kid and a blonde woman. She was older. She said something about going to bed and they drove toward the main street."

His hands closed over the notes. He said, "Careful how you go, Jack. It'll be all over town in half an hour how much dough you're carrying. Stick around and I'll whistle you up a bodyguard. Personal friend of mine."

"Thanks all the same," I said. "Goodnight." I went outside and swiftly down the steps and toward the main street.

I wasn't so drunk any more, but everything happening to me seemed to be happening to another guy. I was walking alongside him, trying to figure him out. The sounds of the night were unnaturally loud and the ground under my feet was wadded cotton. The money in my pocket bulged like a mailman's sack.

It was more than I'd had in my life before. I got a vague idea that I could use it to compensate Kresnik for the loss of whatever was in the suitcase. It was only a secondary thought.

I turned along the main street in the direction from which I'd come. The warty little man with long hair was back on his corner, but he didn't speak to me this time. I went fast, looking into all the side-streets. All at once I had a curious sense of purpose such as I'd never experienced before outside a courtroom.

I was going to kill them.

At that moment I saw the Mercury. It was two hundred yards away, parked outside the tallest of the line of hotels. I was drunk again. I ran.

There was nobody in the car. It was locked. I strode through the entrance of the hotel and into the dazzling white lobby. Around the first floor was a surrounding gallery entwined with some sort of creeper bearing brilliant red flowers. The place was crowded despite the hour. I studied them carefully.

Nobody. I crossed to the desk. There were three men behind it.

The one who approached had unpleasantly knowing eyes and a hair-line moustache that must have taken great pains. I said, "Mr. Fontaine, please."

I was looked over carefully and not approved of. He took up a board, studied it and shook his head. "No one here of that name."

I managed to get the next words out though they nearly choked me. "Then, Mr. and Mrs. Robert Race," I said.

He studied again. "No. Perhaps another hotel."

"You're sure?"

"Quite sure," he snapped.

I walked out. I could feel his eyes following me.

I stood by the car for five minutes, crossed the road, looked up at the hotel windows. Perhaps it wasn't the right car after all. I knew it was. They had to come for it some time and I could wait all night.

Eve giggled in my head. Then I couldn't wait five minutes. Not this time, not the way they'd be passing the hours. I hadn't known before. I knew now. I wasn't going to stand around all night and countenance them.

I looked right along the main street to the bar where I'd been drinking. My car was parked around the farthest corner. If I got the gun from under the driver's seat I could still watch the pea-green car over my shoulder.

I started to walk. The urgency hit me and I almost ran. I reached the bar. I was panting. A hand plucked my sleeve. The light unbroken voice said, "Mr. Race?"

He was a moon-faced kid less than five feet tall and about fourteen years old. He wore the uniform of a hotel bellboy. I stared at him blankly. I nodded. I said, "Yes."

He held out a folded sheet of paper. "The lady said to give you this."

He smiled. He had a front tooth missing. He hovered a moment, but I didn't have sense enough to give him a tip. He nodded, still smiling, turned away, walked off. It didn't matter. I could always find him again. I'd seen the hotel name on the lapels of his uniform.

I leaned against the wall outside the bar and opened the paper.

Hotel notepaper. She'd put the phone number again even though it was included in the letter heading. Underneath was written:

ROOM 422. PHONE ME, BOB. URGENT. LOVE, EVE.

I stared at it. LOVE. I saw our marriage in the way a man grasps his life entire as he is drowning. I entered the bar.

The bartender said, "Out! I told you."

The phone was at the far end. I walked down to it. I stared at the paper again, then dialled the number and when they answered I said, "Room 422." I was surprised at the normality of my voice.

The connections clicked. The phone started to buzz. She must have been waiting beside it.

She said, "Bob?"

"That you, Eve?"

"Yes," she said. "How are you, Bob?"

I don't know what I meant to say. Everything went wrong. I started to weep. I said, "You bitch, you rotten bitch, how could you have done this to me?" I was choking.

She caught her breath. She spoke softly and quickly. "Bob, when you came into the hotel I saw you. I sent the boy with the note. I've made a dreadful mistake, I know that now. Come and fetch me. Take me home. Bob, please!"

"And him," I said. "Where's he?"

"Down in the bar. I got away from him for a few minutes. Bob, I know how you feel. You have every right. But please take me home, please, I'm in awful trouble. I don't ever want to see him again."

I didn't answer. I was fighting myself.

She said, "Do you have the car? Come and fetch me. It was so clever of you, finding us. I'm so glad you did, darling. So glad."

I said, "You and he stole that suitcase."

"I'll explain everything on the drive home. Everything. I promise." Suddenly she sobbed. "Bob, I love you. I've been such a stupid fool. I was lonely and I thought you didn't love me and—"

"Shut up!" I hissed.

"Yes, I know. You're right, absolutely right. There's no excuse for me at all, absolutely none. Divorce me, anything you want. But take me home first, please. Let me talk to you, Bob. Help me. Will you? Will you do that?"

"What do you want?"

"Drive to the front of the hotel. I'll come down with the money. We have to go back to Santapola. We must!"

Somebody broke the connection.

I frantically banged the cradle up and down. The hotel operator said, "Yes."

"I was talking to room 422. You cut us off."

"They hung up, sir. I'll ring again."

The phone buzzed. Fifteen times. She said, "They don't answer."

"Keep trying."

Fifteen times more. Eve might be already waiting in front of the hotel. I hung up the phone and went down the bar and out into the street. I was cold sober.

The green Mercury hadn't moved. There were a lot of people on the sidewalk in front of the hotel, but it was too far away to see if she was one of them. I took three paces. She had asked specifically that I bring the car. I turned about and walked the few yards to the corner. I entered the narrow dark side-street where the car was parked. A curious thing happened.

It was a negative revelation, a slate being wiped clean. I realised I no longer loved her. She had run away with the man who tried to murder me. She was a cold hard calculating bitch and she wanted me to take her back because something had gone wrong.

But neither did I hate her. I'd never feel anything again for her either one way or the other. I hesitated. I didn't want to fetch her. Then I thought of the suitcase.

I stopped by the car. I got out the keys, opened the door and stooped to get inside. Three men came out of the shadows. A gun jammed into my side.

I thought the doorman had been right. The town knew of my winnings. I started to straighten. The man with the gun said, "We waited a long time for you."

The smallest of the three wriggled behind the wheel, unlocked the other doors from inside. I was pushed into the back, the other two either side of me. The man with the gun in my ribs said, "I blast your guts soon as spit at you." He had a Mexican accent. He patted my pockets. The man at the wheel revved the engine.

The gunman said to the man on the other side of me, "Go find the others. Say we find him." Then he said, "Wait!"

He dived a hand in my pocket and closed his fist on the bills. He drew them out, hissing with surprise. He said, "No, first get Esmollet. Bring him to the house. You find the others after."

The other man said, "Okay." He leapt from the car and slammed the door. I caught a glimpse of his face. He was a nondescript grey-haired American of about fifty. He walked quickly toward the main street.

The gun nuzzled deeper. The guy said something in Spanish to the driver and the small man let in the clutch and we turned left. The coloured lights flickered over their faces. They were both Mexican. We went fast past the hotel, but I had time to see that Eve wasn't there.

The neon signs dropped behind then and the night was very dark, but I could vaguely see the tall cactus and I could smell the desert. In a while we turned off the road and bumped a long way over a rutted track.

17

I was sitting on a stiff-backed rush-bottomed chair. I moved and it creaked. The little Mexican who had been driving looked at me profoundly with gentle brown eyes and tightened his hands on the gun. The other man was out in the passage trying again to use the phone. He wasn't having much luck.

My pockets were emptied. The papers and the money were stacked neatly on a table over in a corner next to the shuttered window. The house was small, old and in the middle of nowhere, and I thought by the furniture that no one lived there permanently. The walls were stained brown and flaking. The place smelled of damp.

Out in the passage the other man slammed down the phone. He came back into the room and he was bad-tempered and nervous. He rattled something in Spanish to the gentle-eyed man, then he went over to the table, picked up one of the bills from the pile of money and held it up squinting to the light bulb in the ceiling. He said something else in Spanish. He turned to me.

"Tell again where you get it."

"I won it in a gambling joint."

"Sure," he sneered. "What gambling joint?"

"I don't know the name."

"Where's the rest of the dough?"

"What rest?"

He dropped the note on the table and came over and stood to the side of me so as not to be in line with the other guy's gun. He clenched his right fist. On his hand were three big rings with different coloured stones. They looked something like a traffic light. They'd make an accident of my face.

He said, "I could get tough with you."

"You could."

"You telling me you not Robert Race?"

"You've seen the papers I carry."

His eyes flickered. Nervous men make bad witnesses in court. Out of court they spell trouble. My duodenum contracted.

He said, "Where's the suitcase?"

I knew which one he was referring to. I said, "I don't know."

He hit me. He kept his hand open but the blow rocked me. I fell off the chair. The small man danced over and looked down at me and smiled tenderly. Then he kicked me in the ribs.

I thought it was the beginning of the treatment. I got up slowly, expecting another slam. They watched in silence. I could hear each of them breathing. I wasn't breathing at all.

From outside came the sound of a labouring car engine. The gun jumped into the big man's ringed hand like it was on elastic. The small man slammed me into a corner, jammed the gun in my belly and smiled up tenderly as if we were in love. The rings glinted as the other snatched for the doorhandle. I heard him run softly to the front of the house.

The car outside laboured on more ruts. It stopped grindingly. Two doors slammed, somebody whistled softly. The front door opened.

They came into the room and the nondescript grey-haired American didn't look so nondescript any more with a gun in his hand. He and the Mexican were bundling between them an old man who looked like a sad little gnome, not much bigger than the hotel bellboy had been. He had pale blue eyes and a bulb-topped head with a fringe of blue hair. He was pink and white and shrivelled and thin and nearly dead with fright.

He started to say something. They pushed him hard. He fetched up against a wall and turned around and looked at me with terror. He gave a little sob. He said in a high-pitched voice, "Who's he?"

The Mexican sneered. "Don't you know?"

The old man shook his head violently. The grey-haired American tucked his gun in his pocket and said, "What you find out from Race?"

"Nothing."

"Okay, so get to work on him."

"Button your lip. I give orders here. What you done about finding the other boys?"

"Nothing. Hell, I had to pick up Esmollet here."

"Go find them now."

The American turned red under his grey hair. He looked mean. He said, "Ain't you contacted Mr. Burkhardt?"

The Mexican didn't answer. He walked across to the table. When he turned around he was holding Eve's note. He said, "Check who's in room 422 of the Victoria. Bring them here and be clever about it. Maybe they got the suitcase."

Esmollet said in a thin shriek. "The suitcase? You mean it's back here in Mexico?"

He looked wildly about him, like an elf caught at an all-night party after sun-up. He might as well not have been there. They took no notice. The gentle-eyed Mexican watched me and I watched Esmollet. I saw him catch sight of the money on the table.

His expression altered. His fright didn't disappear, but suddenly he was alert. The tip of his tongue came out and licked at his lower lip. He rubbed his fingertips together. His hands were small and beautiful and he'd taken care of them all his life.

The grey-haired American said sullenly, "Contact Mr. Burkhardt first."

"You do like I tell you." The Mexican suddenly looked evil. The American turned, left the room without a word and I heard the front door slam.

The car started up. It groaned away into the distance. The roe-eyed Mexican gently waved his gun and I sat down again on the rickety chair.

The other one said, "Esmollet! Check the dough on the table."

The old man walked across and picked up the whole bundle. There was reverence and love on his face, but he did no more than riffle the bills cursorily, looking here and there at a serial number. He laid the pile back on the table.

"Beautiful green money," he said.

The Mexican narrowed his eyes. "Recognise it?"

"No."

The big guy exploded. The rings flashed and the fist caught Esmollet in the chest. The little old man thudded against the wall and fell to the floor. He gasped. He sobbed for breath for a full minute. He squealed, "Wait till Mr. Burkhardt hears of this."

"He'll hear." The Mexican reached down and yanked Esmollet up by the lapels. He said, "You crooked lil bastard, we all been keeping eye on you like Mr. Burkhardt said."

He put his hand back of the old man's neck and screwed his head until Esmollet was forced to look at me. He said, "You're mixed up with this guy."

"I never saw him before."

"Sure. That's why you're in Campello. That's why he came down here from over the border. When the suitcase arrived in the States this is the guy stole it."

He flung the old man across the room.

I said, "Leave him alone."

The fist hit me in the side of the head and I fell off the chair again. Gentle-Eyes moved nearer. I got up. I went over and picked up the old man and it was like lifting a skinned rabbit. I sat him in the only other chair.

He shuddered. He was nearly paralysed with fright. He opened his mouth and the words came out in a hysterical spate. He said, "Wait till you see the trouble you're in when Mr. Burkhardt hears about this. You're never supposed to come near me, none of you. That's what all the secrecy was for. That's why we had all the arrangements with the sailor. The Feds know who I am and they told the Mexican cops and I'm being watched. They're probably watching me now. You've picked me up and they'll get to Mr. Burkhardt through your fault. Wait till he hears about that."

The Mexican turned yellow. The soft-eyed one hadn't even blinked. I knew now that he didn't understand, he didn't speak English. I watched the tears spring to Esmollet's eyes.

He broke right down. He said quaveringly, "And what about my five per cent."

"You don't get it," the Mexican snapped. "You don't never get it. No one never had no intention to give you five per cent. What can you do about it?"

The phone rang in the passage.

It rang four times. The gunman looked lovingly at Esmollet and me and covered both of us. The other guy went outside. He lifted the phone. He talked too softly for me to hear.

I said, "Esmollet, what's going on?"

He looked at me speechless with fright. He didn't answer. The gunman snapped something in Spanish.

I said, "I'm on your side."

The gunman moved like a ballet dancer. He wafted across to the side of me and swung his foot and hacked my shin. He spoke again. I didn't understand him. I looked straight into the eyes that weren't so gentle any more and I said, "Esmollet, there's a gun under the driving seat of my car. It's pretty far back."

Out in the passage the phone chimed softly. The other man entered the room looking as if he had suddenly developed jaundice. He was sweating. He chattered something to his buddy, then turned to me. "Okay," he said, "we get going. You go to see Mr. Burkhardt."

"What about me?" Esmollet said.

"You come too."

"But I'm never supposed to meet Mr. Burkhardt. Never. He told me so himself. If the cops see me—"

His voice died in his throat. His eyes grew enormous. He croaked, "What you going to do with me?"

"Move!" The jewelled hand heaved the old man through the door. The little gunman made another balletic move, jammed the gun in my back and eased me out of the room to join the procession. We went down the narrow flaking passage. The big man was only a few paces in front of me and I could have jumped on his back. But the little man was right behind me and didn't have to jump but only fire at my back, and I could feel the size of the bore through the cloth of my jacket. We went out through the front door.

The night was so black it was tarry. It might help. There might be an opportunity. There were only two of them, and they had to cover both me and the old man. One of them had to drive at the same time. In the light from the open door I shot a look at the big man's face. His eyes were jumping around like fleas. He said something rapid in Spanish and changed his position. I realised what they were going to do. They'd use my car again, because it was the only one there. The little gunman would drive, sitting in the front with the old guy next to him until the big guy got in the back with me. Then the big guy could use both guns to cover both of us, while the little guy drove.

It wouldn't be as dangerous as it sounds. It wouldn't be dangerous at all. I wondered how far we had to go.

They were shifting for position. I said loudly, "This is my car." I knew it wouldn't do any good. "My car," I repeated.

The big guy was behind me. He put the nose of the gun precisely between my shoulder blades. The little guy opened the door beside the wheel and waved the gun for Esmollet to crawl across to the far seat. It looked foolproof.

Esmollet let out a scream and tried to bolt.

The little gunman's free hand flicked like a whip end. He grabbed Esmollet's wrist, jerked hard and the old man staggered back and fell and the side of his head hit the car step where the door was opened. He groaned. He writhed over like a worm, hands in the car, and tried to push himself upright.

His backside was in the air. The Mexican kicked it. Esmollet fell.

He was half in, half out, his face on the car floor. He flapped his arms like wings. His small and delicately kept hand shot right under the driver's seat and he went rigid for a moment. Then he writhed again. He rolled right over on his skinny back and I flung myself sideways and down.

The two guns went off simultaneously.

I didn't have time to check anything. I struck up savagely and my fist hit the big guy in the softest part of his groin. He started to double. I was too close under for him to fire so he tried to chop with the gun. His wrist came down. I snatched it. I had a lot of luck. I pulled and twisted and then he was flat on his back beside me and the gun was somewhere away in the darkness.

One of the other men was screaming.

The big guy's hand came over. He got my hair. He could move like a landed shark. I slammed his face, hit him in the groin again, he broke away and made a dive for where the man was screaming. He was going for a gun. I lunged after him.

His left arm was out. I grabbed it. I moved in the same direction as his movement, then I turned his arm and he was so afraid of breaking it that he flipped
right over like a flapjack. His back hit the car chassis. I leapt astride his hips. He
tried to slide from under me and I got his throat and then I banged his head
against the hub of the rear wheel.

I kept right on banging his head. The hub cap gave a dull ring that sounded
even above the screaming. I don't know how many I gave him. He'd gone limp
before I stopped. I gave a last one for luck, let him fall and tried to listen if he
was still breathing. I couldn't hear because of the screaming.

I went to the still-open door of the car.

The little Mexican gunman was on his knees, praying, his head in Esmollet's
lap. The old man was sitting in the car with his feet outside on the ground and
his back against the driver's seat. His chin was up and his eyes popped from his
head. He was screaming his lungs out. His dainty hands were clasped to the
back of the Mexican's head as if he was trying to push it into his stomach.

I loosed the hands, pulled the Mexican up by his collar. The shot had entered
by his left eye and stayed in his head. I let him drop and kneeled by the screaming old man and he had reason to scream. A dum-dum bullet had made a hole
in his stomach.

I reached out and touched his skinny shoulder. I said inanely, "You did all
right, Pop. You were brave."

He stopped screaming.

He lowered his head and turned pale eyes on me. He wasn't frightened any
more. He looked at me quizzically and nodded firmly as if he agreed with what
I said. His lips moved. He said, "I'd have handled it all myself, but I couldn't
distribute it." Then he pitched forward and put his face on the ground and lay
still.

I felt for the pulse in his throat. There wasn't one. It didn't matter then
about moving him. I dragged him clear and pulled the small Mexican beside
him. I went over to the other one.

He was snoring with unconsciousness, bubbling in his throat. I didn't know
how bad he was hurt, I didn't care. He was a bastard. I went through his pockets and got my papers back and the money. Then I picked up a gun, got in the
car and slammed the door.

The ignition key was in the panel. I turned on the dashboard light and I'd soon
be needing some gas. I turned carefully and headed for Campello. The grey-
haired American was about due. I wondered if I'd pass him on the way back. I
wondered if he and his friends had got to Eve yet.

18

I was travelling too fast. The car lurched and bumped over the ruts, the springs groaned. I was afraid for the back axle. I was more afraid for myself, of meeting the grey-haired American and the men he'd gone to find. I had to warn Eve. I'd have warned anybody.

I trod harder on the accelerator. The car cleared the deeper ruts with little jumps. I was travelling without lights and the night swirled like stirred ink. My insides were tied in a knot. I was sweating.

I tried to quit my fear by arranging what had happened into some sort of cohesive sequence. Start with the suitcase. Carried from Mexico to the United States by an English sailor. There were men mixed up with the Mexican end: I knew nothing about them except that one was called Burkhardt and another Esmollet.

The last had said he was known to the FBI and watched by the Mexican police. His associates had neither treated him with respect nor trusted him. But he had been important. They had brought him to examine the money. He claimed he didn't recognise it. He had been horrified that the suitcase was back in Mexico.

And the big Mexican had thought there might be collusion between Esmollet and myself. I couldn't follow that. But if the mob distrusted the little guy on one thing, and had reason for it, they'd distrust him without reason on all things. I'd seen that happen often enough in court. But why had they distrusted him?

The nearside wheel sank into a large pothole. The car leapt. The headlights criss-crossed like fireflies on the main highway about a mile ahead. I was going to Eve. To help her.

I thought about that and remembered her and I was going to help her only because she had been my wife for two years. For no other reason. My love for her was gone. Strangled. Lopped off. Tony Fontaine and Paul Taylor and all the other guys Sam Alford, her own father, had hinted at. My swan had turned into a goose, my butterfly become a caterpillar. She was merely someone I once knew.

It was almost like being released from prison. I wanted to save her, but only from violence. Two men lay dead back at the adobe villa through her indirect fault. I'd go to the hotel, get her, take her to the local police. She must face the consequences. The affair had snowballed too big. I couldn't play it privately any longer.

I'd take the consequences too. Lose my licence. Be ridiculed. Wear my horns all over town for every joker to hang his hat on. So I deserved the lot of it. I should have told Kresnik to go to hell, whatever the pressure. Old sins cast long shadows and small slips tumble you into deep pits. I'd have the consolation of a completely fresh start, none of my former life clinging. Without Eve.

The idea didn't hurt at all.

I got a quick irrelevant vision of Ginny Ferrer. The other thoughts crowded in. I was back to Esmollet, the money, the way he'd been asked to recognise it, the way he'd looked at the serial numbers. A long lead that could take me anywhere. To bank robbery, swindle, theft. To Kresnik. From Kresnik all the way back to Mexico.

I got to the main highway and turned left toward the town.

The night was dark and there wasn't much traffic. The tires hummed. I might pass the grey-haired American and his pals coming from the opposite direction. They knew my car. They knew the number. Sure they did. They'd been waiting for me around the corner from the bar. They were still loose in town and if I stopped for anything they could pick me up before I reached Eve.

A question hit me. *How had they known I was in Campello?*

I was up in the air without wings. I turned on the headlights. The neon lights of the main street threw a gaudy aura into the sky ahead. I slowed. I had to look for side-streets. If I stayed on the main street they'd have me.

The juke-box blasted into the late night.

I saw the narrow street and turned sharply, thankful that Mexicans seldom light anything but their main thoroughfares. I saw the other turning off to the right and turned into it. The main street was one short block away. I was running level with it.

There were doors and windows, boarded up, the backs of gambling joints protected against sneak hold-ups. I smelt the odour of stale cooked food, then I was looking at the lighted back of the line of hotels. They had names over the back doors. The one in the middle was the Victoria.

I pulled up farther along. No lights shone on the car. I got out and retraced my steps.

There was a window next to the Victoria door. I looked through into a large kitchen. There were three waiters in a knot and a cook over in a corner, ladling something into a saucepan. I pushed open the door and walked in.

The cook didn't look up. The three waiters stopped talking and turned in my direction, one of them smiling. I said, "You boys are working late," and headed for the door at the far side. They didn't answer. I glanced down. My left shoe was caked with blood. There were splashes below the knees on my pants.

I went through the door and the service elevator was right in front of me. I stepped inside and punched the button. There was something wrong with the current. The cage ascended jerkily. When it groaned to a stop at the fourth floor I had had a reaction. I was numb. I had lost all interest.

I left the elevator gates open so no one could call it down. I looked for room 422.

The lay-out of the floor was uneven. The architect had got tricky with the corridors in order to pack in as many rooms as possible. I followed the door numbers to 412 and was at a dead end. I went back to the elevator, struck off in another direction and failed twice.

I found 422 finally. It was in another cul-de-sac. The door was slightly ajar.

I felt stupid. I didn't know if they were in there together. I was suddenly assailed by a question of taste. It was a situation in one of those comedies of adultery that are funny in the theatre and nauseating out of it. But I couldn't stand there forever.

I tapped the door with my knuckles. It opened an inch more. No one answered.

There were footsteps somewhere off in the maze of corridors. I slid the gun from my pocket. The footsteps moved away, but they had decided me. I slid around the door and into the room.

It was big, furnished with cheap luxury. A big double bed with a chenille quilt like a pink waffle-iron, lamps with parchment shades and blonde bedside tables. The long window was open. The noise came through from the main street and the neon signs flashed from the buildings at the opposite side. I stepped across and looked out and down. The pea-green Mercury was still parked at the curb. I turned around.

They'd got there first.

Eve was lying on the floor at the far side of the bed. She was dressed for the street, but she had no shoes on. Her hair was disarrayed, her arms spread wide. One leg was doubled under her where she'd fallen and been left.

I put the gun beside me and knelt down. There was nothing I could do for her. She was dead.

There was no blood. The marks showed on her throat where the fingers had tightened. Her tongue was out. That was the worst part. It hung far from her mouth like a bloated sac. It reduced her once beautiful face to an obscene mask.

I'd never known her. Now I never would. The other men were clean away and there was nothing to connect her with a missing suitcase. I had an inkling of what that might mean for me.

I stared at her. I didn't like the way she was lying. I picked her up in my arms, still kneeling, and drew her leg from under her. I kissed her cheek, then lay her down again. I felt nothing. I looked at her for what seemed a long time, but I couldn't bring her back again so I put my hand on the gun and stood up.

The waiter walked in.

I went toward him. He was the one who smiled at me down in the kitchen. He wasn't smiling now.

He said, "What you want, Mister, what you doing here?" He saw the gun. He came to a frightened halt, looked across the bed and saw Eve. He opened his mouth wide to shout.

I hit him in the teeth. He staggered back against the wall and I went after him.

I switched the gun from right hand to left and slugged him again. He went down with a small moan. He lay still.

He might have been faking. I couldn't hit him again. I ran out of the room and around the corridor and the service elevator was gone. Maybe he'd come up to close the doors. I ran to the far end of the corridor and through a small door. I jumped down a flight of narrow stone steps three at a time.

My only instinct was self-preservation. I burst out of the door at the bottom and came to a standstill. I tucked the gun in my pocket. I twisted my face in a smile and entered the kitchen.

The same two waiters were there. The cook was over in his corner, still ladling. The waiters looked at me rigidly. I kept smiling. I nodded like a marionette and walked past them and over to the far door, feeling their eyes on me. I went through the door and hit the street. Then I ran again.

My legs were giving out. The gun in my pocket bounced against my side and the money crackled. I panted for breath. I fell into the car and slammed the gears. I jumped away.

Two miles out I was on the dark main highway leading to the border. I couldn't find a side road. The gas tank was nearly empty. I had to stay on the highway for a gas station.

They were going to catch me. I was a lawyer. I had no illusions about beating the prosecution. The cold night wind of the desert blew in through the side windows and I sweated like an animal.

19

I sat at the table in the dim back of the lunch counter and kept my head down and continued eating. The man from behind the counter brought me a plate of Mexican chile con carne, which he got from a can packed in the States. I had no appetite. I ate with a neurotic compulsion. If I concentrated on food it prevented me from thinking of anything else.

I was cracking up. From the corner of my eye I could see Eve watching me. When I turned my head quickly she wasn't there. I continued eating.

The car was parked off the highway, behind a tall spreading clump of cactus. There was no moon and no stars. The other car that looked like a police car had shot by ten minutes before, and if I gave it time to get ahead I could maybe find a side road. I had to get out of Mexico, away from Mexican jurisprudence.

I thought of the guy who was ten years in a Mexican jail, waiting trial on a charge of unlawfully opening an ordinary parcel. Finally he got six months. The ten years counted for nothing. If I was to be taken I preferred it to happen in the United States. I didn't intend to be taken.

A cold wind blew across the desert. It made little moaning noises around the corners of the isolated lunch counter. I wondered if the place stayed open all night. It didn't seem worth it. Two cars passed close together, going to Campello, then there was nothing at all. Everything was silence except the wind.

I was going to Santapola. Eve had said it on the phone: "We have to go back to Santapola." Maybe that's why she was staying with me. I beckoned the man from behind the counter. He looked tired.

I said, "There a gas station around here?"

"About two miles down."

"Open?"

He nodded. "Yeah. We're the only places till you get to the border. Theory is we catch all the night traffic. Only sometimes there ain't any."

He looked at me closely. "You sick?"

"No."

"Guess not after what you ate," he said, "but you sure look it. Four forty."

I gave him five dollars. "Keep the change," I said. "Be seeing you." He nodded and smiled. He was an ugly man. I went outside and along the road to where I'd left the car.

The wind was blowing strong and cold from the Sierras. It had a bite as if snow still lay on some of the peaks. I walked through the eddying sand and got in the car and started the engine. It took time to warm. The rear wheels slipped in the sand. I had visions of being stuck. Then I was back on the highway and heading for the border.

I tried to concentrate on what was happening to me. My mind wouldn't focus. I was going to pieces. All I could do was watch the gas-tank indicator. It registered empty.

The highway was straight. There were no other cars. I saw the gas station ahead, its lights shining out into the surrounding countryside. It was one of those flat-topped concrete fake-acropolitan places with pillars, standing back from the highway, a line of gaudy pumps in front of it. I drove on to the half circle of concrete and pulled up. The lights overhead seemed bright as day.

The two guys who came out of the office were one tall and one short, one Mexican, one American. The Mexican took a rag and started wiping the windshield. The American was the boss. I said, "Fill her up."

The boss tried to talk to me about the wind. The Mexican, who was young and pretty and moved like a girl, finished with the windshield, checked the water and oil and said they were okay. He fastened the hood back in position, looked away into the night. He said, "Another customer."

The headlights were pinpoints, approaching from the border. I heard the engine purr above the sighing wind. The car was coming fast. I knew it would be the police.

I paid the American with shaking hands. He went into the office for change. The other car hurtled toward us.

It was travelling at about eighty. It was a big yellow Cadillac. It got nearly to the gas-station, slowed suddenly and the brakes winced. Then the driver changed his mind, decided he wasn't coming in. The car leapt forward again and went whining down the highway toward Campello.

The man came out of the office with my change.

The Mexican said, "We lost them." The other man smiled at him and put an arm around his shoulders. They stood like that and watched me drive away. I looked back and they were entering the office, holding hands. The night closed in again.

The desert stretched bleak on either side, hard and naked except for the cactus. There was no side road. The highway ahead led straight to the frontier where I knew the cops would be waiting for me. People sneer. They're wrong. Cops can move fast when they want. I had to find another way across the frontier if it meant wading a river. I had to get to Santapola. I didn't know what for except that Eve had said so.

I drove slowly, peering into the night. I heard the other car and the headlights glinted in my rear view mirror. I drew well to the right. I wanted it to pass. It was coming at a lick. I flicked another glance at the mirror and turned right round and stared through the rear window.

The other car was the big yellow Cadillac.

I stamped the accelerator. I jumped forward. I was going fast, but not fast enough. The Cadillac drew closer with a sneering lack of effort. I slammed on till the engine strained. I wasn't going to get away. I started to zig-zag across the road.

That finished me.

I swung to the road's opposite edge. They hurtled right alongside me and there was no other way out. I turned the wheel and went thumping across the desert.

The wheels skidded. The steering came alive and twisted in my hand and I hit a boulder. The car half turned over. It righted itself with a great bounce. The engine roared, I had no control any more, I saw the other boulder ahead and tried to brake. I hit hard.

I was lifted up. The steering wheel rammed into my guts, the headlights went out. I pushed open the door and fell on the sand. I picked myself up and ran into the darkness.

The lights of the Cadillac spread in the night like a fan. I kept running. I was sobbing for breath. The engine turned off and a door slammed and under the moaning wind I heard the footsteps patting after me. I dug into my pocket for the gun. I couldn't run any farther. In the distance another car came trundling slowly from the direction of the frontier.

Behind me a voice shouted breathlessly, "Turn the bloody lights off. They'll see us."

Truman Capote. The English sailor.

The darkness fell like a blanket. I turned and snapped a hopeless shot in the direction of the voice. I ran again. My legs were failing. I tripped on something underfoot and fell against a tall cactus.

The sharp spines dug into my left hand. The pain brought me to a standstill. I went rigid. I shuddered for breath. The other footsteps halted and the voice beside me hissed, "Charlie!"

The other car came on slowly, rattling like a crate of junk.

Truman Capote called, "The bleeder's got a gun."

"He ain't got far," Charlie answered softly. "We can spread out—"

I didn't hear the rest. The slow car was almost level, making too much noise. Its faint headlights spilled into the night and dispelled a little of the darkness.

I was at the edge of the big grove of cactus, some of them thirty feet high. The one beside me had three thick arms. Two yards away on the other side of it were Truman Capote and the man with dirty hair. If they turned their heads they'd see me.

I stood and looked at them.

They had guns. The man with dirty hair said something and started to move away, farther into the desert. The car rattled past and the throwback of its lights was suddenly no more than a faint glow. I couldn't see a thing. I stood motionless and tried to force my eyes to dilate.

There were two light patches on the ground. I could see them through the arms of the cactus. Capote was still wearing his flashy black and white shoes. I judged where his body would be and took slow aim. I tightened my finger on the trigger.

I couldn't do it.

It was something to do with the murderers I'd defended. Premeditation. And being a coward. I stood petrified with inaction. I heard him take a breath. He shouted in a stage-whisper, "Charlie! I'll turn the lights on again."

He moved.

He was turning. I heard his clothes catch on the spines. He swore softly and the cactus jerked a little and I took two paces to the left. I saw the moving white of his shoes. I grabbed.

My right arm clamped his throat. It happened quickly. I rammed my knee into his back and his hand came up in reaction and his gun fired into the darkness.

The other gun answered.

He gave a convulsive jerk. He gasped. He made a tiny whimpering sound and all the bones left his body and he started to melt. He went down on his knees. He said in a childish whimper, "Oo it hurts. You rotten sod. Oo it hurts, it bleeding hurts. Oh oh oh oh." He fired into the darkness again. The other gun spat back. He gave a last tiny surprised scream. I was running in a half circle toward the flashes.

I couldn't tell where he was. I came to a stop. Ginny Ferrer had implied the guy was simple in the head. Maybe she was right. Suddenly he shouted, "Hey!"

He wasn't far from me. The wind blew. He shouted, "Turn on them lights."

I moved again. "Scrine! Turn on them goddam lights!"

I could almost see. I went round the orbit of the cactus grove. I waited again. He shouted for the last time with a sharp edge of fear in his voice.

"Quit it! Where are you, Scrine? Scrine! What about them lights?"

I reversed the gun in my hand and stepped up behind him. He shouted, "Scrine!" I smashed the butt into the base of his skull and he went down like a sack of wet bran. I leaned over him. I hit him again. There was a sudden movement three yards away. I thought the Englishman had come back.

I lunged.

The man was on the ground. He writhed like an eel, thin but not strong. He gave a sob of fright. A flood of Spanish poured from him.

I pinned his shoulders to the ground, tried to stare into his face. I said, "Who are you?"

I could see the bulging whites of his eyes. He lay without moving. He made a gulping noise in his throat and he said, "You no hurt me. I got much children. I go United States."

He wore a shirt and a pair of pants. By the feel of him he had no underwear. It was a cold night to be lying around like that in the desert. Then I knew.

He was a wetback. Trying to make illegal entry into the U.S.

I held his arm and got up and lifted him to his feet. I said, "I'll take you."

He tried to pull away. "Come on!" I said. He still struggled. I jammed the gun in his side, and then he made no more resistance.

I didn't check on Truman Capote or the man with dirty hair. I marched the Mexican across to the yellow Cadillac and we got inside. I started the engine and backed to the highway and drove slowly in the direction of the border. The guy beside me was rigid in his seat.

I said, "You got papers? Documents?"

He looked at me fearfully from the corners of his eyes. He didn't answer.

I lied to him. I said, "The police won't bother you once you're in the country. But you have to be careful crossing the border. Better to cross where there are no officials."

He said, "I pick lechugas. I make much money. I ten children."

"That's good," I said slowly. "Boys?"

He relaxed a little. He almost brightened. "Ocho. Eight boys. Two girls. I no money in Mexico."

The Cadillac purred softly. We were getting too near the frontier. I reached in my pocket, found a cigarette and gave it to him. I said, "You got Mexican friends in the United States?"

"Sí."

"How did they get across?"

"I ten children," he said.

He leaned back and puffed his cigarette. A car passed us going in the opposite direction. I started to sweat again. I wanted to threaten the Mexican. I was afraid he'd fold back into fear. I said nothing.

He had half finished his cigarette. A big clump of cactus was clustered on the right of the road ahead of us. He tapped my arm. Suddenly he grinned. He pointed.

"Por aqui," he said. I turned sharply.

There was no road any more, no sign of one. The wheels hit rocks and holes. The Cadillac chassis floated around us like an air cushion. We went about eight miles in silence, then he tapped me again and pointed and shook his head. I turned off the lights. We continued in the darkness; small rocks catapulting from under our tires.

I don't know how he knew where we were. He stretched right across me and put his head out of the window on my side. He reached back, tapped me and I turned right. He remained where he was a couple of minutes, sat back in his seat and leaned out of the window on his side. Suddenly he hissed, "Estopp!"

I pulled up.

I could hear the water ahead of us. The Mexican looked at me expectantly and I nodded and he got out of the car. I followed him. Maybe because of the water, but the night seemed lighter. The river was about twenty yards across and I could see the other side. There were trees, there might be someone waiting. The chance had to be taken.

The Mexican looked at me again. I nodded and he walked into the water. I started to follow, but he shook his head. I stood on the bank and waited.

I watched him wade across. The water never went above his calves. He reached the far bank and turned around and beckoned furiously with both hands.

I got back in the Cadillac. I revved the engine. I took off the brakes, slammed in the clutch and gave her all she'd got.

The wheels gave one useless turn on mud at midstream. They caught again. Then the Mexican was leaping out of the way and I was shooting up the far bank.

I was in the United States.

The Mexican strutted over to the car. He put his arms straight out on either side of him as if he were doing exercises and he took a deep breath. He grinned hugely. He pointed to the seat beside me, raised his eyebrows, asking if he could get in again. He sat beside me. He took another breath and chuckled with delight.

He said, "I pick lechugas."

I wondered what were lechugas.

I reached into my pocket, pulled out some of the money and thrust it in his hand. I couldn't see how much it was. He looked at me in puzzlement, then bent forward and examined the notes by the light of the dashboard. He straightened up with his face incredulous.

He said, "They good?"

"Yes," I said.

His eyes and his mouth made three circles in his face. "Why?"

"For helping me."

He nodded like a somnambulist. He said, "I ten children." He made a little noise and flung his arms around me and hugged me first to one side of his chest then the other.

"Gracias," he said. "Adios." He climbed from the car. "Adios," he said again. I got out after him.

I watched him wade back across the river, back into Mexico.

On the far bank he turned and waved. Then he was gone. I got back behind the wheel and headed in the direction of Santapola. I was alone again.

Eve returned. She sat in the back of the car and looked over my shoulder.

20

The track I had taken landed me on the far side of Santapola. I had to drive back down the main street toward the frontier. The hour was late, but the town was noisy as ever.

Some of the bars were full and there were drunks about. I wondered vaguely what troubles obliged them to get drunk. I drove slowly, so as not to attract attention. I passed a cop and my stomach lurched. I turned off the main street, backed the car into position for a quick getaway, parked in a shadow and headed on foot for the Flamenco.

I had no fixed plan. I'd come here only because Eve said we had to. Apart from that I could see no start and no finish. Everything else was a mix-up of Kresnik, the English sailor, the Mexicans, the little guy named Esmollet with a hole in his stomach and somebody named Burkhardt who lived in Mexico and gave orders over the phone.

I wasn't thinking any more of Tony Fontaine. His car had still been outside the hotel. It was his grief if they'd snatched him at the same time as they killed Eve. I wondered if they were trying to persuade him to tell where the suitcase was. Hurting him.

I approached on a rutted back street. Lights shone from the front; the Flamenco was still open: there was a murmur of voices. I ducked into an alley, crossed a yard filled with broken crates, fetched up at the window of the bedroom. It was shuttered.

I stood a couple of minutes getting a grip on myself, took a hold of the gun in my pocket, went out of the alley and on to the street. Then I walked around to the front and straight into the bar. I must have been out of my head.

I saw the two cops but my feet kept going. I was inside before I could change direction. The cops were one young and brash, the other middle-aged and tired. They were down at the far end, talking to the woman, June. There was a line of listening customers between us. The Mexican, José, was serving them with drinks.

His eyes lighted on me.

He gave a twitch and turned pale. His face writhed, but he went on serving. The panic hit me. I turned to walk out. Three men appeared in the doorway and stood in an unmoving block. They looked with interest toward the police. I leaned against the bar and stared down the room. The little bantam of a guy who'd been there before was out cold at one of the tables, his face flaming like a rooster's crest. I listened to what the woman was saying.

She was patient and amiable. She said, "I got no reason to cover up."

She moved her head and saw me. Her face didn't flicker. "Wouldn't do any good," the older cop growled. "The guy left a trail as wide as a highway. If he comes out of Mexico we'll have him like that!" He snapped his fingers to show like what.

The young cop had a notebook. He was bright. He was pompous. He said, "This other guy, this Fontaine. He was your cousin?"

"The son of my cousin," she explained kindly. You would have thought she was a fine woman. "Tony," she said. "He stopped by for a couple of hours. Told us he was running away with this Mrs. Race."

"You denied it when we asked first. Why?"

"I thought you was a divorce case. I'm a good Catholic. I don't want to get mixed up with no divorces. And I didn't know at first she was dead."

The Mexican came along the other side of the bar and stopped in front of me. The dried spit was thick around the rim of his mouth. I said, "A beer." He nodded. His skin looked like a dried lemon peel. He went away. The men at the door hadn't moved. I couldn't get out.

The woman said admiringly, "You're pretty smart, getting here so quick."

"All police are smart," the young one said. "The public should realise that. We got the co-operation and the organisation."

He was giving all present a lesson and a warning. He meant well.

He said, "For example. The waiter in the Mex hotel walks in just as Race has murdered his wife. Race skips off, the waiter recovers, he calls the Mex police, they examine Mrs. Race and find her identity, they get in touch with her home town. The home town cops call her next of kin, her father, and he says there's been some monkey business about phone calls. The local cops check with the phone exchange and find Race made a call from Santapola. They even get the number."

He paused dramatically, announcing his own entrance with a fanfare of silent trumpets. "They call us and tell us the number. It's a drugstore. We go there and the clerk tells us the guy who made the long-distance call was also asking for the Flamenco Bar. Here we are."

The woman shook her head in awe. The Mexican put a beer in front of me and got as far away down the bar as he could. The older cop said irritably, "The guy seem as if he'd commit a murder or anything? Anything funny about him?"

She said measuredly, as if explaining for the tenth time: "He just came in and asked about Tony. He took a beer. I ain't even sure he was Race. How can I be?"

"What did he look like?"

She narrowed her eyes, faking a recall of memory. She looked right at me. "Not too tall," she said. "Thinnish. Brown hair sort of curly in the front and blue eyes and a short nose. Kind of a good-looking guy. He'd be attractive to women, except he had a look that women didn't interest him."

The cop glanced at her shrewdly. "Clothes? From all accounts he was a pretty snappy dresser."

She smiled, opening her eyes wider. "I don't remember." She turned to her husband. All the heads in the bar turned in the same direction. "José?"

He shrugged.

The next guy along the bar had his back to me. He crooked his finger and pointed to his glass for a refill. He didn't make a sound. Nobody made a sound. They were too absorbed. The young cop reacted and strutted and milked his audience. He should have been an actor.

The red-faced little man at the table drunkenly lifted his head. I edged a backward step to the door. The three men still blocked the way, and a move to break the absorption would call attention. I had to wait.

The older cop said, "Fontaine know he was being followed?"

She shook her head. "They were very happy. Like honeymooners."

"Yeah?" The young cop gave a barking laugh. "Well, the honeymoon's over. They're both dead."

His colleague said, "Shut up!"

"The kid's car is still outside the hotel. The Mercury that Race was asking about in the bar in Campello where he got drunk."

"Shut up!" the older cop snapped.

The woman said, "Poor little Tony. Such a good kid."

The red-faced little guy put his head right back on his shoulders and peered down the bar. His eyes fixed me blearily. He said loudly, "Hi!"

I stopped breathing.

He lifted a hand. "Hi," he said again, and waved. I nodded tersely. Everyone was looking at him, including the cops. He put his head on the table and went back to sleep. The spell was broken.

The guys at the door snapped out of their pose and squeezed into the bar. There was general movement. Two men called for drinks. I crushed against the counter to let the guys pass, then eased into the street. I walked slowly to the next corner, turned it and ran.

The Cadillac tank was full, the highway empty. I drove until the tires screamed. I watched the sky lighten, darken again, then come out in the pink and primrose of true dawn. Eve was still in the back of the car.

I drove toward the city because I had a home there and an office, it was a place where I knew people, knew the territory. I couldn't visit the home or the office, nor speak to the people. But they'd give me what I needed most right then; a background of reality.

I drove for hours, never looking back at Eve. I was tired and stupefied and the fatigue ached in my bones. Then in the way you do I got my second wind. I started to think. That made everything worse.

The city was so much my territory that the stones would recognise me. The people I knew were a cop named Jeff Pastor, Paul Taylor who hated me and my father-in-law Sam Alford. And Kresnik. And I was driving a big conspicuous yellow Cadillac that almost certainly belonged to Kresnik.

That nearly did for me. I couldn't go back to the city and I had nowhere else to go. During ten minutes I decided to give myself up. I was mentally wording my own defence. I saw the motel up ahead.

It was a decent looking place, the cabins wide-spread. It had a garage. I drove straight into the garage and parked. When I emerged on foot a man was coming from the office.

He was about fifty and bald-headed. He had a plump, red-skinned, mild face, and though he'd obviously been up all night he greeted me with a smile.

I said, "Got a bed?"

"All you can use," he said. "Slack time of the year." He studied me incuriously. "Driving all night?"

"Yes. I could use something to eat."

"We can manage that too. Anything wrong with the car?"

"I like to keep it out of the sun."

He was satisfied. He said, "Nice looking heap. Grub in about ten minutes."

I said, "Meantime I'd like to make a phone call."

He led me into the office. He stood looking at me, still incurious, not thinking he was in the way, so I said, "Hadn't you better see about that breakfast?"

His red skin went redder. He mumbled something and left. I gave the operator the number.

I had to wait around four minutes. I began thinking she was maybe still at the club, that being Saturday she'd worked all night. I didn't know much about clubs. I didn't know much about anything. The smell of frying ham wafted on the warming morning air and through the open office door. I'd planted the statement about breakfast to get rid of the motel owner. I wasn't hungry. All I needed was a drink. A lot of drink.

She said, "Hello? Yes?" Her voice was croaky as if she'd smoked a lot of cigarettes overnight. "Who is it?"

"Robert Race," I said.

She paused. She said sort of gently, "You move around, Bob. You calling from a police station?"

"From a motel."

"Oh." She waited. Then she said, "I heard about your wife. It's in the late editions. What can I say?"

"Nothing," I answered, and I was light-headed. "I didn't kill her. I can't prove anything."

She said in a tired voice, "Any way I can help?"

"Tell me where Kresnik is."

"I don't know."

"The police get to him?"

"No," she said, "why should they?" She paused again. "You think they'll come to me?"

"Why should they?" I asked bitterly.

I looked at the mouthpiece. A whole minute passed in silence. I had to drag myself back to remembering why I'd called her.

I said, "Kresnik get his suitcase?"

"How could he?" she said. "No. He's still crazy worried, but he says he'll get it in the end. He says he's got a method."

"He tell you what was in the suitcase?"

"Yes."

"What?"

She took a breath. She said flatly, "One million dollars. One million dollars in U.S. currency."

I began to giggle. I sat down on the edge of the table and thought of how I had intended buying off Kresnik with my roulette winnings. I giggled some more. She was speaking again but I couldn't understand her.

I said, "What?"

"You didn't kill her."

"No." It seemed unimportant.

"The cops are looking for you. What you going to do?"

"I don't know," I said carelessly.

There was no eagerness in her voice. "Maybe I could help you. I know where you are from what the operator said. I could come to the motel and get you. We'd figure something out between us."

"You're valiant," I said. "I got you into trouble once before."

"What's the name of the motel?"

I looked out through the office window. "The Sunrise."

"Shall I come?"

The owner was approaching across the yard. "No," I said. "Goodbye, Ginny." I hung up.

The guy put his mild red face around the door. He said, "Breakfast."

I followed him outside. In the brightening sun his skin showed as an intricate red mass of tiny burst capillaries. I said, "And after breakfast I'd like a drink. I'd like several drinks."

His placid eyes quickened slightly. "We might see," he said. "We might see.

Cabin seventeen and the grub's already there. What did you say the name was?"

"Ferrer."

"Yes, we'll see," he said, and nodded sharply and moved off.

I ate a greasy egg and half a slice of ham. I was going screaming raving mad. Eve came and stood shadowy in a corner and lolled her tongue at me. She knew I no longer loved her. She didn't go away even when the owner returned with two bottles of bourbon.

He wasn't hurt that I didn't finish the breakfast. He poured the bourbon in two tumblers and we drank it neat. We didn't talk, we just sat drinking. Eve went away but I feared she would return so we started on the second bottle. After a while I kicked off my shoes and put my feet up on the bed.

I woke up still drunk.

The day was darkening into night. The shadows were thickening. The figure in the corner moved and my mouth opened wide in a dumb shout. The woman swooped at me with her hands out. She turned on the bedside light.

It was Ginny.

Her hair was tucked up under a sort of turban hat and she wore horn-rimmed glasses. I stared at her, thinking drunkenly what a feeble disguise it was. I didn't speak.

She put a hand on my head and moved her fingers through my hair. She said, "I been waiting hours. I'm going to take you home."

I stood up. She led me outside. It was the same car she'd used to bring me from Kresnik's house, five million years ago. She opened the rear door and because there was nothing else to do I got in. She said, "Don't worry, I paid the guy. He's stinking drunk. He said something about a yellow Cadillac. Can you be traced here?"

"No," I said.

She slammed the door and got in front behind the wheel. She looked over her shoulder and said, "There's a bottle back there somewhere."

I groped around and found it. I started to drink again. The road rushed by, the smell of evening, the taste of whisky. I don't know how long passed. We reached the city and I vaguely recognised the streets. The perspective was shot and there were no real people about, only dolls. When Ginny pulled up there weren't even dolls. Or perhaps I couldn't see them for the darkness.

The stairs were dark, too. She put her arm under my shoulders and almost carried me. There was a bright checkered kitchen with a dancing little table in it and a line of bottles. The table stayed motionless a few seconds, the bottles jumped on and I began drinking again. It wasn't difficult once I adjusted the rhythms.

I didn't talk at all. After a long time Ginny explained something about going to the club and would I promise not to go outside. I went on drinking. She came back and went away again several times, but I don't remember seeing Eve again.

21

I moved feebly a few times and sat up. My head was being sawn in two. I was in a big double couch-type bed and there was a smell of perfume next to me, a warmness and another dented pillow. I was naked.

I croaked, "Hello."

She emerged from the little kitchen and leaned against the door. She was wearing a negligee. Her raven hair hung to her shoulders and her skin seemed very white. She said, "Hi! You want to start drinking again?"

"No."

"I was hoping maybe you'd finally be over it. I'll make us something to eat. You've slept fourteen hours right off."

"What time is it?"

"Six," she said. "In the morning. Wednesday morning."

I heard her clinking around in the kitchen, frying something. Wednesday. A week ago since it all started. I sat half turned with my back against the wall and looked around at the apartment's single room. It wasn't much.

The bed on which I lay was the type that fitted into the wall during the daytime. The room was clean, but although she had tried to brighten it with touches of colour it was shabby. I concentrated on everything in view because I didn't want to think of what eventually I must think of. I stared through the open door of the kitchen and studied the line of empty whisky bottles.

She came in and set the tray across my knees. There was orange juice, hot cakes, ham, eggs, rolls, butter, marmalade. The orange juice was cutting cleanly through my fouled-up mouth. She sat down on the edge of the bed, nodding approval. She said, "Eat as much as you can or you'll be ill." She looked and sounded very young.

I started on the hotcakes. I was hungry. She said a little anxiously, "There's more where that came from. I used some of the money in your pocket. I had to do that, to buy your whisky."

"Take as much as you want."

She tried to make a joke. She said, "I should have asked Kresnik for a raise long ago."

I was no longer hungry. I kept eating. I said, "I thought he treated you better than this."

She smiled. She looked uncomfortable. "You mean that stuff I told you about being his mistress and having a luxury flat and everything? It was a gag. He asked me a few times. I guess I could have if I wanted. He's not my type of guy."

Her voice tailed off. She stood up and went into the kitchen.

In a while she came back with two big cups of coffee. She didn't sit on the bed this time. She stood stirring her coffee more than was necessary and looking away whenever she caught my eye. She said, "I've cleaned and pressed your suit and washed your shirt and underwear, and I've been out and bought a razor so you'll look all right. Get some coffee down and you'll feel all right."

I couldn't run away any longer. I said, "Then what'll I do?"

She put the cup on a table. She said, "You angry with me? There's only this one bed. I couldn't sleep on the floor."

I shook my head. Suddenly I felt a rush of affection, almost of tenderness for her. It was a return to the innocence of all those years ago when we took long night walks together and she use to sing to me. I said, "Ginny, you're running a big risk. If the police are still looking for me, you can be hauled in as an accessory."

"They're looking for you," she said grimly. "All over the country. And in Mexico. But you won't be connected with me. You already been here three days and nobody's even asked me a question."

"What'll I do?" I repeated.

She sat down on the bed again. She spoke lightly but tentatively as if she were suggesting an unusual dish for dinner. "I was thinking. We could go away somewhere. Maybe up to Canada, out to the Islands or somewhere. The papers say you're travelling alone. No one expects a woman with you. You'll be safer with me. I've counted the money in your pocket and there's more than twenty thousand dollars. That should last us a while till you get your hands on the rest."

I felt sick. I said, "What rest?"

"The million dollars."

"No," I said, "I don't have it. I've never had it."

She spoke in the same tone as before. "So twenty thousand dollars will last us a few years. I'm used to living economically. I can always take a job singing or something. Maybe you could get a job too when the heat's gone off. It's a good idea. Isn't it?"

She reached out and took my hand. I was trembling from head to foot. I said, "The only good idea is to clear myself. I can't prove a thing against Kresnik. Tony Fontaine's my only hope. I don't know where he is."

"I do." She let go my hand. "We'd better get to Canada as quick as we can."

"Why?"

She said, "He's dead. They claim you killed him."

She went into the kitchen. I pressed my bare back hard against the wall and I shook. The young cop at the Flamenco had said Fontaine was dead. I'd thought he was guessing.

She came back and dropped the newspaper in my lap. It was the previous night's edition and I was still all of the front page. They had reprinted the picture of Tony Fontaine standing arm in arm with me outside the courthouse after I had secured his acquittal on the robbery charge. "Beau Brummel Killer and Victim," the caption said. "The missing lawyer with Anthony Fontaine. Picture exclusive to the *Tribune.*"

The rest of the front page was an exclusive interview with Paul Taylor.

He'd probably harmed himself professionally. Lawyers who denigrate other lawyers queer their pitch both in professional circles and with the more intelligent clients. Paul Taylor had gone ahead anyway. He'd done a good job. He hated me.

He didn't say so in the interview. His tone was that he wouldn't speak at all, but truth demanded it. About my career he made implications worse than accusations because refuting them would entail too many defensive words. He wondered loudly why I'd left the D.A.'s office. He had felt at times that maybe I spoke too freely of my clients' private affairs. He disliked saying it, but he feared I made cynical use of the sensational cases I defended free. I had for instance told him personally that I knew both Fontaine and Garcia to be guilty. I had defended them anyway for their publicity value.

Of my private life he couldn't speak as a friend, though as a neighbour he could speak intimately. Eve had suffered torments through my insane jealousy. She had been a wonderful, sweet-natured person slowly terrorised until she was afraid to move outside the door. She always spoke defensively of me because she was so loyal. But I had slowly and certainly killed all of her love. He hinted that possibly I had unnatural habits.

He knew well that none of this would stand up as evidence in court. Perhaps he shouldn't have spoken at all. He hoped I would soon be caught. I was a dangerous person. He was giving the police all possible help.

I followed the paper's instructions and turned to the centre pages. A picture of Mrs. Fontaine with a handkerchief to her eyes. An exterior of Sam Alford's big house. Mrs. Fontaine had not been down to attempt identification of the body. She was too ill. Reporters had tried to interview my father-in-law without success. He was prostrate at the death of his only child.

There was nothing about Esmollet and the other dead man in Mexico, nothing about the English sailor or the guy with dirty hair. There was nothing about Kresnik and nothing about a suitcase or money. It was all a simple triangle case.

The crazed husband had killed the guilty lovers. I was being tried by the newspaper and the sympathy was with the lovers. A woman feature writer had written a double page spread on jealous husbands of the century. With pictures.

I dropped the paper by the side of the bed.

Canada, the Islands—I imagined life on the run, the disguise, the unending deceit, the rising gorge every time a cop passed, the public certainty of my guilt if I ran away. I couldn't face it. I wasn't the type. I pulled the top blanket from the bed, wrapped it round my naked body and went to the phone.

Ginny said frightenedly, "What are you doing?"

I didn't answer. I dialled the number. I waited.

Jeff Pastor's sleepy voice said, "Yeah?"

"This is Bob Race."

He woke up.

"I was hoping you'd call," he said. "Where are you?"

"Save it a while. You on my case?"

"Not directly. The boys weren't even sure you were out of Mexico. You want to come and see me? I don't go to work till nine."

"What's the charge?"

"Double murder."

"I didn't do it."

"Of course you didn't." His voice was kind and persuasive. "Everyone who knows you says you didn't. Come and see me. We'll talk privately. You'll get a fair deal. What do you say?"

He was coaxing me as if I were a child. Everyone who knew me. The jury wouldn't know me. I remembered Garcia.

I said, "Do you think I'd have been justified to kill them?"

"Well, that's a difficult question. A man in your position always has a lot of sympathy. If you get the right judge—"

"Ten years?" I asked.

"Maybe less. Be sure you'll get a fair hearing in court." The newspapers and a jury and my father-in-law and the public had judged Garcia before he even got to court. I said, "Okay Jeff, you think I did it. I didn't. Make a note of these names. Burkhardt. Esmollet." I spelt them for him. I said, "They're both down in Mexico. Check on them. Then check on Al Kresnik."

"The guys are mixed up in it?"

"Yes," I said, and the hopelessness of the situation fell on me with clammy weight. Kresnik had been hundreds of miles from the murders. Esmollet was dead. Burkhardt might even be an invented name. I had no witnesses. My story wouldn't even make sense.

I said, "I'll call you back."

"Don't go," he rapped quickly. "Tell me about it. I got all the time in the world."

His voice betrayed him. I said, "Time enough for your wife to get to another phone and have this call traced."

I hung up.

It hadn't been a good idea. I had grasped at a last straw. I had no doubt any more. I was stuck, I was skewered, I was an open and shut case. No jury in the world would fail to convict. I hadn't an ounce of proof against anyone else, and my story about Kresnik would sound like an invention of the devious legal mind.

How they'd love convicting a lawyer.

I was thinking all that and at the same time imagining Sam Alford, my father-in-law, the way Eve had been his whole life. Imagining Mrs. Fontaine, the way she'd looked at me when she thought I might hurt her son. I saw the inescapable hole I was in and maybe it was the drink I'd taken, nerve strain, something else. Maybe it was an innate cowardice.

I sat on the edge of the bed and put my head in my hands and started to weep.

She hit me so hard my head rang. I looked up and she slapped my face with all her force. Her eyes blazed.

She said contemptuously, "You goddamned jellyfish, is that all you can do, sit and bawl? Goddamned sissy, take that razor I bought and cut your throat, why don't you? That's a nice easy way out."

She dropped down beside me. She put her hands under the blanket and wrapped her arms around me and put her head on my bare chest. She said fiercely, "God! How I love you. I love you. I always have."

I held her to me. I kissed her. Her hands slid down over my body and the blanket around me fell to the floor. She gave a little sob. We lay on the bed. We made love.

22

It was nine o'clock. The sun was up. Not much of it penetrating the apartment because the only window overlooked a blank wall just across a narrow alley.

I finished shaving and put on my clothes. I thought how well she had cleaned them. I studied myself in the mirror and I looked like any man about to leave for a day's work. Except that my eyes were red-rimmed from alcohol and dead from lack of hope. I couldn't force any hope into them. I couldn't feel any hope.

Ginny came in from the street with the groceries and a morning paper. I saw the misery in her face and regretted she was mixed up with me, thought she deserved better. I suppose I should have gone away, left her, but I didn't have the guts to be alone. She went into the kitchen to prepare more coffee. I read the paper.

I was sharing the front page now with a hit-and-run of the night before. The police were expecting an early arrest in both cases. They contradicted themselves a little farther down by saying they thought I was still in Mexico. I didn't read beyond that. I couldn't take it.

I turned to the second page and studied a columnist's analysis of the internal difficulties of Communist China.

The words skated before my eyes and I took nothing in. I continued reading— the other columnists, the local news, the births, deaths and marriages. The daughter of a client of mine had announced her engagement. A man I once met on a committee had just died.

I was at the page before the sports page and halfway through the paragraph before I realised what I was reading.

It was a jolt of dynamite. I closed my eyes a few seconds, got a hold of myself and went back to the beginning. A news-service item. A great weight slowly lifted.

The local reporters hadn't tumbled or they'd have tied it with the feature story and played it big. A sixty year old man named Sellers had been arrested all the way off in Kansas City. For interfering with children. He had an appallingly long record of similar offences, which was why it was a news-service item. He was certain to get a heavy sentence or preventive detention.

Maybe that persuaded him to confess. He'd made a list of his crimes, long and unpleasant and reaching into many cities. He finished his confession by saying that the previous week another man had been unjustly sentenced to six years imprisonment for offences committed by himself, by Sellers. A prompt investigation would be held.

The name of the unjustly convicted man was Garcia.

I folded the paper. The world had changed. Ginny came in with a couple of steaming cups and the coffee smelled very good. I went across and picked up the phone. She put down the cups and took my arm.

"Careful, Bob. They might trace you."

"I have to do this," I said.

She looked intently into my face. She seemed to relax. I realised how much she was doing for me, feeling for me, suffering for me, and I put an arm around her and kissed her. Then I sat down and dialled the number of my office.

It was after nine o'clock and I knew Miss Cleaver, my secretary, would be there. She'd keep the office open till the crack of Doomsday or till I gave the word to shut it. The receiver was lifted and her voice came on, very middle-aged and calm and sexless. She said, "Mr. Robert Race's office."

It gave me a big lift. I was still a person. I had an office. I said, "Good morning, Miss Cleaver. You know who this is?"

"Of course," she answered immediately. She paused. "I'm quite alone. No one has visited me yet this morning. Is there anything I can do?"

"Thank you, Miss Cleaver. There's an article on page twenty of this morning's *Herald*. It mentions Felipe Garcia. Get out the file on him. Communicate with Jeff Pastor at Headquarters. Garcia is innocent."

The warmth came into her voice. "I'm so glad. How fine! I don't think it will be necessary to communicate with Mr. Pastor. He comes here every day."

He had told me he wasn't on the case. I said, "For what?"

"I'm afraid he's found a legal way to examine your mail. Anonymous letters arrived for you on Friday, Saturday and Monday. He took them away."

"Anything else I should know?"

"Mrs. Alice Tarkington wants to apply for a possession order against the Booth Company lands. I'm going ahead with it."

"You're doing right."

"Mr. Paul Taylor comes in at least twice a day and asks a lot of impertinent questions. I hesitate to say this, Mr. Race, but I think he's your enemy." Her voice changed again. "In fact, I think he's nuts."

"You won't forget about Garcia."

"Of course not. And you, Mr. Race?"

I said, "There's a way out for every innocent man. There must be a way out for me. Goodbye."

I depressed the phone cradle and released it again. If I didn't keep on the move the last words I'd spoken would go mealy in my mouth. I dialled a second number.

Ginny's hand was stroking the back of my head. I smiled up at her.

Laura Taylor said, "Yes?"

"Can I speak to Paul?"

I waited. She didn't answer. I said, "This is Bob Race."

"Oh, I know. I recognised you. But you can't speak to Paul, he isn't around. He doesn't live here any more. He's left me. You might try the YMCA or the Carlton. Anywhere in fact. Funny that you should be looking for him. He's looking for you. He even went down to Mexico on Sunday to find you. Know why?"

I didn't speak.

She said, "He was really in love with that dirty whore. I was so pleased when I read how you'd killed her. I thought Paul would just fall back into my arms." She laughed. "He didn't. Quite the reverse, my dear. He loved her so much that his one thought now is to revenge himself on you. And do you know something. I'd help him if I could, just to ingratiate myself with him. I'd sell you right up the river without a thought. Would you like to comment?"

"No."

"Do me a favour, Bob. Tell me how you killed her."

I hung up.

Ginny said, "You on to something?"

"Not yet."

"Drink your coffee. It'll get cold."

I sat and sipped, still hearing the misery in Laura Taylor's voice. I thought of someone who'd be in even worse condition. It was probably a weakness in my character, but even with the whole country considering me a murderer I wanted those who knew me well to retain a good opinion of me. I picked up the phone again.

"Anything you do is right with me, Bob. I just don't want them to trace you."

I dialled.

The servant answered. He was sorry, Mr. Alford was speaking to no one. I insisted. Maybe he recognised my voice, though he gave no sign. I heard his footsteps going across the hall.

Sam Alford said dully, "What do you want?"

He sounded an old and weary man. I felt a stab of pity for him. I said without preamble, "This is Robert. I called to tell you I didn't kill Eve."

There was a silence. I was expecting a different reaction, something strong. He merely said in a flat voice, "You know what's going to happen to you, don't you?"

"Not if I can clear myself."

"What hope have you got?" he said without heat. "You burned the kid and you strangled my Eve. The cops'll get you. If they don't, you bastard, I will. I suppose you think you're going to get away with a million dollars."

"No," I said. "Neither the money nor Eve. I loved Eve. You know that. I was trying to save her. Kresnik had a bunch of guys waiting down in Mexico. They were looking for the money. They found me and through me they found Eve. She had the suitcase. They killed her for it. Kresnik got his money back."

"You're a liar."

"I'm not and I never was. You've never liked me, but you've always been able to take my word. Take it now. If I had the money I'd be over the hills and far away by this time, like Kresnik is. He's disappeared."

Ginny leapt to her feet in stark panic. Somebody was pounding the apartment door.

I snapped the receiver into place. I stood up. The apartment had no other exit. I ran to the window and looked out and there were four floors down and no fire-escape.

We stared big-eyed at one another. There wasn't even a cupboard in the room. The pounding continued and I snatched up the coffee cup and ran into the tiny kitchen.

I put my back to the sink and pulled the open door on me. Anyone entering would have a full view of the kitchen. Anyone looking close enough would see me through the crack of the door. I stopped breathing.

A voice outside said, "Open up!" Ginny tightened her negligee around her. I saw the gun on the chair where my clothes had been and I grabbed it.

She slipped the catch and opened the door just wide enough to peer through. The voice outside said, "Police." I guess she had no alternative. She stepped back and the two detectives came into the apartment, the beefy one in front still flashing his badge. The bald-headed one behind I'd met once on a case. It wasn't going to help me.

Beefy said, "Miss Virginia Ferrer?"

She nodded. Her voice came out naturally. "Sorry I kept you waiting. I was asleep."

They came farther into the room. They were three yards from me. The detective said, "Your phone number is Bel-Air 6-54326. We want to talk to you about a call."

I nearly quit then, walked out from the door and gave myself up. The bald-headed guy glanced sideways into the kitchen. He looked at the bed. Ginny said, "What call?"

He put away his badge and took out a notebook, thumbing the pages slowly. I felt my finger involuntarily curling around the trigger of the gun. He said, "Saturday night long distance from Santapola. Remember that."

If she denied it, that was the end. There'd be a record at the exchange. She tightened her negligee again, walked across the room, picked up a cigarette. They swivelled their bodies, keeping their eyes on her, turning their backs to me. I loved her.

She said, "Sure I remember it. Why wouldn't I? The guy's been in all the papers ever since. It was Robert Race."

"What would he be doing calling? He a friend of yours?" She shook her head. She was being helpful. "I met him twice. I knew his wife better. She used to come with her boy friend to the *Caracol* where I worked. They were all there together on the Thursday night before the murder and Eve, that was her name, invited me to dinner for the Saturday. Her husband called me from Santapola to see if I'd seen her."

She laughed. "I couldn't understand what he was talking about. He sounded crazy. He hung up in the middle of it."

I didn't know how the cop was taking it. I couldn't see his expression. He said, "You still at the *Caracol?*"

The bald one spoke for the first time. "They closed up a couple of nights back. Went broke. One of Al Kresnik's deals. That guy's sure took a beating this past year."

The other one turned sideways. I could see his profile. He eyed Ginny admiringly up and down and began to smile. He said, "Coffee smells good."

"Fresh out of coffee," she said, smiling back. "Want me to come down to Headquarters or something and make a statement?"

He didn't get rough. He said, "Yeah. Some time today. Look out for yourself. We figure the guy's in town. He's near enough to make a phone call on a dial phone. He's crazy enough to harm anybody."

"If I can't be good I'll be careful," she said flippantly, and led them to the door. When they were outside she said, "Thanks for warning me. It was good of you." Then she closed the door and walked across the room and fell full length on the bed with her face in the pillow.

I waited. The cops didn't come back. I counted off five whole minutes then stepped back into the room, tucking the gun into my pocket. I said, "Where can I get Kresnik?"

She rolled onto her back and stared at me. She had been crying. "He left town on Sunday morning, right after the club shut. He'd read the first editions about you."

"Where is he?"

"I don't know," she sobbed. "I don't know. I haven't any idea at all."

I said, "Roust yourself. Make us some more coffee."

23

I was eating again, beans from a can on buttered toast. I said, "The newstands won't have any back numbers. Tell me what you remember."

She stirred her coffee. By this time she'd drunk about a gallon. "It was in the papers Monday. Some guy driving on the Mexican side of the border saw this car burning up. He couldn't get near it so he went on and told police. When the fire burned out they found Fontaine inside. He was a cinder. He had two bullets in him. The cops could still read the number plates and they checked up and found the car was yours. When the waiter found your wife's body back at that hotel everyone looked for Tony Fontaine because he was with her. They couldn't find him. So the cops figure you already had him dead in the car."

"That car," I said. "And the number plates. Everyone knew them. That's why Kresnik's Mexican boys were able to wait for me in Campello. They got me, they killed Eve, they got Tony Fontaine. The English sailor and Charlie were on their way down, probably to keep a closer check on what was happening, they passed me while I was at the garage, they also recognised the car. They came after me. When I got away the car was left behind."

It was very clear. I said, "By that time they made Fontaine tell where the money was. They didn't need him any more so they shot him. Charlie or the English guy had got through by that time, told them where the car was, and they had the perfect frame. They drove out, put Fontaine in the back and burned him up. I get the blame for both murders."

"They get the money back," Ginny said miserably.

I put down my fork. "Do they?"

"What?" she said.

"Wait." It was a glimmering. I had to take it slowly or I'd lose it. "The couple down at the Flamenco in Santapola," I said. "Poverty stricken as a dried bone. Yet they refused five hundred bucks for telling me where Fontaine was. They denied he'd even been there. All right, call it family feeling, they may have been fond of him. Only they weren't."

I said, "I stood in their bar with two cops. They thought I'd killed Fontaine. They didn't give me away. What did they have to lose? I'll tell you. They had a million dollars to lose, or something near. A million dollars, a lot of notes, a suitcase full, the suitcase I saw under the bed. Tony Fontaine wouldn't have toted a bundle like that across the border into another country. He couldn't."

"I'm not following."

"He'd left most of it behind. That's why they wouldn't take five hundred dollars in the first place. They had a bigger cut coming. That's why they didn't give me away to the cops even when they knew Fontaine was dead. Especially when they knew Fontaine was dead. The dough was still there somewhere in the bar. They were going to get all of it. That's why Eve said we had to return to Santapola. We were going there to get the money back."

I reached for the phone and handed her the receiver. I said, "Jeff Pastor will be at headquarters. He can trace this call in three minutes. Don't mention my name till the end."

"But if Tony Fontaine told Kresnik's boys…" she started.

I dialled for her, still talking. She was nodding. She asked for Pastor and they put her through right away.

She said, "Hello, Mr. Pastor, you don't know me but it's important. There's a bar down in Santapola called the Flamenco, run by a man named José Ruso. If you can get some men there right away quick you might find close to a million dollars on the premises. Ask Ruso how it got there. See if he can explain. The Flamenco Bar in Santapola. Ruso. No, Mister, this is not a gag. I'm trying to help Robert Race. Goodbye."

She hung up.

The smile I gave her was dying behind my face. The police might find the money. They just might. The couple in the bar might crack, connect the money with Eve and Tony Fontaine. Then the cops had to trace it to the little guy named Esmollet, who was dead and could tell them nothing. Possibly they'd get farther. But if Burkhardt existed and they got to him, and from him to Kresnik, Kresnik would do less than nothing to exculpate me.

I had something to go on, but not enough. I had to make an independent movement of my own.

I said, "Kresnik. No idea at all where he is. Not even a guess?"

"No, why should I?" She turned aside, shaking her head. "I'd better go wash these dishes. I haven't made the bed yet."

"I can see that." It didn't ring true. It was all too smoothly evasive. I seized her wrist. "What are you lying about, Ginny?"

"Nothing." She remained turned from me. "What is there to lie about?"

"You tell me."

"After all I've done for you these past days," she said angrily, "and you want to start blaming me?"

I took her chin. I turned her head until she was forced to look into my eyes. "Where is he?"

"I don't know, I told you."

We stared at one another. All at once I knew my next words would not be a lie. I said, "Honey, I don't care if you were his mistress. I love you."

She gulped. We stood a long time with our arms about each other. Then she said, "The dishes," and I went with her to the tiny kitchen and dried the plates as she washed them. She was doing that so she didn't need look at me while she spoke.

"Maybe you don't know how it is when you're looking for night club work," she said. "There's some guys, you can't get a job unless…."

She washed and re-washed the same plate. I took it from her. She said, "It did-n't happen very often with him. I was never his mistress really, if you know what I mean. I'm not trying to pretend I'm better than I am. I might even have been his mistress, except when he offered to set me up in an apartment he kept call-ing it a love-nest. I didn't like the expression. I told him so. I'd have explained all this to you, Bob, honest, but we haven't had time yet. And...."

Again she stopped talking. I said, "You thought I was too much of a prig to understand. None of it matters except where is Kresnik now."

She put down the dish and turned to me. Her hands had gone pink from the water. Suds dripped from her fingertips. She said, "You're going to ask me how I know. I'll tell you. He invited me to go with him. I've been there before. Five week-ends. Just him and me and that Mexican houseboy. It's a place in the mountains, out past Sawchuck. Maybe he's not out there any more."

"We'll go see."

She appeared not to hear. She was looking at me desperately, lips slightly parted, eyes deep with troubled thoughts. She said, "What do you think of me now?"

"What do you want me to think?"

She said, "I suppose I've lost you. There've been others, too. Not many. That's the God's honest truth: not many. I only did it because I had to, to get a job. But I never once did it for love. I've never loved anybody but you." She pursed her mouth and squeezed her eyes tight shut. "Now you won't be able to love me because that's how you are. I shouldn't have opened my big stupid trap."

I took her soapy hands and started to dry them on the dish-towel. I said, "Ginny, I've a double murder rap hanging over my head. Thanks for helping me. How do I get to this place?"

She gave one small uncertain smile. Her aspect changed. She finished drying her hands herself and became brisk. "You can't leave here. Get on the street and someone'll spot you in two minutes. I'll go see Kresnik myself."

"And do what? I want answers to questions you don't even know about. How far is this hide-out?"

"It's a cottage," she said. "Four hours drive. You can't go. You're too well known. Anyone could tell you a block away by your clothes. You know how they always described you in the papers."

"The city's best-dressed lawyer," I said. "The advocate from Savile Row. It's a chance I have to take."

"I could buy you some clothes off the rack."

We stared again. "A raincoat," I said. "A 7¼ hat. A pair of glasses." I dug in my pocket for the money.

While she was gone I read about Garcia. I induced in myself a schizophrenic state where I was gut-worried about my own condition and light-hearted over him. I should have been making plans about how to deal with Kresnik. I wouldn't know how to deal with Kresnik until I was confronted by his attitude.

I sat with a small ache spreading through my duodenum.

The raincoat she brought had been made for a man with a bigger belly. I placed the gun in the right-hand pocket, put on the hat and glasses and stared into the mirror. I looked just the same. I turned back to her and smiled and she put out a hand and touched my arm and the crease of worry disappeared momentarily from between her brows.

She said, "The car's gassed up. I parked it outside the entrance. If we drive fast we should be there by about two o'clock. Shall we go?"

I nodded. All the colour drained suddenly from her face. I took her arm and we went out and down the stairs.

There were three flights. Even in daytime they were almost as dark as I remembered them. The banister was rickety, the passage long, the walls greasy. The blinding sunlight beyond the front door was like a blow in the eyes.

I felt her cringe. She tried to draw back. I dragged her with me. We stepped out onto the narrow sidewalk and I felt fiercely conspicuous in the raincoat. From the corner of my eye I saw the cop.

He was a hundred yards off, looking in a store window. I thought, "He's been left there to watch her," and I smiled at her and opened the car door. Then I walked right round to the other side and got behind the wheel. I started the engine and eased forward. The cop swivelled on his feet and walked into the store.

"Now," I said. "Where?"

"Third on the left. Straight through to the highway. Then left again."

She lit two cigarettes. Her hands were shaking. She put one of the cigarettes into my mouth as we turned the corner. The cop didn't follow and neither did anyone else.

I felt lucky.

24

We stayed on the highway for three hours, turned off and started to climb. The road began winding. It wasn't a good road because it didn't lead to anywhere but Sawchuck and similar places beyond. There was no traffic and I still felt lucky. I started to relax.

Ginny was a back-seat driver.

She knew the route. She warned me fifteen or sixteen times about the coming curves so I pulled up and we changed places. After that we made good time. She was a better driver than I. All I had to do was lean back and watch either her face or the scenery.

It was afternoon but the sun still held a midday heat. The mountains were standing in a shimmering mauve haze. Spring had marched almost to the peaks and there were great scatterings of blue borages and yellow dandelions and daisies. The trees were a blinding fresh green that made me think of Tony

Fontaine's car. Nature was pretty, but I preferred to watch Ginny's face.

The sun showed the faint down on her cheeks, the circles of fatigue under her eyes. She had in indefinable aura of night-club, a transparent pale skin conditioned to cigarette smoke, a look that came from seeing the dawn too often from the wrong side. She also had integrity, an entireness that sculpted her face all of one piece and made her beautiful. She was Ginny Ferrer and aware of it and not trying to be anyone else.

I said, "You're better looking since you died your hair black."

The fatigue wiped away from her face. Her eyes went bright. She said, "Well, you're wrong. I used to dye it before. This is my natural colour. You ought to be able to tell by the texture. Dyed hair is brittle."

"Anyway," I said, "you're beautiful."

She smiled. "So are you. Maybe it's the drink. Maybe it's those glasses. You've lost that punk juvenile look. You're handsome when you're haggard."

"Then I should get handsomer." The interlude was over. A fierce irritation swept through me. "How the hell much farther is this Sawchuck?"

"Here," she said, and skilfully rounded the bend.

It looked like a place with around two thousand inhabitants. There may have been more hiding in the mountains from a sense of civic shame. The main street was a dried creek bed. Nothing moved in it except a pink and apparently hairless dog. There'd be a lot of flies in the summer and I figured the locals were named either Jeeter or Jukes.

We passed a haberdashery full of jeans, a general store, a feed store, what looked like a harness shop, something called *Modes by Lili*, and right at the end of the street a drugstore with a window full of ball-point pens and a plaster of signs mostly by Coca-cola. The trip took about thirty seconds. We turned the exit bend.

The flowers were back with a riot of colour almost mutinous. Ginny said, "I guess you won't want to drive up to the front door."

"What's this?"

"If we take the right fork ahead you can sneak up on him through the trees."

"All right," I said, and looked at her. The fatigue was back. I said, "This is going to sound silly, impossible and maybe tasteless. I really am in love with you."

"Yes," she said, and nodded. "We're pretty damn lucky people."

That made me laugh. I put an arm across the back of the seat and went on looking at her. The trees flicked past. A few stones bounced. The sun was very hot.

We drew to a slow halt.

She looked a long moment into my eyes. Then she straightened. She whispered, "Through there," and she pointed. She started to get out of the car.

"What are you doing?"

"Going with you."

"Anywhere ahead you can turn the car round?"

She nodded.

"Do that. Then wait here. Don't move."

I took off the phony glasses. My eyes ached a little. I smiled at her once, checked the gun in my pocket and got on to the road. There was a small bank. I hauled myself up it and was in a grove of aspens.

The trees didn't grow very close together. Their new leaves made a canopy that cooled the sun and bathed everything in shadowy green. There was a strong smell of earth and wood, and a lot of birds were singing. Some insects rattled and scraped. The car started up behind me.

It made a startling noise. I was convinced Kresnik would hear. I could see his house a hundred yards through the trees and I knew he was there because the back door stood half open. I froze against a bole and I waited.

It was a two-storey house and had a chimney. The doors and window frames were painted cream and bright red. The outside walls had been whitewashed with several coats, but the dark colour of the local stone showed through. Tall trees cast cool shade and there was a flower garden.

An ideal place to spend summer week-ends. I continued to wait.

The birds chattered on. The back door neither opened farther nor shut. Nothing moved except the fluttering aspen leaves above me.

I edged forward. I had the gun out of my pocket and I was sweating like a french fried potato. A couple of sticks snapped under my feet like pistols. I shrank behind a tree ten yards from the door.

Nothing at all happened. I could vaguely see through one window and there appeared to be no one inside. A platoon of men could have been sitting upstairs with rifles trained on me. It was a chance I had to take. I mentally picked up my gear, flitted across the last ten yards and shot sideways through the door.

The Mexican houseboy was waiting. He smiled up at me.

It was the same smile he'd used when alive. He was dead now. He was on his knees, clinging fiercely to the door-handle, going rigid in position. He had tried to run away, and been caught at the door.

The back of his white houseboy coat was caked with congealing blood, but the marks were clear where the two bullets entered. One had emerged from his chest and was embedded in the door. The dent was above his head now because he'd been upright at the time.

I looked at him for what seemed a long time, but I didn't touch him. I went carefully on tip-toe around his outstretched legs and through the narrow white kitchen.

There was a hall with open doors. From somewhere I could hear the slow ticking of a clock. The birds outside sang furiously. The air was thick with the reek of whisky. I had a choice of three rooms and for no reason I picked the middle one. I creaked over the intervening space, crossed the threshold and looked at the top of Kresnik's head.

He was sitting behind a desk. He had fallen forward. There were two empty glasses in front of him. His left hand had knocked over a whisky bottle and the contents had poured on to the floor. His right hand was in the desk drawer.

I went around the desk and lifted him up by the hair.

His mouth was open and so was his forehead. It had been excavated by a bullet. He was as dead as a kippered herring.

I propped him back in the chair. His left hand flopped off the desk, his right hand remained in the drawer still touching the gun he'd been reaching for. I opened the three side drawers and they were all empty. I reached across his thrusting stomach, opened the centre drawer wider and fumbled around his dead head. There was nothing but the gun.

I searched him.

The folded sheet of paper was tucked down his right sock. The list was in pencil. At the top was a number: A81194189A. Alongside was written To 200. The next number was A90967826A. To 900. It went on like that all down the page.

I turned the sheet over. Another list. I folded the paper carefully and put it in my coat. I froze.

The whining voice said, "Drop the gun, Buster. Then turn around."

I could have tried a snap shot. I was too beat. I had no co-ordination. I opened my hand and the weapon clunked down beside me.

Then I turned around and looked at the gun in Jordan's hand.

25

His flaxen hair was bright as ever, the rictal sneer more pronounced. He said, "So now you've knocked off the boss."

He made it almost funny, perhaps because he spoke without moving his jaw. His teeth were wired together, the top set to the bottom. It gave him a fanged look, like a trapped wolf I couldn't think of anything to say. I bleated, "I thought you were in hospital."

"I didn't stay. I'm the restless type." His eyes glinted bleakly. "Not so much as you. You're really having a ball. Your wife and now Kresnik. What did you do with the kid? More important. What you done with the dough?"

I didn't answer. I was standing there thinking Ginny Ferrer had led me into this, calling myself all the fools on earth.

He said, "You sure effed things up, Buster. We heard from Burkhardt about Campello and Charlie-boy's said what happened in the desert. He's gonna to be glad to get his hands on you. Me too."

He forgot himself, tried to open his mouth. The wire clicked around his teeth and he gave a sharp involuntary groan. He took two steps farther into the room. He said, "You bastard, you're going to take a little ride."

"How will you manage that?"

He reached his free hand in his pocket and pulled out a sap. It was made of black rubber and weighted with lead. He said, "Any questions?"

"Who killed Kresnik?"

He said, "You funny bastard." He took another step forward.

"And the houseboy out there in the kitchen," I said. "Cold as old toast."

His face twitched faintly with surprise. He made a quarter turn toward the door, then swivelled back to me. His lips moved. I stared at him and past his shoulder.

Ginny Ferrer was there. She held an empty milk bottle by the neck. It was raised above her head.

I said, "Yeah." Jordan about-faced like a dancer. She was already swinging.

The gun went off and I jumped. She hit him in the side of the face and his jaw fell right open. He dropped the gun and went howling to his knees and she hit him square on the top of the head. The milk bottle exploded. Then he was flat on the floor not howling any more. He was barely even breathing.

I dropped beside him. He had nothing on him except the gun and the sap, cigarettes, matches and eighty-three dollars. No handkerchief. I got up again and Ginny was frozen into position, staring wide-eyed, finger pointing at Kresnik.

She said, "I slept with him. He's dead." Her mouth opened as wide as Jordan's and she was about to have hysterics.

I struck her hard in the middle of the back. I snarled, "Out! Get out!" I seized her arm and dragged her. We bundled past the smiling houseboy. We got outside and streaked through the trees for the car.

I had lost my illusion of luck. She was quitting her hysteria because I was driving and she had to concentrate on me. She wrapped the handkerchief tighter around her cut hand. "I saw Jordan's car in front of the house from farther up," she said. "That's why I came to see."

"Glad you did."

"Kresnik," she said, and shuddered. "And the houseboy. I nearly threw up when I saw him. Who did it?"

"I don't know. The blood was still fairly fresh. It happened in the last two hours."

She said distantly, "Kresnik was about your last hope. What'll you do now?"

"Tell the cops before the trail goes cold."

"You're crazy." Her detachment vanished. "They'll be on you like a pack of pointers. You'll get the blame. They've already got it stacked. The cop this morning said you were crazed enough to shoot anyone."

I said, "If Jeff Pastor has found the money down in Santapola he might make a connection. Maybe he can get a wedge in somewhere, crack the case open."

"Don't overlook that he thinks you killed your wife." She stared down at her hand. It was still bleeding. She said, "When you think of what she has caused it's pretty hard to be sorry she's dead."

"Leave it," I said. "We have to do something about that bleeding."

"It's nothing." She shrugged. "All right, let's be cool and calm. Let's take it one step at a time. Check about the money first. If there's any chance of making a case you can tell them about Kresnik."

"I have to tell them anyway."

I reefed around a bend. We were at Sawchuck again.

Even the hairless dog had quit. Nothing moved anywhere. I took another look at Ginny's hand and slackened speed. I pulled up outside the drugstore.

She made no protest. She followed me inside and the interior was a surprise because it was all spick-and-span and soap-smelling with everything neatly stacked, a phone booth, a flashy little soda bar with five high stools. The little man fitted perfectly.

He came from somewhere at the back. He wasn't a Jeeter or a Jukes. He was thin small and smooth-skinned with a quick intelligent look at my raincoat. His speech was as neat and meticulous as his appearance.

"Good day." He saw Ginny's hand. "Could you remove the handkerchief. Thank you. Ah yes, nothing much, nothing much at all. More blood than damage."

He disappeared through the door into the back and reemerged with a bottle and a box. He swabbed the hand with gentle precise movements, examined the two cuts, plucked out a fragment of glass with a pair of tweezers, smiled happily, carefully applied two strips of plaster. "There!" he said. "Now. Something to drink? We have very good ice-cream."

He was eager. He wanted to hang on to the company. Living in Sawchuck I would have been the same. I said, "Two cokes."

Ginny blinked at me. "I'll make that call," she said. She walked into the phone booth and shut the door behind her. There was no way I could protest.

"Two cokes," the little guy said, and placed them before me. He looked into my face, smiled, wiped the counter from one end to the other and vanished once more into the back. I'd been wrong about him wanting company.

I waited to see if he was returning. I could hear Ginny's voice without understanding what she said. I swivelled on the stool, got off it, went toward the phone booth. She hung up and came out.

Her exhaustion was complete. She shook her head. She said in a low voice, "Your theory was wrong. The police at Santapola found nothing. Kresnik's boys got there first."

"No," I said. "Jordan asked me where was the dough."

We stared helplessly. "You say anything about Kresnik?"

She shook her head again. "The cops would have come up right away, passed us on the road. They may do it anyway. I was a fool. A call from here can be easily traced."

"Let's go," I said.

I turned to the counter. The little man had emerged again. He was standing at the door with a twelve-bore pointed at us.

He said, "It's loaded."

We jelled into an appropriate tableau. The guy was paler than before, but there was an expression of great popinjay delight on his face. He said, "Put your hands up, Mr. Race. And the lady."

I wet my lips. "What was that name?"

"Robert Race. Your newspaper picture has been inescapable these past few days. You murdered your wife and her paramour in Mexico." His shoulder twitched unexpectedly, but the gun remained firm. "I'm not saying that I blame you. I can't strike an attitude, being a bachelor myself. But I must do my public duty."

He stood there looking like an incarnation of all the civic virtues. I said, "Yes, I read about the guy. I think I do blame him." I smiled at Ginny. "So does my wife."

"That's a good gambit," he said, not faltering. "But your disguise is too thin. I warn you not to move while I get from here to the door. I'm going to call for aid. Sorry, Mr. Race."

"Mr. Kingsley," I said.

"Mr. Race."

I said, "I bet a thousand dollars it's Kingsley."

He was in mid-stride with one foot off the ground. He put the foot back into position. Cupidity had washed away all his virtue.

"A thousand dollars? At what odds?"

"Evens."

"Not a real bet."

"Two to one." He shook his head. I was thinking of Jordan recovering and coming down, the cops tracing the call and coming up. I said, "Three to one."

"Five to one."

"You've got a bet."

"Money on the counter, naturally."

"Naturally."

"Then it's in your pocket. The lady can stand behind you and extract it. That'll give me the opportunity to blow off your head with both barrels if she gets funny."

"She won't," I said. "Get it, Ginny."

She stepped behind me. Her hand went into my pocket and closed on the wad of bills. She drew them all out. The druggist cleared his throat and behind the spectacles his eyelids flittered.

"Ten to one," he said calmly, "I'm going against all my natural instincts. I need adequate compensation."

"You shifty little bastard," I said. Ginny was already counting off the notes. She laid them on the counter.

The guy said, "Now lay down the rest. As an apology for the name you called me and an assurance I don't call the police as soon as you're gone."

"Do it," I said.

He nodded. He said breezily, "Well, it looks like someone made a bet and I won it. Goodbye, Mr. Kingsley. Goodbye, Mrs. Kingsley. Have a nice trip."

There was no alternative. "Goodbye," I said, and we walked out.

Four men had appeared at the far end of the street. They were talking in a small knot. They looked at us curiously as we passed in the car, and that was all there was to it. That was Sawchuck. We went on down the mountain and met no police or anyone else. We changed places and Ginny drove and after that we moved like the wind. We didn't speak until we were back on the main highway.

I said, "That was a gay little interlude."

She nodded. "Finishes Canada. I wonder the swine didn't hold you up for the whole million."

"He didn't know about it. It's not been in the papers. No one knew about it except Kresnik and his mob and Eve and Tony Fontaine."

"And me," she said.

"And my father-in-law, Sam Alford," I said.

It should have hit me like a thunderbolt. All I was doing was murmur casually. I tried it again for size. I said, "And my father-in-law. He mentioned the million dollars when he was shouting at me on the phone this morning. How did he know?"

I saw a motor-cycle cop coming from the other direction. I lowered my head, shrinking into the seat. He roared past without a glance.

Ginny said carefully, "Sam Alford knew because his daughter told him. You were certain she'd phone him. That's how you found she was in Campello. She finally got in touch with him and broke the news she was toting a million bucks. Like you said, she told him everything."

"Not everything." The engine roared in my ears. "Not everything. She'd been in the morning to say goodbye. Why didn't she tell him then? Why did she wait till the evening?"

I listened to the humming of the road. The tire treads rippled. I said, "It was the phone call. Sam Alford knew I was in Campello. The telephone exchange told him the trick I'd pulled. He knew the number and the make of my car."

I laughed. I said, "Isn't that something? Isn't it? Ginny, we got to go and hide somewhere until it's dark. I mustn't get caught yet, not now. I think I know why Eve changed her mind and wanted to go back home with me. I think I'm on to something."

"Are you darling?" She smiled. "We'll stay out here in the country. But get rid of that raincoat, for God's sake. It looks funny in weather like this."

A mile farther on we turned into a side road and kept driving. I said, "What did Jordan mean when he asked what I did with the kid?"

26

I was standing tight and unmoving against a tree, twenty-five yards from the entrance to my father-in-law's driveway. I had been there twenty minutes. I had gotten rid of the raincoat so of course it was pouring with rain. I was drenched. My eyes ached from strain.

The driveway entrance opened on to a conjunction where five roads met in a sort of broad, parklike cornerless square. The man standing hidden in the shadows of the driveway of the opposite house was not moving either. He wouldn't be as wet as I. He was wearing a light-coloured raincoat. That was why I was able to see him. That's why my eyes ached, from watching him.

I decided to give ten minutes more. Maybe he'd go away. I felt pretty sure he wouldn't. I felt equally sure he was a cop. And while he stood there I couldn't enter the driveway of my father-in-law's house. There was a street light I'd have to pass under.

The other entrance was round at the back; a street gate leading to a walled enclosure. To get to the main part of the house meant going through the kitchen and the servants quarters. I didn't want to meet the servants or anyone else.

The rain fell, the night was dark, the district was too swankily residential for much traffic apart from an occasional homing Cadillac. I sniffed up the smell of wet linden trees, watched the man across the way, chewed over my situation.

My jaw broke every time on the same item. I couldn't figure who had the money. Not me, not Eve, not Fontaine. Not Kresnik's boys. Apparently not the couple at the Flamenco, though maybe they'd hidden it somewhere before the cops arrived to search. Somehow that didn't ring true. You must at least half trust someone before you hide a million dollars with them. The Flamenco couple looked as if they didn't even trust one another.

The rain dripped off my hat brim. I thought of Ginny, back at her apartment, wondered if she was making herself more coffee. On the far side of the road the raincoat moved slightly. It solidified back into position. It was there for the night.

I couldn't spare so much time. I had to get going. I hugged the shadows of the high wall surrounding the garden and walked softly away from the driveway. I was reciting to myself. A eight double-one nine forty-one eighty-nine A. A again, nine nought ninety-six seventy-eight twenty-six A.

Serial numbers. Plain as a pikestaff. But not from bank robbery nor swindle nor theft. Guys with pretty hands like Esmollett don't get five per cent on deals like that. In Mexico, where they use pesos, people don't have a million dollars American hanging around waiting to be picked up.

The alternatives were almost non-existent. In fact there was only one.

I turned a corner. It was a street of back-entrances and there were no trees any more. The rain fell unimpeded. I fetched up against the gate, set in the end of the wall. It would be locked. Hordes of servants would be waiting the other side. I curled a hand round the gun in my pocket, depressed the gate-catch with my other thumb and heaved.

It opened so easily I nearly fell. I was in the enclosed kitchen yard.

There wasn't a light anywhere. The servants had a night off. Then I figured Sam Alford had gone away too. My sort of luck. I gumshoed across the yard and tried the back door.

This one was locked. I stood and despaired and got wet.

There was no sound from anywhere. I tried two windows, went to a third and all were bolted. I took off my hat, put my fist in it, held it against a small window pane and leaned.

I pushed.

It went off like an explosion in a plate-glass factory. I stood without breathing for a couple of years. Nothing more happened, no noise except the falling rain, and then a passing car. I swung the window open, swung myself up and stood a moment among the splintered glass in the kitchen sink. Faint music was coming from the front of the house.

I climbed down, hit a handle and waited while an empty saucepan spun four times. I fumbled ahead.

He had his hi-fi turned up full belt. I went up the kitchen stairs, left the cabbage smell behind me, and the music got very loud. Second act of *Die Fledermaus*, the entire chorus of the Vienna State Opera singing a schmaltzy waltz about brotherliness and the joys of loving one another. I wondered if Sam Alford had visitors. I sneaked past the staircase and across the carpeted part of the hall.

A lot of upkeep was necessary for a house like this. If Sam Alford had stopped giving money to Eve it meant he had none for himself.

The chorus finished their fraternizing. The orchestra took over and the record continued in strict three-quarter time. I waited. The orchestra finished its second-time-through. I decided there was no one else in there because the music was too loud for conversation and Sam Alford liked to talk while he listened. I eased the door handle and stepped into the library.

He was drunk. In something like a revelation I realised how many people get drunk in times of trouble and how futile it is. The whisky was beside him on a small table. He was wearing a brocaded dressing-gown and sitting in a deep armchair, hands in his lap, head back, eyes closed. He was an old man, beaten and exhausted.

I left the door slightly open. I stood in front of it, waiting for him to move. The music whooped to an end with violins and four bright chords and the phonograph clicked twice and automatically stopped itself.

Sam Alford opened his eyes. He stared at me.

He evinced no surprise. His voice was slurred with drink and irritated, as at a tiresome child who had interrupted his diversions. He said, "What do you want?"

I moved farther into the room. I felt pretty silly confronting an unarmed old man with a gun and I slipped it into my pocket. He followed my movements with eyes expressionless as boiled candy.

I said, "I want to explain about Eve."

He made no answer.

"I traced her in Campello," I said. "I spoke to her on the phone. She wanted to come with me, but Kresnik's boys got there first and killed her."

He didn't move or alter his expression. Only his voice changed. "Did she say anything that might have been a message for me?"

"She was coming back. That's a sort of message. You had spoken to her on the phone. You're the only one could have ordered her return. She was obeying you."

I took a stab. "She told me why you wanted her to return."

He lowered and raised his eyelids. Nothing else.

"She had to bring back Kresnik's money," I said. "For a perfectly straight-forward reason. You and Kresnik were pals. I should have realised it long ago. I was too bigheaded. When I opened my new office I thought Kresnik came to me because of my personal charm. He didn't. Guys that type don't mix with somebody fresh from the D.A.'s office. He was there because you sent him. That's what you meant when you said you'd thrown business my way."

Sam Alford showed not a flicker of interest. He reached out, took a sip from his drink, leaned back again and closed his eyes.

"You didn't do it for me personally," I said, "so much as for Eve's husband. You'd do almost anything for her, and she for you. That's why she was bring-ing the money back."

"Sure. She did it because she was my girl."

He said it proudly. He suddenly realised it was an admission. His eyes opened. He was a serpent peering from behind a rock.

I said, "You made Kresnik my client and without telling you he picked me to collect the suitcase. He blackmailed me and I was weak. I told Eve about it, she told Fontaine, he thought it worthwhile chancing his arm and he robbed me. Meanwhile Kresnik had kidnapped Eve as a hostage. He knew I was in love with her."

Sam Alford reached out, finished his drink, closed his eyes again. I wasn't go-ing to get a thing out of him.

I said, "Everything straightforward so far, except that Kresnik made little use of his hostage. He treated her respectfully. He let her go. He wasn't the gentle-manly type. But he wouldn't let his boys even talk about her. Why? She was the daughter of his pal."

"Proof?" My father-in-law wasn't so drunk.

"We get to the interesting part," I said. "Father and daughter relationship."

His eyes slitted.

"Eve came and told you she was pushing off with Fontaine. You claim she told you everything. She did. About her sex life. I guess you brought her up that way; it was the solid bond between you; you with your pornographic classics, her with her men. But she didn't tell you about the suitcase she and Fontaine were taking with them. You didn't know about that till I came here in the evening, on the run from Kresnik. Then you were afraid for her. You phoned your pal while I was here and you knew where he'd be and you didn't even have to look up the number. You told him the suitcase was still in my possession. Later events prove he believed you. You were really a close pal."

Something nagged me. I couldn't get my finger on it. How close was a friendship that allowed Sam Alford to call Kresnik and broach the subject of the suitcase without any pre-amble? I said:

"Unfortunately Eve picked Mexico to run to. It was where the suitcase had come from in the first place. She phoned you from there and the exchange told you the trick I'd pulled to discover her whereabouts. You knew I'd also be heading for Campello. You told Kresnik. You told him the number and make of the car I was in, he thought I had the dough and you didn't have a qualm about throwing me to the wolves. His boys picked me up."

He sat there indicating nothing. I had to provoke him. I said, "How am I doing?"

"Boring me."

I got it then. Like emerging from Ginny's house again into the bright street. I said, "Eve hadn't told you about the money in the morning, there was no reason she'd tell you on the phone at night. But suddenly she was going to ditch Fontaine, pick up the money they'd left in Santapola and return here. There was one person could make her do that. You. You knew about the money without her saying anything. Either you knew beforehand or you'd learned it from Kresnik. Whichever way, we get to the same conclusion. The Kresniks of this world don't tell things like that to pals no matter how close. You weren't pals. You were partners."

I said, "Less bored?"

He gave me a half smile.

"Kresnik not only had Eve murdered," I said, "he got away with all the dough. That riled you. After you spoke to me on the phone today you drove up to the mountains. You accused him of a double-cross. He denied even seeing the money, he probably denied about Eve. He was reaching for a gun so maybe you can plead self-defence in shooting him. You'll have a tougher case with the Mexican house-boy."

"Proof?"

I tried to bluff, I said:

"You had to go through Sawchuck. There's not much traffic. There's a druggist there with nothing better to do than take the numbers of passing cars. It's a form of hobby. Your number is third on today's list."

"Proof collapsed. I hired a car. It couldn't be traced to me."

"I hope you shot Kresnik because he denied having the money," I said. "It would make a nice twist. He didn't have it. Neither did his boys."

My father-in-law sat up slowly. "Where is it?"

"Don't you have it?"

"You wriggling bastard," he snarled. "Where is it?"

Then he stopped. I watched his face change. His mouth fell open, he turned white, then he became a pale green. I knew there was someone behind me before the voice spoke.

It said, "Get your hands up."

I hesitated. I turned around slowly. Having heard the voice I was able to make the mental adjustment. I knew why Jordan had asked me what I did with the kid. The guy was standing inside the door with a gun in his hand.

He was Tony Fontaine.

27

A small shard of embedded glass winked from the front of his left shoe. He had come in by the same way as myself. He was wearing one of my suits and he looked smart. His hair was neatly parted, he was closely shaved, he hadn't been caught in the rain.

He gave the impression of having come from a college frat-house meeting. Except for his face.

It was stony. It had no trace of normal humanity. He was here for a purpose that nothing would prevent him achieving.

I remembered how I'd got him acquitted of robbery with violence because I'd thought him incapable of it. He was capable of anything.

He wasn't nervous. He said coolly, "Snap out of it, Alford. I'm not dead."

I said, "How did that happen?"

He looked at me directly, without embarrassment. "Shut up, you. I got more important things to talk about."

"Like a million dollars?"

My father-in-law's eyes were glassy. His hands lay still in his lap. He croaked, "Have you got it, Fontaine?"

"What do you think? Who else could have it?"

Each knew what the other was talking about. I dug. I said, "Kresnik might have it."

"Who's Kresnik?"

It was as if someone had thrown me a neatly packaged parcel. Fontaine hadn't been burned in the car. He didn't know about Kresnik. I said:

"You killed Eve."

The stone face cracked. He looked faintly surprised that I'd bothered to mention it. He showed his teeth. He was meant to be grinning. He said, "The papers tell me you did it."

Sam Alford got slowly to his feet.

Tony Fontaine said, "All right, Alford. Sit down again." He came right into the room, signalling me with the gun. I backed up. "Sit down again," he said, and swung his heeled fist and hit Sam Alford in the face.

My father-in-law sat down again.

We had a few pulsing seconds of quietness.

Tony Fontaine said, "This is the deal. You offered me twenty per cent to bring the dough back from Campello. I'm offering the same twenty per cent to know the trick that's being pulled. Twenty per cent is two hundred thousand. You need it. Eve told me."

"What trick?" Sam Alford said.

"Don't play games. I've had to beat it out of three cities in the last two days. The cops were after me. Why?"

Sam Alford put his finger tips together. The corners of his mouth twitched. He nodded his head several times and then he laughed. He said, "You stupid bastard." There was vast satisfaction in his voice. "Sure they chased you. You're going to be chased wherever you go. Every one of those goddamned notes is a counterfeit."

The fist hit him in the mouth. He stopped laughing. He lurched sideways. His elbow hit the table and the whisky glass fell off and rolled clear across the floor.

"Lying get's you nowhere," Fontaine said quietly. "I've changed eleven thousand bucks of those notes in different banks. Hired guys to do it for me. None of them had trouble. What's the trick?"

"I don't know," Sam Alford said.

The fist smashed again. His head banged back against the chair. Blood gushed from his nose.

"Lay off!" I said. "He doesn't know. It wasn't his money."

"Sure. That's why he could offer me twenty per cent of it."

I looked at my father-in-law's bloody face. He was in pain. But he was back behind his boulder again, playing serpent. I said, "I get it. Twenty per cent. You were going to double-cross Kresnik. He'd chase me thinking I had the money, because you'd told him so. He'd probably kill me in trying to find it and you'd feather your nest."

"I thought you had the money."

"Not that early in the game. You thought it only after you decided I'd killed Eve. You had the wrong man."

I looked at Fontaine. He didn't flinch. He said, "You messed up the plans, Race. You were never supposed to come up that cliff again after I sent you over. It was a foolproof scheme. Unknown robber kills lawyer. We were going to lay

low and live normally till everything blew over. But you appeared next morning. We had to hit it out quick for Mexico."

He blinked. "Who's Kresnik?"

"Who did Eve say the case belonged to?"

"She didn't know."

"She didn't say in case you got scared."

"Me scared?" he said contemptuously. "She said it belonged to a client. She
didn't know his name. She thought the case might be valuable and it was. We
got down to Campello, she wanted to call her old man to tell him where she was
at, then she found out the dough belonged to him."

I said, "Then he told her to bring it home and in return you'd get twenty per
cent. She'd do that for him. She liked her father. Other men were just something
inside pants. But you wanted a hundred per cent. You had to kill her to get it.
Maybe you caught her trying to sneak off. You left your car behind because it
was too easily traced."

"Wrong," Fontaine said coldly. "I didn't do anything of the kind. You killed
me, then you killed her. It says so in the papers."

He showed his teeth again. "I'm sitting pretty. Nobody even knows I'm in circulation."

I looked at his gun and a chill ran up my back. He was regarding me with eyes
like pebbles. Nobody would ever know he was in circulation. I said, "Can I put
my arms down?"

"No."

I hated him, not just for the arms but for everything. "Not such a very pretty
seat," I said. "A little guy in Mexico told me he would have kept the dough except he couldn't distribute it. Kresnik told me distribution could be stopped at
any time he wanted. Okay, it's been stopped. You're up a tree, Buster."

"Temporarily," he said, and turned to Sam Alford. "What's the trick?"

"The money's false. All of it."

"Try another tack, something I'll believe. You wouldn't cross this Kresnik guy
for a case of counterfeit."

"It was supposed to be good counterfeit. Undetectable."

"Yeah. In banks but not in clothing stores. They were supposed to send me
around a suit. They sent the cops. Speak up, Alford!"

"He can't," I said. "He doesn't know anything. I do. You probably made the
error of trying to pass bill number A81194189A."

"Tell it!"

"Or bill number A90967826A. Everyone needed that million dollars," I said,
"and it was so well forged you could pass it in banks. Kresnik was desperate.
He took desperate measures. There was only one sure way of knowing where
the money was, and that was by the serial numbers. Kresnik claimed he could
stop distribution. He did. He made a selection of the numbers and somehow
publicised it.

"You were all right in the banks, but in the clothing store you handed over one of the selections. The cops came after you. You escaped. Maybe Kresnik counted on that. I guess he had one of two plans. Either he was trailing you by where the money turned up, or he wanted you to get scared so that you'd come back here and make a deal. Have you, for example, also tried passing A81194200A?"

Fontaine said, "How many more do you know?"

"The lot. Twenty per cent for me and we'll make a deal."

"On what?"

"I've got the list."

"Where?"

"Here." I dropped by arms.

I got both hands into my jacket pockets. I got the gun halfway out and he shot me in the right shoulder. I sat down hard on the floor.

Sam Alford tried to hurl himself out of the chair and across the gaping space to Fontaine. He didn't make it. The gun popped again making almost no noise and my father-in-law smacked down on his face. I twisted my left hand across my body and tried again to get the gun from the pocket. I reared to my knees.

Fontaine shot me in the head.

A cleaver split my skull. My forehead hit the carpet. I rolled on my side and I was dead, but I could still see everything. There wasn't much pain.

Fontaine came and stood over me and examined me. His face fell down like an avalanche. There was blood over my eyes. He kneeled and took the list from my pocket, read it, put it in his pocket, took out my gun, examined it to see if it was loaded, held it tight in his hand and dropped his own gun beside me.

He stared into my face. I remarked the length of his eyelashes. Then he got to his feet and walked out of the room. I sat up.

I grabbed the gun in my left hand, thrust up and made the door in a single lurch. I got round the frame and leaned against the wall in the darkness. I didn't know where he was because I couldn't see or hear him. I took aim in what I figured was the direction of the kitchen door, and fired.

The gun went pop! I slid down the wall and sat on my hunkers. I pulled the trigger a second time just for the hell of it. I knew he was already gone, but I didn't care.

His feet went clacking across the uncarpeted part of the hall. The front door opened.

There was a blank after that. Then I was staggering through the rain and he was running down the drive ahead of me. I lifted my left hand to take another shot at him. I didn't have the gun. I'd dropped it somewhere. I teetered on because if I sat down again I'd just get wet. I reached the gate.

I couldn't see him. Then he passed under the street light, head down, running like a race-horse. I couldn't go any farther. I leaned against a pilaster and prepared to watch him disappear. I had a grandstand seat.

The guy in the light raincoat came out of his little nook and took one shot. Off in the distance Tony Fontaine went up on his toes, ran clear to the middle of the road and fell down. The guy in the light raincoat ran toward him. A dark-dressed man on the farthest corner came out of wherever he'd been hiding and ran after the light raincoat.

I fell over.

When I refocussed the raincoat man was past the light. The dark-clad man ran under it and he was Jeff Pastor. In the middle of the road Fontaine made a sudden movement and twitched himself to an upright position. The gun barked. It was the light raincoat's turn to fall over.

His gun clanked to the ground, he rolled a few times and Tony Fontaine went on firing. Jeff Pastor in the dark suit came to a halt beyond the light.

Everybody had a gun. It was so funny that I laughed. Jeff Pastor pumped away like a well-regulated machine and Tony Fontaine lay down again and kicked his legs. Pastor went to the raincoat man and dragged him to his feet. Fontaine stopped kicking. The street was suddenly very quiet. I got to my hands and knees and started to crawl toward them. I said, "Hey!"

Another blank.

I was being propped against a wall. I got my eyes open and looked at Jeff Pastor. He said, "You hurt bad?"

"I'm dead," I said.

I gazed beyond his shoulder. The raincoat man had blood all over his face, but I recognised him. It was Paul Taylor. He looked as though he was seeing a ghost.

I couldn't think of anything to say to him, so I rolled my head and gazed along the street to where Fontaine was lying. I heard the car.

It was a homing Cadillac. It came sweeping round the corner, heading for wherever it was going. It ran over Fontaine.

I passed out.

28

The sunshine came brightly through the window. I was propped against two pillows with the stitches in my scalp tugging and the plaster around my shoulder weighing a ton. I was reasonably happy all the same.

I was holding Ginny's hand.

I said, "The guy who got burned up was the English sailor."

At the other side of the bed Jeff Pastor shifted uncomfortably on his chair. "We'd have got around eventually to proper identification," he said. "Be sure of that. I admit it's easier now we've picked up this Charlie guy, this Charlie Buller. All we had to do was withhold his narcotics for two days. He squealed his head off. He claims the Englishman was already shot dead in the desert. By accident. He burned the body because he didn't want it identified in case the cops could trace connections. It was pure bad luck we thought it was Tony Fontaine."

"Bad luck for whom?"

"Maybe you got a right to gripe. It was a natural mistake on the face of it. Mr. Buller's going to have a tough time in court though, proving the body was dead when he put the match to it."

"We're all going to have a tough time in court," I said.

"Not so very. The Mexican cops are a good crowd. I don't know their methods, but they've picked up this Burkhardt guy along with a bunch of others and sweated a confession out of them. We ourselves have Mr. Buller and Mr. Jordan. Mr. Jordan can't talk yet. His jaw's broken in five places."

"He went home with the milk," Ginny said.

She lit cigarettes all round and stuck one in my mouth. I said, "What about Esmollet?"

"Smollet. Esmollet is the Mexican way of pronouncing it. You spelled his name wrong. That's why I couldn't trace him right away after your phone call. He was well-enough known to be traced right away. The best counterfeiter in the business and the biggest double-crosser. The FBI was closing in a year ago when he skipped to Mexico. There wasn't enough evidence for an extradition and the Feds had to be content with warning the authorities in Mexico. The Mexicans were watching him."

"He knew it."

"Everybody knew it. The way Kresnik knew we were watching him this end. There was no connection between the two surveillances, but it explains why they had to take such elaborate precautions. Anyone seen even nodding to Smollet would have been followed every inch of the way on any journey in the direction of the border. And all Kresnik's acquaintances were being watched this end. Except those above suspicion, like you."

"Thanks," I said.

Ginny squeezed my hand. "Don't get all bitter and twisted, sonny."

Pastor said, "In Mexico they picked on this corruptible English sailor who was making the trip up here. At this end they selected you. You were to keep the case in your apartment until such time as Kresnik or one of his boys could be sure of being without a shadow. Only your wife and Fontaine puckered the whole works. They left most of the dough at the Flamenco to be picked up later, took enough for a good time and skipped over the border. To Mexico. Hard luck on them."

"Hard luck on the couple at the Flamenco," I said. "Thinking Fontaine was dead, then he turns up after all and collects the money. What happens to the couple?"

"We're relying on your evidence."

"Count me out."

A spasm of irritation twitched over Pastor's face. "And your father-in-law?"

"He's dead. We can leave him out altogether."

"After what he tried to do to you?" The irritation came out into the open. "He phoned his daughter to bring the money back and at the same time was still sending Kresnik after you. That's how they picked you up in Campello."

I said, "Without that his daughter wouldn't have died."

We sobered up on it for a minute.

Pastor said, "The boys in Mexico weren't so bright. Little Smollet's history of double-cross counted against him. He was in Campello that night purely by accident, to do a little gambling. His pals made an imaginative jump and thought he'd made a deal with you. They'd have shot him any way."

"He had pretty hands," I said.

"He made pretty notes," Pastor said. "Even the boys at the Treasury had a tough time identifying them."

Ginny said, "Then how did the cops get on to Fontaine?"

"Kresnik's double-cross," I said. "His method of stopping distribution. He wasn't going to tell Sam Alford about it. He let Alford believe it was really Fontaine who burned in the car, just to throw him farther off the track. Kresnik wanted all the dough for himself, the same as my father-in-law. He leaked a list of some of the serial numbers."

Pastor nodded. "Through a pal he had in high places. The pal is no longer in so high a place. The serial numbers were rushed to the Treasury and the T-men blanketed the whole country. The idea being that the pal was to check where they turned up and Kresnik would have a trail to follow to collect the rest. Risky, but he had no other remedy. He was dead broke."

"So was my father-in-law. Now they're both just dead."

Pastor looked at a notebook. "We found the place Alford hired the car. The mileage checks. In his bedroom we found the gun used to shoot Kresnik. Fingerprints all over it. Fingerprints all over the place in the mountains. The case needn't even reach the newspapers."

He blinked a couple of times. "The newspapers are trying like hell to reach you."

"I know. I'm ready."

"All you need do is tell the truth. That as a lawyer and a public-spirited citizen you collected the suitcase in the first place because you wanted proof of Kresnik's crookedness."

"That I was being blackmailed because I gave a hundred bucks to an old man named Lopez."

"I've seen Lopez. Claims he doesn't remember a thing about it."

We stared at one another. Ginny's hand tightened again.

"Okay," Pastor said flatly. "What about Paul Taylor?"

"What about him?"

"I don't like anonymous letters. I've received too many myself. That's why I took the case over when you could no longer prevent me. Paul Taylor made a statement down at headquarters when he was trying to do you dirt. He signed it. The mystery was solved. No man can disguise his handwriting that much."

Jeff Pastor paused. "The guy hates you."

"I know."

"When he heard from his wife that you were back in town he set out to look for you. The only conceivable place he thought you might go was your father-in-law's house. He set himself to watch. He didn't know I was across the road watching him."

"Glad you were," I said.

"Fontaine came running out of the gate. He had his head down. Taylor shot him. Think that over. Think hard. Taylor thought it was you."

"Fontaine was wearing one of my suits," I said. "Taylor did me a good turn. Was he badly hurt?"

"Shot in the leg. The blood on his face was where he hurt himself when he fell over."

"If you're counting on my evidence against him, don't!"

"How damned stupid can you get?" Pastor said contemptuously. "Come out of that lily-garden."

"No." I looked at Ginny. "It smells too good."

Pastor said, "Gah!"

A nurse put her bright blonde head around the door. "Mr. Race, a man insists on seeing you."

"Newspaper?"

"I don't think so. A Mexican."

"Let him in."

Garcia entered very slowly, a huge bunch of flowers in his hand and a box of candy under his arm. He stood at the foot of the bed and looked at me. That went on for a minute. Then he started to cry. He didn't say anything, he just cried.

After a while Ginny cried. Then I joined in.

Pastor left in disgust.

The following day Ginny visited the druggist in Sawchuck. She claims she had a wonderful time. That's hard to imagine in Sawchuck, but she did bring the money back.

THE END

Cry Wolfram

by Douglas Sanderson

For Eileen and Tom

1

The night outside was filled with sea-sounds and the smell of flowers. The Regatta Club was full of cigarette smoke and expensive perfumes with an underwaft of perspiration. There was a band playing French jazz, loud but good, and a big-chested girl at the microphone singing loud but not good. The dancing couples were crammed hard together and an aerial view of the floor would have looked like a snood of boiling porridge.

It was two o'clock in the morning. I should not have been there.

My new acquaintance was called Sedelquist. He had made undue efforts to be friendly, we had drunk much liquor and he had paid for it all. I wondered what his game was. He was now philosophising that the world's troubles were caused by people holding opinions not based on their personal experience. A few minutes more and he would be talking Kierkegaard and Jean Paul Sartre. His face was red and his light grey eyes goggling from booze. My own eyes were about to fall out. I nodded agreement to everything he said. I wasn't really listening. I was glaring at Julie and trying to make her turn her head.

She did not.

At a table for eight near the door a big man slapped a small man's face. A short clawy brawl started. No one paid attention because the brawlers were only film people arrived ten days ago and soon to be gone. The regular habitués descended nightly from their villas, looking for juicier scandals involving members of their own set. When they stopped discussing money there was little else to talk about.

The brawl petered out. The participants kissed one another upon the cheek.

"And your father?" Sedelquist asked kindly.

I brought him into focus. A big amiable English-speaking Swede such as you find all over Europe. Like most of his nation he had looked suicidally miserable after five drinks. Like most of them he could probably drink any other nationality clean under the table. He was trying to do that with me. He had got drunk himself. I was no better.

"My father is dead," I said.

He shook his head sadly. "But you have Mr. Craddock. I hear he is a fine old man."

I said, "That's a novel view."

"I should like to meet Mr. Craddock. Perhaps you will introduce me." Sedelquist took another long slug of whisky and it made his English slip a little. "I like to meet him varry moch," he said.

"Why?"

"Because I like fine old men."

He boomed with laughter. We had a private joke, but I wasn't in on it. He said,

"But it may not be necessary. In a few days we shall know."

"You might. I won't."

The grey eyes crinkled. He banged down the glass and slopped the drink and I had to jump back. He was as drunk as a man can get.

"You!" he chuckled, and amiably punched my arm and nearly broke it. He got to his feet. "Wait here. I go to be sick."

He went.

Drums thudded. Inspired dancers thrust more fiercely. The girl at the microphone reached for a triumphant E, arrived at something like C, the bandleader smiled at her and I thought he was probably sleeping with her. That made me glare again at Julie.

She was laughing happily and her silver-blonde head was tilted. She was beautiful and yielding and it was killing me to see her happen to someone else. I didn't know who he was. But I hated him.

He was the athletic manly type that looks as if it never drinks. He was as blonde as Julie, well-groomed, darkly tanned, taller than I, handsomer and richer. He could not have been poorer. He was probably the reason she had not kept our date. He was certainly the reason she had made signs that I must not speak to her.

I tried to murder him by will-power. I talked to myself about primped-up goddam frog Frenchmen. I felt I was playing des Griex to her Manon and decided to speak to her when they got off the floor whatever trouble it caused. Then she turned him. She looked straight at me. She acknowledged my fierce signals with a wink of assent.

The world was paper, the sea was ink and the Universe was writing me a love letter. Suave men swirled dancing by with their gay young women, and black-tinted blue-rinsed ladies got closer to their professional young men. I loved them all, even the couples actually married. They all had a right to live. Brass blared and cymbals clashed, the mass convulsed and bubbled. Joy!

The waiter tapped my shoulder.

"Another phone call, Mr. Molson."

"I am not here."

"I said you were."

"I am unobtainable."

He shrugged, bored, and struggled off through the tables. The music jarred to a stop on a screech of saxophones. All the dancers unglued themselves. I stood up and forged for the outside.

In the packed bar I waved to the bartender. I crushed through the press and out the french doors. The terrace was quiet, dark almost deserted, the scented night soft and April, the sea whispering an explanation why people mortgage their souls to live on the French Riviera. I crossed to the dim head of the stone stairway, lit a cigarette, leaned against the balustrade. A flowering creeper was under my hand and somewhere a night bird singing.

'*O Natura!*' as Leopardi once said. 'Nature, why do you not fulfill what you promised earlier? Why do you deceive your children?' But I was undeceived again and now almost fulfilled. When the linked couple murmured across the terrace and descended the stone stairway to the sand I accompanied them in spirit. I swayed to an unheard waltz. Euphoria surged and I went from Leopardi to Campion and murmured, 'There is a garden in her face where roses and white lilies grow.' I had it bad.

She came.

She stood at the threshold, head lifted and hair shining like snared moonlight. She glided across the terrace, a small bright torch, every motion dilating her beauty's flame. I took a stiff half-step forward and smelled her perfume. Then she was beside me. I put out my arms.

"No," she hissed. "What do you want?"

The reality was hard. "Why didn't you keep our date?" I snapped.

"I couldn't. Hush!"

Sedelquist staggered across the terrace and around the corner toward the car park.

"I must go back," she said. "Roger thinks I'm powdering my nose."

"Who's Roger?"

"A guest. He arrived this morning. I'm stuck with him."

"Come down here and explain to me."

"I can't."

"I'll make a scene."

"Johnny, please!"

I could not stop an ocean. I put an arm tight around her waist and led her resisting down the stairs. The sand crumbled under our feet. I dragged her on. The shadows between the pine trees were long and dark. The sea was singing; the night a laving warmth.

I crushed her to me and found her mouth, and then she no longer tried to unseal herself. We had the habit. Her will disappeared. She ceased to struggle and we stood tight together and the night swayed around us.

"I must go back."

"No."

"I must."

"No."

Our whispers were nothing against the sighing sea. We stopped talking. In a little while there was no more blissful couple from the Straits of Messina to the Straits of Gibraltar.

2

I lay with hands behind my head and the sand pressing grittily into my knuckles. The fever had passed. I could think in a straight line.

"Tell me about Roger Lascelles."

"A friend of my brother. He arrived unexpectedly."

"Why do I have to stay out of the way?"

"Johnny, you're drunk."

"Don't dodge."

"You have no right to ask questions."

"I have," I said. "I'm in love with you."

The starlight was caught in her eyes. She was cross-legged, smoothing her short bright hair, a hamadryad, very poised, very lovely.

"What is your job with Craddock?"

"What?" I said. "Listen. I've just told you I love you."

"I'm trying to be practical. What's your job?"

"I don't know."

"You draw a wage for doing nothing?"

"In five weeks I've translated six letters. He says he's grooming me and the work comes later. He won't answer questions. He's old and cantankerous."

"He's a crook," she said.

"Who told you, your brother?"

She smoothed lipstick with the tip of her little finger. "Does he mention my brother?"

"Should he?"

"Perhaps," she said. "Doesn't he confide in you at all?"

"Are you trying to check my prospects?"

I pushed myself to a sitting position. "I have no prospects. When I've earned enough money from Craddock I shall go back to the Sorbonne and study some more."

"Aren't you a little old for that?"

"It's what I want," I said. Then I was quiet.

The man was approaching slowly through the trees. I couldn't see him and the sand muffled footfalls, but he was whistling something tuneless and dirgy.

"Please get up," Julie said quietly.

"Because it may be Roger? Good. We'll have a showdown."

The whistling drew nearer. She was already standing. She looked tense. "Please, Johnny."

"Don't panic. I can do it just as well on my feet." I stood beside her. I started to put an arm around her shoulders. She avoided me.

"I don't want one."

"What?"

"A showdown," she said. "I need to think. We must not see one another for a while."

"Why not?"

"Please."

"Stop saying please." I was seeing her all at once through a plate-glass window; a beautiful desirable model unattainable because I lacked the price. I said, "What makes Lascelles important?"

"I've known him all my life. He's a friend of my brother. He might tell about us."

"Also you're both rich."

"Yes."

"And it might be nice to marry him?"

"Don't be silly."

"What will you do if he asks you?"

She snapped, "Oh go away, you bore me!"

I said, "You bitch."

I grabbed her shoulders. She tried to free herself. We stood struggling and panting with our feet slipping in the sand. She slammed me in the face.

It rocked me. We drew apart. We stared taut like angry animals and the whistling stopped and Louise Morgan came out from between the trees.

There was a pale little smile etched in wood on her face. She cleared her throat and said, "Hello, Miss Chirac," and the smile twitched. "Hello, John," she said, "I drove down for you. Mr. Craddock has had another attack."

We stood unspeaking and unmoving. The embarrassment dropped like a blanket.

"A bad attack." Louise Morgan's voice had gone croaky. "He's decided to drive to Paris in the morning to see the specialist. He wants you with him. I thought you had best get some sleep."

The silence fell again, long, scent-laden and excruciating. Music wafted down from the club on a breath of breeze.

"Well," Julie said. "Thanks so much for the walk, John. I must get back."

We shuffled an uncertain moment. We walked away from the sea with Julie in front and Louise Morgan beside me still branded with her wooden little smile. We crossed the open sand, reached the steps, hesitated again. We looked to the terrace and then we were searching one another's faces. Roger Lascelles was sitting on the balustrade above us with a drink in his hand.

He rose from his seat. We went up.

There were others on the terrace now, a little crowd. They tightened with attention. We came to a halt, a knot jumped into my stomach, I looked directly into Lascelles eyes and waited. I couldn't hit him first.

He had a good face. All the appearances of the upright man, the regular guy, the one who does not deserve the dirty tricks. He looked away from me and spoke politely. His voice was so soft as to be almost inaudible. He said, "Julie, where were you?"

"Hello, Roger." She gave a timid smile, a nervous half-shrug and started to walk away. His nostrils flared. He reached a quick hand and caught her. "My dear, I asked you where you were."

She was turned from him, motionless, the timid smile fading from her lips. Louise Morgan said much too loudly, "Miss Chirac and Mr. Molson and I were at the bottom of the stairs. Smoking a cigarette."

"Oh," he whispered. "I see. That will be where she got the sand on her back."

His wrist jerked. The drink shot into my eyes. The glass dropped and shattered and I stood there wet-faced and squinting and I was still unable to hit him first.

He hit me.

The fist glanced off my cheek. We clinched. We met with too much force and fell over. The crowd poured from the bar, the humiliation was complete, we went rolling and squirming back over back across the terrace.

I was stronger than he, and sober could have beaten him. As it was, we were too well matched. We made half-punches and got scuffed. We clawed girlishly. We rose to our feet, stumbled, clamped together and fell a second time. The feet of the watchers danced around us, someone laughed, we rolled and hit the balustrade in a knot and got up. That was all. The fight was over. Louise Morgan was pressing between us.

We were glaring, unheroic and panting, a hand each on the stone rail. The faces in the watching crowd were waxen with delighted expectancy. Mr. Lanvin came fluttering from the bar with a delicate waving of plump hands. Mr. Lanvin was the proprietor. One or two sighed with appreciation.

Customers were usually permitted to brawl themselves out, particularly on the terrace. Lascelles, I guess, was too well-known and important, too rich and well-connected. I was merely an employee at one of the local big houses. I saw who was to be the culprit.

So solicitously sorry, dear sir. Perhaps Mr. Lascelles would like the police called. It was a toffy club, but few clients received this much deference. Some decided to enjoy vicarious prestige. Lips curled, eyes looked down noses, I was that drunken American who turns up and ruins civilised everything. I looked around for Julie. She was gone.

"Take me home, please, Mr. Molson," Louise Morgan said clearly. She grasped my arm and I allowed myself to be led. We walked around the building toward the car park. The hum broke out behind us. Somebody laughed loud and derisive and I was the small boy with wet pants being led out of company by his nurse.

"Let go!" I snarled. I shook off her grip. The vehicles were gleaming under the stars and the world was rocking. I turned to go back, the footsteps came running, and there was Lascelles again, his hands in his pockets. He stopped. He forced a thin smile. He said, "Mr. Molson."

I hit him.

I drew it from right back in the next province. It hurt my knuckles and jarred clear up my arm. He gasped. His head jerked and I thought I had broken his neck. He stood a split second with his eyes closed, lifted his shoulders, moaned, and crumpled to the ground like a pole-axed bull. I stood and looked down at him.

I felt terrible.

"You dirty coward," Louise Morgan said coldly. It burned like pitch. I took her by the arm and led her to the car. "You coward," she said and changed to savage English. "You coward and fool. All to satisfy your rotten desires with that filthy little creature."

"Shut up!"

We got in the car. I was too drunk to drive, but I pushed her from behind the wheel. We shot through the gate and in the headlights I saw Sedelquist being sick against a tree.

3

"Drive more carefully!" she said

The car was taking the curves of the cliff road like a super-charged serpent. I pulled up altogether, not to please her but to light a cigarette in safety. My pores were trying to open, my skin prickled, I was still very drunk. The atmosphere between us was taut as a strung bow.

"You got the Mercedes tonight," I said, trying to ease the strain.

"It was on the driveway. He was about to go out when the attack came."

I had known. The old man took a drive at the same hour each night to help his insomnia. Always in the Mercedes. He suffered insomnia along with every other psychosomatic ailment in the book. I said, "How did you know where I was?"

"I phoned. Then I came. The barman told me you were outside somewhere. I found you."

Her face twisted. It was a pretty face, but with too much prim and properness, too heavy a coating of piety. I said, "I didn't know you could whistle."

Her lips moved a few times. "You filthy disgusting creature."

"All right," I said, "you saw us. You walked away and came back whistling to give us warning. Very polite of you. Now I'll tell you a secret. People all over the world do that. Your parents did it to get you. You should try it some time. It might change your prudish outlook."

She sat like a statue. The windows were open. Far below at the foot of the cliff the sea sibilated like sand on glass. Spring filled the night and Julie was an ache.

I had to get to the house, telephone to her, apologise. I reached for the clutch.

"Wait!"

Louise Morgan offered me a frozen profile. She was suffering about something. She said, "Just a moment. I'm going to stick my neck out."

"About what?"

"You've been here four weeks. I've been here off and on with Mr. Craddock for four years. You're being deceived."

I knew exactly where we were going. I wanted to shut her up. The subject was too overwhelmingly important to me. "All right," I said, "let's have it. Who is Roger Lascelles?"

"He comes down to stay with them two or three times a year. It isn't with him she's deceiving you. He's only one. She's had all the locals. She picked you because you still rate as a visitor."

"What pretty little thoughts you have for a convent girl!"

"She'll drop you when a new visitor appears. She will make it lingering and unpleasant. She's sadistic."

"And who did she steal from you?"

"Be clever if you wish. You think you know what you're doing. But everyone else knows what you're doing. I should imagine someone dropped a hint to Lascelles tonight and outraged his vanity. Hence the scene."

"Or he might be in love with her," I said. "He might want to marry her."

"No. He's a friend of the brother, but a Lascelles does not marry a Julie Chirac. She's notorious."

"And much prettier than you," I said. "What else did you learn at convent? I begin to understand why people say you're Craddock's mistress."

"People? Do you mean Julie Chirac? I wouldn't pay too much attention. I overheard one of the chauffeurs saying that you are the object of affection. Mr. Craddock has never married. The chauffeur remarked on how you were picked up in Paris."

"Other people remark on how your education was paid for in the United States. And that Craddock got you an American passport."

She said, "Very well. I'll tell you about that, to avoid any misunderstanding between fellow-workers." She turned to me for the first time. Her eyes were expressionless and she looked rather like a young schoolmistress. She said, "When I was twelve years old Mr. Craddock came over to France and created one of his biggest mergers. My father, who was not quite so unscrupulous, got caught in the squeeze. He was responsible to his stock-holders and could not support the strain. He went into the library one night and put a sporting rifle in his mouth. It blew the top of his head off."

"Louise, that's enough."

She ignored me. She continued in the same instructional tone. "I was on summer vacation. From the convent. I was the one who discovered my father and I giggled for hours about it. Mr. Craddock did not even see him, but he wept.

Mr. Craddock had a substitute for conscience even in those days, even before he went the whole hog and got religion. He had to make amends to himself. He did it by financing my education in the United States. When my mother died he offered me this job as secretary. He got me an American passport to make me more portable. I am fluent in French and English, I serve him well, he pays me well. Now shall we go?"

The car slid forward. I stepped on the gas. I could not understand why she had told me. I was shocked. In my pre-employment inquiries about Craddock there had been not a whisper of her father. It reflected on my ability to find things out. I said, "I'm sorry. I didn't particularly want to hear that."

"It will obviate any misunderstandings about my position."

"You must hate him."

"No. But he brings out the un-Christian in me. When he lies on the floor and suffocates, I almost enjoy it. It has nothing to do with my father; I recovered from that ages ago. I think I just do not like Mr. Craddock. He is a living falsity."

"Then leave."

"And go where? He has been too much of my life. I shall escape when he dies."

The night blew at the windows. The cliff road twisted and the rockface hissed at us on every curve. She said, "Don't drive so fast."

"What caused tonight's attack? Cables?"

"Something quite new. A prowler. I have waited six months for a fresh reason, and a prowler is original. Nobody saw him except Mr. Craddock. Nobody doubts his word because nobody dares. He was up in his room, reading his favourite book of prayer, preparing for the nightly drive. He glanced down into the garden and there was the prowler. There is an added touch. The starlight gleamed on a gun."

"Nonsense."

"Yes, but original. The servants scoured the grounds with the dogs and found nothing. No matter. Mr. Craddock had achieved his purpose. Mr. Craddock was lying on the bedroom floor, the centre of the Universe, blue in the face and howling for you, of course, the apple of his eye. In between gasps I suspect he was happy. I once investigated the question of hysterical asthma."

The night hummed past us. The headlights jumped into the darkness beyond the unfenced road. She said, "And yet, at the same time, I know he is a poor old sick man with a bad conscience. I should be praying for him."

"You're tired."

"I'm not a very nice person," she said, and we hissed around the bend.

The nearside back wheel came off.

The car jumped as if a hammer had hit it. It bucked like a mad Brahma bull and started to scream and swung sideways in its own length. I slammed hard over the wheel. We jumped nose first off the road and went bucketing down the slope and Louise was shouting.

It was very quick. I flung gasping upright and stood my whole weight on the brake. We slithered on toward the edge. I saw the shimmering sea. I wrenched open the door and tried to drag her, but her hands tightened on the wheel in terror and stuck fast.

I hit her wrists. I heaved maniacally and for a moment we hung in nothing. Then we hit the shale in a twisting heap of arms and legs. I was trying to dig in with my feet. I rolled on top of her.

We slewed sideways. The car plunged and hit the sea far below. We were still sliding. We rolled, my throat cried out, I clouted my head and then my bones melted. I was off in a deep sleep.

I recited in entirety Shakespeare's Thus With A Kiss I Die. I told Death I was his Friend by courtesy of Beddoes. I wept a little over the Athlete Dying Young, killed by Mr. Housman, then I opened my eyes.

I was still on top of Louise Morgan. I rolled away. I lay a while again.

"Louise," I said. "Louise."

Her lids fluttered, her eyes opened, she lay a moment bewildered. She started to get dazedly to her feet and I helped her upright. We stared blankly at one another, down at the sea and up at the road. Then she drew her hand very far back and hit me hard across the face.

She said, "You filthy beast!"

"What?"

"I know what you were trying to do."

"What's this?"

She started by herself, stumbling up the slope. I stood a deluded moment, trying to orientate myself, then I scrambled after her and got an arm around her waist. We heaved, dragged, slid our way up to the road again. We stood there on the asphalt, floating in the vague. I said, "You hurt?"

"No. No. What happened?"

"Neither am I."

"I told you not to drive so fast."

"That's right," I said. "The back wheel came off."

"You took no notice of me."

"It did," I said. "It came off."

"You drunkard!"

I looked along the road. Nothing. I walked to the edge and peered down. Nothing again. The wheel had rolled after the car. Maybe I had imagined it. I said, "It came off. The wheel!"

"Don't shout. Don't be ridiculous. Where is it?"

"I don't know. Maybe there was a rock in the road. You sure you're not hurt?"

"I'm perfectly all right, thank you."

"Why did you hit me?"

"Are you quite mad? I didn't hit you."

"Down there."

"Where?"

"Leave it! Let's get to the house. Come on!"

We limped along the road. A breeze was rising. We had about a mile to walk.

She said, "I wouldn't tell Mr. Craddock yet. You're in enough trouble, sneaking out tonight."

"He'll have to know about the Mercedes."

"Please yourself. He'll have another attack."

"Was the car insured?"

"Of course. That's part of my duty as a secretary."

"You needn't snap about it."

"What do you expect? After almost killing me with your drunken driving."

"Oh, shut up!"

She said contemptuously, "You are the most nauseating person I have ever met."

We trudged along the cliff edge in silence.

4

The servant came twice to the bedroom to say that Craddock wanted me immediately. I replied each time that I'd be right along. I stayed with a drink at my elbow and a telephone in my hand. I was all right except for a few aches. Maybe the bruises would develop later.

They had told me three times already that Julie was no longer at the Club. This time the waiter said that everyone had gone home and I was forced to believe him: there were no longer any background noises. I sat gnawing my thumbnail. She had told me never to call the house because of her brother, who must not know about us. Her brother was strict, starchy and certain to make difficulties.

She said her defiance of him proved her love for me. That may have been true. It certainly added an extra intimacy to our relationship. But he had to know some time, and the time was now. I could not live through the night without speaking to her. I stuck my finger in the dial.

The door burst open behind me. Craddock crashed in.

He was flamingly angry. He stared down his long pitted nose with bitter satisfaction. "Well?" he snapped. "I'm your employer, I pay you, I sent for you twice. I had a bad attack tonight and might have died. You were supposed to be looking after me. Instead you were tom-catting around with Chirac's strumpet sister down at that brothel of a club."

I replaced the phone. "How Louise does chatter!"

"Louise does nothing but make excuses for you. I've known about the Chirac tart this past fortnight. If you have to satisfy your dirty lusts find something better than—"

"No!" I said. That's enough!"

Maybe he got Puritanism with religion, or maybe he always had it. He talked of sex as the W.C.T.U. talks of drink, with loathing and disgust. It revolted him. Perhaps age and inability were the causes. I don't know. I said, "Shut right up. I don't want to hear from you."

He closed the door with a black flip of his hand. His eyes glittered. Yet in a curious way I could see he liked me talking rough to him. He crossed the room and sat on the bed and in the clearer light his illness was too apparent. He was a sick and ancient tortoise, as haggard as death and as old. His eyes were mica in a mottled face. For the hundredth time in a few weeks I felt an enormous surge of sympathy.

"It's not worth upsetting yourself about," I said.

"I know. Forget it."

He lay back on the pillow, studying me silently from under lowered lids. He could never stay angry with me and he didn't now. His face changed. It went sloppy. These were the times when I earned my wages.

"John," he said, "you get away with murder because I'm fond of you. I've been fond of you since the first moment I saw you. You remember that?"

I remembered it. Notre Dame Cathedral in Paris. And me praying for money to appear from somewhere so that I could continue my studies. The Sorbonne has seventy thousand students. Thirty thousand have to find rooms in Paris. Landladies capitalize and my backlog had disappeared through having to pay sixty a month for high-priced squalor down by the Odeon. In Notre Dame I was delivering a "Dear God, please send me...."

An old man keeled from a pew and lay on the floor and wheezed....

Craddock.

Anyone would have done it. I picked him up and unlocked his tongue from his teeth. I took him back to his hotel after being sure he had enough money to pay the cab. Then he offered me the job. His attacks since then had become more frequent.

I said, "I remember."

"Yes." He was using his special soap-opera voice. "Not only liked you, but trusted you. There was evidence of the Divine Hand the way you appeared in that church. You looked after me, John. The first time in my life anyone ever showed me disinterested sympathy. I'll always be grateful."

If he talked like this to others, no wonder about the chauffeur. But I doubted it. I had made inquiries about Mr. Joseph P. Craddock before accepting his job. Mr. Craddock was a supremely unloved hard case with no reputation for soft words or soft anything else.

He moved on the bed and closed his eyes. He said, "You fancy yourself in love with this little tramp?"

"None of your business."

"Wrong. Everything about you is my business. In God's eyes we are all responsible one for another. Am I my brother's keeper? The answer is automatically and unavoidably, Yes! Written to your sister lately?"

"Yesterday."

"She all right?"

"Thanks, yes."

"I guess she misses you. Well, her loss is my gain. You're going to be a lot of use to me in the future, son, once you've learned the ropes. You're exactly the right type. You fear God, know where you're going and love money. And there's a great big streak of rottenness in you, just like I've got."

"Do these compliments strain you at all?"

"Face it, my boy. You hate it and yet it helps you. It means you'll have to fight consciously for your salvation, and that's the best way to go about it."

He lay right back and put his feet up. His breathing was spasmodic. He was feeling frail, in need of a little more comfort and he was capable of administering it himself.

"I may be an old man," he said, "but I don't whine. Why should I? I've got trust now that God is looking after me. God loves everybody. He wouldn't let anything bad happen to a man who loves Him as much as I do."

It was excruciating, especially considering his reputation in Paris. I said, "It must be a comfort."

"Louise tell you what happened tonight?"

"Something about a prowler."

"You should have been here to look after me. It's part of your job. You're young and strong." He coughed, jerking the mottles of his face to fiercer life. He was an extremely sick man. He said, "Yes, I've made a lot of enemies in my life. God forgives, but man doesn't. You have to be near me always, to protect me."

At the far end of the landing his private phone began ringing in his room.

"Get it!" He half rose and sank back again. "Get it or they'll ring off before I get there." His thin lips curled. He was a querulous doddering ancient. "Who is it? I'm not expecting anyone. I'm coming after you. Hang on till I arrive."

He swung his feet to the floor. I went swiftly out and around the curve of the long landing to the other bedroom. I lifted the phone beside his bed.

"Hello?"

"Craddock?"

"Yes."

The man was standing very close to the mouthpiece. The very British accent was whispering but loud.

"Parker here. Listen carefully, Mr. Craddock. A C.P.A. warrant was issued a few minutes ago. They are trying for me and will soon be after you. I'm leaving. I'll contact you. The others can take their chance."

"Wait!"

"For C.P.A.? My dear sir! There is not a soul to say a word in our defence.

Nothing has come through on the wolfram option. Without that we have not enough weight to carry us through the feeblest crisis. You will now, I suppose, despair."

"No."

"Bully for you, Mr. Craddock, for I have another little pointer. If, that is, we are not too late."

He stopped. Five long seconds passed. He said, "Have you nothing to remark, Mr. Craddock?"

"Yes," I said. "I'm not Mr. Craddock."

The phone went dead.

I rattled the cradle. Nothing. I listened. No sound of Craddock approaching. I dropped the phone and flew back around the landing like a bat. My room was in darkness.

"Don't touch the light," he hissed

He was over by the french windows, peering down into the garden, his profile sharp against the curtaining. "Another one," he whispered. "Get a gun."

I moved beside him.

Over the sea beyond the garden dawn was creeping into the sky. The blonde hair of the man below shone vivid in the dark grey light, and he was making no attempt at concealment. I eased the old man aside. 1 opened the windows, stepped on to the balcony and all of Southern France was in the early morning air.

I called, "You want something?"

He tilted back his head. For a moment he did not speak. "Yes," he said, "I have come to apologise. May I enter?"

He was my rival: I disliked him. "Some other time," I said. "I'm busy. Come after breakfast."

"I swear I shall not start fighting again."

"You think I'm scared? Push off before they set the dogs on you."

I stepped back inside and shut the windows.

"Who's that?"

"Someone named Lascelles. He's staying with Chirac."

"That explains it," the old man panted. "He was the prowler here before."

"He was not the prowler here before. Lascelles was in the Regatta Club all evening."

The man below lifted a hand, dropped it hopelessly, turned around and went slowly down the drive to the main gate. I watched him out to the road. I went across and switched on the light. The old man sank on the bed again.

"Lascelles," he said. "Perfumes. He might have some sort of deal with Chirac."

"I wouldn't know. And I wouldn't recognise Chirac if I saw him."

"He sends his sister along to pump you. But you don't know anything yet."

"And he doesn't know about his sister. What would she pump me about?"

"What does she talk about?"

"What is C.P.A.?"

"Jesus Christ!"

He shot bolt upright to his feet. I felt like Red Riding Hood when the wolf jumped out of her granny's bed. He stood there shaking and his tremor was neither illness nor religion. He said, "Corrupt Practices Act. Bribery of public servants. So they've caught up with him."

His eyes lit up like bonfires of joy. He rubbed his cold hands in glee. "They'll crucify the bastard," he said jubilantly. "Aha! Chirac! Big time financier. Legitimate game for everyone in this country; public, politicians, police, press, everybody. They'll slaughter him. They'll smash him to little pieces. The politicians will smash hardest to save themselves from exposure."

He hugged his ribs. He was out of control. "Aha! Chirac. Aha! Finished! They'll wipe him out. Ahahaha!"

"You," I said. "Not Chirac."

His eyes opened like two large oysters. His hand flew to his throat and the laughter stopped. He whispered, "What?"

"The phone call was from a man named Parker. A C.P.A. warrant has been issued. Parker is running away."

Craddock said, "You cunning little swinish bastard."

I said, "Gee, thanks."

He sank to the bed and bent over slowly as if all his joints were tortured. "No, son," he said. "I didn't mean it. I didn't." He shook his head like a wet dog. "I trust you, son. I always have. If there had been time for me to marry I should have wanted a boy exactly like you. I didn't mean it."

He put his hands on his knees and leaned all his weight forward. Suddenly he no longer wheezed. He was younger, harder, revivified like a vampire who has just sucked blood. "Parker running away," he said. "Bloody fool. We can crush that warrant by lifting the phone."

His face was set in derisive lines; his voice sharp and confident. "Who dares touch me? There's too much money involved, too many big names. They'll fight like hell for me. They have to fight for me, to conserve the deal. It's in my name. Without me the whole negotiation collapses." He lifted his head. "I got the whip hand."

"I hope so," I said. "There was another part to the message. You didn't get an option on wolfram."

"Ah," he said, and stared at me incredulously. Then he murmured something tiny with his lips and slumped back full length on the bed. His mouth opened. His hands flew to his chest. He sucked in a great agonized breath like a child with whooping cough.

"I'll call a doctor."

"You," he gasped, "wait here."

"You want an injection?"

"Wait!"

He lay perfectly still and gazed at the ceiling. He sank right into the bed. He fought for control, the sweat beaded his forehead, his lips compressed a circle of bloodless white around his mouth, and I stood there admiring him. Out on the landing the big clock ticked like a beaten anvil. His breathing came back to normal by sheer force of will.

He lay expressionless and unmoving like a figure entranced. He said, "All in the hands of God." He intoned it. I knew we were in for a real bout of religion and the embarrassment crept into the muscles of my face.

I said, "You all right now?"

"In the hands of God," he repeated. Then he started.

"John," he said, "I wonder if you have realised what week this is?"

"Yes," I said. "Easter."

"Easter. Even more important than Christmas. We all get a second chance this week, every single one of us, even a man like me. Think deeply on it. Think of salvation. We must be contrite and say our prayers."

He moved. I thought he meant right now and was about to protest. He rose from the bed, walked steadily across the room and gazed down into the garden. When he turned around his palms were flat together and he was wearing an expression like a stained-glass window.

"John," he said. "This place. I don't like it. I never have. It's sinful and corrupt and full of people who have turned their backs on the Holy Face. I want to be somewhere else during a time like Easter, somewhere with a more reverent atmosphere." He moistened his lips. "Is your Spanish fluent?"

"Yes."

"You been to Spain before?"

"Many times."

"Pack your bags. We're going down there now. Immediately."

"Immediately," I said. My stomach wouldn't take it. "You goddamned stinking rotten hypocrite. Immediately of course, because if we don't move quick the French cops will be here with that warrant. Count me out."

He looked at me hard. He clicked his teeth, put his hands to his chest and started to keel. I stayed where I was. He straightened.

"A five hundred dollar bonus," he snapped. "You'll go."

"No."

"For five hundred you will. I know you. Let's figure it out. We'll use the Mercedes."

"I smashed it tonight."

"Then the Cadillac," he said, as if to smash a Mercedes was nothing. "No servants. Just you and me. We're Americans. We're allowed in without a visa and don't have to wait. And Louise."

"You can't travel without a doctor."

"Horse—! I'm not as ill as everyone tries to make out."

He walked to the door, the man they had described in Paris, the Ogre of the Bourse, the present head of Craddock Enterprises, the former head of the Craddock Business Consultancy, the former head of Craddock, Craddock & Craddock, the man rumoured to have won and lost three enormous fortunes, the original hard business nut with no soft centre, the guy who never took No for an answer.

"I'm not going," I said.

"Don't give me that bull. Get moving!"

He snapped his bony fingers at me and tossed his head. He went out and I heard his voice calling along the landing for Louise Morgan. She answered from somewhere downstairs. I shut the door, went to the table and picked up the phone.

Lascelles had been alone. It meant Julie was already taken home. I dialled.

"Yes?" A man's voice.

"Miss Chirac, please."

I waited.

"Yes?" she said.

"John."

"Darling, at this time of the morning. I told you not to. My brother is livid. Now there'll be all sorts of questions."

"I wanted to apologise about the Club. I have to know how you stand with Roger Lascelles."

"Darling, call me tomorrow. Go to bed."

"I can't go to bed. I can't call you tomorrow. I'm going away."

"Oh, Paris. Of course. The Morgan girl said something about it. Call me the moment you get back."

"Not Paris," I said. "And I don't know when I shall be back. I'm going to Spain."

"Spain? What about Mr. Craddock?"

"I'm going with him."

"Oh," she said again. I wanted her to plead with me to stay. I would have done so. She said, "Perhaps it is for the best. I shall know better about my feelings by the time you return."

"I thought you loved me."

"I don't know," she said, and caught her breath. "Oh God, Roger is coming across the garden. He'll talk the rest of the night if I don't escape. Please go on loving me until you come back. Goodbye."

She hung up.

"Goodbye," I said to the cold telephone. Someone tapped the door. Louise Morgan came in."

"I'm sorry to disturb you," she said icily. "Perhaps you can tell me to what part of Spain we are going, what the weather will be like, what clothes I should pack?"

"Ask Craddock."

"I did. He went into the study without answering. I don't even know if this is business or pleasure. He is taking only one briefcase. He is packing it himself."

"With prayer books, medals and missals," I said. "Didn't you know? We have a special appointment. Mr. Craddock is going down to Spain to meet God. Good old God."

She flushed. "The remark is in bad taste."

"And you," I said, "can go and get lost, you nasty little convent prig. Go check the oil in your wise virgin's lamp. Get out of here."

She turned on her heel and went. I heard her footsteps recede along the landing. I stood there like Hamlet in the middle of the room and hovered with indecision.

Five hundred dollars, and perhaps Julie was right that we should be better apart for a while. I went to a drawer and took out the pocket encyclopedia. *Wolfram:* the same as *Tungsten:* symbol W: Atomic number 74: Atomic weight 183.92: used in magnets and high speed tool-steels. A list of sites. Heavy deposits in Spain.

I packed. I put in Valery, Pascal and an Italo Svevo. Away from Julie I might start reading again. I went to the bathroom, shaved, examined myself for bruises, showered, cleaned out my mouth. I came back and put on my one good American-cut lightweight suit. Outside the light was strengthening in the sky. I picked up my case and went downstairs. Louise Morgan was already waiting.

We got the old man in the back of the car and made him comfortable with a rug. He immediately fell asleep with the ability shared, I am told, by all great men. We nosed out on to the road-way. "We'll get breakfast somewhere on the way," I said. "It's a long trip."

Louise Morgan did not answer. She sat stiffly beside me. She clearly never wanted to speak to me again. I stood on the gas and the car went like a song. The curry-smelling pines swished past, the morning sang at the windshield and France was beautiful.

We passed the Regatta Club. The sky had turned from pearly to pink: a great lemon-green glow was spreading in heaven like a promise of eternal things to come. We passed the broad iron gates leading to the big villa among the rock-gardens where Julie lived with her brother. I ached for her. I lit a cigarette but its smoke profaned the morning. I threw it away. I made an imaginary hole in the seat, settled in it, the way a driver does when beginning a long journey.

I saw the crowd ahead. My heart jumped to my throat.

There were three policemen. The rest were fishermen, workmen with bicycles and clipped trousers, a woman with a basket; spread over the road and not expecting traffic at this time of the morning. I pulled up because I had to. I was thinking of C.P.A. I saw the blanketed bundle at the side of the road.

The nearest policeman looked at the Cadillac, approved of it, smiled at me, touched his cap and moved nearer. "Good morning," he said. In the rear-view mirror I saw Craddock wake up.

"Good morning. Accident?"

"Hit and run."

I made the right sounds.

"Must have happened some time in the night," the policeman said. "He's been dead a few hours."

"This is a dangerous road at night. I hope he hasn't left a wife and children."

The policeman shrugged. "About that I don't know. He's a foreigner, staying at the *Miramar*. A Swedish gentleman. Name of Sedelquist."

Craddock leaned forward. "Could you clear the way, officer? We are in a hurry."

"Of course, sir."

The sun came up. The sea was a sparkling blue. We hummed along the fringe of coast toward the Pyrenees and the Spanish frontier.

5

It was the capital city of the province; small as cities go, but pretty. The roads deteriorated at the outskirts, the houses got a bit ramshackle, but toward the city centre were shaded squares with flowers and fountains, elegant little parks, some old and noble architecture. A few of the hundred churches showed traces of the Moorish occupation and may have been converted mosques. On most of their corners blind men with white sticks sold tickets for the national lottery.

The day was white hot and full of sharp-edged shadows. The sun was a brass cauldron in a duck-egg sky and the lion-coloured rocks of the surrounding mountain ranges shimmered in heat. The local inhabitants claimed that their year consisted of two months winter and ten months Hell. It sounds better in Spanish. You juxtapose the words *invierno* and *infierno*.

My lightweight suit was not light enough. I thought with longing a couple of times of the white hell of the Klondike. Then I took a beer. The coldness made beads on the glass.

This was the morning of Good Friday. The whole town was out on foot. No one was working, nothing but bars and cafés were open, there was no wheeled traffic. The crowds strolled down the Ramblas, along the Avenida José Antonio, round the Plaza del Caudillo and back again. They moved at a slow pace that would have reduced me to screaming frustration. This because they had nowhere special to go.

The women were mostly silent. The men gesticulated and exclaimed with passionate animation, spat with medieval abandon and publicly scratched with Spanish unconcern the fork of their pants. The shuff of feet, the buzz of conversation, filled the entire town. The subjects of conversation were identical with those that fill all other Spanish towns.

Scandalous gossip about anyone. Films, because Spaniards are the most passionate filmgoers in the world. Bulls. And football. The unparalleled glories of their home town. The unparalleled sexual prowess of Spanish men. And from there to women.

On the last two subjects they were talking fantasy.

Don Juan is a myth, a dream, a wish-fulfillment. The average Spanish bachelor has little chance of practical sex. There are no brothels any more—shut by the Jesuits, says the whisper—the cruising prostitutes are confined to Madrid, Barcelona and American bases. There is nothing else left. The Spanish girl is under constant vigil and unobtainable without marriage. Pure Woman is so closely guarded from Bestial Man that an engaged couple must not ride in a cab together. And the male has such a strong conception of female virtue that if he has his fiancee before marrying her the marriage will probably not take place.

So up and down the street they walk, making talk as adolescents make drawings on a lavatory wall. From the same motive and with the same innocence. I listened. Spaniards talk so loudly it is difficult not to listen. They were describing as true the things imagined before falling asleep the previous night. But their lies were gracious, interesting and enthusiastic. They enjoyed what they were saying and politely hid their disbelief of the other's man's story. They were all, every one of them, nursing the Spaniard's dream, his wild desire, his glorious hope of one day meeting that easy game, that certain pushover, that notorious sexual free-lunch, A Foreign Woman. In the desire and pursuit of the whole, she is It.

I like Spain. There is a unity about it that allows you to slip back after the first visit almost like going home. The subjects of conversation, the cheerfulness, the courtesy—even the streets have the same names in all the cities. They are called after musicians, writers, poets, the more popular Spanish saints. They are always called after the Caudillo and José Antonio.

The Caudillo is General Franco, Chief of the Spanish State, victor of the Spanish Civil War. José Antonio was the ideological father of modern Spain and the man executed by the Other Side when the war first broke out. He is dead; his name and political beliefs are not. They govern Spain. There is a day of remembrance for him each year. His picture hangs with Franco's on either side of the Cross in all government offices. His words are held sacred; he is now regarded almost as a secular saint. He was Founder and first martyr of the Falange Party. I saw some of its members that morning, and very smart they looked. So did everyone else.

Spaniards make the best-looking and best-dressed crowds in the world. The majority don't have a nickel in their pockets, but the street is their drawing-room and they tog up for it. The gypsies alone were making counterpoint that morning. They moved among the others like mice in corn, dirty, ragged, lithe and sly. They were begging. They pleaded piteously and their eyes were insolent.

There were stalls on the jam-packed Plaza del Caudillo. I bought a Toledo dagger with a damascened handle as a souvenir. I bought a pocket of peanuts in the shell, went into a church, said a prayer, went into a cool bar, had another beer. Then I strolled back toward the hotel and looked again at the people who were looking at the posters.

Holy Week posters with blue and white cowled penitentes, scarlet torches, crimson and cream uplifted images. Studied by women. I stopped by a group of men. They were looking at a bursting bullfight poster of the usual tight-but-tocked torero making a veronica. The corrida was due to take place in two days, four-thirty in the afternoon of Easter Sunday.

Nothing is private in Spain. I listened to what the men were saying. I had heard the same conversation at two other posters.

"Him." A middle-aged man tapped the top name. "This so-called torero. Luis Hernandez."

"Everyone knows," said a younger man with pimples. "I was at school with the bastard. He ran away from this town when he was thirteen and never came back."

"Deserted his mother. Think of the money he makes. And she's still a hawker."

"Too old now to hawk what she used to."

They rocked with laughter.

"What?" a boy said. "What? Tell me!"

"She was a ten-peseta whore in a house on Alvarez Street. Everyone in town poked her except me."

They laughed again and moved on, still talking about it.

I said, "No!" to a begging gypsy kid, turned off José Antonio and went to the hotel. Julie had been right. We were better apart for a while. I was unconcerned to the point of feeling guilty. My only worry was Craddock. A man of seventy-three should never have made the trip. I had thought last night that he was cracking up completely.

Our rooms were on the fourth floor; separate entrances and an adjoining door. Louise was directly across the corridor. I went to my own room, examined the dagger, liked it, locked it away in the suitcase which I hadn't yet unpacked. I washed my face, took a glass of water, cautiously opened the adjoining door in the hope that he'd be asleep.

He wasn't. He looked ghastly.

"Where the hell you been?"

"Down to the bar for a beer."

"God, it's cold," he said, and drew the blankets tight around him. "I'm ill."

"Want an injection?"

"No."

"You shouldn't have stayed up last night for the processions."

"I'll do as I like." His voice softened. "I get something out of being with all these devout people. Think of the weight of those statues. Think of the devotion of the men who carry them all around the town. I wish I was young and strong enough."

He paused. He brooded a moment. He said, "How do you stand with God, John?"

"Will you stop mauling me?"

"You're right. That sort of thing is between a man and his Maker. But you shouldn't talk to me like that, boy. I'm fond of you. You'll have it proved to you in the end. You'll pray for me. Do you pray for me now, John?"

I was saved from it. Someone rapped the door.

The guy in the corridor was boiling in a suit of tweed. He had a clipped military moustache, a long horse face and a vague slim air of diplomacy. He flicked me an appraising glance to see if I was a proposition, the way those guys can't help doing. He wrote me off. I was not his meat. He said in his too-clipped, too-British accent: "Mr. Craddock's room?"

I knew who he was. I said, "Come in, Mr. Parker."

"*Major* Parker." He walked breezily past me. "Hello, sir. Still in bed?"

Craddock said, "What's this?"

I shut the door and leaned against it. Craddock struggled upright, looked at Parker, blinked, looked at me and said, "John, get to your room. Move!"

As you speak to a wayward child. I wasn't having any. I said, "Nice trip from France, Parker?"

"Rather bumpy, thanks for asking. And you?"

Craddock said, "None of your goddamned insolence. Get to your room."

I went. I slammed the door behind me. It was a door with noiseless hinges and I opened it again about half an inch.

The bed creaked. Parker said softly, "We can't fail."

He stopped. There was a silence. The door slammed open so violently it hurt my ear. Parker smiled at me reprovingly and wagged a finger. "Bad boy," he said. "You must not eavesdrop, my dear. That really is too naughty of you."

I crimsoned. I said, "Mr. Craddock, I'm going for a walk." I slammed out through my own room and into the corridor, locked the door and went down to the elevator. I didn't look back because Parker was watching me from Craddock's door. I emerged into the bright street, walked around the block, went up by the service stairs and noiselessly entered my room again. I crossed to the door.

They were whispering too low. I couldn't hear a thing. I strained for ten minutes until my middle-ear was pulsing. Then the door of Craddock's room shut. Down the corridor I heard the elevator whack. In Craddock's room there was a light ting! as the telephone lifted.

I waited a couple of minutes and quietly opened the door again.

6

Craddock was speaking Spanish. He spoke it abominably, but that didn't keep the croaking satisfaction out of his voice.

"Yes," he said, "but the situation has changed since yesterday. I am not offering a bribe this time. I am threatening you. I will reveal my identity when you have reached your decision. That will be on Monday. I shall call you again. Meanwhile, dwell on your position."

He listened a moment. "Do not shout, señor. I do not believe you that it is awarded already. Insufficient time has passed. Anyway, you are the Civil Governor of this province. You have the power to change your mind and withdraw the option. I want it. I shall have it. I refuse to discuss it further. Until Monday. Goodbye, Governor."

He hung up, wheezing with excitement. I gently shut the door. I went down the corridor, down the stairs again and out to the street.

The sun was brilliant, the crowd still moving with the lack of Sturm and Drang that is Spain's blessing until it becomes the mañana complex. I went into the first bar and thumbed the telephone directory. No Civil Governor listed as such. I made inquiries of the barman, then went through the streets at three times the speed of anyone else. They were right and I was wrong. I should have kept my nose out.

The Civil Government building was large, modern and ugly. It filled one side of a deserted square lined with other ugly buildings. There was a fountain in the middle of the square with some benches around it and some beds of brilliant flowers. I went up the broad white front steps and smiled at the guard on the door. Before I could open my mouth he said, "No one working today, señor."

He said it amiably, slowly, carefully and with much pantomime. He knew I was a foreigner. It was my suit. I said, "Gracias," he half-saluted me lazily, I went back down the steps and sat on one of the benches. I had guessed wrong. Craddock had known the Governor's private address. I listened to the tinkle of the fountain and took several deep breaths.

The flowers had no perfume.

Up at the door the guard sprang rigidly to attention, snapped a full salute, and the civilian came out of the main entrance. He descended the steps and went hobbling diagonally across the square. To receive that sort of salute meant importance.

I followed him.

He was a short plump harassed-looking man with not much hair. He resembled one of those odd little generals you meet in Russian literature. He was hatless, had gold-rimmed spectacles, a comfortable paunch and a small chin carried high. This made him look odd because he walked as if his feet hurt.

I followed him at a distance as he limped through four empty side streets. He did not once look round. He turned to the left. The street was wider, directly ahead was a tiny fenced park thick with tall flowering shrubs. I walked on ahead of him and round the park on the right-hand side. Then I hopped over the iron fence.

The place was almost empty. Through the shrubs on the far side a dark pretty nursemaid in a starched white apron was with two little boys who played ball. The only other person in the park was a tall burly man in a grey suit standing with his back to me. He was turned toward the entrance of the park, up on his toes a bit. It was nice to be proved right. The plump man came in.

The other man took a quick look all round, didn't notice me and turned back again. I ran fifteen yards bent double and ducked behind the oleander bush. I didn't have to strain my ears this time. The little boys shouted at their play but they were distant. The other two were a yard away.

"Don Roberto." The tall man had a voice professionally deep and silky. "I could have come to your office, sir."

The plump man said, "I do not want you in my office: Scum!"

The little boys and the ball came into view. They couldn't see me.

"I do not understand. Is there—"

"You had it copied," the plump man hissed.

"No!"

"Do not lie: Liar!"

"Don Roberto, copying was out of the question. Anyone in the country would recognise it."

The nursemaid called the two little boys. The eldest went back to her. The youngest, who was four or less, started kicking the ball toward me. He had chubby little bare legs and could not kick very well.

"Blackmailed me for years on the strength of it," the plump man whispered. "I lifted you from the gutter where you belong. I used my influence to put you where you are. You are a rubbishy lying cheating thief not fit for public office of any sort, but I had to succumb because you are also a blackmailer. I find now even that was a deceit. You told me there was only one copy."

"I spoke the truth," the other man burst out. "I gave it to you after my final promotion. I was there when you burned it."

"Lower your voice. Explain me this. I have received an anonymous phone call. Another blackmailer. Another copy."

The little boy was tongue-out with concentration, slowly scuffing the ball straight at me. It needed the nursemaid to come for him.

"Now consider this," the Civil Governor said. "Someone else knows. Even have you retained a copy you have lost your hold over me. A secret shared is no longer a secret."

"Don Roberto—"

"Silence. Consider this also. I have never liked you. I have made a point of not-

ing every misdemeanour committed by you while in office. I have gathered documentary proof. Mark this well. If the copy is made public and I go down I take
you with me. To the very bottom. You understand?"

The small boy halted before me and smiled, a beautiful child.

"What do you wish me to do?"

The small boy lisped with loud and exquisite politeness, "You want to play
ball with me, señor?"

I laughed aloud. I swept him up in my arms and we laughed together. I swung
him in an arc and went "wheeee" and he gurgled like a dove and closed in again
and flung his arms around my neck. I turned and looked into the face of the tall
man.

He was big for a Spaniard. Low forehead, bone-ridged brow, thick features
and two gold teeth. His eyes were a mauve-brown colour like licked gum-drops.
He was handsome in a brutalised way, and yellow with fear. He said, "Who are
you?"

I smiled. I kissed the little boy on his chubby cheeks and laughed with him.
"No speak," I said. "I foreigner. No speak."

"Documents! Show me your documents!"

"No speak."

"Documentos! Documentos!"

"Oh." I shifted the little boy on to one arm and fished my passport from my
inner pocket. The nursemaid was coming. She wailed, "Juaniiiitoooo." The little plump man had his back to me. I said in English, "You want to play ball
again, pet?" and set the little boy on the ground, picked up the ball and bounced
it. The kid crowed with pleasure. He was delighted to find a pal. The nursemaid
called, "Juaniiiitooooo."

I turned around again. I smiled at the tall man and took my passport from his
hands. I said, "Gracias," with bad pronunciation, lifted the ball, caught it on a
drop-kick, sent it clear across the park and ran after it with the happily squealing kid toddling at my heels. "Juanito!" the nursemaid said reprovingly.

I smiled at her with stiffening muscles. "Nice kid," I said. "Pretty." I swung
him once more for luck, put him down, smiled all round and walked out of the
park. I went down the street and around the corner. Then I skittered.

It was a little past noon. It was already sizzling, but the real heat would come
between three and four. On the Avenida José Antonio the crowd milled slow,
gay and unconcerned. I ducked into a long, dim, cool, crowded tavern.

The tables were crowded with yellingly conversational men, the walls lined
with great tuns, there was a fine smell of wine. I stood at the bar and asked for
a small beer. I said chattily to the man next to me, "Nice town."

"Finest town in Spain," he beamed. "Yes, sir! The finest wine and the pret-
tiest girls. We are noted for it. You a foreigner?"

Conversation is never difficult. A Spaniard would talk to a phonograph if it
could answer politely. I said, "You have luck to live in a town so fine. It is all a

question of good government."

"What?" He looked at me in astonishment. Those same Spaniards are scornful of any government. He said, "Government by whom?"

"Don Roberto is a good man."

"Don Roberto Nolasco, the Civil Governor: yes, to him I would give the benefit of the doubt. Nothing yet has been discovered against him. Have you heard of our mayor?"

"No."

"A thief!" He was off. He rattled like a riveting machine. I said, "Fíjese!" several times in shock, amazement and commiseration. I had learned as much as I needed and had no further use for the man. There was one empty table in the far corner. "Yes," I said, "yes. And now, señor, I must wait my friend."

I picked up the beer, went to the table and sat. Mentally I put my head in my hands. I set to work on a small jigsaw puzzle. I had gathered enough pieces to make a pattern.

Corrupt Practices Act: a warrant in France. Craddock thought he had enough power to crush the warrant: until he learned he did not have the wolfram option. Wolfram option the key to liberty. France untenable. Down to Spain.

Craddock had anonymously called the Governor on arrival and offered bribery. Without success. Perhaps that had made him so ill, though any excitement could do it. Enter Parker. Craddock—loveable religious old Craddock with his Easter Week—phoned the Governor again immediately and started blackmail. Instrument of blackmail clearly brought by Parker. Clearly strong enough to force a withdrawal of the option even though already awarded. The power to award the option was entirely the Governor's.

Then the holes in the pattern: the big hole.

The Governor had been blackmailed by the big man for how long? What had been burned after the final promotion? The final promotion to what? How did Parker get a copy? Why would anyone in the country recognise it?

I realised that the hubbub in the tavern had suddenly died.

There was a scraping of chairs. A knot of men crowded eagerly to the front window. I craned. I could see nothing. The noise from the street poured in, then even that diminished. A malevolent little man at the window said delightedly, "They are going to meet."

The quiet fell.

"One of them will cross the street."

"Hombre! How can they with everyone looking?"

"They have to meet."

"This will teach the son of a whore not to presume."

"Well said, man! And now after all these years the whore gets her son back."

"He cannot avoid it."

"Look at his face!"

"Look out!" the malevolent man hissed. "He is dodging in here."

They scampered back to their tables. Every eye turned to the door in an unashamed Spanish stare. The guy stood at the threshold with his back to the street, blinking from the sun. He stepped inside.

He was beautifully dressed. He had long legs, no hips, wide shoulders and was so upright that his back curved inward. He was the best looking man I had ever seen. He was smouldering and dark as Method actors try to be, but without their phony air of being about to kick the furniture. He took three more steps forward and he moved with that unconscious animal grace that Spaniards call garbo.

He came to a halt in the dead quiet. He looked around at all the staring eyes. He saw me, didn't know me, and noted my foreign suit. He smiled. He had to go somewhere and my table was his only salvation. He prowled the length of the tavern and stood looking down at me. His eyes were the black-blue you read about and never see. His smile was a fixed grin of horror.

The sweat was running down his face. He was frantically afraid that I would let him down. He widened the awful smile, held out his hand and said, "Hola! amigo."

What was it to me? I stood up, took the hand and shook it. "Hola!" I said. "I was waiting for you. Where have you been?"

Then we sat down again. I called for some wine.

7

He had swallowed more than a litre of wine. He could carry it well, though not all that well, and he was getting drunk. It didn't relax him. The expression in his eyes was old, even for the member of a profession where men are noted for aged eyes. He was a snarled-up ball of nerve and sinew and I was waiting for the top of his head to blow off.

The row in the tavern had started again, but they were still throwing sly glances. He pretended to be oblivious. He sat there, occasionally calling for more wine with a commanding sweep of his arm, and talking a tense blue streak about nothing. He thought I was a Frenchman at first and spoke a few words of French, badly. Then we jumped around from France, to Holy Week, to our clothes, to the heat, to the condition of the wine. It was easy to drink, but strong: I was only sipping. After a while he ran out of subjects altogether. His need of sympathy was desperate. There was no way anyone could reach him.

"Nice town," I said. "You live here?"

"No."

"Been here before?"

The muscles of his jaw stood out. "Yes."

"Come to visit relations?"

"No." The sweat beaded his forehead anew. His black-blue eyes were brilliant with drink and his mouth an uncontoured line. He said, "All right, now tell me something. Why did you say you were waiting for me?"

"I am always waiting for someone to drink with. Why did you speak to me?"

He gave no answer. I didn't need one. I had merely been a refuge found in panic.

He said, "Who are you? What do you call yourself?"

"John Molson. Enchanted. And you?"

He put his arms on the table and stared at me hard. His low voice carried through the tavern. "I am Luis Hernandez."

At a far table a group of men burst into laughter. They were probably telling a joke among themselves, but it was a bad moment. "Luis Hernandez," I said, and frowned. "It sounds familiar. Luis Hernandez." I stabbed a finger at him and grinned, keeping it soft but excited. "Of course! You! The torero. I have read of you in *El Ruedo*." I leaned across and wrung his hand. "An honour for me." I beckoned eagerly for more wine. Another glass and it would run from his ears.

He said, "What did *El Ruedo* say of me?"

There he had me. *El Ruedo* is the bullfight magazine and as a torero he was bound to have appeared in it. But what it said of him, whether he was good or bad I had no idea.

"That I lack something," he said with a fierce masochistic satisfaction. "Lack something! I spit in their faces. I spit in the face of everyone. They are trying to hold me down. Everybody. They will not succeed. I shall rise to the category of Luis Miguel and Ortega."

"And Manolete," I said, doing what I could.

"Ah, yes, Manolete." He looked at me with dislike and contempt. "When the foreigners wish to pretend about bulls they speak always of Manolete. The French writers, the American tough guys, the English pansies. All of you make me sick."

The fighting was due to break out. Someone had to pay for what he was enduring. He had elected me. It was the reward for my sympathy. It was my own fault for going soft. He said, "When did you see Manolete?"

"I was too young."

"Then you are a liar."

It offered no dividends. I looked for the nearest exit. Standing at the door peering in was Louise Morgan. I stood up.

"Louise."

Every man in the place followed her with his eyes. Something strange had happened to her in Spain. I did not understand it. The smug piety of her face was subtly changed. She was pretty, vernal, fresh as unexpected violets in a wood. But her attitude to me was not changed. We continued like a snake and a mongoose.

Hernandez rose slimly beside me. He was steady on his feet, perhaps because he was holding the table. I said, "Miss Morgan, Mr. Hernandez. Have a chair, Louise," and we all sat down again. The waiter brought another glass. The tavern became a single staring eye.

"I have sought you more than an hour," she said in harsh French. "Mr. Craddock is very bad. He needs an injection."

The customary pattern asserted itself. I said, "So go give it to him."

"I am not accustomed to injecting elderly men in the thigh."

From her fresh innocent face the implied lewdness came strangely. All of a sudden I felt responsible for it. I picked up the carafe, filled her glass and she turned for the first time to Hernandez. I saw his handsomeness strike her like a blow.

She blinked. She did not see he was drunk, I know, because she had a special look for drunken men. She spoke slow Spanish made sweet by her French accent. She said, "You must forgive me, Señor Hernandez. I speak your language not very well."

They smiled at one another for an irritating eternity. He was looking at her as though the sun was in his eyes. Then he changed. It was incredible. He relaxed completely. He said with a wonderful soft formality, "Señorita, you speak well. I understand you perfectly."

"How kind of you!"

"What about the injection?" I said in French.

Her smile wavered and for a split second she gave me two eyes of what looked like misery. Then she raised her glass. Hernandez raised his as if in toast. He drained the drink at a gulp and she did the same through automatic imitation. I said, "Watch out. That stuff is strong."

His hand was trembling. Gravely, courteously he filled them up again. "No," I said, "we have to go now," and stood up. The panic leapt to his face. He was about to be abandoned among the unfriendly natives. That was his look-out. I said, "Come on, Louise. Let's get moving."

She half turned her back. She took another deep draft of wine. "I have told you before, I do not take orders from you."

"Come on!"

"When I'm ready."

We spoke in French. The words escaped him, but not the meaning. She was going to stay with him, a voluntary bulwark against all his enemies. The panic fled and he gazed at her with gratitude, tenderness and what looked like adoration. Perhaps I should have been touched. I was not.

"Suit yourself," I snapped. "You should get on well together. Louise and Luis. He's drunk." I managed a withered smile for him. He did not notice. "Adiós," I said, and walked down the tavern and out into the blazing sunlight.

Crazy. I was jealous. I put it down to the fact that any man always wants all the women for himself.

Giving the old man his injection was a niggling, fiddling job. He made as much fuss as a child taking castor oil. Between heating the hypodermic and getting him moaning back into bed nearly an hour had passed. I presumed the attack was his own fault, brought on by his blackmail of the Governor, but I couldn't stay angry about it. His condition was too bad. He seemed to be entering a decline. I wondered if he would die. A fine thing to be stuck in a foreign country with a dead man on my hands.

I leaned against the window to get a breath of air. The crowds below were thinning a little. I pulled down the blind to cut out the sun, then I went back to my jigsaw puzzle. I said, "What's all this about the C.P.A. warrant?"

His eyes in the dimness were brittle as glass. His cheeks were sunken. "That," he said weakly. "A mistake. Parker came all the way down here to tell me so. We can go back to France next week."

"You have an interesting time."

He looked a long while at the ceiling. He said, "I have a terrible time, son, terrible. And it's my own fault. Years ago it was a game with me. Now it's a way of life. It's the money gets you, son, the money."

"It can get me any time."

"It will," he said. "It will. One day you'll understand why I picked you. It's not the dollar bills and the gold sovereigns, boy, they're nothing. Money in the abstract is the trouble—the columns of figures on the sheets of white paper. They become an obsession. You have to manipulate them, add to them, make them longer, make them bigger. You get to the stage where money has no actuality."

He was rambling. He wheezed like a broken accordeon. "The lists," he said, "that's the trouble. The investors were just another list on a less important sheet of paper. Some of them committed suicide. That's the unforgivable sin. Maybe God forgives them. But does he forgive the men who drove them to it?"

"If they were that soft," I said, "they shouldn't have been in the game."

He didn't hear me. "Governments don't forgive," he said. "I'm as innocent as a baby on that C.P.A. charge. I can prove it. But that Special Branch up there is a bunch of bastards. They've been like it since the Stavisky rake-up. They murdered him, you know, in that chalet, to keep his mouth shut. And who killed Rubenstein in New York? Cops claim they don't know. I know. I know that you can buy and sell anything."

He turned his head from me. He said, "I'm afraid." Then he started to cry.

I stood without doing anything. I said, "What's the matter?"

"Nothing. Nothing. What do you think of this Parker?"

"I'd trust him as far as I can spit."

"You're right. A born ten per center. A twister. His bodge-handedness caused all the trouble in Paris. He comes running to me now only to get himself off the warrant. He thinks he'll hang around and take a big cut. He's wrong. The bastard would sell me to the first man who offered him an extra one-per-cent."

He turned his head to me. His eyes were wet. "See how I talk to you, son? See how I trust you? I'm going to make use of you later on. You're a boy who can keep his mouth shut. You're sharp. You'll be valuable in this game."

"What game?"

He stared at the ceiling again.

"Anyway," I said, "no processions tonight."

"Oh yes. There's a special one I want to see. They bring this statue from a church up on the mountain, all the way down through those narrow streets. People expect it to fall every year, but it never does. The chambermaid says it's beautiful and inspiring."

"You can't walk."

"The manager has a wheel-chair. You can push me."

I said, "I didn't know you could speak Spanish."

"I don't. The chambermaid speaks a little English."

Bad conscience or original sin, but a silly lie and it brought back my ill-temper. I said, "Louise speaks Spanish enough."

He said, "You got the envelope safe?"

"What envelope?"

"The one she gave you."

"She didn't give me any envelope."

He writhed up on the bed like a serpent. He went purple in the face. "Find her!" he gasped. "Get it! It's the most important—" He fell back on the bed with his mouth open. I ran to him.

"Get away! Find her!" He beat me off like a man demented. "Get it! Keep it safe! Go! Go! Go!"

I shot out of the room and along the corridor.

The elevator was in use. I ran two at a time down the service stairs and out to the street. I went up José Antonio, frothing with sweat, charged into the tavern and for a moment could see nothing because of the sunlight. My vision cleared. Most of the tables were empty. The table in the corner was empty. I turned to the barman and said, "Where is Luis Hernandez?"

"Gone. I did not notice. A nice girl that friend of yours. I had not thought that Hernandez would know a nice girl like that."

I stood there and forced Craddock's infectious panic out of me. I guessed what the envelope contained. For a few minutes it was as safe with Louise Morgan as with me, and I don't like panic. It distorts. I deliberately ordered a small glass of beer.

Did I know Hernandez well? Yes, I said coldly. The barman became less eager. He was unable to tell me about the mother being a whore. I finished the beer and walked slowly down the street. I was feeling hungry. It had been quite a morning. I said No to two gypsy kids, saw the souvenir shop over the road and had a fancy to buy another knife.

I stepped into the road. The car honked. I stepped back and it kept honking. The voice called, "Mr. Molson! Mr. Molson. Johnny!" I looked up.

Behind the wheel of the convertible was Julie Chirac.

8

We had a table under an awning. The sun was so hot that the canvas smelled strongly. About a hundred yards away three men had connected a big hose to a ground-level hydrant and were spraying the almost empty street with great sparkling arcs of water. Farther down more men were unloading chairs from a truck and lining them up on the sidewalks in preparation for the night's processions.

"A beer?" I said. I was not yet over the shock.

She shook her head. A shaft of sunlight came through a gap in the awning and her hair was a blaze of light. I tried to count the ways I loved her.

"How?" I said. "Why?"

"I spent a day without you." She reached across the table and laid a warm hand on my wrist. "I realised that another was coming and another and I couldn't face it. I packed a few clothes, got in the car and came away without saying anything to anyone. I had to get to you."

"But how did you know where to find me?"

"You stated your destination at the frontier. I was nice to the official. I told him it was urgent."

"But—"

"Aren't you glad to see me?"

"Sure. I'm thinking of your brother."

"So am I," she said. "You know how he is with me. He may find out where I am and follow. Are you afraid?" Something was wrong; a trick of the fierce Spanish light. She was not the same as in France. A small finger of ache bored into my stomach, a doubt wriggled through my mind like a tiny worm. I didn't love her. It was the unbalance caused by my surprise, my unpreparedness to meet her. I reached over and touched the fingers that covered my wrist.

It was easier then. She turned me the softness of her palm. I said, "Have a drink."

"Not now."

"We'll go somewhere for lunch."

"I'm not hungry," she said, "for food."

Blame the Holy Week poster behind her head. Or the broad daylight, or a lingering American Puritanism. I looked away from her frankness in embarrassment. I could think of nothing to say.

An old vendor was passing on the opposite sidewalk, blowing streams of bubbles through a toy like a quizzing glass, a loop on the end of a stick. A group of tiny Spanish children, alike as day-old chicks, were trotting happily at his heels. They were too young to have money to buy and the vendor was doing it for their pleasure. The bubbles jetted in flights into the still air and caught all the colours of the sun. The children squealed with delight. The bubbles burst.

I said, "Want to go back to your hotel?"

She sensed my disquiet. Perhaps that explained why she looked different. She said, "If my brother has found me there will be a scene. Would you like a drive?"

"Fine."

We got up and started walking to where we had left the car. A gypsy child darted ferret-faced from somewhere and held out his hand. I gave him a peseta. He darted off without thanks as gypsies do. We turned the corner into the narrow side street and Julie suddenly went gay. "Begging is against the law here," she said, "did you know? So is driving a car in town on Good Friday, but a nice policeman gave me a dispensation until six o'clock."

She paused. "What is it, Johnny?"

"Nothing."

"Trouble with Mr. Craddock?"

"No."

"You can tell me."

"I'm hungry," I said, and opened the car door for her.

It was parked by the side entrance of a church. There was a middle-aged woman standing there; I thought another beggar about to swoop, she looked so hungry. Then I saw the ear-rings, intricate, opulent, weighing down the lobes of her ears. I saw her haughty face. She skated her eyes away disdainfully, dropped the shawl from her hair and walked away. She was a tall woman, haggard, appallingly shabby, arrogant.

I got behind the wheel.

We snaked through the mesh of climbing streets and out of the town. The buildings grew ragged and stopped. The road steepened and the surfacing disappeared. A hot dry breeze blew around our faces. The rays of the afternoon sun bounced from the rocks like hot steel shafts.

"Is your work troubling you, John?"

"I'm not doing any."

We drove without speaking. The thin silences of the mountains reached down and drew us higher. The city below was a toy caught in a cup of rock, a theatrical scene painted on a sky of impossible blue. We were losing ourselves in airy space. We climbed higher and higher. The heat was a noise.

"Look!" She pointed. The distant village was clinging to the side of a further slope like a scattering of tiny white boxes. I pulled over to the shade of a single tree. I wanted to take off my jacket. I gripped the lapels and got the shoulders halfway down my back and then her arms were around me and I was pinioned. She kissed me gently with lips as cool as hyacinths. She said, "Johnny."

Her arms tightened. She fell across my lap. We attacked one another like animals. She said, "I can't live without you. And you don't love me."

"I do," I said, "I do! I do! For God's sake let me get my jacket off." The heat seized us and scorched us. We panted with thirst. I lifted her from the car and carried her off the road. We lay upon the earth. The rustle of her dress sounded in my ears like silk ripped by knives, the tree grew larger, a bird sang in the stillness. We smeared ourselves with sand and kisses and love.

We were nearly at the town outskirts again and it was almost six o'clock. An evening illusion of coolness was coming from the mountains at our backs. She was driving. She said, "Oh, what a lovely afternoon it was!"

"Yes," I said.

The whitewashed village inn and cold white wine. Anchovies, olives, sardines, asparagus, ham and cold dried fish. There was a public holiday and no radio. The man in the corner played a guitar while his friend in a high sweet voice sang, "I would I were a vine to climb the walls to your room, to see the sweet sleep that you have."

With the red wine we ate a strong gazpacho. The men in the corner were drunker now, the singer's voice lower and softer. "That my heart were a dove...."

Afterwards we went back to the tree. She said it was our place.

"I liked it," I said, and leaned back in the seat. The crumbling houses whipped by us.

"What shall we do now?"

"I have to go see Craddock."

She made a pouting mouth. "Will he stay here much longer?"

"Until next week."

She said, "You must make yourself invaluable to him, help him in his business so that he pays you a lot of money. There are two of us now. We must think of the future."

"Yes."

"Tonight we'll have a long talk about everything." She yawned. "I'm tired, darling. It was a long drive down. I'll go back to the hotel and have a bath and a short sleep."

"I'll call for you later."

"Better not." She was driving slowly. There was no traffic but the crowds were coming out again, filling the streets. She said, "Imagine if my brother should be there. It's not beyond the bounds of possibility. We'll meet outside our café with the awning. We can watch the processions."

"They don't begin until eleven."

"More time for a long sleep and a leisurely dinner. My God, I can think of food already after what we ate. Love gives me an appetite." She laughed. She avoided a group of smiling men and drew over to the curb. "So out you get."

"Why?"

"That's the main street ahead. If my brother is here—"

"I'm not afraid of your brother."

"I am."

I got to the sidewalk and stood looking down at her. She said, "Darling, don't be difficult after I've made all this long journey just for you." She smiled up at me.

And I didn't love her. I didn't even know her. She was someone I had seen just this once, this now, a mask, a face put on to meet another face. I had loved her in loving her body. Possessing her I had not needed to watch the mask changing. We were dancing a minuet with no meaning at all.

"Something the matter?"

"Nothing," I said. "Eleven, then. The café on José Antonio."

"Goodbye, my heart." She kissed her fingertips at me. She waved and drove away and every man in sight moved his head to watch her go. I turned into José Antonio.

The crowds were thicker, more difficult, the chairs lined six deep on either sidewalk and eating space. Someone had worked during the afternoon erecting low roped-off platforms for local dignitaries. Among the elegance the gypsy children darted begging, more of them now because like the flickering bats they somehow resembled they had come out in strength with the approach of night. A gypsy woman with a shawled baby stood hand out-thrust on a corner, whining. "Limosna, señorito. Por favor, limosna. Alms. God will pay you."

I looked across the road and saw Roger Lascelles.

I had to look twice. A beret hid his blonde hair and his tanned face looked no different from those that moved around him. His clothes were not so foreign as mine. He stood out because he was moving more quickly. He darted around a talking couple and disappeared into an alley.

It was inevitable. He had come with the brother. There would be no fight because I had nothing now to fight about. By the time I reached the hotel I had wiped a clean slate in my mind. Julie was finished.

I turned into the lobby.

There were many people, but few foreigners. The town was off the beaten track. Tourists anyway think Spain more fashionable in high summer when they can fry to death. A woman at the desk was complaining in piercing American to an uncomprehending clerk: a British couple stood aloof, nervous and ill-dressed in a corner: a group of French were exclaiming loudly on the cheapness of everything. All the others were Spanish.

I went up in the elevator.

I let myself into my room, looked at myself in the mirror over the bowl, thought I looked baggy-eyed. I washed my face. I remembered that I needed a clean handkerchief but was too lazy to unlock my case. I went to the adjoining door. I tapped.

No answer.

I knocked, waited again, pushed the door open and stepped inside. The blind was down as I had left it, the room dim. The bed was empty and unmade and the door of his private bathroom shut tight.

I sat down on the bed. My hand brushed the sheets. They were cold. The bed had the seedy look of having been left a long time. I hesitated, walked to the bathroom door and said, "Are you all right?" There was no sound. I turned the handle.

The bathroom was empty.

He might be out in the wheel-chair he had mentioned. He was too ill to walk anywhere. I crossed the corridor to Louise's room. The door was slightly ajar. "Louise!" I said. The word ran down the flat hotel silence of the corridor. "Louise!" I said again. I entered.

He was face down on the floor. He was in his pyjamas. I dropped to my knees and rolled him over and picked him up by the shoulders. I went into a flutter and started shaking him. I was sure he was dead. I said, "Mr. Craddock!"

His eyes opened.

He stared at me unseeing. He said, "The bitch. The dirty rotten whoring little bitch." He twitched all over, and then cracked up. The filth poured from his mouth in a torrent.

9

It took over an hour to quiet him. I gave him another injection and got him in bed, then because I couldn't endure any more of what he was saying I went downstairs instead of phoning and asked for a hot-water bottle.

They didn't have one. They were offended at my asking. They seemed to think it reflected on the hotel.

I got back to the room and the change had set in. He lay mottled and quivering, paying for his bout, an old man afraid of death and full of remorse and religion. I drew up a chair beside him. He reached out and took my hand. His flesh was fishlike and clammy and cold as ice.

"No processions tonight," I said.

"Oh yes." He nodded feebly. "Yes, I must. The one where they bring the statue down all the narrow streets." He turned his head on the pillow. His face was one of those horrors that peer from the murk of the Quinta del Sordo paintings. He said, "I've led a wicked life."

"We all have."

"Wicked, corrupt and immoral," he whispered. "I've been responsible for people dying. Did you know I killed Louise's father?"

"No."

"She shouted it at me when I discovered them in there. She must have been thinking it all these years. That was the most terrible part of the scene."

"Let's not talk about it again."

"It's all right," he said, "I understand now. God gave them the instincts and they're both young. Who was he?"

"I told you I don't know."

"It doesn't matter anyway now. Except that she should round on me like that. I've always loved her, just like her father would have done. That's why I forgive her, the way our Father in Heaven forgives us all. Bring her to me. I want her to know that I forgive her."

"I don't know where she is," I said, and I couldn't take any more. I got to my feet. "But she can't be far. I'll go find her if you'll be all right. Will you?"

"Yes," he said, "yes, if you lock all the doors. I'll pray a while and then have a little sleep. Come back in time to give me some soup. We'll go to the procession."

He waited until I was outside. He said, "Do you think my illness is a punishment for the life I've led?"

"No."

"Then I shall get over it," he said almost breezily. I shut the door.

I got to the street. I walked straight into the bar on the corner of José Antonio and the Plaza Caudillo and called for a large cognac. I sat on a high stool and took a fierce interest in everything about me.

A modern bar with two entrances, outside tables on both sides, long curved bar, shiny bottles, five barmen in immaculate white jackets. A rendezvous for the town hoipolloi, the upper bourgeousie. It could have been a bar anywhere except for the two pictures on the wall. General Franco, Chief of State, looked up in pride; José Antonio, Falangist martyr looked down in sorrow; both in colour. I studied them. I had another drink. The stabbing emotional pangs in my stomach became fiercer.

I didn't want to find Louise. I didn't want to look into that holy Raphael face and tell her I knew she was no longer so pious. Yet I did. Ferociously. I wanted to gloat at her, rub it in, make her suffer, hit her, wipe the lambish look from her pietistic chops, tell her she was no better than I. I wanted to sneer at her, jeer at her. I wanted to invite her to my bed.

My stomach tightened to a tiny knot. I looked around for distraction. Major Parker was sitting outside, boiling to death in his suit of English tweed.

His table was on the far side and he had not seen me enter. He was alone at his table, but not bored. He was trying to pick up the guy next to him. I tried to get back to wolfram.

Parker, Craddock, the Governor, the brutal-looking gold-toothed man in the park. I looked from the windows on both sides. All the social life takes place in the small centre of a Spanish town. Anyone from a radius of ten miles is liable to appear in ten minutes. I waited for Gold-teeth. Nothing. I had another drink.

The affair at the table was advancing. Parker turned a little, gave a gay equine laugh and they played footsie. The other guy was the butch type, young, bristly curly hair, big, flashing white grin, enormous shoulders. He looked unintelligent and a rough-trade professional. I examined closer. He was a genuine tough. He was maybe broke, doing it for the money, saving up to get married. His clothes were too good. I didn't know what to think.

I had another cognac.

By my fifth I was half drunk. They were set to go. Parker slapped the other guy's wrists with the tips of his fingers. The waiter came, they had a little squabble over who was to pay, the other guy did and I wasn't understanding at all now. Parker got to his feet, very trim, upright, a kid-silly look on his face. The other guy stood up beside him and maybe Parker knew before, but if not he deserves his due because he didn't bat a lid.

The other guy was so short in the leg he was almost a dwarf. His hands hung low, his thick shoulders made him as broad as he was long, he looked the way I had always imagined a medieval tumbler. Parker had not known: he didn't mind: his eyes glowed: he liked what he saw. They exchanged a few more words, mutually smiled, linked arms in the way permitted to men in Latin countries and strolled away.

I paid for my drinks. I strolled after them.

A short trip. Over a square, past a pretty tinkling fountain, past gay flower beds, out at the other side. In front of me they talked softly and laughed occasionally, slapping at one another. The population was on the main stems, this part of town was deserted, Parker and pal could have seen me had they looked around. They were too engrossed.

We traversed a narrow street. Through breaks in the buildings mountains were marching purple against a fading sky. Evening was far fallen, the dusk thickening, it was hot again. We reached the other square, everything quiet and still; tall palm trees, globed lights like moons and a tiny bar on the far corner. We could have been in the open country. The mountains were close, there were only three houses and all on different sides. They had fences with gardens beyond.

Parker and his pal hesitated. They laughed a little and went through one of the garden gates. I went after them and leaned against the fence. I had drunk five big cognacs. I didn't know what I was trying to do, except forget.

There was another bigger gate for cars, a long driveway, the house well back. I took an instant dislike to it. It was a big new house and very ugly. If the stumpy pal lived there he was not broke. They halted at the front door, the pal laughed very loudly, he put his arm about Parker's waist and they disappeared around to the rear, to a melon patch perhaps.

End of incident. I started to walk away.

To find Louise or listen to Craddock. I couldn't face either. I walked across to the tiny bar at the corner, sat at the only outside table and called for a cognac. I wondered what the hell I had been at, following two odd pansies through a strange Spanish town.

The barman was proud of his single shadowy table. He came out, dusted it off and stood talking while the darkness fell complete and I had three cognacs more. He was a pleasant man. I was the only customer. We discussed some things at great length, principally the beauties of the town and its superiority over all other Spanish towns. Two other customers entered the bar, the barman poured me another dose of cognac and went inside to make coffee on his espresso machine.

Spanish conversation started.

Beauties of the town again, current movies, the American girl that a cousin of a friend of one of the customers had met two years ago in Madrid. Wow! Savour it! But that was nothing. The brother of the brother-in-law of the other customer had met two German girls on holiday in San Sebastian. Sisters. And what do you think! He had to satisfy both without letting the other know and gee, poor guy, he was so beat up at the end of it, etcetera, but anyway Wow!

They had nothing original. Sisters have been the sexual liar's speciality since Casanova had them lining up at his bedroom door. They started to bore themselves. They changed to football, to last night's processions—not as good as last year's. They arrived at the bulls.

Never anyone to equal Ortega. What about Ordonez? The barman's father had been there in Linares that tragic afternoon that Manolete got his lot. Ah me! Then a hop, skip and jump and they had arrived at their home town boy, Luis Hernandez. They tore him to small pieces.

Something lacking, something always lacking. They had not seen him fight, he had never fought here, but they could strip his technique. Sunday's corrida would be a disaster. A crime to take the public's money. The other two men on the bill were no good either.

Hernandez had run away at thirteen, of course, through the shame of his mother being a whore, and in one of the cheapest houses. So where did he get the gall, the unmitigated hard face to come back now and strut as if he owned the place, not speaking to anyone, pretending to be too good? Cut his own mother dead this very morning. Dodged into a tavern to avoid seeing her. His mother, after all, even though an outcast, and mothers as such are sacred. How was it with all the money he was making that she was lucky to get olive oil to dip her bread in?

My stomach started again. There was too much cognac in me. I was drunk and a bad drunk. I had glibly said that Louise and Luis should get on well together. I decided to kill them.

Major Parker emerged from the gate at the far side of the square.

His shoulders were hunched, his head down on his chest and there was something wrong with his legs. He headed straight for the bar on a run. He almost made it. Then his feet got tangled and he did a soft-shoe shuffle. He fell over flat, crawled a couple of yards like a fly with one wing, rolled on his back and lay still. I ran for him. There was something wrong with my own legs by this time.

He was moaning. I put my hand at the small of his back and lifted him. He gave a little shriek of pain and from his mouth came a spate of words that were neither English nor Spanish. Then he looked at me. He recognised me. He said clearly and distinctly, "Hello, old chap. Wonder if you could give me a hand up. Having one of my spells, I'm afraid. Too annoying."

We staggered back to the table and sat down.

"Frightfully decent of you. Might I have this?" He finished off my cognac in a gulp. His face was taut with pain, but he grinned like a cartoon horse and talked like Cheery Bob Cherry. "Old hunting wound," he said brightly. "On the moors at Bairlochfinnie. Know it?"

"No."

"Lovely place." He shook his head. "Never know when it's going to take me. Jolly lucky for me you were passing by."

"I was following you."

"Really? I say, that wasn't very sporting."

I said, "You dope. That's how these punks dress so well. They lure the suckers home to be robbed. And in a country where your little peccadillo is against the law you can't go to the police."

He said, "Oh stop being so madly hetero. I knew a type exactly like you in Marseilles and he finished up by falling in love with a boy of fifteen."

I brought him into focus. His face was without a mark. I said, "I'll get us another drink. One each." I went into the bar.

They were back to football. The barman smilingly poured the two drinks without interrupting what he was saying. It was a small bar. I lowered my voice. I said, "Who lives over there?"

"Where?"

"There."

"Oh, there. Vidal."

"Vidal," I said drunkenly. "Important man."

"A very important man. The Chief of Police."

"A short man."

"A tall man."

"Oh."

I went out. Parker had disappeared.

I drank both drinks myself and went inside to pay. The barman invited me to another free because I was a good customer and a foreigner. In the narrow street was a velvety darkness, a smell of flowers, a roller canary singing on one of the high balconies. The little fountain in the second square was softly lit now, tinkling gently. The flower smell was stronger.

Another canary sang. Latin countries are full of caged birds: thin cats, gargantuan wrist watches, ashtrays full of smoking butts because no one stubs out his cigarette. The Chief of Police was named Vidal.

I approached the main stem again, picking through the crowds, nearing the flash corner bar. I wanted another drink, to be far away, to see and not see Louise. I hesitated at the first entrance. I turned into José Antonio. In front of the bar, unspeaking at a table, there she sat with the bullfighter.

I went straight over and sat down with them.

Panic went over her face. Sorrow. Fear. She made no preamble. She said, "Is he dead?"

I let her sweat. Hernandez looked at me tensed to liplessness.

I was drunk enough to want to fix his face: not drunk enough to think I could do it in my present condition. I didn't speak to him. I said to her in French, "Come back, little prodigal. He has forgiven you. He wants to forgive you out loud."

"Is he all right?"

"Considering the hours he spent on your bedroom floor, yes. But he said some hard things before the forgiveness stage. Dirty little whoring bitch was the phrase, I think."

The colour went from her face. Hernandez said, "Is he speaking well to you?"

"Sí." She did not look at him. She said in French, "Craddock has told you."

"Everything."

"He is despicable."

"Of course. He caught you in the act after all the years of posing. Did you learn at the convent to fall in bed every time you get drunk? You should have let me know. We could have whooped it up weeks ago."

"Please," she said.

"What a sight it must have been. The old man wheezing his guts out, you standing there like Venus at the bath and lover-boy pulling on his pants. Is he hairy? He looks the type to be hairy."

The misery in her eyes was beyond tears. I was so sick with myself I wanted to turn aside and vomit. I couldn't stop. I said, "Your friend, in case you didn't know, is a son of a whore."

"John, don't!"

"But I mean a real son of a whore. A real whore. The whole town knows it."

"I know it too. He told me. He explained it to me." She stared at me and shook her head bewilderedly. All the expression had fled from her eyes. Then the contempt came and the pity and in fighting a false battle I had lost everything. I knew it.

I said, "Come back to the hotel. There's nothing to worry about. He's all right."

She still stared at me. "I will never go back."

"I'm sorry," I said. "I've talked like the bastard I am. I'll crawl to you. Just come back to the hotel."

"Never," she said. "Never. Never."

She got to her feet. Hernandez rose beside her. "Please, Louise," I said.

A tear ran down her cheek. She said, "John, in a curious way you are responsible for what happened today. It started somehow the night I saw you with
Julie Chirac. And when you bullied me this morning I was morally forced to
stay with Luis."

At the sound of his name he looked at her with reverence and adoration. This
time he was not drunk. She said, "I am not making excuses. None are necessary. I only want to be honest with myself. I thought I was in love with you,
John."

"You are," I said, "you are! I am in love with you."

"No." She shook her head again. "No, John, you couldn't be in love with anyone. Shall we go, Luis?"

"Not with him," I said. "He'll think you're a tart. He's a Spaniard. He'll think
you're immoral."

"But I am," she said, and smiled up at him with wonderful tenderness.
"Goodbye, John."

They walked away.

10

It was a half-hour to midnight. The long late Spanish supper was over. The
crowds were out full strength again, milling in hundreds along the streets of the
processional routes, in thousands on José Antonio where all the processions
would finally converge.

In churches throughout the city costumed men were waiting, penitentes, fra-
ternity members of their parishes who had paid weekly sums throughout the
year for the final privilege of marching in procession with their church's special image. Faces were covered with capuchos—masks that hung from high hats
made pointed by a concealed cardboard cone. Costumes slashed bright with different colours draped from necks and swirled around ankles. Pockets were filled
with caramels to pelt unrecognising friends in the crowd. Some of the men were
barefooted.

Along the routes the thousands chattered loudly and told jokes and laughed.
Josephus Flavius said that the union of what is divine and what is mortal is dis-
agreeable. Josephus Flavius would not have liked Spain. I was not liking Spain
too much.

I was sober again, thirsty, and I ached. The processions were late starting as
everything always is except the bullfights. I'd had a hard job getting Craddock
to the position he wanted. The street of his particular procession was built like
a stairway of wide shallow steps, narrow, crammed black with people. I'd had
to push the wheelchair up various side hills, dodge through bottling little alleys:
it had all taken a long time. When finally I got him settled he was muttering and
chunnering that we must have missed something, he was sure. I had not

wanted to bring him at all. He was in a shocking state. The old-fashioned wheel-chair had hard wheels, an open-work cane back, and was uncomfortable. He was slumped far down. His hands were under the blanket that covered his knees, he was dead white, his eyes were sunken to invisibility and he looked a hundred and fifty. I leaned over him.

"You all right?"

"This is fine."

It was suffocating. People were pouring from the scores of alleys and press-ing to the walls all about us. The only sense of freedom was the alley at our back. I listened to conversations. Some small boys had thrown firecrackers last year at the feet of the men who carried the statue. The image had nearly fallen. This year's firecrackers would be bigger. Olé!

Everyone was gazing farther up to the barely discernible church. The lights in the street were dim, sparse, the indigo sky without stars or moon. I looked to the crowded flag-draped balconies above us. I was claustrophobic. I leaned over again.

"Can you see?"

"Yes." He lay back with his head pressed to my hand. The noise rolled around us. The crowd was becoming more clamorous, the uproar rising. A close-packed mass of ill-seen faces stretched up and down the hill as far as I could see. My thirst was worsening; I sweat like a porous pot. The expectant babble rose to crescendo.

A rocket shot to the sky.

It burst. It fell in great slow cascading festoons of globular light. All down the hill a thousand throats went "Aaaaah." The cymbals clashed. The music began. The procession started.

It came at funeral pace, a descending flicker of tiny candles that threw no il-lumination. The muffled drums thudded; the crowds swayed. The trumpets blew long sad dirging chords at the echoing walls of the high houses. Priests bowed their heads and prayed loudly over clasped hands. Tiny crimson-clad acolytes like red-lipped Renaissance cherubs swung their censers from side to side and filled the air with curling incense.

A nearby man said, "This year it will fall for certain." The image came.

It was beautifully dressed. It towered large and high to the walls. It moved in a blaze of light with torches flaming at each corner of its base. It was top-heavy. The invisible carriers beneath the base shuffled in time to the beating drums. The head and outstretched arms swung high over the populace in a wide and frightening arc.

The man said, "Just let one kid throw one firecracker."

I eased my hand from behind the old man, straightened up and scanned the street. There was too much darkness, too many heads to recognise an individ-ual. Craddock shifted. He picked the thought telepathically from my head. He said, "We won't find Louise in this mob. What did she say?"

"She wanted to take a walk. She'll join us later."

"Did she seem happy? Did you tell her I forgive her?"

"She seemed very happy. Yes, I told her."

"How could she have walked out and left me unconscious? I might have died." He looked up the hill. "Will that thing fall on me?"

"No."

"No, of course not," he said. "No. This is beautiful." Then he twitched. He twisted right round in the chair. "She give you the envelope?"

I had completely forgotten the envelope. I looked into his face and lied again. "Yes, she gave it to me."

"Where is it? You didn't leave it at the hotel, did you?"

"It's in my pocket."

"Good." His breathing became easier. "Keep it with you. You're a good boy, Johnny. One day you'll realise how I appreciate you."

He slumped lower in the chair. His face was peaceful. "Isn't this lovely," he said.

The drums thudded slowly. The trumpets passed. The Roman-dressed soldiers marched in slow time. The people chattered loudly on. Penitentes glided by with gleaming eye-slits and candles held low. One of them dived a hand in his pocket and a gleam of caramels showered into the crowd.

There was a shuffling of feet, a squealing of children, instantly stilled. Incense floated, the priests were drawing abreast, the silence falling. Craddock looked high. In his face was reverential love. The image was almost upon us. The sigh went up and the crowd went to its knees like scythed corn.

I saw Louise.

"Just a minute," I said. She was twenty yards away. I struggled through the kneeling crowd and they didn't mind me. The image passed with a blaze of torches in the corner of my eye. I stumbled over feet and outstretched legs. I was nearly there. The crowd gave another sigh and bristled to its feet and I made a last squeezing lunge and grasped her shoulder.

She swung round. Her big dark eyes looked questioningly at me. She was a stranger.

"I'm sorry," I said. "I thought you were someone else." A man moved scowling to her side. The girl said, "In this light—"

"Yes," I said.

The procession was receding down the hill, the sad chords blowing back long-drawn and doleful. The people were brushing their knees, babbling again, flooding the roadway to follow to the really big parade on the Avenida José Antonio. I started to fight my way back. I said. "Excuse me."

The woman screamed piercingly. Despite the darkness I saw everything.

The wheel-chair catapulted to the centre of the street. A small man made a grab, turned the wheels and missed his hold. A lot of women took up the screaming. The chair leapt at every step like a living animal and went rocketing down the stairwayed hill.

Craddock was bolt upright. His hands were still under the blanket. The chair bumped and rattled and I wondered crazily why he didn't fall out. The screaming rose higher, a man began laughing like an idiot, a half-delighted shout of warning rose too late.

The wheel-chair hit the base of the statue.

It hung only a moment. It careened on down and sliced through the scattering penitentes. The image pivoted and tilted. The crowd surged in front of me and I could no longer see the chair. The man jammed against me in the mob was saying quietly, "Olé, olé, olé, olé," over and over. The crazy man was still laughing. I watched the image.

It swayed. It righted. The feet of the carriers waltzed and gavotted and the acolytes dropped their censers and ran. The image tilted again. The outstretched hands scraped a wall. Then everything was out of control and confusion was complete and the mob was clawing to get clear.

The image hesitated. It made a rush forward, came to a dead stop and gave a curious little jump. Then it went irretrievably sideways and hit the wall and broke at the waist. It crashed to smithereens with appalling noise in the roadway. The flames of the broken torches licked at the clothing. The crowd converged running.

I was wedged. I tried to push forward. The people in front were an impassable mass. They erupted to swell the pack from the scores of alleys. They shrieked from the high balconies. I heaved at shoulders and pulled and shoved and made no headway because this was the most diverting procession of all time and no one intended to relinquish his position.

The carriers were picking themselves from the debris. The crowd blocked the road. I saw the nearest alley and fought diagonally toward it. I could run around the block and reach Craddock from the lower end of the hill. I gained the corner.

I ran.

The enclosing walls were an oven and I sweated. I reached the end of the long alley, turned downward and was in a cul-de-sac. I climbed again, turned into another alley. In three minutes I was lost.

There was a small quiet square. I stood and oriented myself and listened for the direction of voices over the rooftops. I zig-zagged downward, going through short diagonal streets full of tall dark houses. I saw no one. The streets led me steadily away from the voices. I ran hard and kept running. Then I was on a main street.

The crowd was away to the left of me, massed around an ambulance. The policemen were pushing them back. There was a preliminary moan and the crowd divided. The ambulance gathered speed and flashed past with siren whining.

I was panting for breath. I saw the wheel-chair. The crowd was breaking up.

I caught the policeman's arm. I said, "Where have they taken him?"

The man was short, stupid-looking, probably underpaid and exhausted by the uncontrollability of the crowd. He did not like me touching him. He said, "What is it to you?"

"He is my employer. I am responsible for him."

"Prove it."

"Don't be a fool."

"Don't call a policeman a fool."

He didn't know where the ambulance had gone or anything about anything. It made him feel inefficient. He said, "If what you say is true they will get in touch with you." Then he slapped his gun holster, shouldered me aside, turned his back and started shoving at the crowd, shouting to everyone to clear the road. There was nothing to be got from him.

I started off again. I knew where I was now. I had no intention of waiting a summons from the police. I could get phone numbers and call every hospital in town. They might not know how to treat him. I fought to José Antonio. I threaded the entire length and turned left to the hotel. I entered the lobby.

Both the public phones were in use.

I leapt for the elevator. Then I knew why I had come all this way. Louise might be upstairs. I could anyway call the hospitals from my room. The gates clanged behind me, the elevator went down again with its cable thwacking the wall, I went along the quiet corridor and stopped in front of her door and banged hard.

"Louise," I said loudly. I banged again.

I heard the distant Wagnerian chords of the trumpets. I spun on my heel, crossed the corridor and entered my own room. I switched on the light, looked at myself in the mirror. The sweat was running down my face in channels. I needed a clean handkerchief.

I went to my suitcase, snapped open the catches, and something was wrong. I couldn't place it. I called again, "Louise," and I was trying to think at the same time about the case. "Louise," I said quietly, and then I went to the connecting door and opened it on to the darkness and said, "Are you here, Louise?" and I stepped inside.

The roof fell in.

It hit me flat on the top of the head and knocked me to my knees. My palms smacked the floor with a force that almost dislocated my shoulders. I rolled over. The roof fell a second time. It hit my neck. The ganglia of my spine exploded in hot lightning all over my body, the trumpets roared loud to split my ear drums and a grave opened in the carpet.

I fought for breath. I whispered, "Louise." I realised I was lost and tiredly lowered my head into the expanding hole.

11

There was something wrong with the suitcase.

I opened my eyes, relapsed and lay back in a doze. The second time I saw the faint light filtering through the curtained window. I lay and let it grow. I got up and fumbled the switch and the light from the ceiling almost plucked out my eyes.

Craddock's room was wrecked.

Pictures were off the walls, mattresses and pillows slit, drawers and suitcases overturned. I went into the bathroom and gave myself an awkward drink from under the cold water tap. I glanced in the mirror and was normal except that my hair was untidy. I explored my head. One bump, no blood and no skin broken. I had been hit with a professional tool.

I passed into my own room.

Same again. The mattress had spewed a white heap on the floor. The lid of my suitcase was split, the lining ripped out, the contents scattered over the floor. I tried to register the other thing about it. I failed. I went and combed my hair.

My pockets were empty. I returned to the other room, picked my billfold from the corner where it had been tossed and found the papers intact. The money was missing. I had no more money. I got down on my hands and knees and crawled about and found nothing else. The watch on my wrist said one o'clock. I did not know how long I had been unconscious.

I stood a moment. I heard again the distant sound of trumpets. The processions were continuing. I crossed the corridor, tried the door handle of Louise's room and pushed. The darkness was waiting. I was going to be smarter this time. I wiped a quick hand down the wall and flicked the light and darted in sideways.

The place was empty, searched and chaotic. I returned to my own room and sat on a chair and nursed my aching head.

Get the hospital phone numbers.

I had a raging thirst. My throat was too dry to talk. I went to my own basin for another awkward drink, dried my mouth on the back of my hand, fingered my head. There had been something about the suitcase. I turned around.

The man was standing at the open door.

He was the tall gold-toothed man from the park. He had a yellow-papered cigarette in the corner of his mouth which somehow made him look more brutal, and he had a gun in his hand. His eyes flicked the room, he stepped inside and motioned the gun unnecessarily. I didn't move.

I said, "What do you want?"

"So you speak Spanish after all." He twisted his mouth and spat. The wet-ended cigarette butt fell to the floor. "You are John Molson."

"What's that to you?"

He took two more steps. He back-handed me across the mouth and I stumbled against the basin. I straightened with my fists up. I put them down again. The gun looked like a small tunnel.

"I am not accustomed to such answers. We shall try again. You are John Molson."

"What's that to you?"

We stared at one another. He backed cagily and dived a free hand in his pocket. He waved the billfold at me. Behind the cellophane window was writing and a photograph. The card was official. He was Antonio Vidal, Chief of Police.

The distant trumpets blew up a small nightmare. I said, "Señor Vidal, your arrival is opportune. These rooms have been burgled."

"You will tell me what is missing."

"Some money from my wallet."

"And what else?"

"I don't know yet."

"You will come with me and make a statement."

"No," I said, "I am unable. I must contact my employer. He is in a hospital."

"You will come with me."

I put out my foot and trod on the smouldering yellow butt.

I said, "Why?"

He adroitly tossed the gun to his other hand. He swung a bunched fist. It was all one movement. I moved, but not enough. The blow hit my shoulder and I sat hard on the floor. 1 was frightened.

He smiled. He said, "Molson, you will come with me. You are a material witness."

"To what?" I said.

"You were with your employer at the moment he died?"

I closed my eyes a moment. "He is dead," I said stupidly.

"He was murdered. You can tell me perhaps who stuck the knife into his back."

I got to my feet. I knew about the suitcase. It should have been locked when first I went to it. Among the scattered contents was no Toledo blade with a damascened handle. I knew what sort of knife had killed Craddock.

I said, "Is there a warrant to make me go?"

He swung the gun.

It was a heavy gun. His hand curved wide. I jumped inside the arc and the gun went round my shoulder and I brought up my knee.

He gasped. He sat down and rolled and started to raise his hand. I kicked again. The gun hit the base of the washbasin. I ran out of the room and along the corridor.

I hurtled down the stairs to the third floor. Someone was coming from below.

I dodged to the right, around a corner, hoping for more stairs, a fire-escape, any-thing. The wall ended blank.

I spun like a top. I saw the slightly opened door of the last room. I dived for it. The darkness enfolded me. I closed the door quietly and leaned against it. The man snored.

He was lying on the bed in shirt and trousers, faintly visible in the light from outside. A bottle of cognac was on the table and a penitentes costume draped over the back of the chair. I went to the window. I looked down on to a narrow back street and heard the trumpets coming. I saw the fire-ladder, the group of penitentes talking under a lamp, the cop leaning against the corner fifteen yards away. I turned back into the room and the light came on.

The man on the bed let go of the button switch. He pushed himself upright. He said amiably, "Hola! amigo, who art thou?" He was very drunk.

I smiled at him. "Hola!" I said softly. I sat down on the chair and took a long swig at the cognac. I handed him the bottle. "The boys sent me," I said. "After the processions we plan to go somewhere."

"We went somewhere before the processions," he said, and laughed heartily and downed a great gulp. "Thou hast heard? My wife goes to have the first baby. It will be a boy."

"Hombre! Felicidades!" I patted his shoulder and got to my feet, still smiling. "Then thou hast no wish to come," I said, and took the costume from the back of the chair and raised my arms and strained into the purple cassock.

He said something. I could not hear. I was struggling too hard. I swirled the red-lined black cloak around me and it was too short. I pulled the capucho over my head and the cardboard cone inside sat awkwardly. The man watched with bemused interest.

"We shall return afterwards," I said, "to see if thou hast changed thy mind. What sayest thou?"

"Marvellous!" he cried enthusiastically. "Marvellous!" Then he collapsed full length and started to snore again.

I was suffocating. The cone tilted on my head, the hanging mask was tight over my nose, I could see through only one eye-slit. I replaced the bottle, turned off the light and went softly across the room. I opened the door and looked out.

Vidal was down the passage. His gun was out. I ducked back. I crossed to the window.

The trumpets were nearer. The penitentes had moved from under the light and were gazing in the direction of the main street. The policeman had gone. I lifted the sash, climbed to the fire-ladder and began to descend. It quivered. My sweating hands slipped on the smooth rails. My feet scuffed at the rungs. I passed the second floor.

A beam of light shot into the night. A head thrust from the window above. The drunk from the bed leaned far enough out to fall and shouted in an exalted voice, "Viva San Pablo! The best parish in the city!" I took my feet from the rungs and slid.

The iron scorched my hands. The penitentes turned and shouted, "Viva San Marco! The best parish in the city!" My feet hit ground.

"You can all go to Hell," the man at the window shouted happily, and flung his cognac bottle. It smashed to slivers beside me. The penitentes laughed. The policeman came back.

I walked slowly in the other direction. I turned at the next corner and went around the block. The parallel street was full. No one was in costume.

They were all going toward the increasing sound of trumpets. I fell in behind five men, arm in arm, laughing about something. The world was spinning. I tried to hear what the men were saying. I caught something about a woman on a horse, and then we were at the entrance to the Florida Hotel.

Vidal emerged.

He had a companion. The other man was the short thick guy who had picked up Parker.

They were talking quickly and urgently. I passed. I wanted to run. Craddock was dead. The knife was missing from my case. This was a foreign land. I was afraid of Vidal. The realisation of Craddock's death hit me fully. I snatched a backward look.

Vidal and the short man were close behind, following me, still talking. I quickened my pace. The men in front still laughed. I reached the corner where the mob waited and looked desperately from side to side for escape. Then I was finished.

The entire length of the Avenida José Antonio was filled immovably thick on both sidewalks with waiting people. The road was packed with procession. Cowled men on black-draped horses beat funereally on drums muffled with purple velvet. Bannered trumpets wailed. An image passed. Another was approaching. A half-dozen more lay far back in a diminishing cluster of lights.

They dipped and swayed. The torches flickered. The air was full of incense and sad music, the murmur of throngs, the sussuration of the shuffling penitentes. I stood. I could do nothing else. There was no way of movement except back into the arms of Vidal. He was right behind me. I thrust at the edge of the mob.

The man in front looked round in annoyance. He said, "What?" Then he laughed. He shouted loudly, "Hey, let this fellow through. This fellow has lost his procession." The heads turned, the ragged path opened and they waited for me.

I was choking in my throat. I shouldered through. Then I stepped from the curbside and was in the procession.

The image swayed at my back. Then penitentes were all about me. I fell into line, sucking a deep breath, suffocating like Craddock, knowing Craddock was dead. From the single usable slit in the hood I saw Vidal and the short man cleav-

ing a parallel progress through the pack on the sidewalk. I fixed my single eye
on the bare feet of the man in front. Craddock was dead. There was a clicking
sound.

The men under the statue bent almost double and lowered their burden to the
ground to rest themselves. The candles dipped, the band ceased, the whole procession drew to a stop. A woman in the crowd burst suddenly into a frenzied
saeta, her voice cutting passionately through the sudden stillness, her impro-
vised prayer harsh and high and hoarsely sweet. "Ay, Jesus!" she sang. "Ay, poor
sweet Jesus! To what place have the wicked people taken you this night? Come
back and save me. Come back. Come back."

I raised my head.

A million miles away on the other side of the road Julie Chirac was waiting
under the awning of the café. She gazed at the image. She lowered her head and
I thought impossibly that she had recognised me. Then I turned to look where
she was looking. Twenty yards ahead, behind the line of chairs at the curbside,
Louise was talking to the bullfighter.

I moved instinctively. I had to reach her. The barefooted man put out a re-
straining hand. He said, "Where you going?"

He had a very deep voice. He tried to peer into the slits of my hood and his
eyes gleamed brilliant black. He said, "You are wearing San Pablo colours. This
part of the procession is from San Juan. Explain yourself."

The hand tightened sympathetically. He said, "Drunk, Chico?"

"Drunk," I said. Hernandez and Louise were moving away. I dropped a hand
into the pocket of my robe. I found a single caramel. I withdrew it and hurled
it at Louise and a small boy leapt laughing in the air and caught it in full flight.

"But you will be a good lad," the deep-voiced man said, and steered me back
into line. "You will not muck it up for San Juan."

The clicks sounded again. The statue raised. The procession resumed its slow
progress. Louise and the bullfighter walked off down a side street. I could no
longer see Vidal.

I said to the man in front, "I feel sick."

"What? You talk funny. Where you from?"

"I feel sick," I said desperately.

"Wait."

He looked to both sides and pulled my arm. We walked directly into the
crowd. He called in his deep voice, "Clear the way, this chico is sick. Clear the
way." He thrust a protesting passage clear across the sidewalk to the door of the
café. "In!" he said, and thrust. The noise and smoke enveloped us.

It was a small café. It was packed. The people were drinking wine and eating
hot spiced beans. Vidal and the short man were at the centre of the bar. They
had a clear space all around them. The deep-voiced man released my arm and
took off his hood.

He was a boy of about sixteen. He had strongly marked eyebrows and friendly black eyes. He said with gruff concern, "Take off yours. You will feel better."

"The lavatory."

"But take it off." He reached for my head.

"The lavatory," I snapped.

The hurt came into his eyes. "Through there."

"I shall be a minute."

I forced myself around the bar to the doorway. The short man had his back to me. I squeezed past Vidal and looked directly into his shiny gum-drop eyes. I pushed my way on and heard the boy behind call, "Hey!" I did not look back. I got into the passage.

The lavatory was on the right. It was a Spanish café and the lavatory was next door to the kitchen. I walked straight on through and raised a hand to the man who was frying shrimps. He did not seem surprised. I went through the other door, across the yard, and then I was in a deserted back street.

I tore the hood from my sweating face. I writhed from the costume and flung it to the ground. Then I ran again. I didn't know where I was going, but I had to find Louise Morgan. She had the envelope. Vidal wanted the envelope. Vidal was trying to pin a murder on me.

12

I had not found her. I did not know the time because my watch had stopped, but it seemed an eternity had passed. I had crept full circle, through a hundred side-streets and alleys and back to the hotel. It was my only hope. Perhaps she would return. She must return.

I was huddled in a shop doorway. The processions were over, the trumpets stilled, but there was still movement in the town. An occasional bunch of drunks passed, a group of women in black mantillas coming from church. Another woman was sitting at the corner, selling cigarettes from a folding tray like a small card-table. She was hunched almost double. A shawl was wrapped around her head.

I flattened to the wall and edged my nose around the corner. The light in the hotel lobby was still on. It was dangerous to peer, but if Louise approached from the other direction and I was standing back I would miss her. Some men stopped at the cigarette woman's corner and I shrank back into the darkness and waited until their footsteps faded. I put out my nose again. The cigarette woman rose from her stool.

She smoothed her long black skirt and left her tray. She moved along the opposite sidewalk in a shuffle and suddenly skittered across the road at me. I didn't try to run, I couldn't, I hadn't the will left. She sidled to the doorway and turned her back on me. I had seen her face. She was the shabby woman with the ear-rings who had stood at the church door. All those years ago this morning when I was with Julie.

Her voice was rasping and flat as if she drank a lot. She spoke over her shoulder. She said, "I am watching. I see you from my corner no matter how far back you stand. My customers will see you. There is another place in the alley behind me."

That was all. She hurried back across the road. A man appeared at the corner beside her tray. She broke into a shambling trot and shouted raucously, "All right, no stealing," and the customer laughed. He said something else. He took some cigarettes and went away.

The silence pressed back down the street. The woman on her stool was a piece of carved wood. I jumped from the doorway.

My footsteps whispered echoes all around me. She moved a little. I thrust behind her and the dark alley was no more than a slit, a stinking cut. There was a recess in the brickwork. I flattened into it. I could see both approaches to the hotel.

The hot silence fell on us like a cloak. I stared at the hotel entrance till my eyes ached. The light was dim and inside no one moved.

The old man said, "Good evening." He was old-school caballero, courtly, silver-haired, impeccably dressed. He dropped three small coins on the tray and said with great condescension, "A cigarette, please, of the light tobacco." Then he bowed slightly, took a loose match from the tray and struck it on his shoe. His shoe had a hole in it. He walked away inhaling hungrily at his one cigarette.

I said, "What do you want?"

She spoke soft and jeering without looking back. "Well, my lady-killer. Well, my little cockerel. Got two of them on a string, have you? Take my word for it, the one you went driving with is a whore. I know."

I said, "What do you want?"

"I am going to help you."

"Are you? How?"

She said, "And the other one, the virginal looking little miss. Who is she? One of your cast-offs?"

"A friend."

"Then say goodbye to your friend. You will never get her back. Luis Hernandez has her and you cannot compete. He is handsome. He is famous. All of Spain says how brave he is. In Salamanca last year they carried him through all the town on their shoulders."

I knew where the good looks came from. I knew who she was. "You're his mother," I said.

She turned. The eyes were the same. The shawl slipped from her head and the long ear-rings jangled about her ravaged face. She said, "He told you."

"No. I guessed."

"Yes." She turned back again, pulling the shawl over her head. "The bastard of course would not talk of me. In eleven years he has not written a letter to me. Why has he returned?"

"I don't know."

"How long have you known him?"

"Listen," I said. "You knew I was hiding. You did not call anyone. That is why I am here now. But if you want information, I want some in return. Do we exchange?"

"For example."

"Vidal. The Chief of Police."

"Filth," she said. Her gloating smile was full of sadistic malice. She knew about me. "Cruel," she said. "A sewer of mierda. A man without scruples and without pity. A man without intelligence."

"How long has he been Chief?"

"One year. Before that, Jefe Comisario. Before that, Inspector. Before that, the Secret Police. Before that, ten years ago, a nothing, a something from the gutter. And always a chulo, an asqueroso, a bastard. I know. I have lived all my life here. Who is the girl with Luis Hernandez. Is she only another foreign bitch who chases bullfighters?"

"Tell me about Nolasco, the Civil Governor."

"For example?"

"What do you know?"

"They say he is a good man. How do they judge? He comes from the south, from Alicante, a widower with no children. They say he has worked for the Government ever since the Civil War. Perhaps he works hard. I don't know. There are many ways to promotion. When he reached the position to be Civil Governor he was sent here. Ten years ago."

She stopped short. "Wait!" she said. "Ten years ago. And ten years for Vidal. Is there something? Can we make money from it?"

"No."

Footsteps sounded in the adjoining street. I pushed back into the darkness. No one came near the hotel and the footsteps receded. The quietness came back.

"Tell me about Luis Hernandez," she said.

"I know nothing. I met him only once. This morning."

"Of what did he talk?"

"Of bulls, wine and weather. Of the town."

She said, "And the town talks of him. Of nothing else. When he walks into the ring on Sunday they will shout, 'Here comes the son of the Alvarez Street whore.' I shall be there to watch. I shall stand up and laugh and bow."

"This does not affect me."

"It will affect him. It is the reason he ran away from here. He ran away again when he saw me on the street this morning. I laughed. I shall laugh when he runs from the ring on Sunday."

I said, "He is suffering."

"I wish I could believe that. But no. He is suffering nothing but delights with your virginal friend. He is his father again. He will give her a pair of ear-rings and leave her ruined and destroyed. But you must not worry. You will not be here to see."

"Explain."

"The police and the Civil Guard are looking for you. You murdered an old man. You stuck a knife in his back. You bought the knife this morning at the stall of Alfonso Ferrer in the Plaza del Caudillo."

"No."

"Tell me about the girl."

I said, "You brought me here only to speak of your son."

"Is she English?"

The footsteps sounded in counterpoint. The high heels clicked sharply like a typewriter. Louise Morgan and the bullfighter came around the corner on the opposite side and walked swiftly toward the hotel entrance.

"Call them!"

"No."

"Call them. Please."

"I can't," she said. "I can't."

They were at the revolving door. I stepped from the recess. I hissed, "Louise!" They entered the hotel and vanished from sight. I was about to run after them. The second man appeared.

He walked softly. He was still wearing his beret. Roger Lascelles. He was a contact with the world as it had been before the sky fell in. I was tempted.

I got back into the recess.

He paused before the hotel entrance, looked in and changed his mind. He turned aside, reached in his pocket and pulled out a pack of cigarettes. Then he walked back around the corner and out of sight. He left no sound of footsteps. The cigarette woman rose from her stool.

She was not the same as before. Her face had become expressionless as a death mask. The shawl slipped from her head and the ear-rings jangled. She said, "Now get out!"

"I have to see the girl."

"Then go to the hotel. You will receive a welcome. There are two policemen waiting. I think I will shout for them. Are you going?"

"Get a message to her for me."

"Why should I?"

"For charity."

"Who ever showed it to me?"

"For one thousand pesetas. The girl will give it to you. Tell her I am waiting."

"Better. I shall try. But you do not wait here. The alley ends dead. Go to the Plaza Chapí, the third on the left. Wait under the big tree."

Her eyes flicked. She looked both ways down the street. She hooked me by the arm and pulled, and then I was running along the sidewalk, hugging the shadows of the buildings. I skipped the first road, the second road, reached the third corner and ran into the square. The car came in from the other side and its headlights swung over me.

I dived for the shadows. The car went slowly past and disappeared down another street. Darkness filled the square.

The giant pepper tree at the centre threw a great cover of low branches. I pressed myself against the trunk. There was a flowering syringa somewhere that smelled strong. I waited. I thought of the books I had brought with me.

So much for the reading. I had some new infinities that Pascal could explore. Somewhere not far away a church clock tolled the quarters and struck three. The chimes shivered away on the hot air and the town was silent. I had an idea to set my watch. I stepped away from the trunk and lifted my wrist.

An iron vise clamped across my throat.

I tried to shout. I was strangling. I staggered three impossible steps on cracking knees and tried to butt with the back of my head. The church clock began to chime again, my eyes bulged, the bells rang a peal. My throat was released, I staggered one step more, the man hit me on the neck with the edge of his hand and I fell against the tree trunk. I lay down.

He dragged me clear of the tree by my hair. He pulled me to my knees. He got astride my legs behind me and clamped his arm again across my throat. He gave a piercing whistle.

The car started up not far away. It roared into the square and stopped with a screech of brakes. The door slammed, the arm released me. I fell forward and retched for breath.

Chief of Police Vidal said, "Then it was he. We were lucky. Is he armed?"

"No, señor."

"Put him in the car."

The huge shoulders bent over me. I swung through the air. My toes dragged, my face hit a floor, I sucked down the smell of leather upholstery. Someone got in behind me and trampled my legs. The door slammed again. The car started. I lay in a sobbing heap.

Vidal said, "Well done, Orlando! You are sure no one saw you?"

"Certain, señor."

A hand reached down. I jerked upright and fell back gasping in a corner. I closed my eyes on Vidal's grin. "You hurt him too much, Orlando."

"No, señor. Not too much. Not yet."

They both laughed. The car gathered speed and whined into the night. I fought for breath.

13

It did not look like a cellar except that it had no windows. There were rugs on the floor, easy chairs, a table with a mauve cloth, a small bar. A single door opened on to stairs that led up to the kitchen. The only cellar-like object was the single light-bulb hanging naked from the centre of the ceiling.

The walls were a nice grainy colour. They were padded with cork.

I had been searched; I sat in one of the easy chairs. My hands were tied behind me and my wrists turned up and hurting against the chair's back. Orlando was over against the wall smiling more or less continuously with very white and even teeth. Every once in a while he flittered his long thick eyelashes; he smoothed his dark springy hair with an elegant loose-wristed gesture that explained why Parker had picked him out to pick up. Vidal was over at the bar pouring a drink.

"You made the phone call, Orlando?"

"Si, señor."

Vidal swallowed the drink in a business-like gulp, left the gun alongside the bottles and came back and sat on the edge of the table.

He had one of his yellow cigarettes in his mouth. He blew out smoke and looked at me through the cloud with his sticky purple eyes. He was doing well, but doing it on his nerve ends. The panic flicked in and out of his eyes and his voice was breathy with suppressed fright. He was not as frightened as I.

"You murdered your employer," he said. "You were seen leaning over him a second before he went for his little ride."

I said, "Yes, you could probably build that into quite a case. Except that I was twenty yards away talking to the girl."

"You persist in talking about this girl. Who was she?"

"I don't know. She can probably be found. Her boy friend was with her."

"Very good." He blew out more smoke. "Now we shall leave that particular aspect and come directly to the heart of the matter. Where is the photograph?"

I said, "What photograph?"

He paused. He leaned forward and held the burning cigarette one quarter of an inch from my nose. "I advise you not," he said. "I have a very strong method for recalcitrants."

The suave Chief of Police. He was a complete phony. He was thick, ignorant and stupid and should have been driving a truck and was not fooling anyone but himself. But it was better that way. The thought of him breaking down to what he really was scared me spitless.

"A very successful method." He leaned back and waited. He had probably used the method on Parker in this same cellar. Parker had skipped off, was probably a thousand miles away by now, and no wonder. Parker had confessed under pressure that he had brought something from France for Craddock. Something was a photograph. Vidal wanted it, the Governor wanted it, and as soon as they got it where would I be?

On a murder charge. A framed murder charge. I looked up at Vidal. Maybe not even that. There was a gun on the bar. I would try to escape. I would not be left around to babble about photographs in a crowded courtroom. At the moment I was at least alive. I was a key man.

I said, "What photograph?"

His suavity began to fray at the edges. He said, "Why did you follow me to the park?"

"Not you," I said. "Don Roberto Nolasco, the Civil Governor."

He got to his feet. He said, "Orlando, wait outside."

"Si, señor."

The door closed.

"Continue."

I said, "I overheard Craddock on the phone trying to blackmail Nolasco. I followed Nolasco to the park to find out what was going on."

"You knew where to find him. You knew he was the Governor."

"I waited outside his offices and followed because he looked important."

"You had the confidence of your employer?"

"No."

"You knew what was involved."

"No."

"You know nothing of the photograph."

"No."

"In the park you pretended that you spoke no Spanish."

"What would you have done in my position?"

"In your present position I would not be a cretin and tell goddamned lies. Orlando!"

Stumpy must have been waiting on the stairs. He came grinning on the run. They did the next between them with the ease of long experience.

Orlando pulled me upright by my hair. He jerked again and I fell flat across the table. He yanked my bound wrists toward my head and I started to kick, but my arms nearly came from their sockets so I lay quiet. A drawer opened.

My jacket was pulled up, my legs were clamped. I lay there like a stretched pelt. The rubber hose whistled through the air and hit me across the kidneys. The agony was incredible.

I said, "All right." The hose came down again and I yelled. The shout flattened against the cork walls. They hit a third time. The hot wires reached for the back of my head. Then I was back in the chair again and trying not to faint. Orlando was smoothing his hair with the palms of both hands.

"Outside!" Vidal sat on the edge of the table, lazily swinging the hose. The little bout had restored his suavity. He smiled, waiting for the door to close. His voice was almost amiable. "That is for kicking me in the hotel," he said. "And if I make threats you will now be sure that I can carry them out. Is there something you wish to tell me?"

"Yes," I said. I would have told him almost anything. I said, "Listen. Wolfram deposits have been discovered in this province. My employer was working with a man named Parker to get a mining option. This Parker somehow got hold of the photograph. The two of them were using it to pressure the Governor because he has power to award the contract. I was there when they made the phone call this morning. It was Parker sent me to the park to listen. He wanted to know what effect the call had. Parker still has the photograph. I could probably get it for you."

Up on the wall an electric bell rang loudly.

Vidal went to the bar and got the gun without taking his eyes from me. He opened the door and jerked his head, then the door shut and I was alone with Orlando. He approached and stood over me. He looked down. He smiled.

He said, "What lovely hair! Is it a natural curl?"

I said, "You son of a whore."

He gazed at me in horror. His lower lip trembled. "Please do not speak to me roughly."

"You are right," I said. "I am sorry, I apologise profoundly. Would you like to do something for me?"

"Very much."

"Get me out of here and we shall be very good friends. I shall pay you a lot of money."

"I should like to be a friend of yours," he said. The door opened and I was sunk.

Vidal came back with the gun still in his hand. Behind him was Parker, in very high spirits.

"Well," he said briskly, "and good evening all." He crossed the room and patted Orlando's cheek. "Hello, you saucy little thing. Molson, my dear, did you ever see anything like him? Straight out of the *Psychopathia Sexualis*. Delicious! Now what is this I hear that you are telling fibbers about me?"

I said, "Your English is slipping."

Vidal went to the bar and poured himself another drink. He offered nothing to Parker. He said, "Orlando, outside. You, Parker, speak Spanish."

"Dear friend, a thousand apologies. Most discourteous. By-by, Orlando. Now where were we? Yes. Molson was saying that I have the photograph."

I looked at the hose on the table and the gun on the bar. The gun's effect was more potent. "You have," I said.

"If only it were true. Oh, my dear, I would not be hanging around here, much as I love our Chief of Police. The photograph is worth millions."

He turned to Vidal. "Millions, querido amigo," he said, missionizing, trying to convince the other man about something. "We shall make those millions together and be rich. You will retire to a life of luxury. I shall go to South America and a glorious future. Mr. Molson, do tell us where is the photograph."

"I don't know."

"You do, dear. You must."

"Perhaps Vidal has it. He was pretty sharp to the hotel after Craddock was dead."

None of the suavity was left. Vidal said, "We waste time. I went to the morgue as I told you. Craddock had nothing in his pockets. I went to the hotel and the place had already been searched."

"By me," I said. "Looking for the photograph. Which proves I don't know where it is."

"Which proves to me," Parker said, "that you do know where it is. You have just convinced me. Shall we to the questioning, Señor Vidal? Very effective, I know from experience."

"Vidal," I said. "Parker is a liar and a trickster. He is wanted on a warrant in France."

"And you, dear, are wanted on a warrant right here. For murder. Oh, you strange person, you, accusing Señor Vidal of having the photograph and then appealing to him for help. Permit me to unconfuse the situation for you. Señor Vidal does not have the photograph or he would tell me. For without me he can make no money. I do not have the photograph or, believe me, I should not be here. Mr. Craddock did not have the photograph with him and it was not in the ruined hotel rooms when Señor Vidal carried out his search. Why not speak up before we get to the painful part of the process? And it is painful, very, I can assure you."

I looked at the gun. To sing a song and then be shot did not appeal to me. I said, "Who killed Craddock?"

Vidal said, "Where is the photograph?"

"I don't know."

"Where is it?"

"I don't know."

"Orlando!"

Parker said, "My dear, this is going to be awful."

I said nothing. All my pores yawned.

This time I was pulled up by the lapels. I was stretched across the table in the same position and I knew I could not endure it, but I could see the big gun on the bar and I was convinced they would kill me afterwards. I saw the hose beside me; then it disappeared. I sweated with anticipation and put my teeth hard together and the thing came whistling down.

It was worse than I had imagined.

"Where is it?"

Parker said, "My dear, don't leave it too long or you will not urinate comfortably for weeks."

"Where is it?"

"I don't know."

My nervous system traced itself like a red-lined diagram in a medical book. On the fourth blow I started to howl. Then my voice disappeared, my vocal chords buzzed, but no sound got beyond my throat. Blood poured into my eyeballs and everything went a dull blurry red. There was no sound in the world but swishing rubber. A madman began shouting, "She has it, she has it, she has it!"

The hose stopped. The voice was mine.

"Who?"

"Louise Morgan," I said.

There was a buzz of voices. I understood not a word. I was on my feet, Orlando's solicitous arm around me, Vidal in front of me with the hose in his hand.

I said, "In an envelope. Craddock gave it to her to give to me."

Vidal grinned. The hose swished lightly. I dragged away from the protecting arm and swung my right foot. I was too slow.

The pain of the movement went all over me. Vidal stepped out of the way, the rubber hose smacked me on the side of the face and I fell into the armchair.

Vidal said, "The secretary. The girl whoring around town with this Luis Hernandez."

Parker said disgustedly, "Is she one of those? The dirty little bitch."

14

I was standing at a bar wearing a ten-gallon hat and fur pants. There were two big six-shooters slung at my hips. The man at the other end of the bar dropped his hands and I tried to draw. I had no arms. The bullet somehow hit me in the back and I fell down dead.

I was picked up gently. My feet touched floor, I took two steps, shouted with pain and the light came on. The rope had been removed from my wrists. I was standing at a door, looking up the stairs, Orlando's arm about my waist. Parker said behind me, "He is all right now," and Vidal's face appeared at the top of the stairs. I took one more step. I was not all right.

I started to fall. The heavy strong arm tightened, my feet left the ground and Orlando carried me up the stairs as if I were a child, holding me tight. We emerged into the kitchen, a nice kitchen, a large white spacious room full of labour-saving devices. There was an enamel-topped table with a telephone on it and a chair beside it. Orlando deposited me in the chair. The kitchen window was slightly open but the room seemed very hot.

"Well?" said Parker.

"At the hotel," Vidal said. "Two of my men are there on duty. The bullfighter is with her."

"Perfectly simple. One of your men can relieve her of the envelope. It is surely sealed."

"That is no guarantee one of them would not look at it. We should be finished."

"And if the girl has looked at it?"

"Then she is finished."

"You have a plan?"

"The girl has seen you?"

"Never," said Parker.

"You will go to the town and she will deliver the envelope to you. My men have instructions not to follow her."

"Good," Parker said.

"Orlando will be with you and Orlando is armed. You are not."

"Oh," said Parker.

Vidal came beside me and jammed my kidneys with the barrel of his gun. I wanted to burst out crying. He said, "You will telephone this girl. She knows you are in trouble and you will say your friend Mr. Parker is helping you. She will take the envelope to the Plaza Chapí, the square near the hotel where we found you tonight. Parker will be waiting in a car. She will give the envelope to Parker and ask no questions."

He poked me. "Will she do it?"

"Yes."

"If anything goes wrong the hose is downstairs."

"I understand."

He picked up the phone.

He dialled and waited a moment. He said, "Orts, Vidal again. Put me through to the girl's room and then get off the line." He waited while the phone clicked. The voice came on and he handed the receiver to Parker. Parker leaned over me, very close. We were going to listen together. There would be no tricks.

"Hello," Louise said. "Hello?"

"John," I croaked. "John Molson."

"John!" She sucked in a breath. "John, be careful. There are police downstairs. They say you killed Mr. Craddock. Where are you?"

"This call cannot be traced. Louise, please listen carefully. Did Mr. Craddock give you an envelope?"

"What?" she said. "No." Then she said, "Yes he did. Oh God, I forgot. Is it important? Shall I take it to the police?"

"No, don't do that. But it is important. I must have it. I've been looking for you since this morning."

She said, "But you—"

The receiver was snatched away. Vidal stood with his hand over the mouthpiece. He hissed, "I do not understand the language. What is he talking about?"

"Hello, hello, hello."

"Give it back, you fool," Parker snapped. He grabbed the phone again and bent over.

"Yes," I said, "I'm still here. This is what I want you to do, Louise. An Englishman is helping me, a friend of mine. He will drive down to the Plaza Chapí. It is a square near the hotel. He will wait in the car with another man and you must give him the envelope. Don't ask questions. There is no time. Have you opened the envelope?"

"No. Should I?"

"No."

"The police will follow me."

"They won't. Please do as I ask."

"But, John—"

Parker reached out and depressed the cradle. It was the end of the conversation. It was the end of me.

"All arranged," he said. "No need to waste time. Shall we go?"

"Orlando, go with him. See that he does not escape."

"Oh, nasty," Parker said. "As if I would." He put his hand on the back of Orlando's neck. "Come, darling. Off to the races. I hope the girl keeps us waiting together in the dark car, you naughty little rogue."

They went.

The front door shut, the car started. The wheels crunched away down the drive and the silence came and sang at my ear drums. Vidal waved the gun. "Downstairs again."

There was no hope of escape. I tottered to the head of the stairs, looked down and knew I could not manage them. I need not have worried. Somewhere in the house a baby cried. Vidal's foot hit me in the small of the back and I took the stairs in a single dive. It did not hurt me. I was becoming acclimatised. I lay there with my eyes shut and wheezed and thought of Craddock.

Vidal picked me up, dragged me and dropped me in the armchair. Craddock hovered over my head with pitiful pleas that I pray for him. I lay in a pearly grey fog and prayed for myself. Then I lifted my eyelids about two millimetres.

Vidal was in a chair at the other side of the table. He had both hands on the table and the gun between them. I kept still and watched. He was sweating. His tongue continually flicked out to moisten his upper lip. He was thick, dull, stupid and brutal. He was also frightened and nervous.

I started in a low key.

I said, "You won't retire with those millions. Parker will need the photograph in his possession for the negotiations. You know nothing about negotiations. Parker is a double-crosser of wide experience. Be sure he will find a way."

"Shut up!"

I did. I waited.

"Then there are one or two other points," I said. "The unknown quantities always attached to high finance. To clinch the wolfram deal it might be necessary to make the photograph public. Who knows? Or not even that. Someone might publicise it in a fit of pique. There is one other important factor. The Governor will discover that you are mixed up in the deal and blackmailing him for a second time. He might have his own fit of pique and blow the whole works. He is a childless widower with not much to lose. Whereas you have a baby."

Vidal came around the table and hit me across the face. His heart was not in it. He didn't hurt me. I went "Ugh!" and closed my eyes and slumped and it discouraged him. He went back and sat down again.

I waited a long time. I tried not to notice the pain in my back.

"Vidal," I said, "I don't understand you."

"Shut up!" He got to his feet.

"In ten years you have reached high position. The most important man in the city. You live well and everyone takes his hat off to you. Everyone is afraid of you. I am afraid of you. You are about to sacrifice all that for what? I'll tell you. When the wolfram deal is completed the Governor will have his photograph again. That will be the essential part of the deal. He will destroy the photograph before any money begins to flow. And where will you be? Waiting defenceless for your rake-off, if any. With the Governor in the clear and able to use his documentary evidence of your past misdeeds. Which he will do. He does not like you. He will put you so far down in prison you'll never see daylight again. Personally I fancy the idea. I can't see why you do."

Vidal said, "You, my friend, will be dead."

He picked up the gun, went to the bar and had another drink. He returned to the table, put down the gun again, wiped his forehead and dried his hand on the seat of his pants. He said, "I shall divert myself with you before you die."

The next scene took two minutes.

They had a key because no bell rang. The door opened and they came in without warning. Parker was in front, Orlando behind, Orlando with a gun still in his hand. The door closed, Orlando leaned against the wall and put the gun in his pocket. Parker stood on the other side of the table, grinned hugely, rubbed his hands, and talked like a Spanish schoolboy.

"Absolutely wizard. No trouble at all."

"You checked it?"

"Not in the dark, my dear. Not in front of Orlando."

"Where is it?"

"Smooth as oil." Parker went right on rubbing his hands. "The girl flitted up and flitted off again, we folded our tents like the Arabs and silently stole away."

"Followed?"

Orlando said, "Señor, I was driving. They cannot follow me."

Parker said, "Now what will we do with our murderer?"

Vidal said, "Where is the photograph?"

One hand went into a tweed pocket. The other waved free. Parker said, "Sealed in a white envelope, as she said."

"Let me have it!"

"Certainly."

The hand now held the envelope. It halted in mid-air. "And what is our plan?" Parker said.

"The photograph."

"Yes, but our plan."

"Give it to me."

"My dear friend."

Vidal reached for his gun. Parker moved with the precision of a machine. His knee came up and tipped over the table. Vidal's gun clattered to the floor. The free hand gave a tiny flick and then it was holding a little toy gun of its own. Vidal shouted, "Orlando!" and dived for the floor. Orlando grabbed for his pocket and made a lurching jump. The little gun spat like a snake. Orlando did a half somersault.

He slammed in a heap against the wall and started to scream. Parker kicked the table at Vidal's face and there was another spit. The light went out. Then the door opened. I could see the light from the kitchen above. There was a blur of shadow and Parker went up the stairs like an arrow. I forced all my dead muscles to life and ran after him.

I got halfway. A shot rang out from the cellar, the front door slammed, a second shot plucked plaster beside me. I fell over the top of the stairs and stumbled into the airy kitchen. An enormous fat woman hurtled across the room and wrapped her arms around me.

I jerked to avoid her clashing teeth. I spun behind her and got my arms around her waist and wheeled her fast across the room like a big hand truck. She struggled like a bull. She was huge. She blocked the door. Vidal's gun was at her stomach. I peered around her head and said, "Down, or I'll throw her at you."

Somewhere in the house the child began to cry.

The woman shouted, "Shoot him, shoot him in the legs, it doesn't matter about me." Vidal backed a step.

"Down!" I snarled. There was a key in the door. He retreated two steps more, his eyes like slits and all his teeth showing. In the cellar Orlando screamed on. The child's voice rose on a long whine of pain. The woman stopped struggling. She said, "It's Pepito. His ear."

Vidal nodded. He waved the gun futilely and walked slowly backward, afraid to trip. I whispered in the woman's ear. I said, "I'm sorry." I felt her relax further. I heaved her to one side and Vidal leapt up the stairs and I slammed the door in his face and turned the key.

I took it from the lock. I put it in my pocket. The woman made no other attempt to stop me. I pulled open another door, ran along a passage, fumbled at a lock and felt gravel under my feet.

I fell over.

I could not move and I could barely see. The pain gripped me in a vice and locked me up. There was a car on the driveway. The gate to the square was open. The car was a million miles away and I could never drive it. I got to my hands and knees and started to crawl.

I had to get away from the door. I closed my eyes and tried to keep down the shrieks that boiled in my throat. Brickwork plucked my coat and dry soil crumbled sandily under my knees. I dimly saw the light ahead. I struggled toward it and lay down and listened to the noises. I was under the kitchen window.

She called, "All right." She hammered again. There was a sudden splintering of wood. She said, "I tried to stop him, but he's gone. He ran out the front way. I couldn't do anything about it."

Vidal said, "You fat sow, I told you always to keep out of the way. You cow, you whore, you fat stupid bitch."

She said, "You could have shot me, Antonio. I told you to, but you didn't. You didn't want to. You love me, don't you. You love me."

The sound of a blow. She winced. Movement. Silence. Around the corner on the driveway the car ripped into life and hurtled away. In the kitchen she said to herself, "He loves me. I am fat, but he loves me. I know it. He loves me." Then she called, "I'm coming, Pepito, darling. Never mind. Mummy's coming."

I lay still.

After a long while I crawled the length of the back garden. When I was strong enough to stand up I managed somehow to get over the fence. I started walking. I walked and walked.

I headed for the mountains.

15

Vidal had given priority to chasing Parker because I was only another murderer, whereas Parker held the key to position and liberty. I was pleased at figuring that out all by myself. I dismissed the other things that puzzled me and rested on my single triumph.

My ears had popped. Not the height because I was not that far up. But afterwards I could hear an early bird singing. It made me feel good. Not all that good, but better than before.

I lay flat among the rocks, sniffed up great nosefuls of fresh early-morning mountain air and watched the sky begin to lighten. My back had solidified into a lumpy bump that felt like a boulder: invisible suckers were pulling out my eyes. But it was more or less supportable now. Everything was except my position. I closed my eyes and tried to sleep.

The man came up without a sound.

I knew he was there because a little rivulet of shale slid around my ear. I waited, not caring much any more, and in a little while he said seductively, "Señor. Hey, señor! You want to buy a donkey? A very pretty fat strong donkey?"

I kept my eyes closed. I said, "I would have to see it first."

"Si, señor. I'll bring it. Right away."

"Don't bother. I'm not really in the market."

"It is an exquisite donkey."

"We shall not argue."

"Oh," he said. I felt him sit down beside me. I did not move. His hand touched my sleeve and then he took my lapel and rubbed it between his thumb and forefinger. "Nice suit," he said. "How I should like a suit like that. Nice cloth. Si, señor!"

In fact he said "Thi, theñor." It was not a lisp, for when he should have said "th" he said "s". I opened my eyes. He was complete with sideburns, oiled black hair, scarf inside shirt and swarthy complexion. He looked as most people think all Spaniards look, which is the fault of the Spanish Government for using so many in their tourist propaganda. He was a gypsy.

He regarded me gravely with the studied cunning innocence of his race. His eyes above high cheekbones slanted long and handsome and foxlike and sly. He was about sixteen, but not an adolescent. There are no gypsy adolescents. They go from childhood to maturity in a single leap.

He fingered my lapel again. He looked as if he had been crying. "A wonderful donkey," he said. "Very strong."

"I hate donkeys."

The bird sang during a long pause.

"You got a cigarette?"

"No," I said.

Another wait while he thought things over.

"Señor." His voice took on a whine. "For six days now I have eaten nothing but raw potatoes." He drew together three fingers of his right hand and made piteous movements at his mouth. "I am very hungry. You please give me money for food?"

"No," I said, "and next time cook the potatoes. Go away."

He took no offence. They never do. We sat in a long silence as if we had known one another for years. I closed my eyes. He did not go away. He said, "You want to go to a wedding?"

"Nor buy a donkey."

He brooded. Then it came.

"What are you doing up here so early in the morning in your nice suit? Don't you wish to see anyone?"

"I don't wish to see you."

"Very strange you should be hiding up here."

I sized him up. He was of my stature and in better condition. I said nothing.

"Of course you want to go to a wedding."

He had me. I said, "Yes," and started to get up. The pain wired through me and I groaned. He stood without trying to help.

A Spanish gypsy will never help. He will never give thanks. He will wriggle, distort, lie and cheat and rob you down to the buttons on your clothes. But he will not break his word. It is the only rule. It is the only way he manages to live with other Spanish gypsies.

I thought about it. I had to gather rosebuds somewhere. I managed to stand upright.

He began studiously brushing the back of my jacket. I winced. He continued brushing. I said, "Yes. I come with you because I like you. You invited me. I want you for a friend. As a friend I shall call upon you for help. I shall tell you something that you will tell nobody else never."

"And you will give me money."

"I have none."

"Man, you do not tempt me."

"I will give you this suit."

"Yes," he said. "That suit. Right. By Maria Purisima, my mother's grave and the Blood of God, I swear. What?"

"I am wanted by the police."

"Man, I guessed. We all are. Come to the wedding."

"I need help now."

"You come first to the wedding. I invited you and you want to be my friend. We go!"

We went.

There were no tracks. We scrambled up steep slopes and down deep painful declivities. The sky lightened; the air was fine and pure. I felt better physically and left my mental condition to care for itself. I was hungry. I said, "What wedding is it?"

He pulled out the front of his filthy shirt, spat on it and wiped his eyes, leaving lighter tracks around his sockets. He tucked the shirt in again and said, "I am Angelillo. And you?"

"I am Juanillo."

"Juanillo," he said. "We are here."

We rounded a ledge of rock. We were there.

The flat open space was almost completely surrounded by mountain caves. The ground was littered with tins, wood, curled paper, excrement, general garbage, carafes of wine, foul stolen donkeys and ten thin sad silent dogs that were having difficulty in staying alive. In the centre of the circle a group of women were tending a huge cauldron on a crackling fire. One was singing. She turned her head and saw us and came on the run.

Nearer she was a girl of twelve. Her greased hair was drawn back tight, her eyes glowed like lamps, her lips were cherries. A dusky red shone in the soft brown of her cheeks and she was beautiful. She put out a hand and touched Angelillo's arm. She said in her soft singing pseudo-lisping mouthful-of-tongue gypsy voice, "Good. You are in time. Father and brother will be happy. It will begin now."

She did not look at me. She said, "Who is the payo?"

"My friend Juanillo. I have brought him to the wedding."

She said fiercely, "No. No, you fool! Joselillo will kill you." She turned to me at last. She said, "You! — off!"

He took my arm. He was as big as I and stronger. His kidneys had not been recently mashed. "He stays," he said.

The other woman turned from the fire. She saw us.

She shouted, "Angelillo has returned!"

The hand tightened on my arm. The people erupted from the caves like ants from a hill. I was dragged forward, and then the boy and I were ringed by swart clamorous gypsy faces. I wanted out. All the dogs began barking.

The voice shouted, "Silence!"

Even the dogs knew. The quiet fell like a guillotine. The man emerged slowly from the centre cave. He was tall, thin and bony and in his middle thirties and with hair the colour of a sloe. The others stood back for him. He halted before Angelillo without looking at me. His very big, very black eyes had small fires in them.

"You have come back, idiot. I am pleased. Joselillo will be pleased. You have thrown the foolishness from your head?"

"Yes."

"Good! We shall live again like a family. Who is the payo? He wants to buy something?"

"No. This is my friend Juanillo. I have invited him to the wedding."

The man blinked once. He drew back his arm and hit Angelillo an open-handed blow across the face. The boy did not move. No one else moved. The silence was palpable.

The man said, "I tell you this again, imbecile, for the last time. Your brother fished the girl. Her father and I have made the arrangement. Nothing can be changed. Your brother loves the girl and she loves him. She does not love you. I love you and your brother loves you. He has waited the wedding for you. Why do you persist in this?"

I might as well not have been there. Even the small children ignored me. In the mouth of the centre cave I saw another man lurking. I badly needed help, but I had had enough. I was tired. I said, "Now I go me," and turned away.

The boy turned with me. The man slapped him so hard that the blow echoed from the rocks. We came to a halt.

"You do as I say," the man said. "I am your father. I am also the Chief."

"And the payo is my friend. He is my guest. He will give me his suit. He goes and I go."

The man without turning his head called, "Joselillo!" The other man came from the cave.

He wore a dazzling white shirt buttoned to the neck. No tie. A brand-new jet black suit had been painted on him. He was about seventeen years old and the spit image of the boy beside me. He walked with head up and eyes narrowed as if there were compressed springs in him. He had a great deal of dignity.

Angelillo reached in his pocket. Then he was holding a knife. The circle took three paces backward as if they had rehearsed it. A dog whined.

The Chief said, "Joselillo, your brother looks to insult you. He has brought a payo to your wedding."

"The payo stays or I go."

"I heard."

The other boy halted. He held his hands away from his sides like a bird about to fly. He said, "Now! Hear me, everyone! This is my brother. This is a day when I hate no one and speak no harsh words. Tomorrow, yes, or next week or next month. But never with my father and never with my little brother. I have waited my wedding because I wish Angelillo here. He shall stay. The payo has brought him and that is enough. The payo drinks the first wine."

There was a stunned silence and then a sort of massed sigh. Someone put a wineskin in my hand. I upended it and the red stream jetted before I was ready and the wine squirted over my face. No one laughed. I lowered the skin, wiped myself, and waited. Everyone else waited.

Angelillo said, "You would do that for me?"

"Yes," said his brother. "I knew you would come." They each took a step forward. The knife dropped to the ground. They ran sobbing at one another and fell into each others' arms and kissed one another all over the face. I said to the Chief, "I go now."

He was standing radiant-faced with his arms spread. He said, "What two men are my sons! Each has forgiven. What noble, generous manly men are my sons! They have said that you stay, and you stay. You drink like everybody else until we all fall down. But you do not touch the women."

"No," I said.

"More wine."

"Yes," I said.

Things became less clear.

There were nearly a hundred of them if you include the children. There were many children. Most of the women had one in their arms, one at their skirts and one on the way. Everyone was imprinted by poverty: a maximum of dirt and rags and a minimum of shoes. Hunger had moulded their cheeks and taken up residence in the hollows of their eyes. Yet they seemed unconcerned, unaware that they were living in what to others would have seemed a tragic misery.

They were swarthy, happy, flashing-eyed and vivid. They were handsome once you accepted the standard. They were the noisiest people in the world and they drank like drains.

The men sprawled on the ground, tilting skins, gesturing fiercely, talking in shouts. Their conversation appeared mainly a series of fierce personal protests. The women sat apart near the mouths of the caves, combing their hair, picking lice from the heads of the children. I counted eight guitars. There was no music. I was still ignored. The Chief was next to me with his eyes fixed firmly on his two sons. The boys were holding hands and smiling at one another. Joselillo in his smart suit was the only male not drinking.

They didn't want me there. I didn't want to be there. I needed help and I had nowhere else to go. I was prepared to give Angelillo my suit, my shoes, my back teeth. I sat and slugged back the thick black wine and felt my kidneys ease and my head go round. I went back to working my jigsaw.

In a while I said, "Sedelquist."

The Chief turned to me. "What?"

"How old are you?"

"Thirty-four," he said.

Nothing surprised me any more. I said, "A hard life, not being able to find work."

"Work?" He looked at me contemptuously. "Only a gypsy in disgrace will work. We are free. We live by robbing the payos."

"So do some of the payos."

"We hate them with our blood. They have chased us and our fathers through this country like rabid dogs. Our souls have formed in the misery of it. Our hearts carry always the fire of vengeance. We want nothing from payos but their possessions. Stop looking at that girl."

"I'm not."

"One of our girls has anything to do with a payo and we kill her."

He suddenly animated himself. He banged his hands together. "Bueno!" he shouted. "Empesaremoth! Silencio!"

I heard the birds singing again. The brothers unclasped their hands. We all stood up and the boy in the black suit stood up. He looked nervous.

"Good!" said the Chief again, and looked at his son as a mother gazes on her new-born child. "We know why we are united here. The brothers are at peace and we wait no longer. We shall begin. You!" He jerked his head at an old woman.

She rose from the ground in a bundle of rags. She made a half bow at the Chief and another to the general assembly. She ambled slowly around the circle of cave entrances and entered the last with a twitch of her filthy skirts. No one moved. No one said anything. The minutes dragged by and the birds sang. The boy stood stiff as a board and sheet white.

The old woman reappeared.

She held an earthenware crock high above her head. Her face was a great toothless smile. She shouted, "Olé! Listen to me all. I have tested. I have seen.

The good lives. She has had nothing to do with nobody. Olé! Viva lo güeno! Viva lo güeno!"

She shattered the crock at her feet. She kicked aside the pieces and began outrageously to dance.

Uproar followed.

They howled and chattered and yelled. They rolled on the ground and jetted wine into their faces. They seized guitars, there was a flurrying twang of music, a man sang high and everyone was dancing. The boy in the black suit walked stiff-legged to where the old woman still kicked up her legs in abandon. The girl came from the cave.

She was wearing a dress of red polka-dots that fell to the ground in tiers of frilly skirts. She had a sparkling white cloth on her head. She was about fifteen years old, and as she walked to her groom she was very lovely. They did not touch. Two low chairs were brought and they sat side by side, as stiff and formal as a Victorian photograph.

The Chief kissed the girl on the forehead. He beckoned Angelillo. The boy kissed his new sister-in-law on the cheek, his brother on the mouth, and then got far away from them. He sank beside me.

"The wedding over," he said, "and now the drink. My poor brother. He cannot touch a drop until everyone else has fallen over. It may be three days. Poor boy."

I said in a thickening voice, "I need your help."

"Later. Now drink."

There was nothing else for it. I drank.

The guitars were thrumming, the voices rose in derisively happy song. The moon had fallen in love with a gypsy boy and each night she came out to look for him and Olé! to see the saucy look on her face when she caught sight of him. Fingers snapped with incredible speed and fast-clapping hands made music of their own. In the centre of a circle a man and a woman faced one another and danced in an explosion of sinews and movement as pitiless and threatening as the mating dance of two scorpions.

I drank. I pointed to the cluster of black-clad women peering timidly from the end cave. "Who are those?"

They were the widows, he said. Forced to wear mourning always and unable to eat anything but dried cod and sardines. Unable to marry again, or even approach a man. Unable even to sing. If they came near during a carouse like this one the guitars were turned face down and everything stopped until they had passed.

"And if they have other ideas?" I asked.

"Impossible, man. It has happened only once. Her husband had been dead twelve years. We heard her singing. We tore off her mourning and drove her from the tribe. Enough with widows. Drink!"

I did it again.

The sun came up. The stew was ladled from the big pot and I ate and ate. The man told me later that the wedding was hurried because the donkey had died. The sun was a lot higher by then and I didn't care what I had eaten. The drinking was too far advanced.

Several times I went behind the rocks. My kidneys ceased to hurt after the second go. I went back and danced with three other men and nobody minded me now. We were an alcoholic brotherhood. The music played unceasingly and the time arrived when I sang "Home on the Prairie." They were unimpressed but forgiving. We talked of our dead mothers and crossed ourselves a great deal and cried a little. I cried for Craddock, but he was very remote. I was thumped, kissed and hugged by most of the male members of the tribe and told I was the only good payo in the world. It was not surprising that the police wanted me.

Perhaps I told them, wanting to be one of them, as free, as careless. It did not matter anyway. I was very far gone. Some time, somewhere, Angelillo stood with his arm around my neck and told me that next to his father and brother he loved me best of all. We sang wild songs, cursed the police, hatched our plan. He was to deliver the note to the cigarette woman, Hernandez's mother, ex-whore, *he* knew. Tell her to get the note to the foreign girl as soon as possible — *she* would know. Simple. We were brothers. Should we cut our wrists with a knife? I have no scar. The sun was very high.

Then there was no sun. I was on a pile of rags. The cave was dank and I was naked. My watch was gone, my shoes, my socks, and it seemed very funny when I lifted my hand to my scalp to see if my head was shaved. It was not. They had left me my hair. I slept. I woke again.

Angelillo looked very good in my clothes. I taught him how to tell the time from my watch. We had some more wine, he brought the pencil and paper, I began writing the note, no names signed in case he or the cigarette woman was caught. Where would I meet the foreign girl? No, not here at the encampment; the police might be sniffing; bad enough with me here. Better pick the Park Madrid, very dark, very dark streets, not too near the centre of town.

He explained very carefully where it was. I repeated the instructions over and over. Eleven o'clock. No processions tonight and eleven was a good time.

"Eleven o'clock," I said. The music played. The voices outside howled laments for Andalucia, for dead mothers, for hanged gypsies. Eleven o'clock. Eleven o'clock. I went to sleep again. I dreamed.

I woke up dressed in a dirty shirt, ragged trousers and rope-soled slippers with no tops apart from pieces of string. I smelled like a Tibetan monk. The music was wilder, my head was splitting, I was dying of dry thirst. I went outside to where the guitars wept. The bronzed figures leapt madly in the red and orange light of the flickering fire. The 'groom and bride still sat rigid on their little low chairs.

When the man understood what I wanted he told me the time.

A quarter past eleven.

16

The streets were as dark as the promise. I was lost. There were no processions or anything else. The city was a ghost town. There was not even the usual Spanish murmur floating over the roofs.

The ache from my head had gone; the food and long sleep had cured me. I still felt eerie. The silence, the shadows, the lingering fumes of wine gave me the impression of moving against the negative of an undeveloped photograph. I was obsessed with photographs. I was obsessed with the clothes I wore. They were lousy. I itched.

A man approached silent in his slippers and I shrank into a doorway. I was afraid to ask a direction in case my description had been issued. He passed with face unseen. I got on to the street again, moving quicker. The park had to be around here somewhere.

Time was flying. Louise would not have waited. The police had followed her and I was walking into a trap. Even if I saw her safely I had no clear plan. She might know something of Parker, but he had the photograph and would be miles off by now. She might get the car and let me escape somewhere. There was not much else.

I turned a corner.

The street was wider. There were no houses any more, only tall solid walls with small doors and narrow alleys. A man passed with lowered head under a dim street light ahead. I leaned against the dark wall until he was gone. I had a sudden wild ache to be back among the yelling gypsies. I should have stayed hidden with them. They might have liked me even after sobering up. I was briefly sorry for myself. Then for no extra reason I thought of Craddock and the ball-up I was in and I became very frightened.

I flicked past the light, past an alley, past a small door. My heart had risen to my throat. I broke into a soft run and lifted my head, and then my throat closed right over and I came to a dead stop. A man appeared under the next light. He wore a uniform and carried a gun. He was a cop.

I thought he had seen me. He halted. I thought he was going to pull his gun and fire. He reached into his inner pocket, took out some papers, held them up to the dim light and squinted. I stood frozen. I sweated. I prayed he would retreat.

He put the papers back and buttoned his tunic and came straight at me.

I turned around and walked. I had to pass under the light again and he might not recognise me in my change of clothes. I was afraid to take the risk. I trailed my fingers along the high stone and touched the small door. I grabbed the wrought-iron handle.

The bar lifted with a noise like a struck anvil. The door swung open. I fell down two steps. I fumbled with all my fingers, closed the door and lowered the bar into place. There was pitch blackness and the smell of incense. The cop's footsteps sounded softly outside and then I could hear nothing. I did not know if he had faded into distance or stopped. I was afraid to go out and afraid he would come in.

The music started.

It played soft and sad on the treble of an organ. It panicked me. I had no light and could see nothing. I fumbled through the darkness, hit the other door, it swung open into the light and I was inside. I quit. I was with thousands of other people.

They were silent. They clustered solid in great semicircular galleries rising high into the church's vast dome. They were packed in the seats and massed shoulder to shoulder around the massive stone walls. I stood halfway down the nave and waited for the shout. None came. Everyone was turned to the great high altar.

Music played. Incense floated visible on the still air. Against the altar's ornamental gold the vestments of the priests stood out blindingly in blue and white and red. In the choir below the bishop bowed humbly before the twelve ragged men and ceremoniously washed their feet. There was an air of great calm. The congregation was awaiting the Resurrection.

In the forefront of the congregation were the uniforms. There were military officials and officials from the Air Force. There were disciples of the martyred José Antonio, members of the Falange Party, in their black trousers, white tunics and sashes. There was a handful of soldiers, a handful of sailors. There was a mass of Guardia Civiles and uniformed policemen and all of them wore guns.

I waited for one to turn his head.

The music wept for humanity. I turned my own head on an aching neck. On the other side of the church Vidal's wife was sitting with a sleeping child in her arms, her eyes fixed raptly on the altar. She was praying. I prayed for myself. I put a hand behind me and felt for the door again. It opened inward. I grasped the handle, looked at the enchanted faces, tasted the silence and made a half turn.

Roger Lascelles was looking at me.

He was standing against the wall, less than ten yards away, on the same side of the church as myself. He was near enough to the policemen to summon any five with a whisper. I stood petrified and waited for him to do it.

He winked.

He made no disturbance. He edged gently through the crush of people and stood beside me, while the music modulated sadly to the base. He removed the door-handle from under my nerveless hand, took me openly by the arm and led me through the darkness. Then I was back in the dim street again and there was no one in sight.

He looked both ways down the street and hurried me across the road. We entered the mouth of a dark alley. The whites of his eyes showed a faint luminous blue. He did not release my arm. He said, "That was careless of you."

"Thanks."

"One of us had to do something. You were paralysed."

"I thought it was the end."

"I understand. Every policeman in the city is looking for you."

I said, "You could have turned me in."

"Why?" He released me. "I have no reason. I was jealous of you once, but it passed."

We stood peering at one another. I said, "You came down with Julie."

"I followed her. To spy. Not very admirable and eventually unnecessary. I find I am not in love with her. Have you seen her?"

"Not since yesterday afternoon. Have you?"

"Not in the whole time. It is as well. Her brother is a friend of mine. I should not like him to know I followed them."

"Them?" I said. "Did you follow them immediately?"

"I first brooded myself into a state of jealousy. It has passed."

I said, "Do you know where is the Park Madrid?"

He shook his head.

"Molson, where did you get the unusual clothes?"

"Found them."

"They make a good disguise. They might help. We must see about getting you out of this mess."

He said it warmly, but as if apologising for poking his nose in. I said, "Did you ever meet Craddock?"

"Your employer? No."

"A Swede named Sedelquist?"

"No. Why?"

"What did you do that night at the Club after I left?"

"After you knocked me unconscious in the car park?"

"I'm sorry."

"Forget it. You want to know what I did. I put my jaw back into joint, collected Julie from the bar and walked home with her. The atmosphere was cool, but I am a friend of her brother and was staying at the house. We did not quarrel openly. Afterwards I returned immediately to the Club and moped a while. I realised that I had provoked the incident, that the fault was entirely mine and I decided to walk over to your house and apologise. The rest you know."

"A long walk," I said. "Had you no car?"

"Yes, but it was going badly on the trip down from Paris. I had left it in the local garage for overnight repairs."

"Could you prove that?"

"Why, yes, if the need arose. I collected it the following day to follow Julie.

It was on the trip down that my love, shall we say, died. The death was hastened, I suspect, by the suspicion that she did not love me."

He smiled.

I said, "How did you know where she was?"

"When I returned to your house after breakfast Mr. Craddock's servants told me where you were. I guessed the rest."

"Could you prove that too?"

"Yes."

He clearly could. I said, "Well, you had better not be seen with me. It will mean trouble."

"I can risk that."

"Why?"

"A part of the apology not yet delivered. I like your face. Let us say that the affair of Julie has given us a kinship. I should want you to do the same for me."

"I would," I said. "What line of business are you in?"

"Perfumes." He flashed white teeth in the darkness. "In answer to further questions I was born in Carcassonne, just over the frontier. It gives me an air of affinity with this part of the world. My parents are dead, I have a brother who is a doctor and a maiden aunt living in Paris. I went to school at—"

"Yes," I said. "I'm sorry. Why were you following Louise Morgan and her friend last night?"

"I still had vestiges. I was looking for you and Julie."

"Then why not go into the hotel?"

"There were policemen in the lobby. They put me off. I did not know then, by the way, that Mr. Craddock was dead."

"He was," I said. "How can you help me?"

"My hotel is on the main street and your hotel appears permanently full of police. No reason, really, for going to either. The best thing is to get away."

"To where?"

"We can reach the frontier before morning. A native of Carcassonne knows ways of crossing over without encountering guards. Once in France you can lose yourself until this blows over."

"How do we get there?"

"My car is at the hotel garage. I'll check out and come back for you."

"I'll wait here."

"Give me twenty minutes. And good luck to us." He held out his right hand.

I reached for it.

He hit me with his left.

He gave me all he had. I slid down the wall with the brickwork plucking me and the world rocking. I sighed. He reached down and his hands slid around my hips and under my shoulders and he lifted me upright with his arms around me. He propped me against the wall.

"I could not resist it," he said. "Primitive vengeance. Atavistic impulse. Are you all right?"

"Yes."

He reached for my hand. "I meant every word. Give me twenty minutes. Would you like another punch at me?"

"No. We're even."

"Good." He squeezed the hand. "Now don't move. I'll be right back. Au revoir."

He was gone.

He made no sound. There was no sound in all the city except a distant yowling cat. Then I heard the tapping stick. I peered around the end of the alley and stepped out.

The man came briskly, tapping as he came. I waited until he was a few yards away. I coughed. I said, "Sir, good evening."

He stopped. "Good evening, sir. Can I help you?"

"I would like to know where is the Park Madrid."

"I shall take you there."

"Thank you, no."

"It will be no trouble."

"No."

"As you wish." He smiled courteously. "Re-enter the alley from which you have just emerged. Go to the end and the Park Madrid is directly opposite. I am sorry I could not take you. I should have liked company. Foreigners are always interesting. Good night."

"Good night," I said. He strode away, walking briskly, his knees bent, his legs pliant with a blind man's self-protection. I ducked back into the alley.

It was not a long alley. I reached the far end and flattened to the wall. Nothing moved. The park was over the way, a small enclosed patch of greenery and thick shrubs with one dim light hanging among the branches of a tree. She would not be waiting now, but I had to be sure. I took a quick look to either side, got on my toes, ran across the dim road and through the entrance.

The light threw no brightness. I got into the bushes. Against a nearby tree trunk was an empty bench. The whole park was empty. Nothing disturbed the silence. I waited a full minute, then I took two further steps into the darkness.

I fell over him.

He was face downward on the ground. There had been no struggle because the shrubs were flattened only where he fell. He had been hit on the back of the skull with a rock and his head was bloody. The rock lay beside him.

I rolled him over. His eyes were still open. I felt his pulse and took my watch from his wrist. I was overcome with sadness that he would never drink more wine or sing another song or even see the finish of his brother's wedding.

He was still wearing my suit and he was dead.

17

I moved away from him and drew nearer to the dim light and squinted at the watch. If it was right the time was after one o'clock. I stood empty, racking my brains, knowing I must now do something, make a positive action.

The heels came clicking hurriedly along the sidewalk. I got deeper into the shadows.

She paused uncertainly at the gateway. She took four steps into the park, halted again and peered into the dimness around her. She lifted her head and a golden sheen ran over her hair. I watched while she moved again uncertainly. She turned on her heel, her shoulders sagged and she made to leave.

I hissed. "Julie!"

Her head was up again and her eyes wide. I moved through the shrubbery toward the gate. She whispered, "Where are you?"

"Come here."

Then she was with me in the shadows, holding me tight, kissing me. And I was feeling nothing. I was wishing it were Louise.

"John, darling, you wanted me and I came. I'll help you. The police—"

"I know. What time is it?"

"One o'clock. Later."

"Why weren't you here at eleven?"

"Eleven? The little boy has only just arrived at the house."

"What little boy?"

"With the message."

"What house?"

"My brother arrived yesterday. He moved me from the hotel because the police were asking questions about you."

"He knows you are here now?"

"No."

"Good," I said. "Have you seen Lascelles?"

She jumped. "Roger? Is he here? Have you seen him?"

"Yes."

"Darling, be careful. He'll make trouble for you."

"I have it already."

She drew apart and looked up into my face. "You didn't kill Craddock?"

"No."

"Who did?"

"Maybe a man named Parker."

"The police are convinced it was you. They've searched everywhere. There's a road-block on both highways leading from the city. You must hide. Come to the house we've rented."

I said, "And your brother?"

"I could sneak you to my room. He never goes there."

"The house is where?"

"On a square called the Plaza Chapí."

"I know it," I said, and disengaged myself. "Did you ever meet a gypsy boy called Angelillo?"

"No. Why?"

"It doesn't matter. Listen. We can't go together. You go on ahead. I'll follow. I can move more easily alone."

"I want to be with you. I love you."

"Careful of these clothes. They're lousy. What is the number of the house?"

"Eight. In the corner. It has a little garden. Let's go together. I'm afraid to lose sight of you."

"You're a darling. Go now."

She hesitated. She kissed me full on the mouth and her lips were sweet. She said, "I'll be waiting at the back. Goodbye, my love."

She was gone.

Her heels clicked away to nothing. I didn't go back to look at Angelillo. I put my hands deep in my pockets, lowered my head and walked out of the park. The population was still in the churches keeping vigil. The city was silent. I walked along the shadowy street and at the farthest corner looked back.

A little barefooted boy came out of the alley. He flitted across the road and entered the park.

I might have guessed. A gypsy is on to anything that might mean money. The kid had either been sent, or come of his own accord. It was unimportant which. But I had not once sensed that he was following me. Gypsies are smart. Except Angelillo. Someone had been smarter than Angelillo.

I turned a couple of corners. There wasn't a soul in sight. Over the way the little bar had its lights turned down. I looked inside and the man in the white apron was asleep at one of his tables. The telephone was inside the door with a tattered book hanging beside it. I entered.

There are all sorts of phones in Spain. This was one of those where you pay the bartender afterwards. I picked out the number and the dial clattered and chattered like a riveting machine. The man did not wake up. The voice at the other end said loudly metallic, "Hotel Florida."

"Room four-twenty, please."

A pause.

"I am sorry, sir, the person is out. The key is here." Then another pause. And much too elaborately, "Oh, I beg your pardon, sir. Would you care to wait a moment?"

Cops. I hung up.

I thumbed the tattered directory. Don Roberto Nolasco: two numbers, his office address, his private address. Nothing about him being Civil Governor. I dropped the book and turned to go. The bartender lifted his head.

"Pay!"

I turned. "Tomorrow. I've forgotten the money."

He examined my clothes. "Looks like you never had any money. Get out before the paying people arrive."

I said, "Can you tell me where is Sogorb Street?"

He told me.

I went through streets that drew me nearer to the centre of town. I ducked occasionally, but not in panic. The decision to do something had somehow quietened my fear. I anticipated all sorts of trouble, but it turned out to be pretty well nothing.

The house was a big sombre-looking stone building standing in its own grounds, surrounded by a paling fence and a low gate with a padlock. There was one light. It shone from a window on the second floor. There was also a vigilante, the sort you get in Spain, a neighbourhood night-watchman. He was short and old, wore a peaked cap and carried a thick stick.

In Spain they don't care how much noise they make at night. Sometimes the watchman banged his stick on the sidewalk and sometimes he rattled it along the palings. When he disappeared around the block for the second time I came out of my hiding place and went over the padlocked gate. I raced across a dirty brown lawn littered with small rocks and got round to the back.

The garden in the rear had bigger rocks. There were flower beds, a tree down at the bottom and what looked like a rose arbour. But mostly it was rocks. There were no lights from the back windows. There must be servants, but they were either at church, asleep in bed or sitting in the dark. I hoped not the last.

I tried the side door, french windows, three other windows and the back door. All shut tight and locked. The house inside must be a stewpot. I went along a blank wall and round to the far side of the house. Above me, high up, was a fanlight affair, a rectangular frame opened outward on a slant.

I jumped for it. I missed. It was too high.

I crawled around the garden. I got my pile of rocks and stood on them. They fell apart with a noise like an earthquake and I waited rigid for someone to come. No one did. I built the pile more solidly. I climbed up carefully, made a little spring and it collapsed a second time. But this time I had my fingers through to the other side.

My feet scraped at the wall and my back on the opened frame. I wriggled a few times and sweat a gallon. Then I was inside.

It was a bathroom half-tiled in white; very old-fashioned. I opened the door, stepped into the darkness and without the tiling could not see my hand before my face. I waited for my pupils to dilate. I crossed the room, opened the other door and was in a big hall. The house smelled like a widower's house, dusty and not properly cleaned. The floors were mosaic, there was no carpeting and the rope soles of my slippers made little hissing noises.

I slithered up the stairs to the second floor. The light was shining from under a door at the end of the corridor. I slithered some more and eased my ear to the woodwork and listened. Nothing.

My ears hummed and sang. Still nothing. There could have been ten people in there or none at all.

I opened the door and ran across the room.

He was behind a desk with a book in front of him and his glasses in one hand. The finger and thumb of the other hand were rubbing his eyes. His head jerked, his hand dived for the drawer, but too slowly because he was afraid to break his glasses. I slammed the drawer on his hand, opened it swiftly again, and then I had the gun.

I backed. I closed the door softly, felt behind me and turned the key. I stood against the door and aimed at him. He rubbed his damaged hand a moment, put on his glasses, then placed both hands on the desk and sat rigid.

He said, "You are the man from the park. You are Molson."

I said, "I am the man with the photograph."

He was wearing a dressing-gown. He still resembled the comic general of Russian literature, but there was something impressive about him. His face was stony and his eyes cold. He looked deathly ill. He moistened his lips and said, "I can do nothing for you, Molson. The option has been awarded as I told you yesterday on the telephone. The final decision reached Madrid two days ago and will be made public within the next week. It can not be changed."

"I can ruin you."

"I expect you will. There will be compensations. I shall ruin Vidal. You, Mr. Molson, are ruined already. The police will take you."

I said, "Who got the option?"

He was silent a moment. Derision appeared in his eyes. "Don't pretend, please. You know who got it. It was your reason for killing him."

I said, "What?"

"But you made a horrible miscalculation."

I said weakly, "What? What are you saying?"

I felt old suddenly and very tired. There was another chair beside the desk. I walked over and sat in it. I said, "Keep your hands in sight." And then I sat there and looked at him.

"Craddock?" I asked. "Craddock had the option?" I wanted to laugh. The tears came to my eyes. The poor, wicked, rapacious old man had been killing himself, had been killed, for something he already possessed. I said again, "Craddock?"

"I found your conduct difficult to comprehend until I realised you were working for someone else. Or for yourself." His contemptuous gaze bored into me. He said, "More than a hundred and fifty Germans and English murdered one another in Spain during the Second World War for the sake of wolfram.

They were at least inspired by patriotism. Your only motive was greed."

"And your motive was fear," I said. "It still is. Were you at the processions last night?"

"1 was sick at home. But I have received a report. You were seen leaning over your employer and searching him. You pushed the chair to create a diversion and escaped down the alley behind."

"A report from Vidal?"

"The testimony of several independent witnesses."

"Did they see my face?"

"They were distracted by the procession. They saw a man. Who else would it be but you?"

"You."

"I see. A novel idea. But a friend of mine took supper here last night. A doctor. He arrived at nine-thirty and left at two."

We sat and stared at one another.

I said, "Will you try any tricks if I lay down the gun?"

"There is no one else in the house. I shall not raise an alarm while you have the photograph."

I wanted to hear it. But I did not put down the gun. I said, "I'll make a deal. You answer the questions and I give you the photograph."

"That easily?" His eyes narrowed. "You no longer want the option?"

"I never did," I said. "Neither did I kill Craddock. The photograph will prove it."

"Continue. I shall answer such questions as do not betray my country's trust."

"Right. First. When did people start bidding for the option?"

"You probably know it. Two months ago."

"And you decided so promptly?"

"Yes. To terminate the unpleasant pressure of bribery offers of people like you."

"Who did the bidding?"

"About one hundred and twenty companies of all nationalities."

"And how much money is involved?"

"Who can say? A great deal. Start with fifty million dollars. It is why I received so many visits. The final decision was mine and the foreigners came to bribe me. I sent them all away. In my years of public office I have never once betrayed the public weal."

"Except for Vidal."

"Except for Vidal." He flushed.

"Who tried bribery?"

"You know as well as I the ramifications of international finance. No names are mentioned until there is a possibility the bribe will be accepted. You did not mention your own name on the telephone. You like everyone else are afraid of the Corrupt Practices Act."

I said, "I know nothing of international finance. I worked with Craddock as a sort of male companion. I did not kill him. I was twenty yards away, talking to a girl. She might remember. She can probably be found. I mistook her for somebody else. Her boy friend or husband or brother was with her."

He looked at me stonily.

"All right," I said. "Were French companies involved in bids? English?"

"At least ten from each country."

"Do these names mean anything? Chirac? Parker? Lascelles? Sedelquist?"

He shook his head. "I almost believe you know nothing. Names are hidden in these affairs. Personalities disappear into anonymity behind the company front. Except for an occasional man like your late employer who wishes to be boastful. He was perhaps a megalomaniac."

"He was," I said. "Who beside you knew the inside of all these dealings?"

"At this end nobody. There is a susceptibility to corruption in all governments. I was given entire responsibility and conducted the affair in secret. Afterwards I sent my decisions to the National Government in Madrid."

"Decisions? Plural?"

"I was at first undecided. Between Craddock and two other companies."

"What companies?"

He hesitated. "Very well. Bijou Mining of France and Schlesinger of Germany. I sent the three names to Madrid. They still left the choice to me."

"When?"

"A week ago."

"And the news of Craddock arrived in Madrid two days ago."

"Yes."

"And Madrid leaked."

"I do not know. That is beyond my jurisdiction."

"Madrid leaked all over," I said. "But not to Craddock. I don't know why. So he came down here to put on the pressure. It was he, not I, who telephoned you."

"Yes," he said. "You have another voice. You speak Spanish too well. But two different men telephoned the day before and attempted to bribe me. One was the same voice that afterwards telephoned about the photograph. Craddock, you say. I fail to understand."

"He did not have the photograph the day before. It was brought down on Good Friday morning from France."

"France!" Nolasco put his hands together. He clenched his fingers until the knuckles stood out. "Then how many people know of the photograph?"

"There is no way of telling."

He said, "I could explain it, but who would believe me?"

"I might."

"You have recognised what is occurring?"

"Anyone in the country would."

"But you are a foreigner. An American. How did you know?"

"I guessed."

He looked at me closely. Suddenly he slumped. His face was weariness incarnate. He said, "Your clothes are scant and would conceal very little. You have lied. You do not have the photograph."

"No," I said. "Neither did I kill Craddock to get it. I was working for nobody. I am not interested in wolfram. I was just a man trying to earn enough money to continue my studies at university. I had no motive for killing Craddock."

"Did you not? You have just given me another, if another is needed. You have now enough money for anything, except your liberty."

I said, "Explain."

"It was your miscalculation, Mr. Molson. Yesterday morning Mr. Craddock asked the chambermaid to call the hotel manager. The manager speaks English. They witnessed Mr. Craddock's will. He has left twenty thousand dollars to the young French girl, Louise Morgan, and everything else he owns, including his business interests, to you."

I sat in silence. Craddock had promised that one day he would prove his fondness for me. He had done so, and the taste was bitter. I said, "Yes, that would be a motive," and I stood up and walked to the door. I turned the key. I said, "I'll keep the gun, and thank you for the information. Now I'll make a promise. If I lay hands on that photograph, you shall have it. My word on it, adiós."

I went into the passage and locked the door behind me. It was not a strong lock. He would need about five minutes. I ran down the whispering stairs and out at the front door. When I had cleared the nightwatchman I ran some more.

The town was a tomb. The hissing echo of my footsteps ran after me. I skirted a park and fancied I was lost and slowed my pace. I turned the next corner.

One short block away was the brightly lit Avenida José Antonio. I could see clear across its empty width. On the far sidewalk, talking urgently to another man, was Parker. The other man had his back to me, but his hair glinted bright.

He was Lascelles.

I went back around the corner.

18

There was a gun in my shirt and fifty million dollars on my mind. Fifty million dollars. I couldn't conceive of so much money. It made my head spin.

A thin bright sliver of moon was rising late beyond the sombre shapes of the mountains. The long street was lined with tall sleeping houses. I stood in a doorway and looked across the street to the bar. Another bar. Inside were two men drinking coffee with their elbows on the bar, a man and a woman at a table and a bartender. The sodium lighting made them all look green. The telephone was in a booth at the far end and was the type that would need a slug. Fifty million dollars and I did not have one peseta.

I had to get the photograph.

I stood and bit my fingernails. The drunk rolled out of an alley and came down the road on the other side. I staggered from my hiding place and crossed to meet him. I spread my arms wide and grinned and said, "Hombre!"

He was a middle-aged medium-sized man with a pleasantly boozy face. He was a drunk and Spanish and could not resist a greeting. He said, "Hola! Who are you?"

"We were talking about the bulls. You were saying that Luis Hernandez is the best torero in Spain."

"Wrong. Not me."

"You mean you don't know about the bulls?"

"I," he said, drawing himself up, "know everything about the bulls. Catch this!" He put his left hand behind his back and made a pass with an imaginary cape in his right. He went up on his toes, started to pivot and pitched.

I caught him. "Olé!" I said, and put an arm around his shoulders. "Like Hernandez."

"Like?" He thrust me aside. "Like nothing! Like Hernandez, nothing! A friend of mine saw him one time in Badajoz. Neither blood nor eggs, he said. And I can tell you something."

"Do."

"When the corrida was over my friend felt sorry for Hernandez. He went back to see him. He said, 'Luis Hernandez, I come to greet you because we are from the same town.' Hernandez said, 'No.' My friend said, 'Yes, everybody knows about you.' And Hernandez said, 'No.' Then he turned away. My friend was left standing there like a fool. What do you think?"

"Ashamed of the mother."

"Right. The mother. The whore. And Hernandez pretended he was too good to speak to a man who could describe parts of the mother that the son never saw. Minutely. And now we have this Hernandez at the Hotel Carlton, pretending to be too good to speak to anybody."

"Terrible," I said. "Let's get a drink."

"Insolence. Who does he think he is?"

"King Sol," I said. "And yesterday he was overheard telling some foreigners that this is the city most ugly in Spain. That the people are filth."

"What?" The drunk clenched his fists and squared up. "He should say that to me. He should just say that to me. I would tell him, and I would tell him what he is."

We staggered into the bar. I said, "Why don't you?"

"What?"

"Tell him."

"How?"

I snapped my fingers at the bartender. "A slug for the phone. Come on," I said to the drunk. "We'll call the Hotel Carlton and tell him he's a son of a whore."

The man stopped in horror. He said, "I don't want to."

"Then I shall," I said, and went down to the far end of the bar and entered the booth and shut the door. The voice said, "Hotel Carlton."

"Señor Luis Hernandez, please."

"One moment."

I waited. I thought of death and millions and the photograph. He said, "Hernandez here. Speak!"

"It is I," I said softly. "I. Is she with you?"

"Yes."

"I must speak to her."

She came on. She said breathlessly, "John, where are you?"

The door of the booth crashed open. The hairy hand reached over me and depressed the receiver.

The bartender said, "You were calling Luis Hernandez?"

"Yes," I said. "No."

"You were insulting him when he could not answer you?"

"No," I said.

He was a big bartender. He followed me back to the bar. The other customers looked at me in contempt. The drunk's face was pale as paste.

The bartender said, "Pay me for the slug."

I staggered nearer the door. "Give me a drink."

"Pay me for the slug."

I jumped for the street.

Maybe someone followed. There was little time left to check. I ran down an alley and a clock was striking two. I snatched a look at my watch and it was right. I reached the other end of the alley and a firecracker landed at my feet and went off like a cannon.

The whole world exploded.

A burst of rockets filled the sky. Sirens wailed and car horns hooted. Church bells pealed and clanged and light burst forth. Doors flung open and windows, the mob erupted into the street and the empty silence was filled with hundreds of yelling people. Money fell from balconies and small boys fought for coins on the sidewalk in a sprawling mass. A blizzard of flimsy papers filled the air and the voices shouted, "Alleluja." On a high balcony a woman was calling to someone that Christ had risen. The rockets shed a light as bright as day.

The crockery began to fall.

It came from almost every window—jugs, bottles, cups, earthenware, anything to break as the Tomb had broken. A hand caught my arm and swung me. A man thrust a wineskin at me. I shook my head. The voices cried "Alleluja" and the papers drifted like great snowflakes and everyone was laughing. I shook my head at the second man: he dragged me a running distance. Sirens hooted, church bells pealed, fireworks exploded and the air was solid with joy and noise.

I ducked into the first narrow opening. Everywhere was uproar and light. I was swept along with the people who were running for joy, and then we all shot out at the other end and were on José Antonio.

The street was jammed. There were policemen everywhere.

"No," I said to another man. I put my head down and thrust through the pack for the far side. The fireworks burst at our feet. We danced. "No," I said. I reached the sidewalk. I saw the empty side street, got out of the crowd and past the corner and the last man swung me round. "No," I said.

He held me tight. He hugged me. The gun in my shirt pressed against my ribs. His teeth showed, the rocket light gleamed on his fair hair, he slammed me against the wall. He opened his mouth and shouted, "Police! Police!"

Lascelles.

I jerked up my knee and missed him. He opened his mouth again and I slammed with my forehead. The rioting crowd moiled three yards away. No man turned his head. We strained at one another and sweated and I butted again with my forehead. His grip relaxed.

I broke loose and slammed. I hit his jaw and he fell sideways. I did not wait. I ran away from the crowd and down some steps and suddenly the rockets stopped and all the light was gone. I got into an alley. I pulled the gun from my shirt. I jumped down some more steps, twisted my ankle, hobbled on, and then I was in the empty square.

The pepper tree threw its shade. The syringa smelled strong. I ran to the corner, saw the number on the gate and fell through. I used my last ounce of breath and ran to the darkness at the back. Julie was waiting there as she said she would be. I leaned against the wall with the gun still in my hand and I panted.

"Are you all right? Johnny, are you all right?"

I said, "Yes."

"Into the house quickly. No one is home."

I heaved upright, keeping away from her. It was a house with two stories. There was no light. A last rocketburst and I saw the eyes staring from her pale face. She took my arm.

"No," I said, and got behind her. She fumbled at the door and we were in a passage. There was a faint smell of cooking. She said, "Where did you get the gun?" I didn't answer. I followed the glint of her hair for four paces. There was a faint blur and she was gone.

I started to turn, but was not quick enough. I stopped. The barrel jammed into my back.

"I'll shoot," the voice said. The hand came around and knocked the gun from my grip to the floor. My pockets were patted. The voice said, "All right, Julie."

The light came on.

She came out of the room into which she had dodged. She was smiling. The man behind said, "We waited a long time. I am glad you came. You can turn round now." I did. Julie said, "This is my brother."

He was small and pale and between thirty-five and forty. He had nice clothes and tired eyes. He did not look like her.

"Pick up the other gun, Julie."

It scraped on the floor.

"Like a drink, Mr. Molson?"

"A good idea," I said.

The other footsteps came crunching around the side of the house.

He made a small gesture with his free hand. Julie put the other gun hard against my spine and the lights went out. We stood packed in the dark narrow passage, the open door making a faint grey oblong of lighter darkness. The footsteps halted. The man stood framed in silhouette.

"Anyone home?" he said, in his quiet musical voice, and stepped inside. "It is I. Roger. Oh, I see. No, I am not armed." He had stopped moving. The door shut.

The lights came on again.

Lascelles' hands were in the air. Chirac's gun was pushed into his ribs. Lascelles smiled past my shoulder and said, "Evening, Julie, you appear to be occupied. Yes, this is quite unnecessary. The situation is too complicated for parlour games with guns."

He looked at me quizzically, eyebrows raised. I said, "How's the jaw?"

"You swine," he said pleasantly, "we shall even that later."

I said, "Chirac, I could use that drink."

The gun bored hard at my vertebrae. I felt a sense of hurt pride that she had never really liked me.

19

There were outside shutters on the window. She went to the garden and closed them. She locked the back door, brought back the key, poured out drinks and handed them to us over our shoulders to stay out of range of her brother's gun. It was all nearly civilised. She moved lightly and as if the situation was faintly amusing. She broke open the other gun to check it was loaded, sat on the arm of the settee and covered us.

The Chirac family was taking no chances.

The room was pleasantly furnished in dark wood, softly lighted by a single tall lamp plugged in the wall. The whisky was Spanish. It tasted like a varnish remover. Lascelles took a sip and placed his glass on the floor. I nursed mine. We were both in deep armchairs and would need two seconds to rise. The guns would need .01 second. Lascelles seemed unperturbed and so did Chirac. They made polite French conversation.

Lascelles said, "Yves, I puzzle about the guns. I could have used a weapon earlier this evening when I still thought Molson was of use to me. I was afraid to bring one into the country. Was the car not searched at the frontier?"

"Julie was with me. You know Spaniards. They were most courtly."

"Your fatal charm," Lascelles said smiling at her. "As a solitary male my car was almost stripped."

Chirac said, "You followed us down, of course."

Lascelles said, "Yves, that was not a good story about your aunt in Avalon. But no, I was actually following Craddock. It was a surprise to find you here. I had not connected you until then."

"And I had not the smallest suspicion about you," Chirac said.

"No, it is something entirely new for me. I floated the company especially for the deal. A faint chance, but worth taking, don't you think?"

Julie said, "Then you came to stay with us to be near Craddock." She pouted mockingly. "Roger! I thought you were interested in me."

"You were interested in my supposed money," he said.

I said in the same cookie-pushing tone, "And she was pretending to be interested in me. And pretending her brother didn't know about us."

"Oh that!" She smiled. "It was supposed to put Craddock off the track if he questioned you about the questions I was asking. And it did add spice, didn't it? And I am interested in you."

"Let's get down to it," I said. "One of you gentlemen is on the short list."

Lascelles looked blankly at me. Chirac narrowed his tired eyes. He said, "So Craddock knew. That is interesting. Julie, you didn't do so well getting information from our friend here."

"Does it matter now? Johnny, darling, I thought you were telling me everything. After all the work I put in for you."

"Craddock knew you were pumping me," I said. "I didn't mind. I was pumping you. Metaphorically and literally."

She said, "That's not nice."

"I liked it."

Chirac said, "And now explain, Roger, why you came down here."

Lascelles picked up his drink, sipped, shuddered and put down the glass again. "Would it not be better to concentrate on the present? We can begin by handing Molson over to the police."

"No," Chirac said.

"Why not?"

"I need him."

"For what?"

"I need him."

"You do not, Yves. I shall tell you why. He no longer has the photograph. He never had it."

There was a long ticking silence. They examined one another as if trying to guess a suit size.

"No bluff now," Lascelles said. "A short time ago I talked to a gentleman known in Paris as Major Parker. He was not so closely allied with Craddock as I had imagined. He did not give Craddock the photograph. He has it still in his possession. He said he would contact you immediately and sell the picture to which ever of us bid the most. He must be the only man in Europe who knows I floated the company."

"Parker," Chirac said. "I remember. He did an odd job for me years ago. Continue."

"His starting price is fantastic. I would not consider it except that ownership of the photograph means the wolfram. He wants cash. I have not that amount of money."

"I thought you were rich, Roger."

"So did I," said Julie.

"You do not know what he asks. I don't have it, neither do you, neither do most people. I am here to present you with a simple scheme. We shall combine. It will prevent our bidding against one another and thereby rob Parker of his strongest weapon. We share the purchase price and afterwards the profits on the wolfram. Papers can be drawn up now or in the morning."

Chirac said:

"What photograph?"

The silence fell. Somewhere a last rocket exploded. There was a lot of blank staring going on. Lascelles said, "You don't know?"

"No."

"I appear to have been mistaken. It in no way alters the situation. I had considered combining with you even before I saw Parker. I called at your hotel earlier this evening. You had moved."

Chirac said, "Tell me about the photograph."

Lascelles stared at his knees.

"Molson?"

"Freely," I said. "It's a blackmail weapon."

"Against whom?"

I stared at my own knees.

"Well, a little deduction," Chirac said. "It can only be Señor Nolasco, the Civil Governor. There, I think, a blackmailer will be doomed. Nolasco is incorruptible. Two days ago he refused twenty per cent of the wolfram profits as a bribe."

"Another point," I said, "is that Parker does not have the photograph."

Lascelles' head jerked up. The startled look went from his eyes and he smiled. "No, that will not do. You cannot prolong your supposed usefulness. I suggest, Yves, that we give him to the police. Or do we kill him to shut his mouth?"

I was the only one who appeared shocked. I thought of the hundred and fifty Germans and English. I thought of fifty million dollars.

"More important, Roger," Chirac said, "is shutting your mouth."

"You are not interested in a partnership?"

"Very much. But not with you."

"Then?"

"With Mr. Molson. He and I can be of great mutual advantage. You, Roger, are not included."

Lascelles said, "I must confess I am not following."

"Then listen most carefully. Mr. Molson, Mr. John Molson, is now the head of Craddock Enterprises. I am surprised you don't know."

I said, "I'm surprised you do, Chirac."

"My friend, the witnesses to the will are having their hour of glory by telling all who will listen. It was lax of you not to visit Craddock's hotel today, Roger. You would have heard."

"Still it does not change my main point. Whoever has the photograph gets the option."

"No, Roger. Your contention may have been valid a week ago and nearly valid on Good Friday morning. But not on Good Friday evening. The option had already been awarded."

"Nonsense," Lascelles snapped. "So soon? Impossible."

"To Craddock Enterprises," Chirac said.

"Ridiculous."

"Another drink, Mr. Molson?" Chirac asked.

"No. It's bad."

Lascelles said, "Then it becomes even more urgent that we get rid of Molson."

I looked at Julie. She smiled. The light shone on her hair and she was very beautiful. And very nasty. I smiled back at her.

"Wrong again," Chirac said. "If Molson disappears from the scene the company collapses and the award becomes null. Previous lists will become null. All the companies who bid before will bid again, but this time with benefit of past experience. They will offer low bids and ridiculous concessions. There is no telling who would get the award next time. Profits will be cut by millions. I have been too near the centre to resign now. I fight competitors while there is a chance, but when I can no longer fight them I join them. Mr. Molson and I will be partners."

"And I?" Lascelles asked.

"Out in the cold," Chirac said. "So far out that you had better order snow boots. I am sorry I cannot permit you to leave yet. I do not want you to send the police. Mr. Molson and I must first reach an agreement."

"And if we fail?" I asked.

"Anyone can send for the police. You are wanted for the murder of Craddock."

I said, "And who really killed him?"

"In the circumstances the question is irrelevant," Chirac said. "Here is my offer. We shall draw up papers allotting seventy-five per cent of the wolfram deal to my company. Twenty-five per cent will remain with Craddock Enterprises. In return I shall get you out of the country. I shall find you a hiding place in France while I start the wheels turning here in Spain. There is no doubt you will be cleared. I have powerful friends."

"Your leaks in Madrid," I said.

"They can justify the large sums of money I pay them." Lascelles slugged off his drink and lifted the glass.

"Another, please, Julie. I am acquiring the taste."

She looked at her brother. He nodded. I said, "You know how much money is involved?"

Chirac shrugged. "Up to a hundred million dollars."

"Mine."

"At the moment and theoretically yes. Not when you are in jail for murder. Then it will belong to nobody. We shall go back again to the unpleasant hurly-burly of bidding. All except you. The instrument of execution in Spain is the garotte."

Lascelles reached backward for the drink. He said, "Thank you, Julie." He moved like a lizard.

He pulled her by the wrist clean over the back of the chair. He fell with her and hit her in the face and they rolled together. It was quickly done. I was out of my chair and halfway across the room. Chirac was beside me. We were too late.

Lascelles stayed on his knees. Julie was pulled tight in front of him. The gun was in his hand, his arm was tight across her neck and her eyes were bulging. He said sharply, "Everyone still. There. That's much better. Yves, toss your gun in the corner."

Chirac looked at his sister's face. He tossed the gun in the corner. It skidded against the door.

"Good," Lascelles said. He left Julie gasping on the floor. He went cat-like and snatched up the other gun and faced into the room with one in either hand. "Now," he said, "we talk business from my point of view. You made an astute offer, Yves. I repeat it, Molson. I shall want eighty per cent. Make up your mind quickly."

"Or?"

"I shall shoot you."

"You wouldn't." I took a step forward.

He had handled guns before. I came to a stop. He said, "I would and you would and so would Yves. For that amount of money so would most of the population and all of the big businessmen in the world. The present case would not be difficult. You are a known murderer. There are two guns. You would kill Yves and Julie and they with the other gun would manage to kill you."

I said, "And back to the hurly-burly of the bids."

"No, my friend. Yves would be no longer here. Parker would sell the photograph to me and the contract would be mine immediately. One hundred per cent. Do not delay too long. I might persuade myself that the second method is better. Julie, do get up, dear. Have I blacked your eye?"

She lay still a moment. She put a hand to her throat and croaked, "You bastard." She moved.

She seemed to move very slowly. She got to her hands and knees and stopped moving altogether. She widened her eyes. We all widened our eyes, especially Lascelles. The door was open behind him and a knife was along the side of his throat with the sharp edge nicking his flesh.

Angelillo's father said, "Drop the guns, payo!"

Perhaps Lascelles did not understand the accent. He got the message. He did not look around because it would have slit his throat. He dropped the guns.

The room reeked with wine. The three other gypsies crowded in from the passage and they were as drunk as vat rats. But they could walk. And they knew what they wanted. The shutters swung out into the garden and the windows opened wide, and Josellillo climbed in with his white shirt and black suit and blazing eyes, and he knew what he wanted. He had a knife. He was sober. The two scrambled in behind him had knives and were not sober. I had danced with one of them at the wedding. He had been a bosom pal. He was not a pal now.

I unsealed my tongue from the roof of my mouth. I said, "I did not kill Angelillo."

"Who did?"

I said, "Give me time."

The Chief jerked his head. "Get him!"

They moved. Julie was still on the floor and the gypsies came at an angle. Angelillo's father bent drunkenly to pick up the guns. Lascelles brought down his open hand like an axe and hit Angelillo's father on the side of the neck. Everyone galvanized into action. I went clear across the room on my belly and pulled out the light plug.

The lamp fell. I heard the table fall. I heard the oaths. I heaved at a tangle of legs and stood up and slammed at a smell of wine and hit nothing. Then I dived through the window and landed on my face in the dirt. Back in the room Julie was screaming.

The gypsy left outside was drunkest. He came with a gleam of eyes and a flash of a knife, but he was sluggish. I met him with my feet. My legs jerked straight and he flew through the air like a bad trapezist. A thick gypsy voice shouted, "He's gone! He's gone!" Julie was still screaming. I went around the house and bolted across the square and the town was a tomb again. Everyone had gone home.

I got to the corner and snapped a look. The light in the hotel foyer was on. She was the only person in the street. She raised her head and saw me coming, but whether she recognised me or not she gave no indication.

I struggled past her chair and got into the recess of the cut behind her. I said, "For the love of God, say nothing!" Less than a minute later the gypsies came.

20

They came softly, staggering from the wine. They halted at the corner and the Chief's face was a mask of fury. Then the rest came the other way round the block with the white shirt gleaming to the fore. They stood in a group three yards from me. No knives were showing. They all had one hand in a pocket.

The Chief's lips barely moved. "You seen a man?"

"A man?" she said. "I seen lots of men."

"You whore! I know about you. A man came running by here?"

"No," she said. "Get away from my cigarettes, you thieving golfos or I shout for the police. Go on! Get!"

They made no signal. They ran all together up the Avenida José Antonio.

A clock chimed three quarters. Silence fell.

A drunk came first. He bought a packet of Bisonte cigarettes and quarrelled over the price. The distinguished old gentleman bought his one cigarette and he was wearing a cloak this time, but he still had a hole in his shoe. Then Julie came and her brother and Lascelles.

They stood on the corner not speaking. Julie had a handbag. She pulled out some money, dropped it on the tray, took a packet of cigarettes and shook her head at the change. She said in good Spanish, "Señora, have you seen a man pass here, a foreigner, badly dressed, perhaps running?"

"No, señorita."

"Thank you."

She turned back to the others. She said in French, "What now?"

Lascelles shrugged. "We count him out. We leave him to the police. He is finished either way if we catch him ourselves. I go back to my original offer. Fifty-fifty and we use the photograph."

"Perhaps you would like some more whisky," Chirac said. "We shall talk."

They hesitated a moment, then turned and went back the way they had come. Lascelles linked Julie's arm. There seemed to be no ill-will. Their footsteps died away, the silence came back, I reflected on the flexibility of big business and on fifty million dollars.

Without turning her head she said, "Now beat it. I want nothing of you."

I said, "You didn't get my message to the girl last night."

"I couldn't. The police did not go away."

"Tonight you gave the message to the other girl, the wrong girl."

"I was helping you, wasn't I? I had a lot of trouble. I went to her hotel and pushed the note under her door. Then later I found she had moved. I had to make a lot of inquiries to find the house she was in. I sent a little boy with the message."

"How did you know about the Park Madrid?"

"The gypsy boy told me. He was drunk."

"And what time did she finally get the message?"

"I don't know. Twelve-thirty. One."

"Why the wrong girl?"

She did not answer.

I said, "You think the other girl is his. You did it for him."

"I would do nothing for him," she said fiercely.

"You did not want him mixed with the police through my fault."

"What do I care? What is he to me?"

"Are the police following him? Or her?"

"The police have gone. Another man is following. A foreigner."

"In a thick suit?"

"Yes. He is over in the hotel now. So are they."

"Then they are in danger," I said. "Bad danger."

Her head turned. The ear-rings jangled. She was a handsome ruin of a woman and the anguish in her eyes gave her nobility. I said, "Do you want to speak to your son?"

"No."

"We can go to your house. Anywhere. Here. Get a message to him."

"I do not want to see him. He would not come."

"The girl would," I said. "And he with her. Get the message to them."

"I do not want to speak to him. He would not come. It is the place he ran away from years ago."

"The foreign man is dangerous. The boy is your son."

"I can not do it."

"You must."

"No."

"Do you know anyone at the hotel?"

"The night porter."

"He must tell them both to come. Perhaps the foreign man will not attack if they are together. Have they far to go?"

"No."

"Then move."

She shrank.

All her muscles collapsed. Her chin sank on to her breast. "No," she whispered. "No."

I stepped from the recess and struck her. I was impelled by fear and desperation and fifty million dollars. I snarled, "Go, you stupid old bitch. Do you want to murder your own son? Go!"

She sprang across the road.

She hesitated at the hotel entrance and peered through the glass. She waited a moment. I thought she was coming back. She entered. I heard the footsteps and got back into the recess and a man came. He was an honest man, I think, but he was tempted by the unattended tray and all the cigarettes.

His hand stretched, he hovered, his better nature won and he walked away. The mother of Hernandez came back.

She said nothing. She arranged the cigarettes, folded the tray and put it under her right arm. I could not see her face. She tucked the stool under her left arm, entered the cut and still silent walked past me. I followed. The cut was barely wide enough for a normal shouldered man, the light from the street cut off, we were in darkness. I followed the swish of her skirt. We emerged into a sort of patio.

It was about fifteen yards across and filthy. It smelled like a slum and was. Tall balconied tenements cut off all the air. A baby was crying somewhere and a man coughing fiercely. The only light came from a tiny dim bar on the other side. Three men and a barman were all drinking, standing apart, not speaking. They drank from porrones as if trying to drown themselves.

We entered a door. I followed her up stinking dark stairs, feeling the greasy wall with my fingers. She fumbled with a key and we entered the room. The light came on. I looked around. She dumped the stool and tray in the corner, and then she turned and made me a little bow. She said ironically, "Welcome, sir."

She was a clean woman because her clothes were clean. The room had not been clean for ninety years and would never be so again. What was left of the ceiling hung in festoons from naked slats. The window was the size of a book, the walls filthy and falling, the tiled floor a remnant. There was a table, a chair, a bed, an oil cooker, a religious picture and no sign of running water. There was a horde of beetles scuttling from the light. Poverty lived there at its most implacable.

She sat on the chair. She looked at her hands, at the Sacred Heart picture and finally she looked at me. She said, "Can I get you some wine?"

"No thanks."

The silence rang.

"He will not come," she said.

"He will come."

"No."

"I am sure of it."

She started to shake her head. There was movement on the stairs.

She rose from the chair and backed to the wall. The nails of her crooked hands clawed at the crumbling plaster. Then her chin went up and her back straightened. There was nobility in her face and an appalling hunger that had nothing to do with food.

The door opened.

Louise Morgan walked in and Hernandez was behind her. He wore the face of Death. I shut the door and slipped the catch and then we stood perfectly still while the mother and son looked at one another with nothing in their faces.

Nobody else had a right to be there.

21

She said harshly, sneeringly, "So you've finally come home. Isn't that wonderful! I suppose I should be honoured."

He looked away from her.

Louise reached out and took me by both arms. She gazed into my face a moment, then reached up and kissed my cheek. She said, "You don't know how I've worried about you."

Hernandez was watching.

"Louise," I said, "you have the photograph."

She was very well-mannered. She turned around and smiled at the woman. She took a step forward, held out her hand and said formally, "You are the mother of Luis. I am Louise Morgan."

She was left with the hand stuck out in front of her like a wooden paddle. The woman took no notice. She went on looking at her son.

Her voice was ugly as grating metal, her eyes like blue stones. She said, "Make no mistake. I didn't ask you for my part. Why are you here?"

He remained silent.

"Come to refresh your memory?"

He looked at her at last. He had the same fine eyes and the same expression. Spanish pride sat on their faces like a mask of ice. He said, "I need no refreshing. There is no opportunity to forget. I stood around a corner yesterday morning and listened to the people. They were saying the same things that were shouted at me as a child. I have not forgotten, nor they."

"Why did you return?"

"I have a new agent. He arranged the fight without consulting me. I could not explain to him."

"A new agent!" A sneer went over her face. "How important we are! What a great illustrious man!"

He shook his head. "I know what they will shout at me when I walk into the ring."

"And who is forcing you to go?"

He said, "I fight bulls."

"Bulls?" Her lip curled. "Hunger has sharper horns than any bull. I have fought it all my life."

"I know," he said. "I know everything about your fight."

She snapped, "You know nothing. Nothing about a woman looking for work with a bastard child in her arms. Nothing of what good religious people say to her. I should have left you outside the orphanage for the nuns. I had to be brave. I was prepared to do anything."

"I know," he said. "Like Alvarez Street."

"Anything."

"Ten pesetas."

"Anything."

"Bringing them here," he said.

"Anything," she shouted in passion. "Anything!" She lifted a hand and jerked at one of the long ear-rings. She flung it at him. The blood trickled from her ear. And perhaps he had waited all his life to say it. Just once. He said it now to his mother.

He said, "You whore."

It was not gallantry on my part. They were wasting my time. I took one step forward and clouted him.

He hit the wall and the crumbling plaster showered on his shoulders. He came up like an uncoiling spring and stopped dead. Louise was in front of me. We stood like a waxworks group while the misery came into his eyes. The woman lifted a hand to the blood on her ear, looked at her fingers, then walked out and shut the door behind her. Louise said, "Listen to me, Luis."

"There is nothing now to say."

"There is one thing to say."

She was a convent girl. She was in a new field of thought and unable to express herself less directly through lack of custom. Her sweet accented Spanish made the words more brutal.

She said, "Do you know how many times it needs to make a baby? Once. There are many good girls can tell you. And we have done it more than that. What happens if I have a baby?"

He whispered, "Shut up."

"Why? There is no badness when the people are in love. You told me that you loved me. Your responsibility has ended. If I have been unlucky I can go away. In a few years time your child can call me a whore."

"I'll leave," he said.

"Wait."

"Of course. You want the photograph."

I said, "Thank God."

She turned to me. She said, "It was when you told me on the phone that you had been looking for me since the morning. That was not true. You saw us in the evening. I became suspicious and gave the man in the car another envelope. It contained a picture postcard."

"Bless you," I said. "That was dangerous."

"No. Luis was waiting over on the corner."

He had his back to us. His hand was down the front of his pants. I said, "Have you seen the man in the car since then?"

"No."

"He's following you. He has a gun. I don't understand why he's let you get away. He wants that photograph more than anything in the world."

She said, "Luis has been with me since the first moment we met."

"That wouldn't stop Parker. He'd hold up the two of you."

"He couldn't in the street," she said. "And after the time when Mr. Craddock caught us we always locked the door."

She said it innocently, as if it were nothing. I wanted to hurt her. I said, "Do you like it? I knew you would once you got started."

She said, "You don't understand, John. You never will."

"Don't give me that. It's always something special at the time. You always pity people who don't have it. Don't waste your emotions on me. I have other things to think of. I suppose you didn't kill Craddock."

"For what reason?"

"Your father," I said. "And Craddock left you twenty thousand dollars."

She turned away. I took the envelope from Hernandez's hands. I said to him, "Did you kill Craddock for catching you on the job?"

His fists bunched. Louise moved and he looked at her and let his hands fall limp. She said, "I told you, John, he has been with me every minute."

"It does not matter to you that he knows?" Hernandez asked.

"I would tell anyone."

"You want me to go?"

"Yes, and look for your mother."

It was the phrase to make him stay. He planted his feet. I went to the table under the light and opened the envelope and my hands were shaking. I took out the picture and laid it on the table. It was postcard size and very clear.

I think I had been expecting pornography.

It had been shot from a height, perhaps a window. Four men were standing in a walled enclosure in front of a firing squad. Their hands were behind their backs, their heads high, their eyes not bandaged. Along two of the walls, behind the squad, was a line of watching men. Their faces were distinct.

Not one of them looked vaguely like the Civil Governor. I went sick. I said, "Does this mean anything to you, Hernandez?"

"No."

"Louise?"

She said, "Is it a shot from a movie?"

I sat down on the only chair and put my arms on the table. I put my head in my hands. I wanted to cry. The door opened.

Her ear had stopped bleeding, her face was as hard as before. But she had found an excuse to return. She put the carafe of wine and the four glasses on the table. She said with derisive gaiety, "The house is poor, but the hospitality rich. This must be a night to remember. Who will drink?"

I pointed to the photograph. "Tell me what that is."

She picked it up. She examined it. She shook her head and the remaining earring dangled and glittered. "How should I know? You want a drink?"

"Parker would know," I said. "The man in the thick suit, the man who was following."

Hernandez's mother said, "The man who is waiting down there now in the dark of the alley."

I stood up. Louise grabbed my arm. "John, he has a gun. He will recognise you."

"You want a drink, señorita?"

"No, thank you."

The woman said, "You want a drink, little son of a whore?"

He gave a last look at Louise and the door shut behind him. She started to move. I held her tight. I said, "He'll recognise you, too."

The woman turned her face to the wall.

She gave one awful gasping sob and it was over. She went to the table, poured three glasses and sat down in the chair. She took a sip. She said lasciviously, "What is he like in bed? His father was not much."

"Stop," Louise said. "Please."

"He'll leave you. They never want you after they've had you. He'll be afraid of the disgrace. Not yours, his. The same as his father. He looks like his father."

"He looks like you," Louise said. "He's handsome."

"Fifty million dollars is handsome," I said. "The garotte is ugly. I have my own troubles." I picked up the photograph again. I stared until my eyes ached. Nothing. But the Governor wanted it, his career hung on it, my money hung on it, my life. There had to be a method of using it as pressure.

I said, "Is there a phone near here?"

"Down at the bar where I bought the drink."

"No, Louise," I said, "I have to risk it. Wait here." I put her from me and crossed the room. I opened the door. Parker was standing outside.

His face was curled in pain and his knees were bent. His mouth was bloody. His arms were twisted to breaking point up his back and Luis Hernandez was standing behind him. Hernandez heaved. I shut the door.

The bullfighter was holding both wrists in one hand. In his other hand was the little gun. He said contemptuously, "Your friend will not be hurt now, Louise," and he jerked the wrists higher and Parker fell on the bed with a squeal.

I said, "Thanks, Hernandez." He looked at me with hatred. Parker sat upright on the bed and dusted his knees.

He tentatively dabbed his bleeding lip with his fingers. He said brightly, "Good evening, señora, Miss Morgan, Mr. Molson. Good evening, strong handsome sir. I knew who you were, but didn't think you knew me. Careless of me. I was probably influenced by your pretty face."

I said, "I knew you didn't have the photograph, Parker. You'd have got away out of danger. Now I have it."

"My dear, I know. A naughty trick you played, Miss Morgan."

I said, "What is the execution scene?"

He blinked. He fluttered his eyelids. He looked delighted. "Molson, you mean you don't know? Oh. Oh, pretty good. Now where does that leave me?"

I went over and pulled him to his feet by his lapels. I felt the bulge and put my hand in his thick jacket and pulled out the cosh. I knew who had hit me in the hotel after the murder.

I said, "You women go and finish your drink down in the bar. Both of you, out! Hernandez, stay here."

He scowled. But he leaned against the wall with the gun in his hand. Louise took the other woman's arm, smiled at her and then the door closed. I swung the cosh experimentally in the air.

Parker said, "Well, I don't mind. I speak from a deep personal knowledge of my own psychology. I can think of no greater pleasure than being mauled by two big handsome men."

I swung the cosh and hit his kidneys.

He gasped. He fell back on the bed with his face white and his lips standing out like offal on a butcher's slab. He whispered, "I say. That's not fair."

"What's on the photograph?"

"I don't know."

I pulled him up by the hair and hit him again.

"My dear, it's the shooting of Dan M'Grew."

"Your last chance."

"But I don't know what it is."

I hit him. He went back on the bed. I hit him twice more. He whimpered, but he was brave and I couldn't continue. I snatched his hair again and pulled his face up. I said, "Listen, I can keep this up longer than you. But before we continue I want to tell you how Craddock loved me."

"My dear," he said weakly. "Really."

"He loved me so much that he made a will and left me everything he had. That's why I'm prepared to beat you to death. Craddock Enterprises and all its contracts are now mine. I, John Molson, am the boss."

I released him. He remained on the bed staring at me. His eyeballs were yellow with little red veins all over them. He said finally, "Well, that would change everything of course if you told me that I'm hired."

"You are."

"You'll never regret it. I'm a very useful person."

"You've a job for life."

"Then, my dear, it's another complexion. Naturally I'll tell you. The Civil Governor is fourth from the end on the left wall. The chap with all the bushy hair. He's lost it since then, poor darling."

"What are they doing?"

"Oh that, yes," he said. "Doesn't it prove how the actuality of history soon fades! It's José Antonio Primo de Rivera: you know, the Falangist martyr. They're executing him."

22

Luis Hernandez had the gun in his pocket. He was sitting silent on the table and slowly working his way through the carafe of wine. Every so often he took a quick glance around the room. He was sweating, though it was not that hot.

Parker remained on the bed. Every two minutes he threw a coquettish glance at Hernandez. In between times he talked fast with his most British accent.

"You realise, my dear, that a man in my position lives by what he can discover. I cast my net in whatever waters and afterwards try to sell the fish. Usually tiddlers. Recently a whale."

"How?"

"The wolfram deal was coming up. There was a normal possibility that Craddock would get the option, but he wanted to diminish the risk. He hired me. I circulated Paris. I put out feelers about everything relevant—wolfram, mining equipment, Spain, the name of the Civil Governor. The last was the bait that caught the monster. It led me to Santos."

"Who is Santos?"

"I'm glad you asked. My dear, he lisps terribly. Ill-fitting dentures. All his own teeth were knocked out during a questioning in an army cell toward the end of the Spanish Civil War. Who did the knocking and questioning? Our friend Vidal. Santos was the Other Side, Vidal on the side that later won. Franco's side. Santos is not a nice person. When he took the picture at the execution even his own side didn't know. And when Vidal later removed the pictures from Santos in the cell nobody would have known of that either except that an air raid started. The barracks collapsed and Santos escaped with his life. He fled to Paris."

"No negative," I said.

"Lost even before the cell incident," Parker said. "So if any pictures remained in existence they were the two in Vidal's possession. Two. I came down to pay him a visit. I met him terrible casually in a bar and we chatted. I was an English historian, very interested in the Civil War period. He checked my passport and believed me. He's terribly stupid, you know. Do you like Vidal?"

"No."

"An avaricious man. Greedy. Do anything for money. My dear, his eyes when I told him the prices I was prepared to pay for photographs! He offered me the copy eagerly and of his own free will. The only stipulation was that I would never reveal where I got it. My dear, I was only too willing, I gave my British word of honour, I never wanted to see the silly beast again. I paid him with my last penny and skipped back to France."

"Why didn't you make a negative?"

"Why, oh why? And the times I've asked myself that in the last two days. But these things are dangerous if they start to spread. I was working on the rule of the less people the better."

"And in France you told Craddock."

"Well, dear, no. Having used my own initiative and my own money I decided I was entitled to a little of my own profits. I had gathered a notion of the size of the wolfram deal by then. I realised that once I had a list of the principal bidders I could start a little auction. There was plenty of time so I began to make inquiries. The first and only thing I discovered was that Lascelles had floated a company and was making a try. Then the bomb fell."

"C.P.A."

"C.P.A. All my sources immediately closed up. They were afraid of entanglement. I could find out nothing. I held out as long as I could, then was literally forced back into Craddock's arms. Most trying. The charge has nothing whatever to do with this wolfram. It harks back to another little job I did for Craddock almost two years ago. But only Craddock now had the power to save me."

"He had the power only if he had the wolfram option."

"Aren't you quick! What a boss you'll make! So down I came helter-skelter to Spain to give him the photograph to save my neck. Disappointed, of course, but resigned. Life's lessons and not the first time. I sighed a little and hoped for a big check. I didn't know the trouble was only beginning."

"Vidal caught up with you again," I said. "Through Orlando."

"The nasty little thing!" Parker shuddered. "The shock I had when he stood up and I saw how short he was. But always a gentleman: I was too well-bred to turn on my heel. I strolled home with him. What I thought was home. Vidal was waiting."

"For your kidneys," I said.

"Don't mention it! A man can only stand so much. I told the whole story. I mentioned the sums of money involved. Rapacious Vidal immediately decided to enter the photography business as a partner."

"He'd been in it before," I said. "That's why he had to keep everything so private."

"Should I know what you're talking about?"

"No."

"Well." Parker beamed a bright gaze at Hernandez and got no response. "Well," he said undamped, "in what a pickle was Parker. I couldn't tell Craddock and I couldn't run away. The only road out of Spain is through France. There was a warrant waiting in France. I was flat broke. Craddock I thought was ill in bed and you with him. What was I to do? I was brooding my way late through the streets, not at all edified by the religious spectacles, when suddenly with clamour and uproar I heard that an old foreign man in a bathchair from the Florida Hotel was dead. Reason it out for yourself. There were not that many sick foreign gentlemen at the Florida. I improved the shining hour and zizzed around to the hotel on the off chance of getting the photograph back. Easy locks and empty rooms. I was having a thorough old uncomfortable search striking matches, I heard a noise and somebody came in. You. Calling 'Louise' so prettily. It hurt me to cosh you."

"Forget it."

"Most generous of you. But you threw me into an awful tizzy. I simply went mad and switched on all the lights and ripped the place to pieces. Had I found the photograph I should have been on my own again without the beastly Vidal. But nothing. Nothing at all. Except of course your little bit of money, and I had to take that because I hadn't a stiver. I fled despondent."

"And contacted Vidal again."

"No. He contacted me again through darling Orlando. I spoke to Vidal on the phone and suggested you might know where the photo was. I got to his house much later and there you were all tied up and tortuous. I had a reason for being late. I had seen Lascelles and Chirac."

"Together?"

"Apart. Well apart. But you can imagine the ideas they gave me. Two men in the same business as Craddock. The customers coming right to the door. I begrudged the fifty per cent for Vidal, but what could I do so long as he was willing to play? Then, my dear, he wasn't willing. It all blew up. I returned with the envelope after that painful scene with your kidneys and Vidal got tricky. I could smell it the moment I walked in. He wanted a hundred per cent. Though how he could have got it without knowing the customers—"

"He had changed his mind," I said. "He had a private axe to grind."

"You know, I guessed it. I guessed it the moment he told me he had lost his own copy of the photograph. Something not quite right here, I thought. I was on my guard from the very beginning. Thank heaven I had the gun."

"It was a nice trick."

"*Isn't it neat!* And the delight of putting a bullet into that deceiving little monster Orlando." Parker turned back the cuff of his jacket. "It works like this, you see? One two! Granny's faithful friend." He looked reproachfully at Hernandez. He said in Spanish, "Much safer up there than in my hand as I know to my cost, you brutal thing."

The dark eyes looked at us equally with dislike and contempt. Hernandez said, "Have you finished with this maricón?"

"Wait." I turned back to Parker. "What then? You found you had a picture postcard."

"A view of a gorgeous baroque church. Not quite what I wanted. Imagine me, my dear, alone and weeping in the dark of the mountains, peering at the wretched thing in the light from the dashboard. Major Parker foiled again. Such chagrin and woe. And what could I do? France was out. Your little bit of money might have bought me a third-class boat ticket across to Italy, but France has extradition rights from every place in Europe except England. I wanted enough to get me direct to haven in South America. My only remaining method was bluff. I buried the thought of Vidal, hard though it was, and came back to start negotiations with Lascelles and Chirac. I hoped they would pay me a deposit on the photograph sight unseen. I hoped at the same time to snaffle it from your Miss Morgan. Ah me, the times I have lived solely on hope. Lascelles, incidentally, already knew of the photograph's existence."

I said, "Why didn't you go to a British consul? He could have got you home by a direct sea or air route."

"Oh, the British," Parker said. "The wretches can recognise a false passport from twenty yards distance." Suddenly he giggled with delight. "My dear, I fooled you. Doesn't it just prove what I've always said. If you want to disguise yourself in Europe, be British. Simplicity itself. Wear uncomfortable clothes, insist on marmalade and kippers for breakfast and always take your afternoon tea. Be formal and polite and never mix. You will not be expected to mix. And other Englishmen will not betray you, because they never speak to one another when abroad. I remember this terribly good-looking boy in Vienna with his father. One day in the Prater—"

"Cut the vaudeville," I said.

"Your whim is my command, boss. Anything you say. Let's to business. We must first clear you of this silly murder charge. Leave it to me. Not too difficult, I imagine, now that we have the photograph and are certain of getting the option on the wolfram."

I said, "The option on the wolfram has already been awarded."

His jaw dropped. I had heard of this happening but never seen it before. He said, "Then what are we— No, my dear, it can't have been. Impossible. It's much too soon."

I said, "Didn't you hear of the short list in Madrid?"

"What short list? My God, no! Once the C.P.A. rumour got around I couldn't get a leak from anywhere, especially not Madrid. Everyone was afraid of implication. What short list? What names?"

"Schlessinger."

"Of course. One man affair. No partners to consult. He can take risks and make a better offer. A German fronted company, manipulated solely by that Swede. What's his name?"

"Sedelquist," I said.

"That's right, Sedelquist," he said. "What other names?"

"Bijou Mining."

He slumped. His face sagged. "Well, toodle-oo to you and toodle-oo to me and call the nearest policeman. This sudden darkness is caused by the fact that we have both just fallen down a deep deep sewer. Bijou is another one-man concern. The man in question is here now and on the job."

"Yves Chirac," I said.

"Yves Chirac," he said.

I thrust the cosh into Hernandez hand. I said, "Keep the gun on him. If he tries any tricks, hit him across the kidneys." I ran out the door and down the stairs.

They were sitting at a table in the filthy bar, hands clasped and heads close together. Louise jumped to her feet. The woman told me where the phone was. The bell rang five times at the other end, and then I talked to the Civil Governor.

He thought me mad at first. I said he could send any police for me except Vidal and it convinced him. I told him where I was. I didn't tell him that the police were for my protection.

We went back upstairs. I had two glasses of wine and the others stood around not talking. Parker looked at everyone in stark panic, the two women looked at one another and Hernandez looked at no one.

Six police came in three cars. They brought Hernandez along, but not his mother. We piled into the cars and the drunks from the bar came paralytically to watch us go. We all drove off to the Governor's house.

23

We were alone in a small room across the big hall from where the others were waiting. The Governor struck the match, the flame licked, the paper curled, then there was nothing on the plate but ashes. He put his fingers in at first. In a sudden fit of ecstasy he put in his fist. He crunched the ash to a fine grey powder, took the plate to the window and blew. When he turned around again he looked as though his feet had stopped hurting.

He said, "You see, I am a native of Alicante. I was caught there when the Civil War broke out and had to be discreet until I could get to the other side. I was a man of importance. The Reds wanted to compromise me. They forced me to attend the execution. When finally I got away my wife could not accompany me. They killed her."

"It's over. There is no other copy."

"Thank you," he said. "After all these years. You have no idea how I feel. Perhaps I should have confessed to the authorities when the Civil War ended. But feeling was too high. Afterwards it was too late. The memory of José Antonio rightly became sacred. The new and better system of government was based on his teachings. I was a coward. The longer I waited the more impossible confession became. I would have lost certainly my position. I might have spent the rest of my life in prison."

I said, "But I have seen the photograph. Have you no fear that I will talk?"

"No. Too long has passed. No one would accept your story without the pictorial evidence. I should deny everything. I have fortunately a long reputation for strict honesty. They would believe my lie in answer to an accusation so ridiculous."

"Good for you," I said. "What about me?"

"You can prove who is the murderer?"

"I don't know. Proof is the job of the police. Vidal was in personal charge and made no attempt at investigation. He wanted only me."

"Vidal," the Governor said, and dusted the ash from his hands. He took my arm. "Come."

We went through the door and across the echoing hall. The three armed policemen straightened to attention. The Governor said, "Sergeant, are there more men in the garden?"

"Two, sir."

The Governor nodded. We entered the other room.

It was a big room. It had a grand piano, gilt mirrors, a long settee and a lot of chairs upholstered in red brocade. There was a film of dust over everything and no air. The company was sweating. It may not have been the heat.

Julie Chirac and her brother were side by side on the settee with Lascelles behind them. A group. Vidal stood bolt upright with his hand on the piano and his forefinger picking the threads of a decorative yellow shawl. Louise and Hernandez were on chairs at opposite sides of the room from one another. That pleased me. Parker, less a horse now than a rabbit, stood against the wall and sweated hardest of all.

Beyond the french windows stood a cop.

"Good evening," the Governor said urbanely. He closed the door behind him. "I should say perhaps good morning. Thank you all for coming voluntarily at this hour. I have no legal power to hold anyone but Mr. Molson."

"Would you like warrants, sir?" Vidal said.

He was ignored.

It was all briefly like a tea-party. There were murmured introductions, decorous bows exchanged and a spot of hand-kissing. I sank into an easy chair and scratched myself. I didn't mind the chair this time. There had been a general frisking. No one in the room was armed except the Governor. I hoped he would have no cause to shoot me.

Julie said, "It is terribly hot, señor. Might we—?"

"Of course, dear lady." He opened the french windows and murmured to the man outside. The cop saluted and tramped off round to the front of the house. The Governor wanted no unnecessary eavesdropping.

He came back in and perched himself on the arm of a chair. The weight recently lifted from his mind had made him jovial. He was everyone's polite uncle. "I shall speak Spanish," he said. "If there are any who do not understand they will seek the help of a friend."

No one spoke.

"We are here to discuss wolfram and murder. We shall begin with wolfram. Mr. Molson has offered kindly to fill in any gaps as we go along." He looked up at the ceiling.

"Two months ago," he said, "this government made public the fact that it was open to bids for the mining rights of the wolfram deposits in this province. The final decision was mine. Communications from foreign companies arrived in shoals and representatives of foreign companies in small armies. They attempted to bribe me. I am unbribable. The pressure became insupportable, the situation repugnant and I worked with great speed. I reduced the long list to three companies. I communicated the fact to Madrid."

"From where," I said, "it was communicated to two of the companies."

"The fact will be investigated," the Governor said. "The list consisted of Schlesinger, Bijou and Craddock Enterprises."

Parker brightened.

"Craddock," I said, "Sedelquist and Chirac. And the last two knew they were on the list. Craddock didn't find out because he was in bad odour and his leaks had dried up. Craddock and Chirac lived in the same district: Sedelquist came from somewhere to be near them. I imagine he was waiting the final result. If he failed to get the option he would try to make a deal with the winner."

"Old stuff," Parker said. "If you can't beat them, join them."

I said, "Chirac decided to beat them. With Sedelquist he was lucky. He found him drunk and made him a hit-and-run victim. With Craddock not so lucky. Chirac lived nearby and knew the old man went for a drive every night in the same car. He arranged that the car be wrecked. The old man wasn't in it."

Chirac said gently in French, "Ridiculous."

"Very well," I said. "A large-sized and uncanny coincidence. We'll leave it to the Riviera police."

"My friend, you are absurd and laughable," Chirac said.

The Governor leaned forward. "Please repeat that in Spanish."

"I do not speak Spanish."

"But you have understood what is being said. Repeat, please."

Chirac flushed faintly. "My friend, you are absurd and laughable."

"Yes," the Governor said. "You are the other man who phoned to bribe me the day before Craddock was killed. Does that help you, Molson? Nothing else you have said yet comes under Spanish jurisdiction."

"It will," I said. "We first deal with Lascelles. He also wanted the wolfram option. He had not much hope, but was prepared to work. He somehow heard of Mr. Parker and a certain photograph. He knew Parker was currently employed by Craddock and thought therefore that Craddock must have the photograph. Lascelles wanted it. The first move was to get near it. He came down from Paris to stay with his friend, Yves Chirac. He did not know that Yves was also in the field. Yves on the other hand knew nothing about the photograph."

Chirac was very polite. "Could not Lascelles have killed Sedelquist?"

Lascelles said reproachfully, "Yves!"

I said, "Lascelles did not know about Sedelquist. He knew nothing of the short list. He was a beginner with no leaks in Madrid. His further conduct proved it. Sedelquist was trying to get to Craddock through me. Lascelles had the same idea of getting to the photograph. Julie scotched his plan by being feminine that night. But Lascelles still tried to be friendly. Too friendly. His attempt to enter the house with an early-morning apology was feeble. Especially so because Craddock did not at the time have the photograph."

Parker sighed. He was fully recovered. "The trouble it would have saved," he said. "O greedy me."

I sat and stared out of the french windows. I was suddenly glad that the governor was between me and the darkness. I spoke more precisely. I said:

"Now we shift to Spain. Craddock came here partly because he could not stay in France, mainly to make a last desperate bribe at the Governor. Craddock didn't know he was on the short list or any list. He didn't know that on the day he arrived he had been awarded the option officially. Before leaving France I told Julie on the phone where we were going. She told her brother. They both took out after us. Lascelles was not much interested until he went to Craddock's house, maybe to make another apology. He came down to Spain on the trail of the photograph."

"And Craddock was murdered," the Governor said.

He wanted to skip the next part. I didn't blame him. But I had to tell it all if only to get it straight in my own mind. I looked out into the night again.

I said, "The murder doesn't come yet. Several new elements are introduced. Chirac phoned offering a bribe. Craddock phoned offering a bribe. No luck for either. Then on Good Friday morning up pops Parker, introducing for the first time the actual photograph."

"Perforce," Parker said.

"Which he had previously bought from Vidal."

"And, my dear, the price!"

I said, "Craddock phoned the Governor again. The Governor realised Vidal was implicated and got in touch with him. They were both in danger. But Vidal had a starting point. He had sold the photograph to Parker and Parker was back in town. He probably thought Parker was doing the blackmailing. They had a short sharp session together and Parker told about Craddock. A little later Craddock was murdered."

"By?" Julie said.

I stared out of the french windows. I was not deceived. I said, "Four men wanted the photograph: Lascelles, Vidal, Parker and the Governor. Chirac had tried to kill Craddock in France because Chirac wanted to be the only man on the short list. A total of five people. Someone went to the hotel and stole the murder weapon from my room. In the crowds, in the dark, it was stuck into

Craddock's back. When I got to the hotel Parker was already there looking for the photograph. Parked slugged me. When I recovered, Vidal turned up, also looking for the photograph. I did a lot of dodging after that. I dodged right back into Vidal's arms. He hadn't found the photograph yet and neither had Parker. Vidal had the idea of teaming with Parker and making a fortune, but I changed his mind. Then I dodged out of his arms. I wound up at a gypsy encampment."

I had their attention. I also had the murderer.

"There was a boy at the encampment," I said, a bit louder. "A nice boy. In return for a few services I gave him my suit. A mistaken appointment was made for me with Julie at eleven o'clock in the Park Madrid. A note was slipped under Julie's door at the hotel. The mistake was discovered and a message delivered much later to the house her brother has rented. But somebody read the note and went early to the park to wait for me. The gypsy boy, being a gypsy, had the same idea. He probably went to the park with the idea of eavesdropping his way into a little money. It was a dark park and he was wearing my American-cut suit. He was mistaken for me. He was killed."

The Governor sat up straight. "Does anyone else know of this?"

"Oh, yes," I said. "Yes indeed."

"Who did it?"

"The same person who killed Craddock, and for the same reason. Looking for the photograph."

"Who?"

"The person who went to my room and got the knife. The knife was locked away in my suitcase. The fact that it was found proves the person was searching thoroughly. For what? The photograph. If we take it slowly it all comes out simply. Was it the Governor? No. He was sick at home with a first-class alibi. Parker? No. He came to search after the murder. The murderer had searched already, before the murder. Vidal? No. He came too. He also went to the morgue, which indicates he was summoned from a known address in an official capacity. Which indicates a phone. Which puts him off the streets."

"I can prove it," Vidal said.

I said, "And Hernandez is an alibi for Miss Morgan, and vice versa. And she didn't need to search for the photograph because she already had it. Whom have we left?"

"Yves Chirac," said Lascelles.

"Right. Yves Chirac. With his leaks in Madrid. The same leaks that told him on Friday that Craddock already had the option. Which left him where? With the idea of trying to make a deal with Craddock as he afterwards tried to make one with me. But not to kill Craddock. That would mean the bidding beginning all over again, with the other companies this time more experienced. So who is left now?"

"Me," Lascelles said.

"You," I said.

"Prove it."

"You were wearing a beret to hide your blonde hair."

"Prove it."

"Finding the murderer is usually the difficult part," I said. "The proof follows naturally. It may take time, but it'll come. I began to suspect because you were in the church so near to the park. Then when you slugged me in the alley you ran your hands over me, feeling for the photograph. I didn't have it. But it might have been hidden somewhere. You made plans to take me off in your car to where I could be better questioned. Very solicitous of you. In complete contrast to the next time I saw you and you yelled for the police. In between times you had seen Parker. He had told you that he had the photograph. You had no further use for me except as a scapegoat. And a little later you told Chirac you had visited his hotel. He was gone. But you had entered one hotel room the night before and you did it again. You found my note and went to the park. You killed the gypsy boy. One thing puzzled me. Of all processions in town how did you know which one Craddock and I had gone to?"

He smiled. "Governor, there is no need for me to answer questions?"

"No," the Governor said.

"You have no legal reason for holding me?"

"No."

"Then goodnight all," Lascelles said, and walked out of the french windows into the dark of the garden.

"Let him go," I said. "Let him go."

Vidal said, "He'll run for France. I'll get him."

"You will do nothing, Vidal," the Governor said. "You have just been relieved of all your official duties. There may be a job for you on the municipal garbage dump. I doubt it. The rest of you must not be worried. Lascelles cannot leave by the back way because the wall is too high. While attempting to leave by the front way he will molest a policeman and provide legal grounds for his own arrest. I suppose now that everyone would like to go home."

He stood up. I didn't want them to go out yet. I said, "You need sleep, Hernandez. You have a big fight this afternoon."

He didn't answer me.

I said, "Coming Louise?"

Neither did she.

Chirac said in French, "Molson, we must talk seriously. You are new to this business. You will need advice. Perhaps we can—"

I said, "Shut up!"

Parker said, "So rough, my dear!"

I stepped into the garden.

The back garden wall was not all that high, not too high for the man who had listened outside the window. He had come and gone with a blur of white shirt and no sound. I turned back to the Governor. I said, "Sir, you had better come out here."

Lascelles was lying dead among the rockery with his throat cut.

24

We had seats down at the front near the barrier. The ceremonial march was over, the first bull was in, the third trumpet had sounded and one of the picadors was leaning from his old blindfolded nag and was jabbing at the bulls tossing muscles with an eight-foot spiked pole. On the rising stone tiers around and behind us twenty thousand people were crammed. They sweated in the heat and shouted with impatience. They were a very bad crowd.

Louise was not looking because of the horse.

I said, "In Alcoy last year a man caught his wife in bed with a kid of twenty. He shot them both as they lay there, gave himself up to the police and in twenty-four hours the case was finished and the man free. It's the Spanish idea that Family is sacred. Even a gypsy's family. I don't suppose the police will press too hard. If they do they'll get no help from me. They'll certainly get none from the gypsies."

Louise said, "How did they find the girl?"

"With a broadcast from the local radio station. She remembers that I spoke to her. She has identified me. So has her boy friend. They prove I could not have been the man seen bending over Craddock before he went for his ride. Not that their evidence was necessary. Lascelles left a trail a mile wide. He was seen in the hotel corridor by the chambermaid. It was she who told him which procession we were at. That, by the way, was why he didn't know about the will. The whole hotel was talking about it, but he was afraid to go back in case he was recognised. He had shot his bolt."

"All for money," Louise said.

"For fifty million dollars and up," I said, and laughed. Why not? The money was mine. I said, "He was seen, too, in the other hotel when he found my note. He had been up to Julie's room. The manager remembers that Lascelles came down in the elevator before asking where the Chiracs had moved to. How did he know they had moved unless he had been in the rooms?"

She said, "What about Parker?"

"Fixed," I said.

"Are you pleased about that?"

"Yes," I said. "Parker was too shifty. I didn't want him in my hair. I enlisted the aid of the Governor. The local authorities phoned France this morning. Parker has been arrested and now awaits deportation to face the C.P.A. charge."

She said, "Oh."

"I'll see what I can do about Chirac when we get to France. I'll work on it, believe me. I'm an influential man now. I'll get results."

"Yes," she said.

"We leave tomorrow morning."

She didn't answer. She was staring across the ring again. The horses were gone, the fourth trumpet had sounded, the peon was sticking the banderillas into the bull's withers and the crowd was jeering him. He wasn't really bad, but the temper of the crowd had unnerved him. They were a foul crowd. I was sorry I had come. I was bored.

I said, "I'll wipe out all opposition and make a clean start. Just you and me and fifty million dollars. I know nothing about the business so I'll need your help. Maybe we'll both need help. In which case I'll say nothing to the French police until I've picked Chirac's brains. He's been in the business a long time. He'll know the wrinkles."

She said, "You've talked of nothing but money since this morning."

"Why not? It's nice to talk about money. I'm rich. I'll buy you everything you ever wanted."

She made no answer. She was still staring across the ring.

I said, "Have you seen him since he walked out on you last night?"

"No."

"He was jealous because you helped me. He's not an educated man and I imagine he has a bad temper. Not that I'm blaming you, Louise. He's handsome, a bullfighter, he's got glamour. But it's over now."

"Yes," she said.

The fifth trumpet sounded.

The silver note died away, and then I thought I had gone deaf. It was incredible. Twenty thousand people all stopped talking at once. Their necks craned. They grinned. All the greedy eyes stared in one direction.

He came out from behind the burladero.

God knows what it cost him. He showed nothing. He walked a slow half circle of the ring with his head up and his suit of lights glittering yellow and green and the silence screaming at him. Admirable. He struck fear into me, but my heart swelled for him. He came to a halt directly below us and I saw the sweat streaming down his face. Then I hated him.

He took off his hat. He was going to dedicate the bull. I thought I had lost.

He looked up into her face, into her eyes, for five long seconds of the howling stillness. He looked above and beyond her and his right hand flicked and the hat skated over our heads. Then he pointed. He kept pointing. He jabbed his finger long-armed as if it were a pick. I turned and the whole crowd turned. His mother was standing on her feet in the cheap seats up at the back with the hat clutched two-handed to her breast and the silence lapping all around her.

Her head was as high as his. They were a mirror of one another. Her gaze swept the entire amphitheatre, her face was calm and impassive. I have never seen a figure so majestic nor shall I see one again. She bowed her acknowledgement to Hernandez. Neither of them smiled. He took his cape and went out to meet the bull.

He was catastrophically bad.

He started with low passes, which is what he should have done, they mostly all do. He made five veronicas and finished with a chest-pass. Had he been another torero the public would have drowned him with catcalls. There was only the silence, horrible and empty and sneering.

He made three more passes and there was nothing wrong with them. There was something wrong with him. He worked the bull at least two yards from him. He was deathly afraid.

Somebody laughed.

It made a hole that quickly closed again. We could all hear the sound of the bull's hooves. It came on a slavering run and he made another pathetic natural. He was bad. I closed my eyes with shame.

Up in the cheap seats she started shouting all by herself. Her voice cut across the arena cleaner than the notes of the trumpet.

"Olé, son! Olé, hijo mió! Olé, my son! Olé! Olé!"

Louise moved from beside me and was gone.

The bull went clear to the other side of the ring. It stood a moment huge and brown in the brilliant sun, tongue out, flanks heaving. Then it charged. It was enormous. He took it with a natural, then parted his feet and lifted the cape in an attempted molinete. I was sweating.

The voices of the two women sounded in all that silence. "Olé, Luis! Olé, torero! Machote! Olé! Olé!" They were standing together, their fists clenched and their faces fierce. He heard them.

He looked at me first. I had lost and he had won. Then he looked upward. He smiled. His smile was stamped there forever. The bull charged once more and Hernandez dropped to his knees. He made the most beautiful and courageous kneeling molinete I ever hope to see.

The sky split. Twenty thousand throats went, "Olé!"

He stood them on their heads after that. He made history.

He was glorious and poetic. He ignored every rule of safety, demonstrated every pass in the book and invented one of his own. He worked so close to the bull his suit of lights was bloody from knees to neck. The public screamed for him. They screamed to the band for music to inspire him. He took off his slippers and laid one on its side and planted his toes dangerously and immovably in it and everyone went completely mad.

Always with that smile of happiness on his face. And his mother and Louise up there in the cheap seats with their arms around one another, crying into each other's shoulders.

That was that. I quit.

I went out through the empty alleyways and down the street. The cries of acclamation were deafening from five blocks away. I stopped and had a beer and went on to the hotel. Julie was hanging around waiting for me.

She was terribly charming. We drove up the mountains again at her suggestion to what she called Our Spot. This time there was no malarkey about being in love. She did what she did to ingratiate herself with me. I was not fooled.

Later I looked for Louise to say goodbye, but failed to find her. Maybe I did-
n't look hard enough. In the streets and the bars and the cafés—everywhere—
they were talking with brilliant eyes of the triumph of their local boy, Luis Hernandez, their very own torero. I saw one old man crying with pride over it.

By six o'clock the following morning I was in France. I figured they would
soon be treating me much more politely at the Regatta Club.

THE END

THE END